AF241944

THE PATRIARCH

The Crockett Chronicles: Book 1

JENNIFER LYNN CARY

Praise for the Crockett Chronicles

"This book is so good! If you like Christian Historical Fiction, you will love this book. It hooked me on the first page and I couldn't put it down." —Ann Ferri

"I thoroughly enjoyed the book! A big fan of Christian Historical Fiction, this one was absolutely great! Looking forward to the rest of the series!" —Amazon Customer

"I was drawn in by the idea that this series chronicles the descendants of Davy Crockett written with the fictional imagination of a direct descendant. The time period and a glimpse of the Huguenots made for an interesting story. I am excited to read more." —Jennifer Berry

"Exciting and grabs your attention from the first page! You find yourself there! A must read!" —Nova Forrest

"Excellent story of the Crockets. I could not put it down. The characters touched my heart." —Mary Rima

Also by Jennifer Lynn Cary

Available now:

The Patriarch: The Crockett Chronicles: Book 1

The Sojourners: The Crockett Chronicles: Book 2

The Prodigal: The Crockett Chronicles: Book 3

Coming soon:

Tales of the Hob Nob Annex (May 2020)

Relentless Heart (July 2020)

Wedding Bell Blues (September 2020)

Relentless Joy (November 2020)

© 2019 by Jennifer Lynn Cary

Published by Tandem Services Press

Post Office Box 220

Yucaipa, California

www.TandemServicesInk.com

All rights reserved. No part of this publication may be reproduced or transmitted for commercial purposes, except for brief quotations in printed reviews, without written permission of the publisher.

Scripture taken from the NEW AMERICAN STANDARD BIBLE®, Copyright © 1960,1962,1963,1968,1971,1972,1973,1975,1977,1995 by The Lockman Foundation. Used by permission.

This book is a work of fiction. Names, characters, places, and incidents are either products of the author's imagination or used fictitiously. Any similarity to actual people, organizations, and/ or events is purely coincidental.

Cover photo credit: Depositphoto

Cover design by Tandem Services

This book is dedicated to my loving family.
Thank You, Lord.

Know therefore that the Lord your God, He is God, the faithful God, who keeps His covenant and His loving kindness to a thousand generations with those who love Him and keep His commandments.

— DEUTERONOMY 7:9

Chapter One

No!" Antoine's brain screamed. He had worked so hard, come so far. There must be a misunderstanding.

However, the look on Albert's face told the truth. Antoine had a baby-minding assignment. How else could he think of it?

"The king's cousin, albeit a distant one, needs to be chaperoned around the chateau during the fête and after when we return to Saint Germaine. His Majesty is sure you are the one for the job." Albert crossed his arms over his chest, not bothering to hide his grin. He enjoyed this far too much.

Probably some old maid cousin with sour breath and a face like a persimmon. Or perhaps, a dewy-eyed prepubescent who could not seem to decide whether to be twenty-one or three.

"What about Jean-Luc? He—" The glint in Albert's eye stopped the words before Antoine could plead his case, but not before he caught the faintest hint of a . . . what was it? A smirk? Possibly. Or maybe Albert was aware of something, something ... funny? Something that could undoubtedly be held over him.

If only Antoine could believe he would survive all this, the boredom or even the humiliation of having to be a caretaker and away from the action usually afforded his position.

That was the worst part.

At the age of twenty-five, Antoine thrived on the excitement he usually found in his work. Devoted to his duty to country and king, he did not like to be away from his responsibility.

Or opportunities for adventure.

For his king, he would even walk through fire. But this?

"The request comes straight from His Majesty himself." Albert poked his finger into Antoine's chest for emphasis. "He specifically asked for you and would take it as a personal affront if you were to refuse him." Antoine's friend and mentor smiled. "Think, man, two weeks of escorting his cousin to special events does carry some privileges with it. Access to the best of the carriages and stable, dining on the best of foods, and who knows how His Royal Highness will remember you when this is over?"

"So, I will be stuck here and there, bowing to her every whim, while you and Jean-Luc and the others will probably have the best adventure of your lives and—Stop laughing at me!" Antoine ground his teeth. It took all his willpower not to punch Versailles' illustrious captain of the guard in the nose.

Albert gained control of his face—everything, that is, but his eyes. They continued to twinkle with amusement. "Come, your king expects you right away. Do not keep him waiting."

They traveled down the hallway, Antoine dragging his feet with every step. Had it been anything requiring nerve, he would have put on such a brave face that even demons would have backed down in fear, or so he would like to imagine. But mind the baby? *Fi donc!* He was a soldier, not a nursemaid.

A voice drifted from the next room. The speaker seemed to be displeased, but considering it was someone in conversation with the king, the voice also sounded very respectful and controlled.

And definitely female.

Albert held the door.

"I appreciate your thoughtfulness in procuring an escort for me, your Majesty, but in truth, I do not need one. There are my books and my needlework. Or perhaps I can amuse myself with my sketchbook while *Tante* Marie goes about her business. I do not want to be a bother."

The speaker turned her head. Tingles ran up Antoine's spine. He soaked in the vision as if he had never seen a woman before. At that moment, he was not sure he ever had. *Please, let her be the assignment.*

His Majesty's voice pierced through Antoine's fog. "You do ride, do you not, my dear? I own the finest stable on the continent, and many of my horses have been brought from their home at St. Germaine for use during our stay. Surely you would not turn down an opportunity to ride while here?" The king caught Antoine's gaze. Though not a word was passed, Antoine knew he had been caught in His Majesty's web of matchmaking.

Rather than being annoyed, Antoine was more concerned for the lady's answer, which seemed an eternity in coming.

"I do enjoy horses." Her fingers picked at the folds of her gown.

"Let me assure you, my dear, that it is no bother at all." The king winked at Antoine.

"Merci beaucoup, your Majesty. You are most gracious." The lady curtseyed, a picture of grace and elegance.

"Good, then." His Majesty clapped his hands once, his eyes twinkling and his smirk modest. "I should now like to present your escort, Monsieur Antoine Desaure Permonette de Crocketagné. Antoine, this is my beautiful cousin, Louise de Saix. She was named for me, you know."

Antoine bowed over her hand and kissed it, daring to look up at her sweet face as he did.

A true beauty. Her light brown hair was pulled up on her head, with soft curls on each side framing her face. Dark, thick lashes rimmed her pale blue-green eyes.

Those eyes immediately captured Antoine's attention. He

liked to pride himself on his ability to read volumes in others' eyes. The lady's, though exquisite, were unreadable. She had a mystery about her. The challenge drew him. "The pleasure is mine, mademoiselle." Antoine knew he spoke the truth.

"I would have you know, ma petite, Antoine is one of the finest horsemen in the land. In fact, the first time I saw him, he was riding so magnificently, I demanded to know who he was and immediately offered him a position. He quickly proved his worth and is now second-in-command of our palace guard, currently stationed here at Versailles."

Heat crept up Antoine's neck at His Majesty's praise.

Louise glanced at him. Her eyebrows rose before she glanced away again.

"My dear, I am sure your bags have already been taken to your chamber." The king rubbed his hands together, seeming anxious to proceed to the next part of his agenda. "I will have one of the servants show you the way so you may rest from your trip before dinner. Antoine will meet you later to escort you to the dining hall. However, I now need to speak with him. You as well, Albert."

His Majesty motioned for Antoine and Albert to walk with him.

Antoine followed, looking over his shoulder at the captivating but diminishing sight.

⚜

THE HALLS OF VERSAILLES TEEMED WITH PEOPLE, EITHER those who lived there, visited, or unobtrusively worked on the never-ending project. Everyone went about their business of making the chateau an oasis of luxury and peace.

Louis had loved the place from the first moment he stepped foot on the premises. "Did you know Versailles was originally built by my father? Now soon, this chateau will host a palace."

He glanced at Antoine and Albert, who followed a respectful

distance behind, and led the way through another hall. At a door, he waited for Albert to open it. "I do love this place. In fact, when Monsieur Colbert wrote suggesting the Petite Chateau be razed and rebuilt in a fashion more in harmony with the newer structure, I adamantly opposed. I approved the restorations needed but warned him that if repairs are botched, the new structure will have to be rebuilt identically to the original." He smiled. "Good, we are here." Louis sat, and the men stood facing him.

۞

AN ELBOW JABBED ANTOINE'S RIBS. HE JUMPED.

"Do you not agree?" His Majesty's eyebrows rose, his head tipped to the side while his gaze narrowed.

Realizing he had missed a question, Antoine looked to Albert for help.

The king smiled. "I said, our guest is beautiful, is she not?"

Heat raced up Antoine's neck, rising to warm his face.

"*Oui*, your Majesty, I believe Antoine agrees." Albert chuckled.

His Majesty joined in the laughter.

"I am pleased, Antoine, that you find my little cousin such an appealing sight. I hope, in fact, you will enjoy your time with her and become very close."

He would enjoy it more if he did not find himself pinking up like a schoolgirl every five minutes.

The king sobered, vertical lines appearing above the bridge of his nose. "She has been traveling with another cousin of mine who, shall we say, keeps me informed about many things. I find it uncanny how one little old lady can uncover things my well-paid spies cannot." He snorted a chuckle and shook his head. "This cousin has been concerned of late about Louise who has always been a quiet, reserved young woman, even quite pious. However, Marie has not been able to draw her out." With a sigh,

His Majesty leaned back into his throne. "They have been traveling together for some months now, and although polite, Marie feels Louise is hiding something. The sole clue has to do with a half-finished letter to someone named Matthew Maury. I've learned there is a Matthew Maury who, along with the Fontaine family, operates a salt and wine business in the south."

The king stood and clasped his hands behind his back. "I believe he makes his home near Alsais, although he travels a great deal. That could be how Louise knows the man. If he is who we believe him to be, this Maury person is one of those Protestant Reformers. His business could be a clever way of passing information to and from different Huguenot cities." He spun to face Antoine. "I am fearful for our sweet Louise. This possible traitor could be influencing her in a most unhealthy way." The king paused, placing a jewel-encrusted hand on Antoine's shoulder. "I hope you will be able to put my fears to rest, my friend."

Though Antoine's ears had taken in each word, he could not believe anything less than angelic of Mademoiselle de Saix. Her graceful form, her lovely countenance, her innocent demeanor bloomed in his mind.

Ah, but her eyes. Oh, they held a mystery, all right. Was it as dark as espionage? He hoped not. It would be a shame to see that pretty neck stretched.

However, Antoine had pledged his allegiance to his king. "I will do my best, Your Majesty."

Chapter Two

The young maid led Louise down one hall and then another. When she had just about given up hope of ever arriving at her room, they stopped before a chamber. The maid opened the door.

Louise's jaw dropped. Her sheltered upbringing had not prepared her. This was her room? A gilded mirror over the marble fireplace, embellished on each side by twin sconces of gold, reflected the sunlight streaming in between heavy velvet drapes of deep lavender. The canopy over the massive bed, of the same hue but made of silk, draped elegantly from the head and foot. Two chairs and a *petite coucher*, upholstered in a darker-violet brocade silk, stood near the fireplace, and a large armoire and vanity took up the other side of the room. To think the place was under construction. What would it look like when finished?

"Excusez-moi." The maid slipped in past.

Entering the room, Louise stopped at the bed and let her hand trail over the silk brocade bed cover.

The maid busied herself with putting clothes into the armoire.

How thoughtful. "Merci." Louise's voice sounded more like a croak.

The maid bobbed a curtsey and continued with her work.

Louise leaned against the bed. "What do I call you?"

"I am called Michele, Mademoiselle." The girl continued unpacking, keeping her eyes averted downward. Then she glanced up with a tentative smile. "To my sisters, though, I am Mimi." The young woman blinked and looked down, returning to her work.

Sisters. "It must be nice to have sisters." Louise realized she spoke aloud and clapped her hand over her mouth.

Mimi smiled a little bigger and lowered her eyes. "Would Mademoiselle like to rest before dinner? I will come back and wake you to prepare for the evening."

Louise ran her fingers over the spread one more time. "Oui, I would like that very much." She started to sit on the edge when she stood to her feet. "Oh, do you know what room is for Tante Marie? I should look in on her before retiring."

"Do not worry, Mademoiselle." The maid gently guided Louise to a chair, indicating she should sit. "Her room is next door to the right, and I already know she is resting. My sister sees to her needs. I will leave word for your aunt that you are here and resting as well." Mimi knelt and began to remove Louise's shoes. "Would you like a bath poured before you retire?"

The idea tempted. "Oui, please." Who was this puny, compliant woman? Only two more weeks and she would be returning home. Two weeks. She wearied just counting the days.

Mimi arranged the bath, and Louise was soon clean and quite comfortable between silk sheets.

❦

THE CLOUD INVITED, SOFT AND FLUFFY. LOUISE ROLLED HERSELF up in it, cozy and warm. Birds winged by with iridescent plumage soaring high over green islands of treetops. She stretched and rolled to look over the other side.

Far below there was a sparkling blue mirror and ahead . . . what was that? Shiny and bright, the brilliance nearly blinded her.

Something did not feel as it should. Could it have to do with what was up ahead? The cloud seemed to drift toward whatever it was.

Then, on her right, a most wonderful sight appeared. A winged horse! Sparkling white with silver mane and pearlescent wings, it flew ever closer.

She saw a rider. Also dressed in white, he flew nearer still.

It seemed the rider motioned to her, beckoning her. He drew closer now to her cloud and held out his hand. "Louise."

"Mademoiselle." A hand shook her shoulder.

Where was the cloud, the rider? Where was she?

Louise opened her eyes and remembered. Versailles. "Oui. I am awake." She sat up, rubbing her eyes to clear away the vestiges of the dream.

The shy maid who had helped her get settled waited at the side of the bed. What was her name? "Mimi. Merci for waking me." She tried to stifle a yawn.

Now alert, she remembered. "Oh, Tante Marie! I must go to her."

"Mademoiselle, do not be bothered." Mimi handed her a cup of water. "My sister, Danielle, is waking her now. Didi will help her while I help you. When you are ready, I will take you to her."

Louise put the cup on the stand and swung her legs over the side of the bed, dangling them. "I need to see her now."

"You will, but Monsieur is coming. You must stay here until I have dressed you." Mimi took her by the hand, assisting her from the bed. "Didi, your aunt's maid, will be getting her ready so she can go with you and Monsieur to dinner. It is all arranged. Would you like to wash your face before I help you into your gown?"

"Oui, I suppose so, merci." Louise fumbled with her chemise, trying to accept this arrangement.

Mimi poured water from a delicate porcelain pitcher into a matching bowl. Louise's gaze caught the bouquet of lilacs painted on the bottom. A smaller version of the same spray was duplicated on both sides of the pitcher. Louise registered this barely an instant before the water hit her face.

The maid handed her a towel before opening the wardrobe in the corner to reveal the dresses Louise had brought with her. Most of them new and unworn.

"What do you choose to wear this evening, Mademoiselle?"

Louise stared at her new dresses while a nervous flutter teased her stomach. "I have never dined at court. I do not know what to expect." She turned to Mimi. "What do you think would be most appropriate?"

"Oh, Mademoiselle," Mimi flustered, "I, ah…"

"Please, Mimi, you are here. You know. I do not want to stand out like the rustic boor that I am. What would you choose?" Deciding then and there to trust the girl, Louise ran her fingertip over a pink silk skirt. "I have been very nervous about this trip. Tante Marie says I have been too sheltered. She took me shopping for these new clothes at a very exclusive dressmaker's shop in Paris. Never had I seen anything like it, and I cannot remember a thing the dressmaker told me about when to wear what. I want to look nice and not want to embarrass my aunt, but I do not want a lot of attention. Please, please help me."

Mimi nodded. "I will do my best, Mademoiselle." She sorted through a few frocks.

Louise released a sigh of relief. "I just want to get through this trip and go home where everything is familiar and I know what to do. I must sound ungrateful."

"Oh, no, Mademoiselle, not in the least." Mimi held out a sky-blue satin-and-velvet creation with a boned, brocaded bodice. "Possibly this one?" The selection had delicate white-lace trim at the modest neckline, and the three-quartered sleeves were fringed with ribbons.

Louise relaxed. It would flatter, but not be over-revealing. "A good choice. What shall I do about my hair?" She slipped into the gown Mimi held.

"It is far too beautiful to be covered up." Mimi tapped her chin. "Do you have any pearls or matching ribbons?"

Louise pointed to a white enameled box sitting on the bed stand. "In there."

The box held delicate carvings on each corner that worked into feet. There was no handle on the lid, only matching carvings in an oval surrounding a pink enameled rosebud. Mimi lifted the lid, searched, and then returned to the vanity with a white velvet bag. A long strand of small, perfectly matched pearls dangled from her hand.

"They were my mother's." Even after all these years, a hoarseness thickened Louise's voice just speaking of the woman who had given her birth and then left her to grow up alone.

"They are beautiful, and I know just what to do. If you please, Mademoiselle, sit here." Mimi indicated the chair at the vanity table, and Louise sat. The maid pulled the brush though Louise's thick hair that tumbled down to her waist. Then she began an intricate set of braids, working in the pearls and finishing off with small clusters of curls on each side over her ears. The effect was soft, feminine, and not overly showy. A velvet ribbon choker tied at the neck completed the look.

"What do you think?"

Louise gazed in the mirror. What did she in all honesty see? True, the hair and clothes were pleasant to the eye. Perhaps, she might even be inoffensive to look at. No matter. What did people see when they looked at her?

"I do not know," she murmured aloud.

Mimi's face, reflected over Louise's shoulder in the mirror, seemed to crumble before her eyes.

"Oh, Mimi, I am so sorry. My mind was elsewhere." Louise

spun around. "You did a wonderful job. You have been so helpful. I am glad you knew what to do. It is only that I am far more comfortable with a needle and thread or a good book in a quiet corner." Louise stood, the words tumbling out. "Please forgive me if I gave you the notion I was not pleased. Nothing could be farther from the truth. You have performed wonders. I am so grateful." Louise put her arm around the girl.

Mimi's eyes filled with tears.

"Oh, Mimi, do not cry. I am so sorry. Oh, please . . ."

"It is not that, Mademoiselle." Mimi wiped her face with her sleeve. "It is just that I have worked for Her Majesty for two years, helping guests all the while. You are the first to touch me in kindness. I will always remember."

The comment embarrassed Louise. She could not say why, so she stood in silence next to the maid.

Mimi cleared her throat and smoothed her attire. "Shall I escort you to your aunt?"

Louise nodded and mutely followed the young woman out into the hall, stopping at the first door to the right. Mimi knocked. The door opened. A young girl, who shared the same chestnut-brown hair and fawn-colored eyes, as well as the liberal sprinkling of freckles across a pixie nose as Mimi waited. She could see the relation.

"Didi, Mimi, that will be all." Tante Marie took charge. The girls curtsied and moved to the other side of the room where several dresses lay strewn about the bed and floor. "Didi and Mimi and would you believe there are more of them? Their father thought it the grand joke to give all his girls nicknames. All seven of them."

Louise eyes grew wide. "Seven girls? Mimi has six sisters?" To an only child, it was unimaginable.

"Oui. And each one has some pet name or other. I cannot keep them straight in my mind, but much more time with Didi and I will know their entire family history. My but that child can talk." Her aunt waved her fan to and fro, creating a small wind.

"Tante Marie, people find you easy to talk to. It is just the way you are."

"Why merci beaucoup, child. And I must say, the way you look this evening is lovely." She closed her fan and circled Louise as if judging a horse. "Quite lovely."

Louise's cheeks grew warm. "Merci."

"Now, Louise, you must relax while we are here. Didi, or one of her sisters, will take good care of me. You are to enjoy yourself. Investigate the horses, take walks in those breath-taking gardens, get out and do. Take advantage of that escort your king so kindly provided for you. What was his name again?"

"Antoine." The whisper caught in her throat. If her aunt wanted her to relax, this was not the way to encourage her to do so.

"Ah, oui. Antoine," Marie repeated. "I understand he is one of the king's favorites."

"Oh." Louise hoped her aunt was not fishing for a more elaborate answer. Her stomach wanted to tie itself into knots, and there was nowhere to bolt.

❧

ANTOINE, DRESSED IN HIS BEST JUSTAUCORPS, CARRIED two long-stemmed roses—one red and one pink. The whole way down the hall, he rehearsed what he might say. This cousin of the king certainly looked nothing like a spy. However, should she be involved with Huguenot espionage, he did not want to be deceived by her innocent demeanor.

Arriving at the room without a full strategic plan, he at last decided to provide a good ear. Perhaps then the lady would trust him and share her secrets. That would have to be enough of a plan for now. He cleared his throat before knocking.

The maid opened the door, allowing him entrance. The older woman, presumably the aunt, offered her hand.

Antoine bowed and presented the red rose to His Majesty's

older cousin, Madame Marie du Sine. "Madame, my name is Antoine de Crocketagné. I am here for you and Mademoiselle de Saix. Would you allow me the privilege of escorting you to dinner?"

About that time, the vision from earlier in the day moved away from the window, turning to face him. Antoine's vocabulary evaporated. He realized he stared, slack-jawed and stupid, yet he could do nothing else. Grinning like a fool, he thrust the pink rose toward Mademoiselle de Saix.

"For you, Mademoiselle. A rose for a rose." *A rose for a rose?* Where did that come from? She must think him an idiot.

La Mademoiselle took the flower, burying her nose in it, and curtsied. "Merci, Monsieur." Those incredible eyes glanced up at him before she turned and walked over to one of the maids. "Mimi, would you please put this in my room?" With one last sniff, she handed the rose to the girl.

The little maid nodded and slipped past him into the corridor.

"I believe we are ready, Monsieur." Madame du Sine smiled as she took his left arm.

He offered his right to the mademoiselle, and the three of them started down the halls to dinner.

Antoine hoped neither the young woman nor her aunt could feel how the mere touch of this quiet girl electrified him so. Twenty-four hours earlier, he had no clue of her existence. Now she filled his thoughts.

Jean-Luc always had his ladies, perpetually in love but not constant in his affection toward anyone except himself. That was not Antoine's way. He was no stranger to feminine wiles, but Antoine chose his service to the Crown as the more important.

When had he lost control? This was not the first beautiful woman he had met and yet, without so much as a by your leave, she overtook his senses. This was ludicrous!

Irritated, he stiffened and forced himself to shore up his reserve. Thus began a maddening cycle. The more he thought, the more irritated he became; the more irritated he became, the more he tensed.

The hand of the mademoiselle quivered and slipped from the crook of his arm.

He wanted to reach for it but hesitated. How did this girl bring about such feelings? He had seen his share of battle, even faced an enemy far more terrifying yet stood his ground. How had she gotten past his defenses?

Madame du Sine, oblivious to all this, chatted merrily on to the hall. Then suddenly, twenty feet from the doors she stopped and turned, her eyes flashing out a warning.

"I do not know what has gotten into the two of you, but for heaven's sake, *smile.*" Her urgent whisper penetrated Antoine's whirling thoughts. "We are here to have an enjoyable time. Relax, laugh. For if you do not improve your behavior, His Majesty will think something is wrong and will end up in an ill humor. You can then well imagine the rest of our evening."

Antoine's face burned. "Forgive me, Madame, Mademoiselle. I do not know what came over me or where my manners flew. Please forgive a silly daydreamer. I promise to be a gregarious companion for the rest of your stay." He gave the most sweeping bow he knew to do before peeking up with a big grin at the ladies.

Marie beamed back. The smile of Mademoiselle seemed tremulous at best.

Antoine reached for her hand, kissing it before tucking her smooth fingers back on the crook of his arm. Her smile grew stronger and Antoine knew, at that precise moment, he wanted to get to know this gentle woman. She was so unlike the other women who populated his circle. As a rule, they were social climbers, only caring about themselves and preening like peacocks to get the most attention from anyone with status.

When Mademoiselle de Saix at last relaxed, he wanted to sigh with relief.

Once again, he smiled to the women before opening the

door to the terrace for them. As he ushered them through, Antoine could not help but watch His Majesty's young cousin as she exited. The view from the back was also quite nice. He hoped the mademoiselle held no guile.

Antoine's heart skipped a beat. He was not cut out for this type of duty.

Chapter Three

Such a large and noisy gathering caused Louise's stomach to flutter again. Or was it merely the very masculine arm she noted beneath her escort's sleeve? She stood among thousands of other guests at the allée royale waiting for His Majesty to appear. The late afternoon sun did nothing for the chills of anxiety. Nor did the realization that so many in attendance could not stay at the chateau. Why had she, among so few, been allowed lodging?

The massive doors pulled apart, and His Majesty arrived with his court. Tante Marie leaned in front of Antoine to whisper. "The Dauphine is being allowed to attend for a short time. He is looking more like his father every day. His Majesty is so proud of him. He has already begun training the child to be the next monarch. Oh, and look who else has decided to join the festivities."

Louise glanced where her aunt nodded. A stately lady with sad eyes walked near the king. A few of the many nobles Louise could put a name to, but the majority were complete strangers. She turned back to her aunt and mouthed, "Who?"

Tante Marie nodded in direction of the woman again. "Her Majesty Marie Therese."

Louise turned and watched the lady again, struck by the melancholy emanating from her queen. She bit her lip and continued along with her aunt and escort once protocol allowed.

The royal entourage led northward to a rectangular building with three tall arches along the wide face. Wrought iron gates in each arch were flung wide, allowing the royals to enter. His Majesty stood in the center arch. A sun sporting a man's face worked into the wrought iron shone above his head. "My friends. Welcome to you one and all. We wish to commend our dear friend and designer extraordinaire, Monsieur Le Norte who has graced our gardens with this—le Grotto de Thétis." His Majesty flung wide his arms.

Louise jumped as spurts of water pounced at her and all in attendance.

Monsieur wrapped his cape about her, and they scurried away from the water jets. Laughter rang everywhere.

Her hair! Her gown! Then Louise caught sight of other nobles, frolicking in the water. If they didn't mind, perhaps she should not worry. Even Tante Marie played with others.

"This way, Mademoiselle." Monsieur patted her hand, still tucked at his arm, and led her along the path. "Our next stop is to see the new Basin of the Dragon."

Louise nodded and tried to smile. She didn't want him to think her unsophisticated, but if she opened her mouth, he wouldn't think it. He would know it.

The gilded figures in the basin reflected the rays of the dipping sun, making the whole pool appear golden.

"Do you hunger? I believe our next stop will help with that. Come, I will show you the Bosquet de l'Etoile."

Again, Louise mutely nodded. He must think her mute.

The Bosquet de l'Etoile was a junction of five allées. Long buffets stretched down each one, heaped high with meats. In the center of each table, a castle of marzipan and sugar stood triumphant.

Monsieur tapped her hand. "Look up." He pointed to the trees.

Louise gasped. All sorts of fruit, both preserved and fresh, hung from the branches. Apricots and peaches, pears and Dutch gooseberries and Portuguese oranges all begging to be "picked." She looked to Monsieur for permission.

He smiled, plucked a pear, and took a bite.

She reached up, her hand grasping a peach. A giggle escaped, and she bit into the sweet fruit, juice dripping down her chin.

A servant directed them to their chairs. Louise found herself seated between Monsieur de Crocketagné and a quiet man, dressed with less flamboyance than the others. He seemed to take in his surroundings with all his senses, always watching, always listening, as if trying to understand and store the knowledge. Before she realized it, the man had her deep in conversation.

"I have been traveling with Tante Marie for the past four months, Monsieur. She is my mother's sister. My mother died when I was three, so my father raised me."

"I am so sorry, my dear." The man patted her hand.

"It is the way of it." It still hurt, though. Yet the man's sympathy felt genuine and comforting. "I hardly remember her. Rather, I have impressions of a soft scent and a gentle touch. My father, though, is wonderful." She looked down, tracing the outline of design in the tablecloth with her fingertip. "I think a part of him always wanted a son, so he let me do many things other girls my age were never allowed to do. He also insisted I learn to read, write, and understand mathematical equations—in other words, to think. I believe he hoped the mothers of my friends would handle the process of making a lady of me." Louise smiled at the thought of how upset Tante Marie had become seeing her ride astride when she came to visit. In fact, that was probably how her aunt convinced her father to let Louise travel as her companion. "To be perfectly frank, I am not comfortable with all the trappings."

The intense look from Louise's dinner companion caused the butterflies to dance in her stomach again. "Perhaps I should not be confessing all this. I am sure Tante Marie would remind me that I am not being very ladylike."

The man smiled. "On the contrary, my dear, I find you quite the lady."

"Merci, Monsieur, but, in truth, this all seems more than I can take in." Louise sighed. "My tastes are much simpler."

"Just how would you prefer to spend a relaxing vacation, Mademoiselle?" The voice of Monsieur de Crocketagné startled her, so intent was she in the conversation.

Louise looked to the other man, who appeared to be awaiting her answer, and back to Monsieur de Crocketagné. Now they both would, without a doubt, think she did not belong here.

Taking a deep breath, she plunged in. "I would spend my time leisurely reading, taking quiet walks, laughing with a friend, or taking a brisk ride, perhaps to a place by a brook— somewhere to have a meal outside and perhaps sketch a little. I prefer the companionship of one or two close friends to a large gathering, a good book to the latest gossip, and the out of doors to formal rooms no matter how beautiful." She shrugged. "I hope I have not offended anyone. The company of this night is quite enjoyable, but then, you did ask."

"You are correct, Mademoiselle, I did." Monsieur de Crocketagné's gaze held no condemnation.

⚜

After dinner, the assemblage moved to carriages. Antoine helped Louise inside, catching a glimpse of His Majesty riding by in his calèche. Her Majesty, carried in her sedan chair, followed. Everyone rode around the *grand roundeau* to the theatre of Vigarani.

As seating was prearranged, Antoine quickly found their

places, still enjoying the lovely view his assignment made. The quiet dinner companion, who with amazing skill drew out the story of Louise's life, walked to the front of the stage and began to speak.

Louise stared, her eyes wide. She leaned in close and whispered. "Who is he?"

Antoine quietly laughed. "You just had dinner with Monsieur Jean Baptist Poquelin."

The look of confusion on her face told him that information meant nothing.

"You have most likely heard of him by his pen name. Molière." Just when he thought Louise's eyes could not get any rounder, she proved him wrong.

"You mean I just poured out my life to a famous playwright? And not just any playwright, but the greatest comic playwright in France." She gripped his arm, and his pulse raced.

"I take it you know his work." Antoine found it harder and harder to bite back the laugh wanting to erupt, though whether it came from the situation or his nerves, he could not say.

"I told you I like to read. I have never seen a performance, but he makes his social commentaries so humorous. It is a guilty pleasure I acquired in Paris, though my priest at home would be appalled."

Antoine winked. "I will not tell."

She turned in her chair to face him. "What are we viewing tonight?"

Ahh, she does know how to have fun. "*George Dandin.*"

Now Antoine believed Louise's eyes would pop from her sockets. "Ooo, that is new. I so enjoy his satire."

"Then I am sure you will enjoy this. It is otherwise known as *The Fool Who Chooses Not to Be Wise.*"

Louise nodded and turned back to the stage just as the curtain opened.

All through the play, Antoine could not keep his eyes off her. When she turned her head, he quickly made sure his focus returned to the play. Such a dichotomy, this one. She changed from well versed to innocent in a finger snap.

৩৩

AFTERWARD, ANTOINE NOTICED THE QUEEN HAD TAKEN leave before the final curtain. The king escorted another woman. He led the mademoiselle in their king's direction.

She curtseyed, and Antoine, hat tucked under his arm, bowed.

"Marquise," His Majesty began, "may I present to you my lovely cousin, Louise de Saix and her escort Monsieur Antoine Desaure Permonette de Crocketagné. Louise, this is my friend, the Marquise de Montespan, lady-in-waiting to the queen and the daughter of the Duc de Mortemart."

"Madame, it is a pleasure." Mademoiselle curtseyed again, this time to the woman, while Antoine bowed over the lady's hand.

"The pleasure is mine." Although the Marquise returned a smile, it never seemed to reach her eyes. "Are you staying long?"

It did not escape Antoine that the question calculated time rather than offered a friendly inquiry. Had Mademoiselle done something to offend the woman? What could she have done in so short a time?

"We are here only two weeks before we begin our trip back to our home."

"We?" The Marquise's brows rose.

His Majesty patted the Marquise's arm. "Oui, ma petite, Louise and her aunt, who is also my cousin, are my guests for only this short visit, unless Antoine and I can convince them to enjoy court hospitality a bit longer. N'est-ce pas?"

Mademoiselle smiled, and Antoine's heart fluttered. "That will depend entirely upon Tante Marie. I am only along for the fun, as they say."

"Are you having any?" Again, the Marquise's smile appeared forced.

"Oui, tonight has been lovely. Merci beaucoup, Your Majesty, for including me."

"You are quite welcome, my dear. Antoine will see that you enjoy the rest of your evening, as well. The Marquise and I have some unfinished business to attend to, and so, if you will excuse us."

As the couple left, Mademoiselle again curtsied, and Antoine bowed before tucking her fingers onto his forearm. "Would you enjoy a walk by the fountains? They are exquisite in the moonlight."

She agreed.

What had gotten into him? Much of the evening surprised him. The lady could be both introverted and open. For one so private, she had revealed much. He must remember to thank Monsieur Molière. Perhaps it was due to the opulent surroundings.

"Your mind is far off, is it not?" Antoine realized he had let his mind wander. When he looked over at her, it seemed she had as well. "You are thinking too much for such a splendid night."

"I apologize, Monsieur." Mademoiselle looked around. They had wandered through the fragrant gardens of the southern façade and stopped near a fountain of mythological nymphs and sea people caught in the act of raising a cascade above their sea home. It looked playfully lifelike with the dancing moonlight reflecting off the water. "This is wonderful, Monsieur."

"It is called The Fountain of the Pyramid. I think it is Girardon's masterpiece—my favorite of all the fountains on the grounds."

She sat on the edge and stuck her fingers in the misty spray. "You are right. It is too lovely a night to be lost in thought." She closed her eyes and sighed.

Antoine stared. The moonlight paled in comparison to her beauty.

Mademoiselle traced the edge of the fountain's pool with her finger. "Perhaps you should tell me about you."

"Moi? There is not much to know." He kicked a pebble into the grass.

"You are too modest, Monsieur. I am sure there are many things you could tell me of your life here." She brushed her fingers dry on her skirt and folded her hands in her lap. "Seeing that you have already heard my life's story, it is only fair you oblige me."

"As you wish." Antoine smiled, clasping his hands behind his back. "You already know my name—all of it, since His Majesty likes to use it in its entirety." He laughed, and she joined him. Propping a boot against the edge of the fountain, he leaned against his knee. "I grew up in the country around Montaban in Tarn-Et-Garonne. My father has a villa there where he raises horses. My mother died when I was four, so my two sisters became my mothers. They now have families of their own." He pushed off from the fountain and straightened, hands behind his back, keeping memories at bay. "I have been employed by the king here at Versailles since my twenty-first birthday. My favorite color is blue, and I have two weaknesses—one is horses and the other I cannot tell you."

"You do not trust me? And after I have answered all of your questions so honestly."

"Oh, I do trust you, Mademoiselle, I do. But no, I cannot. You would think I made it up." Antoine shook his head and winked at her. "I believe it is better if I do not reveal everything to you. Think of what happened to Samson when he gave in to Delilah and revealed the truth. No, some secrets are better kept."

"Very well, then. It shall be my vocation while here to discover the mystery of your hidden weakness." Mademoiselle smiled and then shivered.

Antoine removed his cape, concerned that her clothes had perhaps not completely dried. "The evening has cooled. Perhaps I should escort you back before you become chilled."

"Oh, it is so beautiful here." She sighed in tune to the music. "Perhaps you are right, though. I wonder about the time. It must be getting rather late. How long do these parties usually last?"

"They can sometimes go on all night." Antoine held out his hand, suddenly anxious for her touch. "This one looks as though it might. Are you tired?"

"I guess I am a bit." She chuckled and accepted his assistance.

A lovely jolt raced up his arm.

"I am not used to such late evenings. Would you mind terribly if I went back to my room? I am enjoying your company but would be embarrassed if I fell asleep on you."

"It would be my pleasure to walk you back. I have also enjoyed your company very much, Mademoiselle." Antoine tucked her hand back into the crook of his arm. "The morrow is soon enough to begin seeing the rest of Versailles."

They walked, Antoine filing away every nuance of the evening until they arrived at her room. "Mademoiselle, I look forward to seeing you again on the morrow. Sleep well." He bowed and kissed her hand, again lingering in that position an instant longer than necessary to peek up at her.

Chapter Four

I said, hello. Are you awake?"

Antoine looked over at Albert and realized his friend had been speaking to him, but he had not heard a word. He could not even remember how he arrived at the barracks so quickly. One minute he told Louise goodnight at her door, and then, voila´, he stood next to his bunk.

"You are home early, my friend." Albert had that twinkle in his eyes again. "The special duty is not to your liking?"

He was not going to play cat and mouse with Albert tonight. "The mademoiselle was tired, so I took her to her room. We had a nice evening."

"That was all?"

"Oui, that was all."

"Then I believe you, that was all." Albert grinned with a wink.

Antoine got ready for bed. "Really. We ate, we watched, we talked, we walked, we said au revoir. A nice evening by all accounts. And *that was all*." He did not even give Albert the satisfaction of looking up.

"I am happy to hear it. His Majesty will be pleased." Albert paused. "Especially when he finds out you are becoming infatu-ated with his young cousin."

"What?" Antoine spun and glared. "Who says I am infatu-ated with her? We had a *nice* evening. I am just performing my duty." Then, after a minute, he punched Albert on the shoulder. "Fortunately, the duty has turned out to be quite pleasant."

"Oh?"

"So, merci. I will thank His Majesty when I next see him." Antoine grinned.

"You are welcome, my friend." Albert chuckled. "You are quite welcome."

Antoine plopped down on his cot, lacing his fingers beneath his head. "Mademoiselle de Saix is quite different from the other women we meet at court."

"Before you get your head too high in that cloud, you need to remember who employs you."

Antoine sat up. "What do you mean? I know who employs me."

"So, you understand that although His Majesty might enjoy playing matchmaker with you and the lovely mademoiselle, he will not take kindly to you putting her wishes ahead of his."

"We only met this very day." Antoine lay back again. "I fear you are getting ahead of yourself."

"Perhaps, but I would be cautious when it comes to affairs of the heart and state. Allowing Mademoiselle, or anyone for that matter, to have more importance to you than His Majesty would have dire consequences."

"I will be on my guard, beginning on the morrow. For now, I would like some sleep, if you please, *Vieille*." Antoine punched his pillow and rolled to his side. "Old woman," he muttered under his breath.

But the warning still echoed in his head.

LOUISE FLOATED INTO THE ROOM AND LEANED BACK against the door, closing her eyes. She could almost hear the music whispering in her ear while the heady fragrances of the garden carried her thoughts away. Gently, under her breath, she hummed the tune and stepped from the door, swaying to the rhythm. The romance of the evening danced with her, twirling her in invisible arms.

A soft cough froze her mid-twirl, her eyes popping wide. Directly in front of her stood Mimi. Then, as she turned her head to look to her right, there stood Mimi, as well. Louise turned her view from one Mimi to the other. Her brain could not assimilate the information. Perhaps the whole evening had been a dream and she continued to sleep in the luxuriant bed.

"Pardon us, Mademoiselle." The Mimi on the right spoke. "We do not mean to intrude."

"Oh, ah, no—that is fine. I must have looked silly." Which one was Mimi?

"You had a pleasant evening, oui?" The Mimi on the right continued to speak.

Louise nodded, still looking back and forth between the two girls. "Oui, yes I did."

"I should explain. This is my sister, Monique. We call her Momo."

"Oh!" Twins. That explained it. "I should have known. Momo, it is nice to meet you."

Momo curtsied but remained silent. Louise quickly studied her. The resemblance to Mimi proved identical; no one could notice the difference without previous knowledge and a practiced eye. Yet, as Louise studied the girls, she noted Momo appeared less gentle, less sweet. Or perhaps, Momo was not as shy as Mimi.

"I have just received information from home. It is important I return there, but only briefly. Momo has agreed to be here so you will not be left alone. I will only be away a short while. I promise to return no later than the morrow's eve. May I have permission to go?" Mimi's voice quivered as she asked.

"But of course."

"You cannot tell anyone." Momo's assertive statement bounced around the room.

"*Pardonnez-moi?*" Though Louise was not one to stand on position, Momo's outburst belied a lower class than her sister.

"Mademoiselle, I am sorry for Momo's bluntness. You have been nothing but courteous to me. I am sorry to surprise you with this. Her Majesty would not understand my need to leave in the middle of my duty. I would be in much trouble should it be discovered. Could you please pretend Momo is me until I return? No one can tell us apart." She glanced at her sister. "Usually. So, as long as you do not say anything, we should not be found out. Please?" Mimi's eyes grew round with fear.

"Of course, I will help you." Louise reached for Mimi's hand. "Is there not something more I can do? What seems to be the problem? Is it one of your sisters? Or your parents?"

"No, you are kind—"

Momo cut her off. "It is none of your concern."

"Momo! Mademoiselle de Saix has only been kind and considerate to me. I will not have you speak with such rudeness. Her word is good. She will not give us away." For a moment Mimi's gaze left her sister and stared back at Louise, begging for affirmation to her statement of faith.

There was never a question that Louise would help. Mimi had befriended her and now made this request. "Momo, I will not give you away. You do not have to fear me. I know what it is like to have to take care of another person. Usually I serve as companion to my aunt. This is a very different experience for me, but I will not look to bring you trouble. Aside from that, Mimi was the first to befriend me here at Versailles. I would not want to cause her trouble. You can trust me." Louise held out her other hand to the girl.

Momo looked at the proffered hand and to her sister, whose

eyes gleamed with tears. Biting her lip, she returned a steady gaze to Louise, but never offered her hand. "Can you remember to call me Mimi?"

"I will try." Louise smiled, drawing her fingers back to her skirt.

"Bon." Mimi visibly relaxed and dropped Louise's other hand. She moved to the bed, turning down the bedclothes.

"Are you sure there is nothing else I can do for you?" Now worry began to set in. There must be something very wrong for Mimi to attempt such a risk.

"Oui, I am quite sure, but merci. I will return as soon as I can, and I will not leave until you are asleep so I will know you are comfortable."

"Oh, there is no need—"

Despite Louise's protests, Mimi insisted. "This is how we planned it, only you were not to find out. I am relieved that you know. It is one less thing off my mind. So, if I may help you out of your gown, Momo can put your things away. Then we will step out while you say your evening prayers."

Louise agreed.

Soon, alone and on her knees beside the spacious bed, Louise dutifully went through her catechism of evening confession and prayer. As usual, it felt inadequate. Did God really hear her? Was she doing this the correct way? Thinking of Mimi and her sisters, she wondered again what could be so important to put the kind maid at such risk. It must be most urgent to Mimi since her sisters were staying here in her stead.

Louise spoke a blessing on Mimi and her family. Her mind drifted to Monsieur, and she said a sincere thank you for the evening, spoke a brief prayer for him, and closed with "Amen."

After finishing her evening toilet, she climbed into bed and quickly drifted off. Somewhere, as if in a dream, a soft touch brushed her shoulder, and she heard Mimi's whisper. "I will soon return, Mademoiselle. I promise."

Louise floated again. The air on her face felt cool, but as she allowed herself to sink into the cloud, she warmed. Peering over the side, she again noted the sparkling blue mirror far below surrounded by a sea of green treetop islands. The birds' wings shimmered in the bright light and the fragrance of roses wafted through the petal soft breeze. How pleasant and peaceful to just drift away through time and space.

Sounds came to her ears—the gentle whoosh as glimmering feathers thrust ethereal winds down and away, a distant splash of a fish breaking the surface of the mirror into billions of shards that quickly repaired itself, her own heart pulsating to the rhythm of the breeze. She could not imagine anything more tranquil or soothing.

Louise rolled onto her back. The stars twinkled high above. Something about the incongruity of the light to dark seemed strange, but it did not bother her. The universe all made perfect sense, and she watched, mesmerized, as the constellations joined into sparkling works of art, separated into a dance of their own making only to join again, each picture more exquisite than the last. Sighing, she knew she was smiling. She felt beautiful and a part of the beauty around her.

Louise rolled back onto her stomach. The night became day again. Looking forward, she noticed something brilliantly blinding in the distance. The cloud began to pick up speed. The beat of her heart picked up in kind. Something inside her whispered of danger, but she could not put a name to the peril.

Then she heard it again—the whinny—and looked to see the winged horse and rider headed in her direction. Excitement rose in her chest, but not from the danger ahead. There was something stirring about the rider.

Eagerly, Louise tried to reach out to him. She wanted to grasp his hand, to see who called to her. Her arm stretched as far as she dared. Her brain told her to wait for him, but her excited heart overrode common sense. She stretched out even farther and . . .

Thump!

Louise landed in a heap. On the cold floor of her darkened room. Amid the hallowed halls of Versailles.

Her hip must be bruised, but not as much as her heart and sensibilities. The dream had been so real. How stupid to fall like that. All the emotions that had flamed before still smoldered within her. Her cheeks were hot enough to glow in the dark. Realizing she was alone in the big room, she did not know whether to feel grateful or abandoned.

Gingerly she rose and found she could stand and walk about. Nothing broken, thankfully. Louise felt her way to the velvet drapes and tentatively parted them. The waxing moon shone distant in the lightened sky. Far over on the other side of the gardens it seemed bright as day, while the area near her side of the chateau lay shrouded.

There was also movement throughout the gardens and near the fountain. She could hear no noise but could make out activity. Not exactly animated, it was more like shadows moving with continued steady purpose.

"Whatever could be happening down there?" If it were not for the coolness of the flooring beneath her feet, she would have been sure she still dreamed.

Louise padded across the room and tried her door. It soundlessly opened. She peeked into the empty corridor. Trimmed sconces gave off a soft glow, creating a surreal, but inviting effect. Did she dare explore the chateau? If she did, could she find her way back?

She looked at her rumpled bed. It did not invite as before. So be it. She would just take a little walk. Only, how did she make sure to return to the correct bedchamber?

Her gaze lighted on the dim outline of Monsieur de Crocketagné's rose in the pitcher. If it had been on the other side of her bed, she would have never noticed it in the faintly lit room. She also would have probably hit it when she fell. The pitcher would have been in ruins and her feet bloody ribbons. "I do not know why you take such good care of me," she whispered to her guardian angel, "but I am grateful you do."

The hall remained quiet and empty. She tied the belt of her wrapper about her as she went out, dropping a petal of the rose onto the side of the corridor and moving in silence down the passage. With the construction going on she feared becoming lost. Therefore, every time the hall turned, she dropped another petal. When she ran out of petals, she would have to go back.

She strained to hear any sound. At one point, a door creaked. Flattening herself against the wall, she waited. One of the elegantly dressed men from the evening's party tiptoed down the corridor in front of her, and with shoes in his hand, slipped without a sound into a room twenty yards ahead.

Louise could guess what was going on but was sure she was not supposed to have seen him. She counted to ten under her breath and then resumed her quiet walk. After about five minutes, she was down to her last petal.

"Louise."

Jumping in her skin, Louise spun around and gasped. "Oh! Your Majesty!" She pulled at her wrapper, making sure it revealed nothing, and smoothed her hand over her hair.

"What are you doing?" His question held no rancor, but his presence made her nervous.

"I am sorry, did I do something wrong?" The rose's stem bent and snapped in her fluttering hands. "I awoke and was unable to go back to sleep, so I thought to take a small walk, but then I was afraid I would not be able to find my way back, and then I noticed the rose in my room and thought I could leave a trail back, so I decided to give it a try and . . ." *Breathe, ninny.*

"Ho!" His Majesty held his hands in surrender. "You are welcome to be here. You are my guest." His fingers fluttered about his chin, and his eyes narrowed. "I generally enjoy a small meal about this time of night. Would you like to accompany me to my suite? We can see what has been delivered."

"Oui, merci beaucoup, Your Majesty." Louise looked down

at her hands. The shreds of rose stem lay mangled in her hands. "Oh, no, I had better not." Her cheeks warmed to the inevitable blush. "I do not think I could find my way back if I went any farther."

The king laughed. "I assure you I will not let you become lost. Please, honor me with your presence at my nocturnal repast." He proffered a gallant arm.

It would be nice to have someone to talk with. Louise shyly linked her arm with that of His Majesty and proceeded to his suite.

The room they entered was his living quarters. She noted a lounge with a few chairs, several bookcases, and a small table with papers stacked next to a silver, filigreed ink well.

Cold pheasant, truffles, a large chunk of ham, and a vessel of wine lay assembled in the center of a small dining table set for only one. Louise could not have eaten that much food in a week.

His Majesty pulled a ribbon of deep green on the wall, and a valet entered immediately.

"Set another place for my guest." His Majesty spoke and it was so.

The valet held the chair for her. Before she could protest, her plate and goblet had been filled. Now she was certain she was dreaming. Amazed at the efficiency of the valet, awed by the opulence of the room, and overwhelmed by the presence of the king, Louise knew nothing of this kind of life. How had she found herself here?

"Eat. The pheasant is excellent." The king picked up a great hunk of the meat with his hands, bit off a mouthful, and smiled broadly.

Louise giggled and mimicked her cousin. The pheasant was as delicious as he had stated, and she took another bite. She had not realized how hungry she was until the flavorful meat touched her lips. None of her new dresses would fit if she continued to eat this way.

His Majesty laughed at her contented sigh.

"It is excellent, Your Majesty." She dabbed her mouth between bites. "Merci beaucoup."

"My pleasure. Try the wine. It also is excellent and comes from one of my vineyards in Bordeaux."

Louise took the goblet into her hand, sensed the sweet bouquet of the ruby liquid, and held a sip in her mouth to savor the elegance. Although she did not often imbibe, her father had taught her the fine art of wine tasting. She recognized a great wine when she encountered it, and this wine was truly excellent. As the velvety fluid went smoothly down her throat, she savored the superb flavor on her tongue a moment before taking another bite of the appetizing food.

"Ma *amie*, you are enjoying your meal, no?" The king wiped his sleeve across his mouth. "What of the rest of your trip? Have you enjoyed your time here at the chateau? I trust Monsieur de Crocketagné is entertaining you."

"Oh, oui, your Majesty. I am having a wonderful time. Monsieur de Crocketagné has been the perfect escort." The warmth creeping up her neck was not from the wine. The handsome face of Monsieur with his kind eyes sparkling flashed in her brain. "We went for a walk after the play tonight. He showed me the gardens and your Majesty's newest fountain. I must say, it is breathtaking in the moonlight. I am so pleased I can see it from my window."

"Then I, too, am pleased."

They continued eating in silence. Louise could feel His Majesty staring at her. Each time she looked up, however, he seemed intent on his food. It unnerved her. But then he was the king.

After a few more bites of the meal and half of her goblet of wine, her eyelids grew heavy and sleep began to overtake her.

His Majesty noticed and pulled on the velvet cord. The valet reappeared, and the king instructed him to escort Mademoiselle back to her chamber.

"Ma amie, I can see you are tired. I hope the food and wine

bring you pleasant dreams." His Majesty enveloped her in a fatherly hug.

"Merci, Your Majesty. I wish you the same."

Louise followed the valet out of the royal chambers and back to her own room. As she snuggled under the covers, she giggled. She would have to write Matthew in the morning. He would never believe this. A midnight meal with the king. Oh my! And he had thought she would not even see His Majesty while at Versailles. Oui, she definitely would have to tell Matthew.

Chapter Five

Louise awoke to Momo opening the velvet drapes and taking care of the housekeeping duties that awaited her.

"Good morning, Mademoiselle." Perfunctory, if not friendly. "May I assist you with anything?"

"Good morning to you, Mo . . . Mimi." Louise caught herself. She knew no one else was in the room but was determined to do her best not to give her maid away. Therefore, she had decided to refer to Momo as Mimi in all situations until Mimi returned. She hoped it would keep her from slipping up in an embarrassing situation. "I believe I am satisfactory for the moment. I would like to wash my face and get my hair out of my eyes, and I need an opportunity to say my morning prayers. Other than getting dressed after that, I have no plans. Do you know of an itinerary for today?"

"I have not been informed. I assume Monsieur de Crocketagné will arrive soon. What would you like me to lay out for you today?"

"Perhaps my riding costume would be a good idea. I have been considering what His Majesty said about his stable. I should like to become acquainted with it I think." Louise smiled, imagining a ride on one of His Majesty's renowned horses. When Momo did not return the smile, though, she questioned her decision. "Do you agree, or do you have a better idea?"

"This is your day. I am only here to serve. If you want your riding costume, you shall have your riding costume."

The young woman turned away to the armoire.

How could someone be so identical and yet so different from her twin? "I am sorry, Momo, if I have offended you in some way . . ."

Momo spun around. "I knew you could not remember. Already, you have had to correct yourself once and you did not even try to say Mimi this last time."

"But you are the one to whom I am speaking. You have been abrupt since we met. I do not know what I have done to offend you, but I would like to know. I would never purposefully offend you or your sister."

"How would I know that?" Momo's fists clenched and unclenched at her sides. "I do not know you, and yet my sister chooses to put our lives into your hands. This is not some silly little game we are playing. If we were to get caught, it would mean extreme difficulty for our whole family and others we care about." She turned back to the armoire. The maid's back remained rigid, hard.

"Why will you not let me help you?"

"Why would you even want to?" When Momo turned back to Louise, her eyes glistened, but no tears ran down her cheeks. "When we speak of my family, we are speaking of a middle-class merchant whose daughters are allowed to work at Versailles only due to a favor the king's father granted to my grandfather. Ah, but you, when you speak of family, you can even include His Majesty Louis XIV, the Sun King, in your little genealogy." She swiped at a stray lock dangling over her forehead. "We are not of the same class, and you have no inkling of what life is like for us." Momo snorted. "Yet you want to be my friend. How sweet. I cannot even call you by name. What kind of a friend is that?"

Louise opened her mouth and then shut it. She had no words. The accusations were true enough, although a bit out of context. It did not matter that she already felt awkward at the class distinctions. Momo was not ready to hear any of that.

Blinking rapidly, Louise turned away to the nightstand, feeling for something to hold back her hair. With the ribbon tied, she poured clean water from the pitcher and splashed her face. Hot tears ran down her cheeks mingling in the basin's tepid water. She splashed a bit more vigorously and felt for the towel. Nothing but air met her blind search. Then at once the absorbent cloth was thrust into her hand.

Louise dried her face and looked up to see Momo. Their gazes locked. A silent truce declared.

Momo laid out the riding costume and left Louise to her morning prayers.

Kneeling by the bed, Louise tried to put her mind on things holy, desperately wanting to be good and loved by God. Confused, she was sure she must have done something dreadful for Momo to react in such a manner. However, she had no idea of what it could have been. Last night had been so lovely. A bright light in a rather closed and secluded life. Goodness! She had even spoken with strangers about things she held tight in her heart.

Wrapping her arms about her, she pondered the thought. Perhaps that was the problem. Could God be punishing her for letting her guard down?

She must try even harder to become a better person.

And there was something else she needed to do. She needed to talk with Matthew.

Dear Matthew. He never condemned her or thought ill of her. He just listened when she poured out her thoughts and fears. Oui, she needed to talk with him. She scratched her knee.

But how? How could she get word to him? No one was

allowed into Versailles without an invitation from the king. She would have to meet him somewhere else. Her knee itched again.

Where could they meet? How would she let him know to meet her? She would have to think about that for a while.

Oh, no. Again, her mind had wandered. If she wanted to be a better person, she would have to keep her mind on her prayers, not plans. If she could get out for a ride and clear her head, then she could come up with a plan and maybe be more focused on her prayers.

"Merci Father for the horses and for Matthew. Please help Mimi and her family. Bless Tante Marie. And Monsieur de Crocketagné. Forgive me for my wandering mind, Father, and every evil thought I had against Momo. Help me to be better, Lord."

Louise closed with an "Our Father." Though she was not sure she had been heard, it was all she knew to do. Having done her duty, she rose to get dressed.

Momo returned to help tie Louise's laces and brush her hair up under her hat. A knock sounded just as the last strand had been tucked. Momo opened it to Monsieur de Crocketagné, also dressed for riding.

"Do you have plans, Mademoiselle?" His dark eyebrow cocked and his friendly smile gleamed.

"Not really. I thought perhaps I might investigate the horses." Louise had trouble meeting his gaze, and her nerves tingled in a most unusual way. "I am in the mood for a ride and thought I would take advantage of His Majesty's offer. Do you think that is permissible?"

"I was, in fact, coming to see if you might be interested in a ride. It is beautiful outside, and I know of a little spot you might like to see. Would that be to your liking, Mademoiselle?"

"Indeed, it would." For although the gentleman might have denied it, Louise wondered if he stood there as an answer to her prayer. Could God have heard her? If so, perhaps the rest would resolve itself as well. She smiled and placed her trembling hand on Monsieur's proffered arm as they left for the stables.

Chapter Six

The woman stumbled but stopped in time. She had no minutes to spare for a fall, nor energy to right herself if she did. Her goal lay down this road.

She would be heard. No matter what, she would be heard.

The bitter gall of her loss burned through her chest where her heart used to be. She could keep silent no more. Enough had been sacrificed for this monstrosity. Now someone would understand.

What kind of law stated that the work on the gardens must be done in such a way that it did not bother the fancy royals? How ridiculous. Did they not realize the required silent night work meant working without enough light to be safe? Did *he* not realize?

Now her husband and son were both silent.

Her Gaston gone, and her son injured, perhaps fatally. She wanted to scream, to point the finger of blame at the one who set all this in motion.

Today was the day.

She continued up the allée to the servants' entrance. There were enough people who would make sure she received an audience. A maid admitted her and guided to the public hall. Already several stood in line, waiting.

One way or another, she knew she would be heard. It would happen.

She glanced about. The morning sun gleaming through high windows brought no joy. No one in line spoke to her. She wanted it that way.

The day grew warmer. A chill ran up her spine at the impact of her mission. She drew her shawl tighter and closed her eyes.

Men carrying a limp body burned through her mind. She squeezed her lids tighter and dragged in a ragged breath, remembering. The hand of her son, or what was left of it.

A tear escaped and trickled down, splashing on her own hand. She opened her eyes and wiped her cheek.

Why had God let this happen to him, to her? Why did He not care? How much was she to sacrifice?

The line dragged. Maybe another hour, and she would get her turn. Would it be soon enough? Outrage had spurred her here, yet she never would have left his side without someone she trusted with him. Her stomach knotted tighter with each passing minute.

Why? Why? The question pounded at her ears as if they were anvils. Her brain had no answer.

A part of her knew that should her son regain consciousness, he would forever be changed. She could not dwell on that now. The important thing was for him live, to open his eyes, to speak to her one more time.

What was she doing here? Precious time streamed past. She must return home.

"Madame LeSuere, it is your turn."

Stay or go? The massive doors towered over her, taunting.

The guard touched her elbow.

She swatted his hand away.

He opened the door, unfazed.

So be it.

Walking toward the throne, her mind churned. There sat King David on his throne, thinking his sins were hidden. Yet nothing was hidden from God. Nothing. The spokesman of God proved that. Nathan, the prophet, confronted King David. Was she God's spokesman? The thought justified her.

Vengeance is Mine. A still small voice.

She tried to dismiss it.

The voice persisted. *Vengeance is Mine.*

She would be the voice of God to this realm.

Vengeance is Mine. The voice whispered one more time as she heard her name announced to the King of France.

Protocol expected her to curtsey. Instead her body began to tremble uncontrollably.

Oh, God, help me!

As His Majesty awaited her curtsey, a page entered, bringing an envelope to one of the ministers. The king's attention wandered to the transaction. The minister brought the message to His Majesty, who read it. He stood and motioned for his entourage to follow.

The whole matter concluded swiftly, fanning the flames of anger in her soul. "You dare to leave?"

The king stopped.

"You dare to turn your back on me?"

A gasp waved throughout the room. His Majesty rotated until he faced her. His stature loomed larger while the rest of the room shank away.

The words were unleashed. She let them fly free. "Your people mean so little to you? We, who do your bidding, building your monument to you, mean nothing to you? Our men lay down their lives. We women lay down our children and husbands on your altar. We make sacrifice after sacrifice for you and you dare to walk out on me?" The venom spewed from her belly. She spat on the Persian carpet. "I spit on your luxury. I spit on you and your state. May you outlive your children!"

Her breath came in ragged gasps, and her blood boiled to

the point of blindness, but every sound pulsed through her being.

"Remove her. Give her thirty lashes, and see to it she never steps foot on Versailles again."

Drained, she collapsed to the floor.

ALBERT AND JEAN-LUC CARRIED MADAME LESUERE OUT TO where her punishment would be carried out. Conscious by this time, she stoically refused to speak.

Neither did Jean-Luc. However, his eyes pleaded with Albert to think of something, anything to stop this madness. Both men knew the king prided himself on his civility to women. Never to Albert's knowledge had such an order as this been given. It was unthinkable. Yet he was expected to carry out the command. Such was his duty.

Albert tied her hands to the ring on the pole. He refused to let Jean-Luc inflict the punishment. Albert commanded the guards, and he would not ask one of his men to do something he would not do himself. Yet, if he could think of a way, he would not carry out the sentence.

No ideas emerged. He stepped back and picked up the whip. For a male prisoner, the back would be exposed. But this was a woman. A woman already in obvious pain. He would not add to this by removing her modesty.

Albert let the whip unwind and lay still on the cobblestones. He took a breath. With the flick of his wrist, he let the whip crack, landing the first blow.

An intake of breath, her only sound.

Crack!

Again, she softly gasped.

Three, four, five.

With each vicious bite into her back, she took in a quick breath. At twenty-five, she fell unconscious again.

As Albert unfastened her bonds and took her down, he thought he heard her mutter, "Pierre."

Jean-Luc left without a word, returning with a wagon and a few blankets. As gently as they could, they placed her in the wagon bed. Albert climbed in next to her while Jean-Luc drove.

The horses' hooves made soft clopping sounds on the road. Albert remembered hearing her announced in the throne room. Being members of the household guard put him and Jean Luc in a unique position.

The gossip grapevine carried only the workers and tradesmen's news to those of similar social standing. The same went for the gossip about the nobility—it rarely reached the ears of the artisans and tradesmen. However, those who served in the chateau in special positions such as valets, ladies-in-waiting, and guards often heard the stories from both fronts.

Albert could guess what brought Madame LeSuere to the chateau that morn. She must be out of her mind at the loss of her husband, and possibly her son, to the building project. There was no other reason he could think of to bring about such insane bravery.

Yet, His Majesty probably had no knowledge of what had led up to the incident. If he had known, would he have given the same sentence?

Madame LeSuere moaned.

Could he have spared her? Albert flinched. There was one way.

Looking at the unconscious woman, Albert sent up a silent prayer for someone to be sent to care for her.

❧

MIMI SAT ALONE, ALMOST. YESTERDAY HER LIFE HAD purpose. Now she looked down on the still form of the man she loved, the man to whom she had given her heart. There was no purpose.

She stroked back a curl of Pierre's thick chestnut mane, hearing her own heart break. Again. *Wake, Pierre!*

He did not hear her heart this time.

She longed to see the sparkle of life in his gold-flecked eyes. Yet if he ever opened them, they would reveal a fathomless well of pain. She knew that as sure as she knew her name. The thought of seeing him in such agony ripped air from her lungs. Would he shut her out? Would he still want to live? *Oh God, please let him want to live.*

None of this was relevant, though, unless he woke up.

Madame LeSuere should have arrived back some time ago. A band tightened in Mimi's chest. This woman was almost a second mother to her. She would never leave Pierre this long.

Mimi glanced through the shutters. Still no sign of Madame LeSuere. Mimi could not just leave Pierre. Yet she had promised Mademoiselle de Saix to return soon. If need be, she would beg to come back to Pierre. Mademoiselle would understand. She would. But would Momo?

Momo hated working at the chateau. She wanted to live at the chateau but not work there. Mimi's twin was sure she would one day live in luxury, having all the things she envied of those invited to Versailles.

Mimi shook her head and held onto Pierre's good hand. Her dreams were much simpler. A life with Pierre. A home filled with the laughter of their children. "Oh, Pierre, do not leave me. I love you so."

The *clip clop* of horses' hooves echoed on the cobblestones outside, but she did not get up to look. She could not spare the second. A wagon stopped outside the house. A moment or two later, a firm knock rapped at the door.

"Come in." Her gaze never left Pierre.

"Where shall I put her?" The masculine voice jolted. Two men stood on the threshold, one carrying a limp bundle.

"Oh, no, what has happened?" Mimi dropped Pierre's hand and jumped to her feet.

"It is a long story. Are you here alone?"

"No, I am caring for Pierre." Was he blind?

"I mean, do you have any help? You will need help in caring for them both. Jean-Luc will fetch anyone you want. I will stay to help while he does."

The indignation drained. The man looked so wretched, his shoulders sagging and his mahogany eyes weary.

She took in the other man. Much larger, he stood behind the speaker who carried Madame LeSuere. "I am sorry. You are kind to help. I have two sisters at home right now. If you could get word to them, that would be much appreciated. I live two houses to the east. Another sister is at Versailles. I need to get a message to her to explain—."

"Consider it done." The big man responded, exiting quickly.

"Here, let me help." Mimi moved to the guard, directing him to another pallet. She helped him lower Madame LeSuere, face down, before setting a pot of water to boil at the kitchen fireplace. Rummaging in the other woman's trunk, she gathered clean strips of cloth and laid them a metal bowl, adding a dipper full of the hot water. She let them cool to touchable before pulling out a strip and wrapping it about some coltsfoot leaves, forming a poultice. The warm, pungent odor fought with her tears.

Mimi located the guard. He stood over Pierre, his back to the women. At least he had manners. She cut away what was left of the back of Madame LeSuere's bodice and chemise. Ever so gently, she placed the first poultice on a wound before wiping a tear from her own cheek. Another cloth, another leaf, another wound.

Madame LeSuere stirred and began to sob, quietly at first but building with such intensity Mimi thought Madame would surely die of a broken heart.

"Oh, God, oh God, where are You? Where are You? Oh, God, I cannot see You? Where are You?"

Mimi turned at the guard. Silent tears glistened in his eyes.

Her heart ached, and her soul whispered, "Oh, God I do not understand either. Where are You?"

Only a stifled sniff replied.

Chapter Seven

Antoine tucked Mademoiselle's fingers in the crook of his arm as they strolled to the stables. The horses waited ready. One glance told him something was amiss.

"An interesting saddle." Mademoiselle looked away.

"If you do not like this saddle, I am sure there is something else." Antoine stared at the stable boy until the lad squirmed. He could not blame her. The medieval sidesaddle, covered in burgundy velvet with gilded trim, appeared as uncomfortable as it was gaudy.

"I know of a different saddle." The stable boy raced back inside.

"I am sure he does not relish the idea of re-saddling my mount." Mademoiselle's toe twisted and poked at the dirt.

Antoine leaned over. "His Majesty's cousin, La Grande Mademoiselle, prefers not to ride sidesaddle either. I believe she keeps a saddle here that you may be able to borrow." The sweet scent of her perfume in the middle of the stable yard shocked his senses.

"I see." She began to stroke her horse's nose. "What is your name, mademoiselle?" The mare nuzzled her hand.

"She is called Étoile, due to the white star on her forehead, and she is probably hoping you have a carrot or two hidden away for her." He scratched behind the ear of the mare.

"Étoile, how lovely it is to meet you. Shall we run today?"

The horse whinnied and nodded her head, bringing a musical chuckle from the mademoiselle. By the time the stable boy arrived with an astride saddle, her happy disposition had firmly returned.

Antoine helped her mount the black mare before swinging aboard his own stallion of pure black.

"What is the name of your horse?"

"He is called Vent, as he can fly like the wind."

He patted Vent's neck before leading the lady out of the yard at a slow canter. When he stopped at the road, she drew up beside him. "We will head out that way." He pointed east. "Would you like to give them a bit of a run?"

"With pleasure." Louise smiled and kicked her heels, starting off at a gallop in the direction he indicated.

"Oui, Mademoiselle, you do know how to ride." Antoine laughed and spurred Vent forward. He soon caught up to her, but as he tried to pull into the lead, she matched his pace.

Riding through the countryside, he barely noticed the land-scape fly past. Meadows in summer green and copses of oak and elm running in the opposite direction intensified the deep sense of freedom rising from his soul. The wind in his face brought scents of forest loam and summer grasses. He flew on, elated and moving in harmony to the horses' gallop. His heart pounded in his ears.

At last Antoine slowed, coming to a stop at the edge of a gentle valley.

She stopped beside him.

"That is where we are going." He pointed.

Mademoiselle stared at a lush meadow area surrounded by oaks. And there, in the very center of the meadow, stood two chairs and a table. Atop sat a basket. She looked back at him, eyes shining.

"I arose early and recruited help. I thought perhaps you might enjoy out-of-doors dining." He winked.

She let her horse take the lead and slowly trotted to the meadow. Dismounting before he could reach her, she finished the walk to the table still leading Étoile. "This is so wonderful." Her finger trailed down the stem of a crystal goblet. "You did this for me?" Her eyes grew so large, Antoine thought he could read her soul.

"Ah, but my lady, it is my pleasure." He held her chair for her with exaggerated gallantry. "What will be your delight?" He began going through the basket. "I see we have cheese, bread, some delightful grapes and strawberries, and, let me see . . .ah . . .a wonderful champagne to tickle your fancy, as well as your nose." Smiling his most charming smile, he waggled his brows at her.

With a wave from his hand, a dark-haired gentleman appeared and approached the table, a towel over his arm. "How may I serve you, my lady?"

"I will serve the lady, merci. Please bring the rest of the food."

Finally, a smile teased at her lips.

"Might I pour?"

"Oh, but can I trust you to know quality champagne?"

He slammed his hand over his heart. "My lady, you do cut me to the quick. I will have you know this is the finest champagne in all of France."

"Very well then, I suppose you may pour. I must say, those strawberries do look inviting. Do you not suppose I may have a few?"

"For you, my lady, your wish is my command." He popped the cork with much flourish and poured for her.

Mademoiselle sampled the sparkling wine. "*Ma foi!* I believe you may be correct. This champagne is exceptional."

Antoine sputtered on his champagne. "Where did you come to be such an expert, my lady?"

"My father is a connoisseur." She blushed, and he enjoyed it. "I, ah . . . He has taught me how to appreciate the difference between what is passable and what is truly good. Due to business, he spent much time in England where he became adept at wine tasting. Without sons to train in the art, my father made do and handed down his wisdom to me."

Antoine smiled and nodded. "Your father must be a very wise man. I hope I will have the pleasure of meeting him one day."

At once her countenance clouded as if a rain of melancholy poured over her spirit. "I do not see him often enough. Ever since I began traveling with Tante Marie, I have had little to no contact with him. He sends the occasional letter, but it is not the same. I miss him terribly." The edge of the lace tablecloth had wound itself about her fingers. "He hoped Tante Marie could help refine me. I have been through so many changes that I wonder if he would recognize me?"

"I am sure he would know you anywhere." He briefly wondered what changes she'd experienced and poured more champagne.

"Merci." She released the tablecloth, smoothing out the wrinkles she had caused and changed the subject. "I can see you are no stranger to horses. You are quite skilled."

"I seem to recall I mentioned my weakness for horses. They are a passion with me. I dearly love the chance to ride without worrying about anything else. It is a good way to clear my mind and relax—my favorite distraction." He leaned his chin on his fists, elbows planted on the table.

"I understand. There is nothing like outriding your troubles. I always feel like I can come back with a fresh view if I can just get away for a while. I was even thinking that just this morning." Her eyes widened, and she popped a grape in her mouth.

Either she was too open to be a spy or a brilliant actress. Antoine leaned toward believing the first choice. "From what troubles would you escape?"

She shook her head and swallowed. "Nothing really. In fact, I think this ride and pleasurable company have put them right out of my mind." Those lovely fingers became fascinated with her goblet.

Again, Antoine smiled and nodded. *What secrets do you hide, Mademoiselle de Saix?*

The conversation lagged while they ate in silence. All Antoine had learned about her—her abilities and shyness—only told him she was a delight. He still believed she harbored a secret, but he enjoyed his time with her so much, he was less inclined to worry about any mystery. Perhaps it even made her more attractive. If that were possible.

Antoine stood and held out his hand. "Shall we?"

She hesitated but took his hand and stood with him.

He led her to his horse where he removed a leather pouch. Linking her hand through his arm, he guided her toward the stand of trees to the north of the clearing.

"What are you doing?" Her steps slowed. Her gaze never left him.

He stopped. "Do you trust me?"

A fight of emotions showed in her eyes. She nodded.

As he led her a short distance among the trees, her grip tightened on his arm. He patted her hand and stopped before turning her around and pointing.

Louise brought her hands to her lips with a sharp intake of breath. "Oh, if only I had my sketch book. The way the oak branches curve around—it is almost as if they are framing the view."

Antoine pulled the pouch from beneath his arm and opened it, removing a set of charcoals and paper. With a bow, he handed them to her. He then removed a small blanket and spread it on the ground.

Her mouth froze with a little o on her lips.

Antoine took her hand, kissed it, and then stepped back out

of her way. She stood until he pointed to the blanket. "You now have your materials. Sketch and delight your heart."

Louise lowered herself to the blanket and began. Once started, she never looked down at the paper but stared straight ahead, her hand moving continually. In a few short minutes she paused. Antoine moved behind her to observe.

"No, this is incomplete." Bending over her work, she hid it from his view. "Go, stand over there."

Antoine chuckled and headed where she pointed.

"No, no, no." She popped up and pulled him by the elbow. "Over here." Stepping back, she surveyed and shook her head. "That will not do." She playfully pushed him.

His heart beat faster. "What?"

"Down. Sit and lean back against the tree."

Antoine obeyed, laughing at her.

Posing him, she nodded her approval. "Now stay there." She shook her finger at him as she returned to her seat on the blanket to begin sketching again.

"When do I get to see it?" Antoine scratched his ear.

"When I am done—if I ever get done. Sit still. I cannot do this if you keep moving." She continued drawing the whole while.

"I am not moving, see?"

"Well, you were. Do not do it again."

"Very well. Please, just finish." He wiggled his toes. She could not see that. Delightful, that was what she was. One minute shy, and the next she bossed him with ease. He could not remember the last time he had such fun.

"Hold still only a moment longer. I am nearly through." She finished with a few quick strokes and held up the sketch. "Voila`."

Antoine shoved himself up and returned to Louise to view the finished product. It was by no means a masterpiece, but the lady's talent showed through. "I am honored, Mademoiselle."

"My pleasure, Monsieur. It is for you." She presented him the sketch.

"I most sincerely thank you." Holding out his hand, he offered her assistance. "You do know we will be spending a certain amount of time together over the next two weeks."

Her eyes grew wide. "Oui?"

"Perhaps if I knew a few other things you like, I could arrange something else for your pleasure. I know you enjoy riding, and I could easily do that every day. May I include some of your other interests? Are there places you would like to go, things you would like to see or do? I am at your disposal, Mademoiselle." Antoine bowed over her hand that he still held.

She pulled away. "This has been such a lovely day. I think I could do this over and over."

"Then this is what we will do until you choose to do something else."

She reached to pick up the blanket, and he noticed her shapely curves. This beautiful girl-woman was an enigma. Sometimes she seemed to relax in his company showing humor and fortitude. At other times, she withdrew.

He took the folded blanket from her and stuffed it along with the pouch of artist materials under his arm and tucked her hand under the other arm, leading her to the table.

She did not seem as nervous as before. Perhaps she was beginning to trust him.

Trills of a lark broke the silence between them. The warmth of her smile dawning at the sound rivaled the sun.

When back at the table, Louise began to pack up the basket, but Antoine stopped her. "Leave it be. Someone will retrieve it all after we depart."

Louise stared at him.

He moved a loose tendril away from her face, tucking it delicately behind her ear. It was so natural. It was too intimate. She did not pull away. His fingers skimmed the surface of her velvet cheek as he pulled his hand back. He reached for her hand, capturing her gaze the whole time. He was earning her trust. He knew he should be glad about that, and he was in a way, though he also knew he was deceiving her. His duty demanded he obtain her confidence.

Imperative though it may be that he learn of her connection to the Huguenot movement, if any connection existed, at the same time he found himself wanting her trust solely because he found her delightfully fascinating.

She was beautiful and intelligent and talented. Yet there was something more to her, something he had yet to identify, something very special. He could see it when she threw caution to the wind. Soon he hoped to understand it.

They retrieved their horses and led them off in the way they had come. There seemed to be no hurry to leave. She allowed him to hold her hand. The thrill running up his arm powered the thumping in his chest.

They spoke lightly every so often—not much, just little things. The silences in between were comfortable, as if their thoughts needed no verbal help to be shared. A woman who appreciated the quiet of merely being together both intrigued and elated him.

Antoine spotted a small, purple wildflower and picked it.

"For moi?" Her smile became a grin.

"But of course." He pushed soft tendrils out of the way and tucked it behind her ear. Such a delicate ear. Such a lovely shade of rose climbing up her neck to her cheeks. He must stop now or he would be no better than Jean-Luc.

She ran to the other side of the path and picked a similar flower. As she turned back to him, her eyes had taken on a mischievous gleam. "For you, Monsieur."

A warm heat spread up his neck and face at her touch. Her fingers brushed his ear lighter than a butterfly as she tucked the flower in place. Thought and breath left him.

She laughed, a pure melodic sound, and he joined her. They walked on. What had taken them twenty minutes to cover in the morning now took much longer. Antoine did not mind, though. There was no other place he would rather be.

By mid-afternoon, they arrived back at the stables and left the horses with the stable boy. Antoine escorted Louise back to her room.

"His Majesty is having *appartement* tonight in the royal suite. We are invited." He enjoyed watching how she rested against her door. Leaning in more intimately, he propped his arm over her shoulder on the doorjamb. "There is to be a concert, followed by games, with supper most probably around ten o'clock. You may want a small bit of food and a nap before we go. Shall I call for you at seven?"

"Oui, merci. And, Monsieur . . ."

"Antoine, please." It would be nice to hear her say his name.

"Antoine, thank you for today. I had no idea I could enjoy myself so much here. I— " She stopped herself as if to say more but changed her mind. A soft pink tinged her cheeks. "Merci. I will see you at seven."

She smiled.

He straightened, kissed her hand, and left.

Louise opened her door and carefully checked for others before hugging herself and making one big twirl around the room. She did not want to again be caught behaving the fool.

Being alone in her room allowed her more time to stretch out and daydream about her wonderful day. Humming to herself, she plopped on the big bed. Two seconds later, she was up pacing the room, too full of life to take the time to rest.

A knock at the door put an end to her flights of fancy. She opened it to a young woman, a maid she had not yet met.

"Mademoiselle de Saix?" The maid curtseyed.

"Oui, may I help you?"

"The Marquise de Montespan requests the honor of your presence in her chambers at your earliest convenience." The young woman turned to go.

"Oh, wait, please." Louise stopped her. "I do not know how to get to her suite, and I could go right now, if you would be so kind as to show me the way."

"As you wish." The maid spoke no more the whole way, stopping only at the door to announce Louise. "Mademoiselle de Saix to see you, Madame."

"That will be all, Simone." The maid was dismissed with a wave. "I am happy you could come so promptly, my dear. Please have a seat." The Marquise lounged on a *petite coucher* in only her chemise, obviously quite comfortable.

Louise chose a chair with a straight back and waited. Why had she been summoned?

"I understand you have been out today with that fellow, what was his name? Ah, Monsieur de Crocketagné. This is correct?"

"Oui, Madame. We went riding." What was this questioning about?

"I see. Do you know the man's intentions?"

"Madame, I am sorry, but I only met him yesterday. I believe he was assigned to escort me, so his intentions have to do with doing his duty to the king." Funny how that thought just popped into her head. Louise surmised the statement was as much to herself as to the Marquise.

"Oh, I see." The Marquise fell silent for some time.

"If there is nothing else . . ." Louise rose to leave.

"Oh, but there is. You need not be in such a hurry. We have only begun to chat."

"Oh." Louise sighed and sat once again. Little hairs at the nape of her neck tightened while thoughts of danger whispered in her ear. What had she done?

"I also hear you like to take nightly strolls through the halls of Versailles. Is that also correct, my dear?" Her tone became as frosty as the coldest day in January.

"I could not sleep and went for a walk. Is that a problem? I understood it was permitted." Louise's temperature rose, but she tried to control her anger. If she got angry, she would, without a doubt, start to cry. The Marquise would pounce on any weakness.

"No, no that is not a problem. Who am I to say what you are permitted? I merely asked." Smooth, like oil. "Oh, by the by, is dining with His Majesty in his boudoir also going to become part of your nightly routine?" The razor-sharp smile seemed almost as lethal as the daggers shooting from the Marquise's eyes.

"Excuse me? I am not sure I understand." Louise's anger increased her courage. She stood and took a deep breath. "Do you have a problem with my accepting an invitation from my cousin, who also happens to be the king, to have an evening morsel with him? Perhaps if *Her* Majesty, his wife, asked this I might understand the problem, although it was just an innocent meal in the outer living quarters of the Royal Suite. You, Madame, are not his wife, and I see no reason to explain things to you."

"Sit down." The Marquise stood, anger marring her cold beauty. Her face contorted, and the smile returned. "You really do not know who I am, do you?" She gave a mirthless laugh. "My dear, I am the king's favorite. Before me, there was a young woman whose mother brought her to the court for the sole purpose of giving her to the king. She has borne him four children, and because His Majesty felt sorry for the public humiliation cast on the little wretch, last year he made her a duchess. He keeps her where he can keep his eye on her. I make sure that is all that goes on."

"But you are married. The queen's lady-in-waiting." Tante Marie always said she was too innocent. She should have called her ignorant. How could His Majesty do such a thing? She wanted to go home.

"Poor, doe-eyed little thing. Have you not even a clue? My marriage brought me to the palace. The queen's chambers brought me to the king. One day my marriage will be over and so will his. I carry his child right now, and I will be his next queen."

Did this really happen? Were the nobles this shallow and callous? What kind of people lived here? She did not belong at Court.

"So, do not think, for even one second, that you can oust me with His Majesty. I have worked hard to be in this position, and I will not be thwarted from my goal by you and that *Mademoiselle Innocent* act." The Marquise sat and arranged her chemise. "Have I made myself clear, my dear?" The frost chilled more like an avalanche now.

"Oui, quite." Crystal clear, in fact. Louise wanted only to leave this place.

"Bon. Now that we understand each other, I think we might be friends. Oui, that could be quite fun with your innocent view of life. For now, I must rest. When we have appartement, it takes much skill to play the games, and I so enjoy winning. Perhaps we might talk later."

Louise stood, knowing she had been dismissed. She stepped out the door just as the maid, Simone, returned to the room of her mistress. Very well. She would have to find her own way back to her chamber.

A mixture of fear and relief flooded over her. As much as she worried about becoming lost in the construction, she did not want to see anyone. She could not hold back the tears another second. With a little effort, she should be able to retrace her steps and make it back to her room by herself before anyone found her with red eyes and stuffy nose.

She caught herself twice as she was about to make a wrong turn, but she at last made it to her chamber. The success of that feat only slightly helped to alleviate the humiliation she wore like sackcloth and ashes. Nothing could wipe the scene from her memory.

Louise closed the door to her room. Not at all like the last time she had entered here. No happy feelings, no urge to dance.

Changing out of her riding costume, life drained from her. She poured water into the basin, rinsed off the dust from outside, and then lay down on the bed in her chemise.

The cruel words of the Marquise returned to her, again and again. There was truth in them. She was innocent. So many things went on at Versailles, things the residents took for granted. They understood the rules of this game. She did not. Did they merely look the other way?

Innocent, a good description of her.

She had not appreciated to the full the implication of the conversation at first. When the king invited her to dine with him, that is all she thought would happen. That is all that did happen.

If the Marquise thought something else might have transpired, might someone else think the same thing? Who else knew about her late-night meal? What if someone told Antoine? Would he think of her in that same light?

That was another thing. She enjoyed her time with Antoine and believed he was enjoying his time with her as well. However, they had only met the day before. It was his job to be her escort.

Maybe he did his job well.

She closed her eyes and begged for sleep.

Chapter Eight

The cloud was not as fluffy or comfortable as before. Joy dripped from Louise's heart like the last bit of water in an empty pitcher. As she gazed over the edge, it began to rain on the green islands and the blue mirror. No birds sang. In fact, there were none to be seen. The only sound came from the splash of each raindrop as it hit the landscape below.

She rolled onto her back to find the stars had dimmed. In place of the dramatic light show she had previously enjoyed, now only a handful of blinking lights hummed a sad, vibrating dirge. The weariness of the scene merely added to her own melancholy. With a sigh, she rolled back over again.

The sight below had not improved. Air darkened, signaling a storm brewed ahead. Lightning pierced the sky and a sudden crash of thunder made her tremble. She was afraid, and she did not know why. Storms had never frightened her. This one, though, she already knew was different. She had nowhere to hide, knew of no way to get down.

Louise was at the mercy of whoever controlled the cloud.

The familiar whoosh of wings sounded as the mysterious rider appeared flying towards her. She could hear him calling out to her. She reached out toward his outstretched hand.

At the same moment, he began to raise his visor. She realized she did not know the identity of the rider. Was he someone she could trust? Would he save her from the danger or just make matters worse?

Louise withdrew her hand. She inched away from the edge. The rider still drew closer. He continued to call her name.

She backed up more.

He continued to come towards her, pleading for her to take his hand.

Louise retreated further still, falling backward over the edge.

At first, she floated. But as the rain pelted her, she became too heavy. The ground rushed up to greet her. She braced for impact.

Louise awoke with a gasp. She bolted upright. Her hair stuck to her sweaty face. Her chemise molded to her flesh, her heart raced as if she had run a marathon, and her body trembled uncontrollably.

Oh, God, I feel so alone. I just want to go home. Please let me go home. Louise sobbed and fell back. She wrapped her arms about her pillow, hugging it close while tears streamed down her face. "I want to go home, please."

Louise lay like that for what seemed hours. Time slipped away, and the shadows in her room deepened. She had no desire to get up and change. There was nothing to look forward to—it was all just a part of Antoine's job.

Now, without intent, it was possible she had given herself a reputation. The type of which was only whispered about in her circle of friends and to be avoided at all costs. Of course, the one person she hoped would not believe it might not even care one way or another, since she was only an assignment to him. Would it change the way he acted around her? Would he look at her differently? What would she see in his eyes the next time they met?

There was a knock at the door, and Tante Marie charged in. "Dear heart, you have not even begun to get ready? See, Didi, I told you she was in here. Why in the world did you not answer

Didi's knock and come to me? Are you ill?" Tante Marie strode to the bed and placed her hand on Louise's forehead. "You do not feel warm. What time is Antoine coming for you?"

"He said seven, but I am not feeling very well. I do not think I will go tonight." Louise pulled her covers up higher.

"Where is Mimi?"

Louise caught Didi's worried gaze.

"I sent her out. I told her I wanted to be alone." Louise lied smoothly. The thought of Mimi had jarred some caring back into her. It would not be fair to punish the young woman because of her own problems.

Tante Marie's hands planted on her hips. "Then what seems to be the problem, child? You have never been ill a day in all the time I have known you."

"It is nothing. I would just prefer to stay here tonight by myself." The melancholy still weighed heavy in her heart.

The older woman sat on the bed beside Louise and put a comforting arm around her. "Come here, child."

Louise fell into her embrace. The sobbing began anew.

When the tears subsided, Tante Marie wiped them from Louise's eyes. "Now, tell me what dire thing has happened."

Louise described the wonderful morning, and how she had enjoyed herself. Then she shared about the summons to the chambers of the Marquise de Montespan and the horrific conversation. In the end, she confided her fears about her reputation and the fact that Antoine was only doing his job.

"My, my, you have had quite a day, have you not?" No judgment tainted her aunt's words. "I am so sorry for the rudeness of the Marquise. There was no reason for her outburst. I do not know at all what His Majesty sees in her, although I can imagine.

"I know poor Louise-Françoise—the duchess she referred to —and I must say, Louise-Françoise may be empty headed, but she is sweet and loves His Majesty with her whole heart. She never has put designs on him to be his next queen, being satisfied with his attention. No one can say that about the Marquise. Her manipulations are well known. It would be a good idea to steer clear of her in the future, if possible."

"I agree." Louise rested with her head on her aunt's shoulder. "I should not have any problem doing that if I stay here tonight."

"Ah, but my dear one, you must not do that. I know that staying here feels like the better solution, but sadly you are the guest of the king and have been invited specifically. If you do not show, he will want to know why. You were right to think that illness might be a good excuse—outside of death, perhaps the best. However, my darling, if His Majesty thinks you are sick, he will send his surgeon to come and check on you. You could probably use a good bloodletting to rid you of your extra melancholy and put your humors back into balance. However, I would not recommend it."

"What? He would not." Louise sat up straight. One look at the face of her aunt told her. "He would. Oh, *now* what am I to do? It must be almost seven, and I do not want to face Antoine. What should I do, Tante Marie?"

"Do not worry, dear heart." Marie patted her hand and whisked back the bedclothes. "Didi and I will help you. You should not have sent Mimi away, but never mind that now. We will get you ready."

Marie turned into a whirlwind of efficiency, ordering Didi what items to find. She put Louise to washing her face and body, while she chose from the closet of new gowns. Pulling out an aquamarine silk with a shirred bodice studded with small, white seed pearls and a deeply scooped, off-the-shoulder neckline, she held it up and pronounced it perfect. The overskirt was of fine Venetian lace while the underskirt shone of a darker version of the original hue. The sleeves were trimmed with matching lace cuffs. Tossing the dress on the bed, she looked through the white velvet bags Didi had laid out as per instruction. She found a matching pair of combs, earrings and necklace, each studded with aquamarines, and set them out on the vanity along with a length of aquamarine ribbon.

Louise changed her chemise, and Didi helped her to slip into the dress.

"Come sit. Let Didi arrange your hair." Marie nearly pushed Louise down at the vanity seat, and Didi began to brush through her tangles. Although the strokes were gentle, Louise had already given herself a nagging headache with all her crying. Every movement of the brush heightened the pain. She bit her lip. Yet the thought of the surgeon gave her the stamina she needed to go through the ordeal.

Tante Marie's fashion ideas were far less conservative than Louise's. "Didi, I saw a woman in Paris with her hair piled high in curls and ringlets at the side. That is how Louise should wear her hair tonight. Make the curls on top pile very high. And use the combs to hold it."

Louise closed her eyes tight, fighting an urge to yank the brush from the maid's hand. It would have hurt much less just to pull each strand out from the root.

"Ah, that is exactly what I described. The highest fashion. Monsieur LeBrun would be thrilled to put you on canvas, dear heart."

Louise peeked with one eye at the mirror. The view jolted both eyes wide open. "Is that . . . me?" A very fashionable stranger with bright eyes and rosy cheeks stared back.

"Oui, of course it is you." Tante Marie turned her away from the mirror to look directly at her. "Any duty-loving escort who can resist you tonight is beyond the hope of even the Almighty. Antoine will not be focused on his job but on you, my dear— trust me. He would gladly pay to be the one to escort you to appartement tonight."

"Oh, *Tante* Marie, I am not out to work my wiles on him." Louise pulled up the lace of her chemise. "I just want to know he likes spending time with me because of who I am and not because it is his obligation to the king."

"Dear heart, I believe that is the case." Her aunt placed a *mouche* to Louise's upper left cheek.

The paste holding the small silk dot in place felt strange. Then so did her hair and reflection.

"Do not be concerned about his reasons at this time. Enjoy yourself, and let things happen as they will. Are we agreed?"

Louise nodded.

Tante Marie applied pearl powder to Louise's cleavage and then her own ample one. "And you will stay away from the Marquise—I know, I know, it is a small private gathering, but do your best." She picked up a small vial of perfume and touched the applicator to Louise's wrists, throat, and between her breasts.

"Oui, I will." Louise tugged up the lace of her chemise even more.

The knock at the door came the next instant, right at seven o'clock. The women looked at each other. Louise took a breath and nodded her head slightly. It felt top-heavy, and she was not yet used to the feeling.

Didi opened the door. Antoine stood there in elegant splendor—his justaucorps was midnight blue with white satin trims and red lining. The sword hilt, sticking out from his embroidered baldric gleamed, and his plumed hat lay neatly tucked under his left arm. He presented Louise with a nosegay of wildflowers. Louise noticed his own wavy black hair fell to his shoulders. He wore no wig. Was it possible he had grown even more handsome?

❧

LOUISE LOOKED MORE STUNNING THAN IMAGINABLE. Antoine could have stared at her all evening had not Madame du Sine taken things into her own hands.

"We need to be going now. His Majesty will be wondering

what has become of us." The older woman gave him a pointed look.

"Oh, oui." Antoine came to his senses. "Please allow me." He opened the door for the ladies and held it while they walked into the corridor. "Shall we?" He offered each lady an arm. Louise's gentle touch at his elbow sent a vibration through his soul. The heady fragrance of her perfume, something floral but spicy, made concentration difficult. Their time today had already become a favorite memory to be viewed over and over in his mind. He had discovered a treasure. The thought that she would be leaving Versailles in less that two weeks was one he shoved with determination to the back of his mind.

He wanted to know this woman. And not because she was any kind of assignment.

What if she really were a Huguenot spy? Could he turn her in?

Antoine did not know what he would do.

Closing his mind to the possibility, he shoved that thought away too. Why dwell on the problem since it most likely would never present itself?

⊗

Louise was grateful to her aunt for keeping the banter light. As they ambled arm in arm to the Royal Suite, she recalled the look in Antoine's eyes when Didi opened the door. Could she trust it? He seemed sincere about wanting to be with her. The possibility of finding out he was merely a good actor left her nervous, jittery, silent. If she could just be out in the glade alone with Antoine. There she could be herself, away from judging eyes and inhibitions. A lump formed in her throat, and the sting of forming tears scared her. An involuntary sniff escaped her.

Antoine paused.

"*Foin*! Are you crying, Mademoiselle?" His concern appeared genuine.

"It is nothing, I am sure. I am right, am I not, dear one?" Tante pointedly caught her gaze.

"Excuse me, Madame, but I think it must be something." Antoine shook off her aunt and turned back to Louise. He enveloped her hand. "Mademoiselle, I am correct, n'est-ce pas? Please, Mademoiselle, I thought we had become friends. Can you not trust me with what is bothering you?"

"I will go on in and let you two talk." Marie patted Louise's cheek. "I will be inside should you need me. For anything." She looked straight at Antoine before turning on her heel and walking into the Royal Suite.

"I am sorry, Monsieur—"

"Antoine."

"Antoine." Louise smiled briefly. "My afternoon after you left has been quite trying. I am fighting a small headache."

"What happened this afternoon?" He held her hand, his voice filled with genuine compassion.

"I had a conversation with someone who--" Louise focused on the floor. She could not meet his gaze and explain this. "Someone who seemed to think I had intentions other than the ones I actually have."

He rubbed the back of her hand with his thumb sending shivers up her spine. "You are being evasive. I do not know if it is due to what was said or who said it. I am not looking for gossip and do not want to pry. I had thought that after today, though, we were better friends than this."

"Are we?" Louise searched his face for truth.

"What do you mean?"

"Mon— Antoine, we met only yesterday. I know I am assigned to you while I am here. It would be nice to think we are true friends, but I would not presume to take liberty where your duty was concerned."

"Mademoiselle," He wiped away a tear and dropped his

voice to a whisper. "Louise, look into my eyes. Believe me when I say this: You are the most remarkable woman I have ever met. I consider it a privilege to be your escort and hope our friendship will be a very, *very* long one."

When he spoke her name, it might as well have been angels whispering. Magical music sang in her ears, and her eyes knew the truth of his words.

"I believe you." She took a deep breath. "Oui, I trust you. I will tell you all about my difficult afternoon, but not here. On the morrow, when we go back to our glade, I will tell you all about it."

He nodded and handed her his lace-trimmed handkerchief. "So, we are friends again, correct?"

"Did we ever stop being friends?" She gave him what she hoped was a smile of friendship.

"Ah, that's the lovely Louise I have grown so fond of." He laughed. "Are we ready?" He presented his arm.

"We are." She placed her hand in the crook of his arm and walked with him into the Royal Suite.

❧

ANTOINE LEANED IN TO WHISPER IN HER EAR. "MESSIEURS Lully and Quinault have composed a new opera. The soloist will be performing an aria from Act One." He guided Louise toward their seats. "Seating is arranged so that the invited are placed with care according to rank. It avoids problems." He read the question in her eyes. "It would not have been the first time a legal issue came about over where someone chose to sit."

"Surely you are making fun. Can people be that petty?"

Antoine shook his head. How much she had yet to learn about court life. He hoped her innocence and candor would not be destroyed before it came time for her to leave.

An ache nudged his heart.

Louise waved to her aunt as they found their seats, smiling sweetly. Madame du Sine looked relieved and smiled back.

They had been given chairs with arms, generally held for the nobility. They sat, and Antoine took her hand.

She did not pull away.

Now that he had her trust, did he deserve it?

❧

LOUISE'S GAZE FOLLOWED THE SINGER FROM THE TIME HE entered the room. He came to the front, signaling everyone to their seats. As the room quieted, Monsieur Lully introduced the vocalist, and then moved to the side where he could conduct the string quartet.

The music transported Louise back to a time of ancient gods and goddesses in long ago Egypt. Closing her eyes, she could visualize the passion of the piece from the opera *Isis*. The melody's spell entranced her.

At the final note, she leaned to Antoine. "Oh, I do not want it to end."

"Neither do I."

She caught his intense gaze and fanned her face.

People stood, giving an ovation. She stood and joined in the applause.

Monsieur Lully came to the front again. He bowed. "Your Majesty and honored guests. I thank you for your enthusiastic reception." Another bow, and he returned to his musicians.

"You do know this is only a small part of a full opera." Antoine's breath tickled her neck. She nodded.

"Next week they will present the full production."

Excitement charged through her. "Next week? Are you sure? I will still be at Court. I will be able to attend, or at least I hope I may attend. I cannot imagine any reason why I should not be allowed to but—"

She stopped. Again, with the blathering. Antoine must think her an idiot.

But no, his eyes twinkled, and his laugh came gently. "I believe I can arrange it. Just possibly."

She laughed with him. "*Bon.*"

Just the same, it seemed if she counted on something, something else came along to spoil her plans.

However, the opera would be next week. For tonight, she must to get through the game period before dinner without having to face the Marquise again.

Antoine guided her out of the way while servants rearranged the room for appartement. Servants arranged whist and trictrac tables and moved into place a billiards table.

It was well known that His Majesty favored the card games. So did many others, for they could sit while they played as well as spend time with the king. Her Majesty was not fond of gambling and merely watched.

Antoine led Louise around the tables so she could observe.

She enjoyed trictrac the most, since she was familiar with the backgammon-type game. Many a winter's eve she and her father had played it to pass the time. It did not take her long to surmise the real expert and deduce his strategies.

As she turned to Antoine, about to suggest giving the game a go, she spotted a servant heading in her direction.

"Mademoiselle de Saix?"

"Oui."

"Would you come with me, please?

Antoine cocked an eyebrow. "Is there a problem?"

"I do not know. If you would excuse me a moment, I will find out."

"Shall I come with you or wait for you here?"

"Stay here. I will return momentarily."

The servant led her outside the king's quarters.

Stepping through the door, Louise found an almost frantic Mimi waiting for her.

"Mademoiselle, I am sorry to be so late and to pull you away. Please forgive me, but things are much worse than I had first imagined. If it were not for what might happen to my family if I did not come back, I would have stayed away." Mimi trembled.

"Please calm yourself, Mimi and tell me what is your problem? I promise I will help you all I can."

"That is very generous of you, and I need to talk with someone. Please, Mademoiselle, could we speak privately?"

Louise looked back at the door, knowing Antoine waited beyond. She paused but a moment more. "Oui."

With a sheltering arm about the maid's shoulders, Louise guided the distraught girl to the safety of a nearby alcove.

Once there, Mimi spilled out the entire story of her love for Pierre, how they were to be married when his time of working on Versailles was complete, the accident, and what had happened to Madame LeSuere.

Louise shook her head in disbelief. "What can I do for you, Mimi?"

"I need to find a way to stay with Pierre. He has not regained consciousness yet, and his mother needs care as well. Momo will only help for so long. I hate to be away from him, and I do not know what to do, Mademoiselle."

Louise squeezed the girl's hand. "I have an idea. Stay here until I return. I will not be long." She hugged Mimi and hurried back out the door and down the hall. First of all, she must speak with Antoine. Maybe with his help, this would work.

He waited at the trictrac table where she had left him. On tiptoe, she leaned to his ear. "Could we step outside, please?"

He nodded and escorted her out.

"What is the problem?" His eyes probed.

Louise trusted him. She must.

"I need your help. Mimi, my maid, is in the hall. I need to find a way into town. She needs my help."

His brow wrinkled, but he continued to listen.

"I do not know what to make for an excuse for having to miss dinner, but it is important that I take her home and help her right now. Do you have any ideas?"

He nodded. "Do not worry. Go back to her, and I will come to your room in a few minutes. Be ready to leave as soon as I get there."

She hoped he could read the gratitude in her eyes before she turned away.

"You have returned." Mimi's face showed relief when Louise ducked back into the alcove.

"Oui, Monsieur de Crocketagné will meet us momentarily."

Mimi's face became pale. "You told him?"

"No, Mimi, I merely asked for his help to bring us to your home. Come."

Louise led the way to her room as fast as she dared without causing a scene. Once there, she comforted Mimi until Antoine could arrive.

The maid calmed, only to jump when she heard the knock at the door.

"I understand there are two ladies here in need of a carriage and escort." Antoine sounded lighthearted, and Louise appreciated the attempt. However, she could see that Mimi did not.

"Where are we going, Mesdemoiselles?"

Mimi gave directions while Louise grabbed up two shawls before they went out the door. Antoine walked them to the carriage, helping them in before directing the driver to the LeSuere home, and following the women aboard.

⁂

THIS TRIP MADE NO SENSE, BUT IT WAS APPARENT FROM Mimi's demeanor something serious was afoot. Antoine longed to question Louise, but this was not the time. Upon arrival, he helped the ladies out, and they all went inside.

Mimi ran through the doorway first. "Has there been any change?"

He followed the maid and Louise into the room. What went on here? Why did Albert and Jean-Luc stand just inside the door?

Albert shook his head. "No, nothing."

Mimi went straight to a young man who lay sleeping. Louise moved to an older woman lying face down on a pallet. Another woman knelt next to her.

Antoine scanned the room. This made no sense.

Albert nodded for Jean-Luc and Antoine to follow him outside.

Antoine pulled the door closed behind, leaving them in the dark. "So, do you want to tell me what is happening there?"

"Did you hear the report about Pierre LeSuere yesterday morning?" Albert's voice floated through the night.

"I do not know . . . oh, oui, was he not the one who was hurt the night before last while working on the fountain sculptures? Is that he?"

"Oui, his hand was crushed in the accident. I think he also must have hit his head. He has been unconscious ever since."

"What of the woman? What has Louise's maid to do with all this?"

"The woman is his mother. A widow who lost her husband to the project a few months back. She chose to vent her outrage to His Majesty. He had her whipped."

Antoine stared, unable to breathe, as if someone punched him in the stomach. "Whipped? His Majesty? Are you sure?"

"Of *course*, we are sure." Antoine recognized Jean-Luc's voice. He had been silent for so long, Antoine had forgotten the man was there. "We were there, my friend. We were *there*."

At first, Antoine understood him to mean they had seen what had happened, but truth slowly dawned. "You? You did this?"

Albert interjected. "His Majesty gave the command and left

it to us to carry out. I had no choice. We brought her home, and at least one of us has been here with her ever since."

Even without seeing, Antoine knew his friends' faces were etched with pain. "I am sorry. What do Mimi and Louise have to do with all of this?"

"Mimi and Pierre were to be married next year. Your guess is as good as mine about Mademoiselle de Saix."

Then Antoine understood. It was her compassionate, tender heart. Only here in Versailles, that could be a very dangerous commodity.

Chapter Nine

The walls closed in around Antoine. Three grown men standing about left little space. Tension filled the room. He convinced Albert and Jean-Luc to go back to the barracks. Their day would begin early. In turn, he promised to keep them informed of what took place in their absence.

Mimi's mother needed to return to her family now that there were others available to help. Antoine escorted her to her home, returning within minutes.

Madame LeSuere awoke to Louise caring for her. The older woman tried to move away, but the pain proved too great.

"Who are you?" She spoke with difficulty.

Louise glanced at Antoine before answering. "I am Louise de Saix, Madame. Is there anything I can get for you?"

Madame LeSuere merely closed her eyes. Antoine gave Louise's shoulder a squeeze and stepped back to be available, yet out of the way.

When Madame LeSuere opened her eyes again an hour later, she stared at Louise. The transformation must have been a shock. While she slept, Louise had taken down her fancy curls and pulled her hair back with a ribbon. The mouche fell off somewhere along the way. Antoine preferred this simpler look.

"Drink." Madame LeSuere's voice croaked.

Louise obediently poured water from a pitcher and held the cup for her. More spilled than was imbibed.

"How is my son?"

"He is the same. Mimi has been beside him all night."

Madame LeSuere pierced Antoine with a look. "You there, come to me."

He walked to her pallet.

"Help me up that I may go to my son."

Antoine bent and gave her his arm for support. Though he took care not to touch her back, the pain of her own movements was obviously excruciating. Still, she never let a sound of the agony escape.

Once she was upright, she walked to Pierre's side. Madame LeSuere could not bend over him, though, so Antoine found an old crate that was low enough for her to sit on without so much bending.

She took her son's undamaged hand in her own and simply held on. "I am here, my son."

Mimi continued to bathe his face and to softly speak to him. She brushed back his hair with her fingers, encouraging him to wake.

Antoine drew beside Louise, whispering in her ear. "Let us step away a moment." Her hair smelled like flowers, and he hated himself for thinking such a thing at this time.

Louise held his hand and let him guide her outside the door. "I do not know how to thank you for all your help." They stood outside and watched the morning star shine heralding the new day. "There is not going to be a happy ending for either of those women, is there." It was a statement rather than a question.

In his heart, Antoine agreed, but longed to give hope. "We do not know that. All we can do is pray and wait."

"Then what? What will they do?"

He drew her to him and wrapped his arms around her. She melted into his embrace. "I do not know. Let us take it a step at a time, shall we? Today has enough trouble in it."

"Of course." She buried her head in his chest.

So shapely, her curves molded to his body like a glove. He loved having her so close. She had awakened fires in him, despite the barricades he had erected. If not for the tragedy inside the door, he could have stayed this way forever.

Time crawled along when abruptly there seemed to be a flurry of movement from inside.

Antoine held the door for Louise as they reentered the home.

Pierre's breathing had become much shallower.

Madame LeSuere rubbed his good hand. "He is growing cold. Rub, rub his feet and hands. Keep him warm."

Frantic, Mimi checked his feet, rubbing them briskly and adding more blankets.

Antoine pulled Louise aside and whispered, "It will not be much longer now. I will go for the priest."

❦

LOUISE ACHED FOR THESE WOMEN. THOUGH SHE COULD not understand their pain, she hurt for them nonetheless. It also put her own hurt feelings into perspective. Not knowing anything else to do, Louise knelt in a corner and began to pray. She prayed for Pierre's soul, for his mother's comfort, for Mimi's peace. Last, she lifted Albert, Jean-Luc, and her king, praying they would find forgiveness. It was the right thing to do.

Antoine returned with the priest, and the cleric began to offer the Last Rites. The little group stood quietly together.

Pierre breathed a last ragged breath. The rattle from his lungs gave finality to the vigil of silence. Mimi and Madame LeSuere held one another as they gave themselves over to their grief. The priest prayed.

Antoine wrapped his arms about Louise, and she threw herself into them, drenching the front of his justaucorps. His chin rested on her head as the sun popped over the horizon.

The new day began with goodbye.

⚜

ONCE OTHER NEIGHBORS CAME TO STAY WITH MADAME LeSuere, Louise was free to leave. She and Antoine escorted Mimi home to her family.

They were met at the door.

An older version of Mimi pulled her into an embrace. "Oh, *le pitoyable*, you poor thing." A younger version wrapped a blanket around her shoulders and guided her through the doorway.

Louise could hear more sympathies from inside.

"We are so sorry, Mimi."

"Mama, Mimi is back!"

Momo stood just outside the door, eyeing Louise with distrust as if she blamed her for Pierre's death.

"I suppose you want to come in as well." Curt and rude. Had Momo ever done anything without rancor?

Antoine stepped up and put his arm about Louise's shoulders. "We wanted to make sure that Mimi safely arrived home."

"How noble of you." Momo's sarcasm cut.

Louise wanted what was best for Mimi and had done what she could to prove that. Yet where was Momo when her sister needed her? Not at her side or helping to make others think she was at the chateau.

Momo stood as sentry to the house. "She is here and no longer your concern. You may go back to your noble friends." Momo locked gazes with Antoine.

He squeezed Louise's shoulder. "Let us go back." He began to guide Louise to the carriage.

She stopped. A niggling thought started an alarm in her

brain. "Wait and think, Momo. There still could be trouble if Mimi is found to be away from Versailles. As long as I am away, it is natural for her to be with me, but—"

"I cannot believe this. She has just lost the man she was to marry, and you expect her to come back to Versailles and care for you?"

"No!"

All eyes focused on Louise as if she were naked. If only the floor would swallow her. Sighing, she tried to explain. "I want her to come back so I may care for her."

"But of course." Momo did not believe her, but Louise became more concerned the longer she thought. It could be dangerous to Mimi's whole family.

"Momo, she needs to be cared for. She needs a place to cry and grieve. Yet if she is not seen at Versailles, your whole family could be in danger. Do you not see? It is the best way. I want her to see her family and talk with all of you—to cry with all of you. However, you know as well as I do, it is best for everyone if she returns to Versailles with me." Louise stepped toward the girl and put out her hand. "Do you not think it is time you started to trust me a little?"

Momo refused to meet Louise's hand. "I see your point. Still, she needs her sisters near her. I will come back with you. That way I will not have to trust you."

Very well. Louise resigned to Momo's plan.

"You might as well come in and meet the family before we leave." The invitation held little warmth. When Louise hesitated, Momo added, "We do not bite, nor do we have the plague."

"Merci." It was the only thing Louise could think to say. She followed Momo into the house holding tight to Antoine's hand.

The girls' parents appeared surprised to see Louise and Antoine enter their home, though they greeted them warmly.

"Bon, so you are the royal cousin our Mimi has been caring for. We are pleased to meet you, Mademoiselle." The older man, presumably Mimi's father, sounded more welcoming than his daughter. "Allow me to introduce my family. I am called Robert, Robert Roché. This here is my wife, Annette. And these here are Mimi's sisters." His arm swung wide indicating the young women surrounding Mimi. "I am supposing you have already met with Momo. This here lovely is my Beatrix."

"Bibi," sang out a voice.

"This is my sweet Cecile."

"Cici."

"My eldest beauty, Genevieve."

"Gigi."

"And my baby, Violette."

"Vivi, that is me." The voice ended in a giggle.

The child peeked out from behind her father. She looked to be only seven or eight years of age. Old enough to understand the loss of a man special to her older sister. Yet still young enough she could not hold her grief for long. Winsome and innocent, Vivi seemed too full of life to remain sad. Soon she would be an adult with adult burdens, but for now, it was good to allow the child to be a child. Perhaps her joie de vivre would help to soothe her family's pain.

"Enough, Papa." Momo's anger at the friendly reception pulled the attention of everyone. "They have come to take Mimi back to the chateau."

"What?" Mimi's mother pushed past her daughters, hands on her hips.

"It is the way it must be, Mama. It is necessary for everyone. I will go with and make sure Mimi is receiving proper care." Louise was not too sure who would do the caring for Mimi but held her tongue.

"We can properly take care of her. She is my daughter. I do not need strangers to come into my home and take my baby away." The woman eyed Louise up and down.

"Mama, listen." Momo softened in a way Louise had never seen. "It will be all right. I will be there to care for Mimi, and Didi will be there too. If they find she is not taking care of

Mademoiselle de Saix—" she glanced at Louise with a curled lip — "we could all be in trouble, and where would that leave us? Do you not think that we have suffered enough tragedy today? Do we need to lose everything else as well?" Momo put her arm around her mother's shoulders. "Hug her and kiss her goodbye. For now. She will come back home soon, and then we can all take good care of her. Are we agreed, Mama?"

Monsieur Roché had remained silent through all this. Now he turned to Antoine. "Monsieur, this is my child. She grieves so. Can you assure me that she will be well cared for? Can you guarantee that she will not be hurt more?"

"You have my word of honor, monsieur, I will guard and protect her. Mademoiselle herself will comfort her and care for her. We will also look for opportunities to bring her home as often as possible. You have my word." Antoine put out his hand.

The worried father slowly clasped the outstretched hand, a peace offering and gentleman's agreement all rolled into one.

The family said their goodbyes, and the three women were helped into the carriage. Antoine woke the driver, and they returned to the chateau. Pulling up to the entrance, Louise was glad for one thing. Not many were up and about.

Pulling Louise to the side before she entered her room, Antoine lowered his voice and held her hands in his. "You will need to get rest too."

"I will, once Mimi is made comfortable."

"You will also need to be very careful not to get caught. One slip and a curious question could lead to things you cannot imagine."

Louise wanted to refute, tell him not to worry. Yet she did not. She knew deep inside he was correct.

"I will be careful."

He pulled her close again and kissed the top of her head. "I will return this afternoon after you have had time to rest."

She nodded, her face buried in his chest. She could smell his manly, secure scent. More than any time in her life, she was where she belonged.

He pulled back, his hand caressing her chin. "Get some rest."

She nodded, and he was gone.

Chapter Ten

Antoine entered the barracks, searching for the words to say, only to find his friend pacing the floor.

As if preparing to receive a blow, Albert faced Antoine. "Just tell me."

"Pierre gave up the ghost this morning at dawn. Madame LeSuere was at his side. Her neighbors are with her now." Antoine rubbed between his brows with the heel of his palm. "Her body will heal, but I do not believe her spirit ever will."

He sat on the edge of his cot with his head heavy in his hands. Weary both in mind and spirit, Antoine did not think there was enough sleep in the world to fix that problem. "Where is Jean-Luc?"

Albert sat across from him. "I put him to bed in the other room. He came back and found a bottle to crawl into. I have not seen him drink this much in a long time—not since that night after we lost Gustave in the siege."

"Does he not have duty soon?"

"Michel is taking the day for him. I wanted to wait for you. It will take the two of us to wake him and make him sober—or at least somewhat sober." Albert rubbed his eyes.

Most people did not know what a tender heart resided in the

big man. Most people did not, but Antoine knew. "He is taking this very hard."

"He nearly refused to do his duty. It was that abhorrent to him. It is not in his nature to lay a hand on a woman unless he is trying to bring her pleasure. The big ape is so compassionate, his responsibility in this mess is destroying him. He pledged his allegiance, as we did, and he knows what we did was wrong. Yet, to refuse to carry out the order would have been to break his vow. So instead he feels like a coward for not standing up for what is right."

Antoine knew to have disobeyed would have meant more than their jobs. It would have cost Albert and Jean-Luc their personal freedom, and brought torture, prison, and perhaps, death. "What else could you have done?"

There was a pause. Albert's jaw worked with no voice. As if from the depths of his soul, Antoine's friend and mentor dragged the words free. "I should have taken the punishment for her."

"Jean-Luc is not the only one to suffer."

They sat in silence, the what-might-have-been speaking loudly around them.

Jean-Luc snored.

Antoine looked at Albert and stood. He held out his hand. "Let us go minister to our friend before his noise rattles the roof on top of us."

Albert made a small attempt at a smile and pulled himself up with Antoine's assistance.

In the next room of cots, the sleeping giant droned on, his mouth slack, drool spilling from the corner. Still with his boots on, one leg hung down with the heel resting on the floor. His right forearm covered his eyes, and his left hand dangled an empty bottle.

Antoine shook his head. It was not a pretty sight. If any of Jean-Luc's ladies could see him now, they would run and hide.

He met Albert's gaze. The captain of the guard nodded. Simultaneously, they grabbed the side of the cot. With one terrific pull, they dumped the unconscious Jean-Luc on the cold, exposed barracks floor. The bottle crashed into a million pieces. Jean-Luc continued to snore as noisily as before.

Antoine nodded toward the corner.

Albert understood and smiled. Grabbing the bucket of water, he upturned it over the sleeping form.

Jean-Luc jumped to his feet, gasping and sputtering, and slipped, landing on his backside. Fortunately, the overturned cot covered the shattered bottle.

"Time to wake up, Monsieur Sleeping Beauty."

"I am up, I am up." Jean-Luc swiped his dripping hair from his face. "Why am I all wet?"

"We were just wondering that, were we not, Albert?"

"What have you been doing Jean-Luc? You have water everywhere in here, and you are on the floor. What is going on, my friend?"

"Enough. Just help me up."

Albert and Antoine each took an arm and helped the bearlike Jean-Luc to his feet.

"Tell me how goes it for Pierre and his mother?"

Antoine paused. "I am sorry, my friend."

The cry, animal and basic, tore at Antoine's heart. Jean-Luc fell onto another cot, sitting with his hands grasping his hair and his face to the ceiling. When at last he looked back to Antoine, tears still glistened down his cheeks. A guttural whisper broke through. "Tell me."

Antoine related all, even the part concerning Mimi staying in Louise's room to keep from suspicion. "It is for the best."

Albert and Jean-Luc nodded in agreement.

A finality descended like a blanket over the room. Antoine bent to right the cot. Albert returned the bucket to the corner. Jean-Luc grabbed a broom to sweep up the broken glass. Life would go on. However that was possible.

LOUISE TRIED RESTING ONCE THEY GOT MIMI TO SLEEP but, though her body was exhausted, her mind would not quiet.

Momo lay next to Mimi, and the twins slumbered in each other's arms.

Pacing the floor, trying to find the sense of the last couple of days, did not work either. Agitated, Louise opened her writing kit. The words seemed to pour from her quill.

My dearest Matthew,

I hope this letter finds you happy and well. Tante Marie and I have had some exciting travels, but I long to just sit and talk with you. I miss your wise and comforting words. I have met several people while here at Versailles, some worth knowing and others I wish I had not met at all. Yesterday I realized how much I long to speak with you. I know you will think me silly, but I have even been having a strange dream. There are other things going on as well, and I wish I could hear what you have to say about all of this. You know you are more of a Father Confessor to me than anyone. I understand you cannot come to Versailles, but there is a glade just on the other side of the town to the northeast. I will be there alone on Saturday of next week, all afternoon. If it is possible, would you please come meet me there?

Ever your loving friend,
Louise

The written word still did not satisfy her. Louise looked over the letter. She missed him very much. What if he thought she was being infantile? Here she was a grown woman, and still she could not sort out her own thoughts and feelings.

Momo stirred. She must be getting up.

Louise folded the note and sealed it with wax.

Momo came and stood behind her. "You should be resting as well. Mimi said you were up all night with her."

Louise shook her head. "I could not sleep. I needed to get something down on paper."

"Oh."

An idea came to Louise. "Perhaps you could help me. Do you know someone trustworthy who could deliver a letter for me?"

Momo's gaze became guarded. "It is possible. Where does it need to be delivered?"

"To Alsais, to a Monsieur Matthew Maury. Do you know someone?"

"Oui, I know someone. It will cost you. That is almost two hundred miles from here."

"I understand. How much?" Louise went to her white box and pulled the velvet bags. She lifted out a false bottom and removed some gold coins. "Will this be enough?"

Momo's eyes gleamed a bit too much at the money.

Louise started to regret even asking.

"For now. I will let you know whether he has any expenses that may require more."

"How soon can he leave?"

Momo glanced at her sleeping sister. "If you will stay with Mimi, I will take it now. I will be gone about an hour. Do not leave her."

"You can trust me."

Momo nodded and went out the door.

An uncomfortable niggling started at the nape of Louise's neck. But could she trust Momo?

Chapter Eleven

Antoine got little sleep. Both Jean-Luc and Albert left, and he did not want to remain in the barracks alone. Or, more importantly, he did not want to be there when others came in.

Perhaps Louise would be up.

Wandering to the door of the barracks, he glanced out in the direction of the fountains, specifically toward that fountain where he and Louise had stood in the moonlight.

Could it be his imagination? No, there she sat on a garden bench.

She was not alone. Antoine could tell from the way they sat. The other person most likely was Mimi.

Drawn, as if by a magnet, he moved closer.

The scene looked too intimate to interrupt. He forced himself to stay back and observe from behind a statue.

How tenderly Louise cared for Mimi.

Antoine's heart enlarged at her gentleness.

Mimi, he could tell, was in great pain and that, too, touched him. These two women, whatever else might be said of them, had good hearts.

He continued his silent vigil until he noticed they were ready to move on. Taking that as his cue, he headed in their direction, calling out to them. "Mesdemoiselles, what a treat to find such beauty among these blossoms. May I walk with you, ladies?"

Louise started to object, no doubt to protect Mimi. Not wanting to intrude, he would go on his way if that is what they wished. To his surprise, Mimi said, "Please do, Monsieur."

She held out her hand, and he took it when he caught up to them. "Monsieur, I want to thank you for all you did. I know it was not the way you had hoped to spend your evening. You do not even know me, or my family, or—" She took a breath and squeezed her eyes tight for an instant. "Your help was very appreciated. I will light a candle for you that God blesses you for your goodness."

Antoine did not know what to say. The silence grew awkward.

Louise timidly put her hand on his arm. "I wish to thank you as well, Antoine. I do not know what would have happened if you had not been there to help."

"I am glad I could be of service." Though he tried hard not to, he found himself looking more at Louise than Mimi. "Where shall we walk?"

Antoine held out an elbow for each woman. The women linked arms with him and they began to stroll the gardens once more.

It was not long before Mimi lagged slower.

"How fare you, Mademoiselle?"

"I believe I would like to return to the building."

"Are you sure that that is what you want to do?" Louise looked concerned.

"Oui, I am ready to rest again. Please, might I lie on the petite coucher?" Mimi held up a hand at Louise's mounting argument. "No, please. The bed belongs to you. I will see you when you return."

Louise agreed.

Mimi paused. "And Mademoiselle?"

"Oui?"

"I thank you too."

"You are most welcome. That is what friends are for—and I am your friend." Louise pulled Mimi to her for a quick hug and whispered in her ear.

Mimi walked toward the chateau door. When there, she turned, gave a brief wave, and then went inside.

"Oh, she is hurting so badly, and I do not know what to do to help her, Antoine." Louise leaned onto his arm.

How could his heart flip-flop like it did when so much sadness surrounded them?

He pulled his attention back to her question with much effort. "There is not much anyone can do. However, I believe that your being here and listening have given her a venue for her grief. It is just going to take time to learn to live with it." He kicked a stone down the path. "My eldest sister lost her husband fighting the Spanish in Franche-Comté last month. They have five children and a sixth on the way. It has been very difficult for her."

"I am so sorry. I did not know." Her eyes shone with sympathy.

"It has been frustrating. I can do nothing to take her pain away. I want to make it right for her and the children, but it is not in my power." Antoine's jaw tensed as visions of the loving sister who had raised him danced in his memory.

Louise moved her delicate fingers over his arm and his tension eased.

They walked on toward Le Vau's garden façade where they stopped to rest again.

Louise's stomach growled.

Antoine chucked.

She blushed, admitting she had not eaten for a while. "I believe our feast in the glade was my last meal."

"It sounds as though your stomach is in need of attention, my lady."

"My stomach does not rule over me. I will eat later. For the moment, I am content to sit here."

He should argue and make her take nourishment. Yet, she looked as content as she stated. "As you wish." Antoine selfishly enjoyed her company. A remembrance floated to his consciousness. "Perhaps you are ready to share about the difficult conversation that bothered you yesterday."

She paused.

He became concerned she might to say something about the fact that *he* did not rule over her either. "Not that you have to, but I am here, and look, two ears."

She smiled. Bon.

Folding her hands neatly in her lap, she took a deep breath. "It does not seem as important today, after last night." Louise cleared her throat. "I was summoned to the suite of the Marquise de Montespan after we returned yesterday. She wore her crocodile smile and warned me not to fawn my attentions on the king."

"Pardon?"

"It seems she is jealous of me because I had a late meal with His Majesty in the Royal Suite. I do not think she could believe it was a chance meeting or that we only had something to eat."

"I do not understand. She thinks you were in the Royal Suite? When was this?"

"My first night here. You brought me back, and I went to bed. However, I had a nightmare. I woke up unable to return to sleep. So, I went for a walk. His Majesty was also up and about. He invited me back to his suite where he had already arranged for a meal. He offered to share it with me. His valet walked me back no more than half an hour or so later."

An ugly green snake wrapped itself around his heart, and his breath grew warm on his tongue. "You were alone with His Majesty? In his suite?"

Louise stood.

He stood as well.

"Antoine, what is this? He is my cousin, family. He invited me to have a bit of food and wine. I hope you are not accusing me of anything improper."

His head told him she could be lying. It would not be the first time His Majesty had a liaison with one of his cousins. However, his heart did not want to believe that of Louise. "No, no, my apologies. I had no right to ask."

"Are you sure you believe me?"

Antoine paused long enough to make sure he told her the truth. "Oui, I believe you." He led her back to the bench and sat after she did. "Yet I can see how the Marquise would be upset. She is zealous in her attachment to the king."

"I do not want a battle. My preference is to stay clear of her. It was not a good choice, but I never once thought something improper might occur. Now, what bothers me most is that someone might view things as she did and, with how gossip can travel, I would not have the best of reputations."

Antoine's heart tightened again, but not due to a jealous monster. "Oh." He needed to make this right.

"As long as you believe me." Her eyes clouded with worry.

"Oh, I do. It is just that..."

"Is there something you want to say?"

"No, it is nothing." It was the first lie he had told her, and he hated himself for it. "Let us talk of something else."

"As you wish." Louise looked confused by Antoine's behavior but spoke agreeably nonetheless. "Oh, I know. Whatever did you use for an excuse for our missing dinner with His Majesty last night? I wondered about that before I dosed off this morning. It must have been sound for even Tante Marie has not questioned me."

Antoine's face burned and knew the time had come. "Ah, well . . ."

Concern radiated from Louise's face. "What is the problem, Antoine? Have I said something wrong?"

He shook his head. "No, no. In fact, it may be that I am the one who has said something wrong. I am very sorry."

"What do you mean?"

Antoine stood and began to pace. "I needed to think of something that would not be questioned or challenged, and I did not have a lot of time to do it. You know, His Majesty is trying to play matchmaker with the two of us. Did you know that?"

"No, I did not know that for sure, but are you not changing the subject?" Her gaze followed his pacing.

"Not exactly. You see, I thought others would not bother us or question things if they believed we were..." He cleared his throat.

"Were what?"

"Ah, *detained* elsewhere."

"Detained elsewhere?" Louise shook her head. "Where would that be?" She did not understand, and he did not like explaining.

"Well, I led them to believe I was taking you for a romantic drive under the stars."

"Romantic drive."

"One that might end in a, well, you know."

"A...?"

Antoine knew the exact moment when it fully dawned on her.

"You did *what*?"

"Louise, I am so sorry. Please, it is not as bad as you are making it out to be." Yet he did not believe that himself.

She stood. The brief thought that she might attack flitted through his mind. "Oh, it is not? I am worried about my reputation being ruined by a vindictive witch when I should have been concerned about the chivalrous escort my family hired to keep me company."

"Louise, that is not fair. It was not like that." Though it was like that. Exactly like that. "Anyway, here at Versailles, no one would think a thing about it. There are many people sharing other beds here. They would think you were just…" He could not say it.

"Just what? That I am a brazen hussy of loose character whose morals can be swayed by the company I keep?"

"No, I did not mean—" He had not thought far enough. Never would he want anyone to think that of Louise.

"Antoine." She faced him squarely. "One day my father will give my dowry and my hand to the man I will marry. I will vow to be faithful to until death. That man deserves to know his bride is his, and only his. I plan to carry orange blossoms, not because I enjoy the scent or because they are so popular, but because I have earned the right to carry them. As a virgin. I do not want my future husband to have any doubts due to some filthy gossip whispered about my stay here."

"I sincerely apologize, Louise. I am very sorry." And he was. More than he could say.

"As am I." She sighed and turned away.

"Louise?"

She paused a moment and then turned back. "Oui?"

"Do you know who that man might be?"

"It is possible. I am not sure."

He reached for her, and she pulled back. "No, I think I want to be alone for a time."

Antoine stepped back and watched her walk away toward the chapel. He sat back down on the bench and watched his future walk away with her. What an idiot. He should kick himself for his stupidity. She had asked for help, and that was all he had wanted to do. Instead he had hurt her. Deeply.

And there still was his assignment to accomplish. Yet he was not sure whether Louise would let that happen. What if Louise requested a different escort?

That is when it all became so clear. It was not the job he feared losing. It was Louise.

Chapter Twelve

Louise entered the small chapel, moving in silence to the altar. Few candles were lit, leaving the room dark and somber. She picked up the wick and lit a candle for poor Pierre. The light did nothing to change the gloominess in the room or her heart. She knelt and began to pray. As faces came to her mind, she recited prayers for them.

At the altar, the pain of what was said between her and Antoine began to overwhelm her. The silence became so loud it nearly drowned out a small voice from inside.

"What about you?"

What about me? She had no clue how to pray for herself. As she tried to think, tears dripped down her face. She felt lonelier than she could ever remember being.

Oh, Jesus, Matthew says You have promised to never leave us nor forsake us. I feel so alone. When I try to help, it seems I just hurt others. When I trust, I find betrayal. Matthew says that it was the same way for You in the garden and on the cross. He says You felt deserted. What did You do about that? What do I do about that? I have so many questions, Lord. Right now, though, I need comfort. I need someone to hear my heart. Can You do that? Please help me.

"My child."

Her eyes flew open with a gasp. She jumped up, hands to her heart. Turning, she found the gentle priest who had given Pierre his Last Rites.

"I startled you." His hand steadied her. "Forgive me, my child. I only wished to know if there was anything I could do for you." His kind eyes calmed her frayed nerves.

"Just pray for me, Father," she asked. "Just pray for me."

"I have already, my child. What is your name?"

"Louise. Louise de Saix."

"Ah, oui. I recall hearing that His Majesty's cousin was to come for a visit. I will remember you in prayer, my child, and you remember to trust in our Maker's mercy and wisdom. He will never leave you nor forsake you."

A peace flooded over Louise as she heard the promise repeated. Her prayers had been silent but heard by God above. He did hear her prayer. Warm tears dripped down her cheeks. She hugged the kind priest. "Bless you, Father. Bless you."

⚜

LOUISE RETURNED TO THE ROOM TO FIND MIMI STILL sleeping on the petite coucher. Just as she had said. Momo was not there, and for that Louise was glad. Something about that girl made her uncomfortable.

She tossed her hat on the bed and, pouring water from the pitcher into the basin, began to rinse her tearstained face. Praying and talking to the priest had helped. She still did not know what she was going to do the next time she saw Antoine. At least she was thinking about forgiving him. She wanted to forgive him. It was what she was supposed to do.

Could she trust him again? He had been trustworthy with the situation with Mimi. His kindness drew her. So, why such a terrible excuse for the missed dinner?

The knock at the door jolted her back to the present. Didi

slipped in with a note from Marie. As soon as Louise grasped the paper, the maid rushed to her sister's side.

"How does she fare?"

"It hurts my heart to see her. We walked in the gardens and she spoke of Pierre. Momo encouraged her to eat something, but she took in very little." Louise's stomach tightened. "I offered the bed. She would not hear of it. I should have insisted, though."

Didi looked back to Louise. "No, Mademoiselle. This is best. You are very kind. Do not worry."

There must be more she should do, though Louise had no idea what.

"Your note, will you not read it?" Didi's gaze indicated the paper still in Louise's hand.

"Oh, but of course." She opened it.

My dearest Louise,

I hope you enjoyed your romantic rendezvous with Monsieur de Crocketagné last evening. Was it not wonderful?

What a terrible question to ask. Images of the ordeal of the previous night appeared in her brain. She shook them away. One moment came back that was almost enjoyable. She could feel Antoine's arms as he held her secure and safe under the stars outside the house. At that moment she had felt so protected and… loved?

Was she reading more into his kind gesture than was there? Oui, of course she was. Still, that was the way she had felt. She smiled as she remembered.

I hope so. I also hope you are up and about. Come with me.
A group of us are meeting on the lawn for a game of pall-
mall. Come and play with your poor old Tante this fine
afternoon. We have not had enough time together since we
arrived. I miss your lovely smile. I am waiting in my room.

Ever your loving aunt,
Marie

Games. Everyone here played some kind of game or intrigue. What were the rules?

With a sigh, Louise knew she must go to her aunt. She owed Tante Marie much.

One last look over her shoulder at the sleeping Mimi, and Louise left as soundlessly as possible, following Didi to the room of Tante Marie.

"Dear heart. I am so glad you are able to join me. We will have fun, no?"

Louise plastered a smile on her face. "Oui, we will have fun, Tante."

Marie looked past Louise. "Where is Mimi? Will she not be accompanying you?"

"No, Tante, not today. I left her sleeping."

Didi's eyes grew wide, and all too late Louise caught her blunder.

"*Fi donc!*" Marie grabbed Louise by the elbow and pulled her to the side. "Louise, you cannot let servants behave in such a manner."

Louise's brain whirled, spinning out ideas beyond her reach. At last she grasped on to one. "Tante, we were out so late last night. The sweet girl acted as my chaperone, keeping my reputation pure. Since she was so kind as to do this for me, I must allow her needed sleep." The lie flowed easily, maybe because it helped in more than one place. Would it be believed?

Marie shook her head. "My dear, you must not treat servants as equals. It will only confuse the poor girl. However, it does tell me what a sweet, kind child you are." The kisses, one per cheek, stunned Louise, and embarrassed her, adding to the guilt she already knew.

"Come dear heart, let us go to the games."

Louise followed her aunt, posture perfect as she had been taught. Inside, though, her head hung low.

An open courtyard held several of the nobility, ready with mallets in hand, watching while servants set up the croquet-like amusement. Louise had not played the game before but soon picked up the knack and found herself tied for the lead with the Marquise.

A difficult decision pulled her. A part of Louise wanted to throw down the mallet and head for anywhere else. Another part wanted to beat the icy smile off that perfect face. Either decision carried deeper meaning.

Resolved to take a stand, Louise chose to stay and play. The ladies' long skirts made it difficult to always see the ground, but Louise had the strong idea the Marquise used that to her advantage.

The train of the Marquise's gown glided past an opponent's ball, bumping it into a more difficult position. None of the players raised so much as an eyebrow. Did they not see? Not one word of protest. Then, in a flash, Louise understood the silence. No one was about to speak a word against the king's favorite. So far, the Marquise had not been caught doing anything to Louise's ball. Now the two spheres came close, and it was the Marquise's turn. Louise put her foot upon her own ball.

"I believe it is my turn, my dear." The Marquise expected no impediment.

"I believe you are correct." Louise smiled but did not move.

"So, why is your foot upon your ball?"

"I thought to help you have a clear path. I did not think you would want my ball to accidentally roll into your path. You do not mind my help, do you, Marquise?"

"No, we would not want any accidents, would we?" The Marquise turned away with a withering look.

The part of Louise that had wanted to run away, now tried to bolt. In spite of her emotions, she continued to stand her ground.

The Marquise took her shot, a rather successful one, and stepped aside for Louise.

Now came the moment of decision. Should she choose to miss the shot and let *le mégère* win? The shrew. Or should she take the shot to the best of her ability and quite possibly win the game? The Marquise could be a powerful enemy or ally. Louise did not want her as an ally, but to resolve to make her an enemy was foolhardy.

She glanced up at the other players. Most would not make eye contact. Her heart begged for help. She found no answers. Louise glanced at the Marquise. The king's so-called favorite galled her. The nerve of that woman.

Lining up the shot, Louise held her breath and took it. She forced her eyes to remain open to see whether the ball would cooperate.

The Marquise never stopped to congratulate her.

A tiny smirk crept its way to Louise's lips.

Tante Marie, standing at her side, whispered in her ear. "Be on your guard, dear heart. You have just made a powerful enemy."

Chapter Thirteen

Antoine did not like moping around the garden. He needed action. Determined to talk it all out, he strode to Louise's chambers. No one answered the knock.

Where could she have gone?

Taking a chance, he headed towards the stables. Perhaps she had decided to go for a ride.

A storm brewed inside him. He should not have used that excuse. He knew the second the words left his lips he should have thought of another reason. Could she not at least understand he wanted to help her?

He rounded the corner and stopped in his tracks. A pall-mall contest played out in front of him. He recognized the players, his eyes drawn to the one dressed in pink.

Stepping behind a shrub, he kept his eyes glued on the game as Louise stood her ground. When the Marquise threw down her mallet and stormed off, he wanted to shout. Louise had bested her nemesis.

Should he go to her now? Should he wait until she returned to her room? As he debated with himself, another man approached Louise and her aunt. The Marquis d'Heudecourt. Antoine's stomach turned. Obese and florid, the man had a nasty habit of spitting over his shoulder wherever he was—inside or out. Antoine shuddered. He had learned the hard way one evening watching a card game at appartement.

What did the Marquis want with the women? How could Antoine find out without appearing overly interested?

Rather than learn more, Antoine turned on his heel and retreated to the barracks.

Once again in his quarters, Antoine decided to regroup. Why could he not approach this in a military fashion? He understood military matters. Perhaps he should look at this situation from that point of view. He sat on the edge of his cot, letting his analytical mind take control while he pulled off his boots.

First, he needed to establish his goal. What was it?

Two days ago he would have said it was to do his duty as assigned by his king. Now Louise had become more than an assignment. Much more so.

So, the question remained, what was his goal?

Perhaps he should analyze his feelings. Very well, then, how did he feel about her? At once his very soul flooded with a foreign emotion.

No, he must remain detached and figure this out. He took a deep breath. The tumult in his chest calmed only slightly. How did he feel? He felt protective of her. After mulling that over, he decided he could live with feeling protective of Louise.

What else? The storm inside grew again. This trying to understand his feelings was a lot harder than a battle. A part of him knew his feelings for her. Did he really have to admit it?

Louise would be leaving in less than a fortnight. The storm inside now grew painful. How did that play upon his feelings for her?

He could not accept the fact he would not see her again after this visit. Very well then, if he were honest, he would have to admit he looked to make her more than an acquaintance.

So, what then?

His father's voice rang in his thoughts. "Son, what are your intentions?" Before he could tell himself he did not know, he realized he did. His heart had known all along.

He intended to love Louise for the rest of his life.

It was the most frightening thing he could imagine. He only met her two days ago. What was he thinking? He could not speak this yet. It would take some time for this knowledge sink into his thick head.

And, just because he felt this way did not mean she did. In fact, that brought him back to the original problem. What was he to do to mend this situation with Louise?

Without an idea, he rolled to his side and tried to figure out his next step. If he only knew how she felt, he might know what he needed to do.

"Andouille!" Antoine threw his boot. Why was this so hard?

How did Jean-Luc fall in and out of love so freely? If somehow this all worked out, he would be so grateful. However, should he ever be free of this feeling, never again would he fall into its trap. He had been content with the duties assigned him, happy to live his life as a bachelor, and enjoy the lack of complication.

What happened?

Louise happened. With her quiet, sensitive manner. With her gentle touch, her exquisite eyes. Captured by her spell, he was helpless to remove himself from it. Nor did he want to.

Would it frighten her to know that he loved her? Or repulse her? Had she forgiven him enough to hear him? Would she ever forgive him?

He had enough of the suppositions. Standing, he fetched his boot and put it and its brother on. Determined to speak with her one way or another, he strode out the door.

Louise turned to follow her aunt from the pall-mall area when a fashionably dressed gent hailed them. Tante Marie waved in return, and the man joined them. After kissing each other's cheeks, Marie offered introductions.

"My dear Marquis, may I present to you my niece, Louise de Saix. Louise, this is my friend, the Marquis d'Heudecourt."

"You are as enchanting as you are clever." Did he purr while bringing her hand to his plump lips? "I have never seen anyone stand up to the Ice Princess like that. You are to be congratulated."

Heat radiated from Louise's cheeks. "Oh, I, ah, merci." Louise sputtered, feeling like an idiot. "I am afraid I overstepped my place. I let my anger get the better of my senses, Monsieur."

"Humble, as well. Well, well, Marie, you certainly have a jewel here."

"Oui, I do." Tante smiled and patted Louise's arm before turning her attention back to the Marquis. "Now, tell me, what have you been up to? I missed you at appartement last night."

"I have been here. In fact, I was at appartement for a short while last evening but was having a bit of an off night. I left the table before the hole in my pocket grew too large."

"I see. What are your plans now?"

"I have not made any at the moment, but I did overhear Prince de Condé saying something about putting together a trip to the Baths."

"We are going to Vichy?" Tante Marie giggled with obvious delight. "Oh, how wonderful! I have not been in ages. Louise has never been, have you, dear heart?"

"No, Tante." And neither did she want to go.

ↁ

Antoine nearly ran Albert over as he charged around a corner.

"Ho! Antoine, where are you going in such a hurry?"

"Oh. I …" No, not now.

"Ah, ha. Mademoiselle de Saix, no doubt. Now I understand. I will see you later, my friend. I am sure you do not want to keep her waiting."

"Actually, she does not know I am coming." Why did he say that?

"Oh?"

Antoine made an immediate decision.

"Albert, might we speak?"

"But of course. What is it?"

Antoine confessed what he had done concerning his poor choice of an excuse and Louise's reaction to it. Albert remained silent.

"Are you not going to say anything?" Antoine expected to be insulted or ridiculed. However, he was not ready for silence.

"What would you have me to say?"

"I do not know. Tell me what a churl I have been."

"So be it, you behaved as a churl. Now what?"

"What do you mean, 'now what'? I have no clue how to fix this. What if she asks for another escort? What then?"

"Then she asks for another escort. Do you have a problem with that?" Albert's eyes twinkled like the day he introduced him to Louise.

"What would His Majesty say?"

Albert put his hand on Antoine's shoulder. "Is that your true reason for concern?"

"Oui, ah, I mean…" Antoine's gaze met Albert's, and he could see the truth. "You know, do you not?"

"Anyone who had seen the two of you together last night would know. I think you two are the only ones who did not know. So, tell me, my friend, how bad is it?"

"How bad is what?" Antoine still could not bring himself to say the words aloud.

"Amour. It is the source of epics, music, and wars. So, what is it like?"

"It is like living on a precipice and being drawn to look over the edge, knowing that if you do you will fall. Yet, you have to look anyway."

"So, have you fallen or are you hanging on by your fingertips?"

Antoine laughed. "Oh, I have fallen, my friend, I have fallen." He might as well confess the rest. "The problem is that I have no idea of what to do about it. Louise is angry with me, what makes me think she could ever love me?"

"Maybe she is angry because she has feelings for you."

The idea was foreign, strange. All Antoine could do was stare.

"What are you waiting for, man? Go."

Antoine obediently took two steps and stopped. Turning, he found Albert still watching. "There was one thing she said."

Albert gave an impatient glare.

"No, really. When we were in the garden, I asked her if she knew whom she would marry. She sounded like she did."

"What does that mean, 'sounded like she did'?"

"Well, she said she might. Maybe. That it was possible." Aloud this sounded so silly.

"Then she does not know anything for sure, and both of us know that things can change at a moment's notice. So, get out of here and talk with her. Now."

"I am going." Antoine flashed a grin and left for Louise's suite.

෴

LOUISE PACED. NOW BACK IN HER ROOM, SHE DANGLED AT the end of her wits. She could not go to Vichy. It would be a trip of a fortnight or more one way, covering almost two hundred fifty miles and then staying for any length of time. She would never see home at this rate. Plus, how could she go to Vichy and still be here on Thursday to meet with Matthew?

How did she get out of this trip? There had to be some way.

The knock at her door startled her. There always seemed to be someone at the door when her emotions ran high. She answered it herself.

Antoine stood there, kneading his hat.

"Louise, I have come to apologize. I was stupid and inconsiderate. Can you ever forgive me?" Antoine looked so humble standing there with her heart in his hand. She wanted to melt at his feet, but she was still in a dither.

"Oui, of course, I forgive you." She grabbed his sleeve and dragged him into the suite. "I must confess, I am no longer worried about that anymore. Mimi was with us, and I can always point out that nothing inappropriate happened since I brought along a chaperone."

"That is true." Antoine grinned, then sobered. "What is the problem? You look disheartened."

"It is that Tante Marie has planned a sudden trip to Vichy for me, and I do not want to go." That sounded petulant even to her own ears.

"Why is that?"

Why, indeed. She could not tell him about Matthew. "Because of Mimi." The lie poured from her as smooth as His Majesty's wine. "We need to be able to take her to see her family as often as possible. She cannot be left alone here nor dragged so far from her loved ones. I do not think taking her to Vichy would be the best thing for her."

"I see your point." Antoine nodded.

"You do?" The words came out of her mouth the same instant she thought them. She could not understand how he believed her so readily. "So, what should I do?"

"Ho, I have been in enough trouble where making up excuses are concerned. Are you sure you want to ask me?"

It broke her heart that he would say that. Especially when she had just lied to him. Maybe she should explain. Still, she had promised Matthew. "Antoine, I trust you. I know you were in a difficult situation, quickly needing an excuse. I do forgive you, and I can use some ideas. I will be the one to give out the excuse. You will not get into any more trouble." She did not want anyone to get into trouble on her account.

Antoine snapped his fingers. "You could say you do not feel up to the trip?"

"No, the last time I suggested not feeling well Tante Marie reminded me of the Royal Surgeon. I do not want to be bled just to get out of going on this trip."

"You are right." His forehead scrunched. "When was it that you used that excuse?"

"No, that is my secret. Back to the point, what can I say to be excused from this trip?" Louise began to pace. She turned and ran straight into the broad chest of Antoine. She could bury her head in that chest and be content forever.

She jumped back.

Antoine took her hand. "What if something is about to happen here that you do not want to miss?"

"Such as?" Louise's heart pounded in her ears. Could he possibly know about Matthew?

"Perhaps a concert, or play, or I do not know. It is a bad idea."

"No," Louise answered slowly. "I do not think it is a bad idea at all. Actually, I think you have figured out the perfect thing. Do you remember when we were at appartement? Monsieur Lully announced he would be presenting the full opera this next week. Tante knows I have wanted to see *Isis* for a very long time. It is a true excuse. I will not really be lying."

There was something strange about the look on Antoine's handsome face. "But you were willing to lie, is that it?"

Why did he have to ask this? "I do not want to, no. However, I feel the need to be here, and if a lie is what it takes…"

She could not look in Antoine's eyes. They spoke to her heart, seeing her lie and not liking it. She could see herself in his eyes, like a mirror to her own soul. It was not pretty sight.

"Antoine, I am sorry. You are right. I do not think I like myself very much right now. Here I am concerned about my reputation, but very willing to lie to get my way. It sounds a bit manipulative even to me."

"No, I understand. Protecting Mimi has put you into some unfortunate situations." He put his hands on her shoulders. "Do not become skilled at lying. Like everything else, it can improve with practice."

She could not bear to look into his honest gaze. "I feel ashamed. Antoine, there is something I should tell you, but it is something I cannot share with anyone. I do not want to lie to you, and I would tell you if I could. It would mean divulging a confidence. Please do not think ill of me. I promise it is not something bad, but the secret belongs to another. It is not mine to tell."

"You have nothing to be ashamed of." Antoine put two fingers under her chin and lifted her gaze to his. "I trust you. If you cannot tell me without breaking a confidence, then do not tell me. I think higher of you for keeping that confidence than if you would share someone else's secret with me."

"Truly?"

"Truly."

He reached for her hand, and she went to him, burying her face in his chest. Their arms went around each other, and he kissed the top of her head. Surprised, she looked up at his face. His hand went to her chin and, tipping it up, his lips met hers.

She had not anticipated his kiss but welcomed it as the most natural thing in the world. Her first kiss brought tingles down her spine, making her toes curl with new and exciting sensations.

A quiet cough shattered the moment. Louise pulled from his embrace.

"I am sorry." Mimi sat on the edge of the petite coucher. "I did not mean to interrupt. Would you like me to leave?"

"Oh, no, ah," Louise sputtered, her face warmed.

Antoine shook his head. "No, Mimi. You remain here. We

are going for a walk." Snatching Louise by the hand, he led out the door and straight out of the chateau. They ran, fingers laced, to the garden bench.

❧

WHEN HE SAT, HE PULLED HER DOWN NEXT TO HIM.

"We are not walking."

He waggled his eyebrows. "No, we are not."

Her smile, her innocence, oh, oui, he loved her.

Antoine grew serious. Now was the time. "About the kiss."

She cut him off, her forefinger to his lips. "Do not talk." Her whisper mesmerized. She pulled his head to hers. Her arms went around his neck, and he responded, pulling her close.

He kissed her thoroughly, completely.

The sweetness of the moment began to give rise to alarm. Antoine needed to take control now. Later would be too difficult. He pulled back from her and gently cupped his hand to her questioning face.

Her cheeks grew pink, and she turned away. "Did I do something wrong?"

"Louise, you are far too tempting and desirable right now." He bit his lip and tried to calm his breath. "Just sit here with me." He turned her to him and covered her hands in his own. "You must not have any idea of what you do to me. I know we have only known each other for a short time, but my feelings for you run very deep."

"They do?" Her eyes sparkled more blue than green, opened wide and innocent. In just two days, she had captured his heart.

"Oui, they do. Louise, I want, ah ..." Now he was embarrassed.

"You want what?"

"I want to know you better. I want to learn all about you, what you think and how you see things. I do not want to spend all this time with you for two weeks and then just say goodbye. I need you in my life, and I want to be a part of yours."

"What are you saying?"

"I guess I am telling you that, or rather I am hoping you feel the same way." He was not saying this well.

"It has only been two days." She was withdrawing, and he could feel it.

"I know. This is how I feel, though. How do you feel?" *Hear my heart, Louise, and tell me how you feel. Do I have a chance?*

"You have not told me how you feel. You have told me what you want. I do not know how you feel." Was that fear in her eyes?

"I thought I had, that I just did. I told you how I feel. I do not want to lose you." How could he make her see?

"Again, that is what you want. If you want me to know how you feel, you will have to tell me." She pulled her hands from his.

Antoine could not stop her. He could not say anything. His eyes pled with her to understand but no words came out.

She stood and turned away. One step. Another.

Before she could take a third step, Antoine stood. "I love you."

She turned back to him.

"Do not go," he whispered, "I love you, Louise."

"Truly?" Her eyes grew tender.

"I love you. Even if you never say it, I love you."

"Oh, oh, Antoine, I love you too." She threw herself into his arms.

He kissed her with all the passion he knew.

Danger.

The thought flitted through his mind and he forced himself back. He stared at her, breathless and shaken.

"We had better walk." His voice sounded unsteady to his ear.

Louise did not argue. Looping her arm through his, she

allowed him to lead her around the gardens and listened while he told her of the plants and flowers.

Antoine could feel his heart pumping faster than galloping horses' hooves. Not only did he not scare her away, she said she loved him too.

And now, what? Keep a cool head. Tell about this flower. Think things through. Name that tree. Determine the rest of his life. Point out the interesting facts of this shrub. Never let her go. *Breathe.* He was elated and terrified all at the same time. He did not know what to do.

"*Cheri!*"

Antoine turned to see Louise's aunt waving to them. The Marquis d'Heudecourt escorted her.

"Tante Marie." Louise waved back. Under her breath she whispered to Antoine, "Please do not say anything to her. This is so new. I do not want to share it with anyone else yet."

Antoine patted her arm and smiled his agreement. He was glad the suggestion came from Louise. Madame du Sine had a reputation as a bit of a gossip, but she was Louise's aunt. At least she would not be interfering.

"Where have you two been?"

How could she tolerate the Marquis?

"Just walking here in the garden." Louise squeezed his arm.

"Oh, Pet, I have spoken with the Prince de Condé, and it is all arranged. We can leave for Vichy on Monday. Is that not wonderful?"

"Tante, I had hoped to see the production of *Isis* this next week when Monsieur Lully presents it. I understand there is even ballet within his opera, and that it is magnificent."

Antoine covered Louise's nervous fingers in the crook of his arm. Could she feel his strength for her?

"Remember, when we were in Paris, Tante, you mentioned it might be possible we would be here to see *Isis,* and now it is my opportunity. Please, though, you go on to Vichy. I do not want you to miss out on your trip, just because I want to stay."

"Are you quite sure, dear heart? We will be gone at least a month or more. I would not want you to miss out on anything, either." Madame du Sine began to eye Antoine. "As you wish, then. I promised you that you would not have to care for this old woman while we were here so, if this is what you want, so be it."

"Oh, merci, Tante." Louise gave her aunt a hug. "You are a dear, and not old in the least."

"One thing, though." Madame du Sine's smile resembled a mouser toying with its prey.

"What is that?"

"Since I am going to Vichy, we will not be able to leave as planned. You do not mind staying an extra month or so, do you? In fact, I believe the court will be back at St. Germaine within the next week."

Louise looked at Antoine.

He met her smile and held in the laugh.

"No, Tante, I will not mind. I am sure Monsieur de Crocketagné will think of something for us to do to pass the time."

"I am sure he will." Marie threw a wink at Antoine and waved goodbye on her way back to the chateau.

What had he gotten himself into?

Chapter Fourteen

The dusty rider pulled to a stop at the edge of the village. Alsais. Now he needed to learn exactly where this Matthew Maury person lived so he could deliver the letter and return.

A house with a well on the side stood on the outskirts. Perhaps the master of the house might allow a thirsty traveler a cup of water. He might also supply the information needed to find the addressee.

Tying his horse to a tree in the front, he hailed the house.

"You there, inside, might I trouble you for a drink of your water?"

"Help yourself, if you are of the mind to, and then state your business." Though in shadow, the speaker was a male, tall from the deep voice.

"I kindly thank you." The rider walked to the well and drew up a bucketful. The rusty dipper hung from a nail at the side, but he was too thirsty to care about the condition. He dipped and greedily drank three times before getting his fill. Once he had rehung the dipper, he set the bucket on the edge of the well where he had found it.

Walking back toward the front he called out, "Do you know where I might locate Monsieur Matthew Maury?"

"Who wants to know?" That disembodied voice again.

"I have a letter to deliver to him."

"From whom?"

Before the rider could answer, he overheard what seemed to be parts of a discussion in the house.

A new voice called, "I will be right out."

Minutes later, a tall, well-built gentleman exited. Obviously, the master of the house.

"You have a letter for me?" The gentlemen spoke friendly enough.

"No, I have a letter for Monsieur Matthew Maury. I am looking for his house. If you could point it out to me, I will not trouble you again."

"I am Matthew Maury, and this is my home. May I have my letter?" Now he held out his hand.

"How do I know you are who you say you are?" The ride had been long and hard. He was not about to give this note to the wrong person now. "This letter might be something important."

"As you wish. You may ask anyone here in my home, or I could take you into town where you might ask people. I believe the quickest way, however, would be for me to tell you who sent the letter. Would that be satisfactory?"

"You say you can tell me who sent this letter?"

"I believe I can." The master of the house seemed certain.

"Agreed. If you can do that, you must be Monsieur Maury."

"It would not by chance be from a lady staying at Versailles? A lady by the name of Mademoiselle Louise de Saix, would it?"

Relief lightened the rider's load. "I stand corrected, Monsieur. Here is your letter." The traveler smiled and turned to leave.

Monsieur Maury started for the house. "Wait, I may need to send a response. You do not mind, do you?"

He did, but... "No."

"Bon. Come in then and I will have Giselle pour you something proper." Maury held the door for him.

He followed Matthew into the house and looked around. This Monsieur Maury may be working class, but he did very well.

A servant girl brought a glass of wine to the grimy man and glared at him when he set his dirty self in one of the dusty-green-colored velvet chairs. Saucy wench. He stretched his red heels out in front of him and smiled a taunting grin.

She retreated to the back of the house with her nose in the air.

Maury reentered. "It appears I will not be writing back."

"Well then, I will be off. Thank you for your hospitality." He shoved his body out of the chair. It was nice while it lasted.

"Oh, you do not need to leave right away. I will be returning with you. Make yourself comfortable since I need to pack something."

"As you wish." He sank back into the chair.

"What is your name, man?"

"Bealieu, Claude Bealieu."

"Well, then, Claude Bealieu, I will return momentarily. Then we can pick out some fresh horses." Matthew ran up the stairs.

Claude had just finished the glass when, true to his word, Maury reappeared with a medium-sized bundle. He led the way out the door and around the back to a stable. Choosing three geldings, Maury saddled two, tying Claude's horse behind one. The extra horse he tied behind his own. He mounted, and Claude followed suit, trailing the man out of the yard.

Monsieur Maury spoke little as they rode. He could have had the decency to let Claude in on why he decided to ride back with him, but instead they just rode. After a time, they slowed and rested the horses. Matthew pulled out bread and cheese from the pack and offered some to Claude.

Claude had scrounged for food on the trip to Alsais, so even basic bread and cheese looked to be ambrosia about now. He took the food and sat leaning against a tree.

"How did you come to be the one to deliver the letter, Claude?" Maury's eyes shone with interest.

"My girl, she sometimes works at the chateau and your lady there asked if she knew of anyone. I was volunteered, I reckon." Claude wolfed down bites between words. "So, what is this lady to you, anyway?"

"A friend."

A short answer. Maury was not going to divulge more. Claude decided to focus on eating. For now. Yet he had to admit, his curiosity was piqued. He now wished he had looked at the letter before delivering it. Maybe he still could get a chance. If necessary, he could lift it long enough to take a peek. It would not be the first time, and he was pretty good. They had a long enough journey before them. If an opportunity presented itself before they reached Versailles, well, he could rise to the occasion.

Claude slouched down against the tree he had been leaning on and, pulling his hat down over his face, he readied for a short nap.

Something nudged his toe.

Claude uncovered his eyes.

Matthew stood over him. "Let us go."

Claude plopped his hat on his head, stretched, and stood.

Monsieur Maury mounted.

He, too, climbed aboard his own horse and followed the man once more.

Chapter Fifteen

26 July 1668

I have not written in several days. Not for lack of activity or thought, though. My days with Antoine are sweet. He is attentive yet allows me to be myself. I do not have to follow conventions and pretend to always be the grand lady. We have been to the lovely glade several times. Each trip has been a delight. I know the reason is his company. Has there ever been a truer love? I have given him my heart and know I possess his.

We have also spent several hours with Mimi's family. They are kind and good, pampering the tender girl with sweets and stories to bring a smile to her face. Antoine has become friendly with Monsieur Roché. Mimi's father is also a lover of horses, and it gives the men something to talk about while we women gather together in the house.

The evenings have been quite exciting. On Sunday last we attended a masquerade ball. His Majesty set the tone by calling for clownish costumes. The whole court attempted to outdo each other, dressing with outlandish abandon. Antoine and I dressed as horses. It was our private folly, and one of the tamest of costumes present.

Monday and Tuesday last we joined the nobility in the evening for appartement. I made a chance with the trictrac table and won quite handily, enjoying myself greatly until the Marquise joined my table. It was clear she expected to win. I would not throw the game to her and played to the utmost of my ability. As luck would have it, I won, but the Marquise let slip a thinly disguised accusation, and I was thus branded a cheat. Very few chanced to play at my table after that, and I confess I cried when alone. But Antoine proved the hero showing me other entertainments. In truth, I much prefer his company to any game.

This evening a rumor spread that the Duchess of Montpensier should arrive on the morrow. La Grande Mademoiselle, as she is called, has led such a colorful life. I would like to meet her but am almost afraid. Like myself, she is cousin to His Majesty, and I heard that at one time it was thought they would wed. Antoine told me she had actually commanded an army during the revolt of the Fronde yet survived her period of disgrace to now be a great favorite at Court. Tante shared that not everyone is looking forward to her arrival, though. It seems Her Majesty and the Marquise de Montespan both see her as an interloper. However, the general consensus is that La Grande Mademoiselle is witty, fun loving, and brings joy to the Court. I believe I should like anyone with those attributes.

I will close this entry for now and write more perhaps on the morrow.

Louise

◈

The riders stopped to water their horses by a stream and take a rest. Claude noticed Maury had been careful not to overwork the horses, not riding the same one each day. They still made good time by staying on a schedule. Neither spoke much on the trip, and that suited Claude. As a rule, he learned a lot from people who liked to talk, but he could tell that this man, when he spoke, wanted information rather than revealing anything about himself.

With that as the case, Claude preferred the silence to the questioning. Still no opportunity presented itself to look for the note. It only increased his curiosity. A fact that made him more determined than ever to know what was so important that this man would drop everything to ride for days to see a woman, who by all accounts, was relative to the king and nobility of some sort.

As usual, Maury undid the pack and broke out the bread and cheese. It had been a steady diet of such, and Claude did not feel as grateful as he originally had. Could not they have stopped somewhere and purchased something? But, no, they had to stay away from towns and villages where they could have gotten something else to eat. That was another thing Claude did not understand. Why had they stayed so far from others?

Monsieur handed the bit of food to Claude and sat down under a tree. He looked preoccupied, bothered by something. Well, he could keep it to himself, for all Claude cared.

If only he could find the note. Claude slid down under another tree and began to pick at the food. A pigeon braved close enough to peck a crumb. At least he would be back at Versailles quicker than if he had returned on his own. For that, he was almost grateful.

He finished off the cheese and left most of the bread for the birds.

"I will be back." Maury's statement broke the stillness.

Claude looked up to see him head into the trees. This was the perfect chance. He hopped up. Stealthily moving to the horses, Claude scanned the area. No sign of the man. The pack on the back of Maury's gelding was not that big. He opened it, feeling around quickly. It should not take that long to find the note. Yet the note did not seem to be anywhere in the pack. Claude rummaged more overtly.

"May I help you?"

Claude jumped, spilling the pack over the ground. He stooped, quickly shoving everything back in place. "I thought I would have a bit more cheese, if you do not mind."

"Help yourself. Are you ready?" Maury's voice held no rancor nor suspicion.

"Oui. Let us go."

Claude mounted up and followed on. At this rate they would be at Versailles by the morrow's morn. The letter was not in the pack. Therefore, if Matthew brought it along, it was on his person. Did he want to see it enough to take that gamble?

Of that, he was not sure. If the opportunity presented itself, perhaps he would chance the risk. If not, then he would not. He had learned to be patient over the years, and he could wait this out.

Chapter Sixteen

Give it back!" Louise jumped, reaching as high as she could. "Do not read it. Please. Give it back."

"Hmmm, I am not sure I should." Antoine grinned, turning this way and that to keep away from Louise's outstretched hands. With broad gestures, he began to open up the book.

Louise jumped and grabbed again.

Antoine cleared his throat. "Let us see. It says here on the first page that this journal is an account of a visit to Versailles and is the private property of one Mademoiselle Louise de Saix, begun this sixteenth day of July in the year of our Lord 1668. A nice introduction, my dear. Shall I turn the page? I wonder what wonderful and terrible secrets you have shared with your journal."

"No! Do not! Antoine, *please!*" Her heart lodged in her throat.

She noted the twinkle in his eyes had been joined with a gentle caring look. He returned the book with great exaggeration.

Louise took it, hugging it to herself. A part of her did want to share some of it with him, but she had written of Matthew in there. That was not her secret to share. She hoped her note had found its way to him and that he would meet her at the glade. She would know soon enough. Though she wondered about Momo's ability to carry out anything Louise desired. She had no way of knowing if Momo hadn't just opened the note herself. She never should have trusted Momo. But what choice did she have? *Please, Lord, let no harm come to Matthew due to my actions.*

Antoine touched her arm. "You know, I would not have read it without your permission. I only teased."

"I know." She stared down at her beloved journal. He had no way of knowing how it held all her intimate thoughts and feelings. Things she could not even voice were recorded for safekeeping. She was not ready for Antoine to see that deep into her soul.

"Do you really?"

Looking up, she met his gaze. "Oui, I do know. Antoine, I have always been a very private person. If I were to choose anyone to read this, it would be you. I am just not ready yet."

"Have no fear. As I said, I merely teased." He grinned mischievously. "I will have to remember you have no sense of humor."

"Antoine!" Louise squealed and attempted to punch him. However, she could not hold back a laugh.

They continued their little dance of her trying to hit him and his moving just out of reach. Both laughed, scrambling among the garden mazes. Louise made an extraordinary leap to which Antoine jumped backward.

Louise gasped, covering her mouth just as Antoine fell back onto another couple.

"So, this is how you treat my guards. Or, perhaps is Antoine the culprit? Shall I have him arrested and put on the rack, Louise?"

Unable to hold it in any longer, Louise broke into nervous giggles.

Antoine seemed to quickly recover.

"Your Majesty." Pulling off his hat, Antoine made a sweeping bow.

Louise tried to curtsey but still shook with giggles so much Antoine had to put a hand under her elbow to steady her.

Glancing first at Antoine, Louise got her voice under control. "Merci beaucoup, your Majesty, but not at this time. Perhaps if Monsieur de Crocketagné does not behave himself, though, I will consider Your Highness's offer." She then turned to Antoine and smiled.

"Have we disturbed you?"

"Oh, no, your Majesty, it was, ah it was…" She looked to Antoine, who merely grinned back.

"Never mind." The king laughed. "I would like to introduce you to my guest. Anne Marie, may I present my lovely cousin, oh, excuse me, *our* lovely cousin, Louise de Saix. And, of course, her escort, the second in command of my very capable palace guards, Monsieur Antoine Desaure Permonette de Crocketagné. Antoine, Louise, this is Anne Marie Louise d'Orleans, the Duchesse de Montpensier."

Louise curtsied again, this time with perfection. Antoine bowed over the lady's hand saying, "My pleasure."

"Louise, how beautiful you have grown. I was there at your christening, although I was still a child myself. It is nice to see you again—especially now that we are both grown enough to remember." La Grande Mademoiselle took Louise's hand and looking at her, spoke to the king. "Your Majesty, whatever else the history books may say of us, they will have to admit we are a very pretty family."

"I believe that would be considered bias coming from you, my dear. Antoine, would you care to comment?" His Royal Highness winked at Louise.

"I believe the duchess is correct in her assessment. I have no argument."

Antoine's intense stare caused Louise's cheeks to flame.

"There we have it, a non-biased opinion. It appears, my dear, you are correct." His Majesty smiled.

"You will be at the opera with us this evening, will you not? Louise, my dear, we have much to catch up on."

"Of course, they will be, my dear." The king responded first. "I will make a point of seating you two so you may chat between acts."

"Oh, merci, Your Majesty." Louise smiled. It would be nice to have a woman here closer to her age with whom she could talk. Someone who was open, friendly, and warm. Plus, she was family.

Now, more excited than ever, anticipation for the night mushroomed. She had questioned up until now whether she was in fact invited. Nothing official had been mentioned to her, but now, it was allowed, and it would be a night to remember. Of this, she was sure. "I cannot wait."

Soon after, Antoine walked Louise to her room and left her there to rest and prepare for the coming evening. She entered humming a tune and saw Mimi placing the bowl of fresh fruit on the night table.

"Mimi, how lovely." Louise could smell their sweet scent as she entered the room. "How did you know strawberries were my favorite?"

"I did not know. They looked good. I am glad you like them. They are from Momo too. We want to say thank you for all you have done."

"I have not done anything, really. You are the one who is always doing. Here, let us both have some." Louise tossed a strawberry to Mimi.

"Oh." The surprised girl fumbled to catch the berry.

Louise bit into hers and motioned for Mimi to do the same. "I have met a long-lost cousin, just a few minutes ago."

"You did?"

"Oui. She was as pleasant to me as the Marquise is not. Apparently, she has seen me before, at my christening. We must be related on my mother's side. Anyway, she is the Duchess de Montpensier. Have you seen her here before?"

"I have not served her, but, oui, I have seen her." Mimi looked away.

Louise recognized the answer had been worded with care. "What is it that you are trying to keep from telling me?"

"Mademoiselle, it is not my place to gossip."

"I do not ask for gossip. Just what is it that you are hiding?"

"I will not try to sort out all the rumors or the reasons, but I can say that neither Her Majesty nor the Marquise de Montespan is very fond of the Duchess. However, His Majesty seems to be genuinely happy when la Grande Mademoiselle arrives for a visit."

Louise ate another berry. Squinting her eyes, she chewed and swallowed. "Something that Her Majesty and the Marquise agree on. That is very interesting." She wiped a drop of juice from her chin. "His Majesty said he would have us seated close together this evening so we might chat. Do you think that will cause problems with Her Majesty?"

"I do not know. My understanding is that she will be attending. I do not think she is spiteful. The Marquise on the other hand…"

"Oui, I presumed she would be displeased. The question is what will she try to do because she is displeased?" Louise wiped her hand across her mouth and tossed the stems onto a tray. It was time to rest for the evening's festivities.

⚜

AFTER MADEMOISELLE DE SAIX LAY DOWN FOR A SHORT nap, Mimi arranged everything she needed to help mademoiselle become ready for the evening. Surveying the room and the time, she realized she had a few moments for herself.

Mimi eased the door closed behind her and went to the chapel. It had become a place of a refuge over the last few days. She would light a candle for her Pierre and Madame LeSuere. Then she would pray at the altar. After a while a quiet peace would come, and she would gather a bit more strength to see her through a few more hours. Often the gentle priest was there, and they would talk when opportunity lent itself.

Today, the priest was not around so Mimi began her routine. It was not long before she sensed another person in the room. Assuming it was the priest, Mimi continued her prayers.

When finished, she stood to speak with the cleric. Deep shadows cloaked the little chapel. She could just make out the form of a man down at the other end of the altar. She walked to him and put her hand on his shoulder.

Mimi withdrew her hand quickly. It was not the priest. Embarrassed, she stepped back and hesitantly studied the man. There was something familiar about him. He had lit two candles and knelt in silent prayer.

She should not stare. It violated the privacy of the refuge. Mimi turned to retreat.

"Mademoiselle."

She stopped, slowly turning to look into the saddest eyes she had ever seen.

"Oui?" Now she remembered the man. He was one of the guards who had brought Madame LeSuere home.

"I …" He paused. She could see in his face he needed to say something to her.

"I recognize you." She wanted to help. "I remember you from Madame LeSuere's home. You want to speak with me?"

"Oui, if you do not mind." He stood and stepped closer.

Mimi's heart could have broken again from the sadness in his eyes. If she still had a heart to break.

"Not at all. Do you want to speak in here or perhaps outside?"

"Would you mind if we went outside?"

Instead of answering, Mimi walked out in front of him.

When they were beyond the chapel doors, Mimi turned again to get a better look at the man. Even in the afternoon sunlight, he appeared very sad, as though he suffered a great deal.

"Mademoiselle, I have thought of you and Madame LeSuere often since that terrible day. How do you fare?"

"I survive. Sometimes that is good and sometimes it is not."

"What do you do?" She knew he was not asking about what work she did, but how she survived her pain.

"When it is not good, I hold tighter to my faith. When it is good, I say a prayer of thanks and try to store the moment in my memory so I will remember I will get through."

He nodded. "I want you to know I am very sorry for your loss. If there is anything I can ever do for you, please do not hesitate to ask." He touched her hand and then turned to go.

"Monsieur."

He turned back.

She needed to know. "What is your name?"

"De Grillet. Albert de Grillet." He smiled his melancholy smile, tipped his hat, and walked away.

Chapter Seventeen

Louise stretched in her bed and smiled to herself. On the morrow she would go to meet with Matthew. He would call her a big baby.

She had to agree at this point.

Things had improved so much. She did not feel as burdened as she had when she first wrote the note. Now, though, it was too late to get word to him. So, she would go meet him. It would be wonderful to see him again.

Then there was tonight. Louise grabbed a pillow to her chest. Oh, she looked forward to a glorious night. Young and in love, she rubbed shoulders with the highest nobility of French society in the most fascinating court in the world.

Could life become any better?

Her journal sat on the night table. She picked it up and thumbed through. As she read the first few entries, it surprised her how different she sounded. What had happened to the quiet, shy creature who hated crowds and bother? Louise still preferred to ride a horse than socialize with many of the nobles present at Versailles. However, she was finding royal court life exciting and fun. Was that so bad?

That first evening getting ready for dinner and the theatre, she had been terrified of too much attention. Now it did not bother her. Usually.

Of course, the attention the Marquise tried to show her was not the most pleasant, but others helped make her stay enjoyable.

That was something else she realized. At some point, she had given up being afraid of what the Marquise might do. She had Antoine. He loved her. That was all that mattered.

Oh oui, life was good.

The door opened, and Mimi peeked in. "I see you are awake. Would you like to bathe before getting ready?" She came into the room.

"Oui, please." Oh, how delightful. To soak in a hot bath and then prepare to go to the opera. And not just any opera. This performance she had wanted to see from the first moment she had heard of it.

Mimi lugged bucket after bucket of hot water to the tub.

She should get up and help Mimi. After all, Mimi was doing this for her. Mimi would not accept her help, though. Louise knew that. Yet she could offer. Or she could argue with herself until the tub was filled.

When had she become so hard hearted as to make someone as sweet as Mimi waited on her hand and foot? The evening lost some of its luster.

When the tub was ready, Louise stepped out of her chemise and into the water. Sliding down, she let the warmth soak away her culpability. A short time later, when she stood, she had pushed her conscience out of the way.

Mimi handed her a towel and helped her out of the tub. A clean chemise waited on the bed. A burgundy-colored dress of satin and velvet lay beside it. Two combs of garnet and pearl sat on the vanity alongside matching earrings, necklace, and a bracelet. Mimi had even included a folding fan of oriental motif and a mouche next to her bottle of perfume and jar of pearl dusting powder.

Louise stepped into the skirt and then Mimi fastened the boned bodice in back, tucking in the flaps. The outer skirt of lace was brought back at the sides to reveal the underskirt. Lace from Louise's white chemise peeked out at the sleeves and neck. This was not the lowest neckline in her closet, but it definitely would be considered low-cut among her friends back home. Louise adjusted her chemise at her cleavage for modesty's sake but dusted her neckline liberally with her powder.

Mimi fashioned Louise's hair into a braided coronet at the crown and added masses of curls over each ear topped by a comb on each side. The necklace was fastened in place, a dab of perfume touched behind each ear, and the mouche pasted into place on the right cheekbone.

"Let me help you with the bracelet." Mimi took her wrist.

Louise's conscience squirmed. She pulled her arm back. "Mimi, you do not have to help with everything." The knock at the door effectively cut off the rest of what she wanted to say, though it could not hide the look in Mimi's eyes.

Adjusting her cap, Mimi opened the door.

A very debonair Antoine, dressed in black and white, stood with knuckles raised. His plumed hat stuck out from under his arm, and he carried a long-stemmed red rose.

Louise met him at the door where he offered her the flower. "Merci beaucoup." She curtseyed and accepted the rose, taking a deep breath of its scent. With Antoine, the world became right. The rest did not matter. After putting the rose into her pitcher, she picked up her fan and wrap. "I am so excited. I do not think this is real. I keep pinching myself to wake up."

Antoine smiled. "It is real, my love," he whispered in her ear. His breath against her neck sent delicious chills up her spine. "Shall we?" He offered his arm and they left.

By now, Louise was confident in most of the halls of Versailles. It would one day be a very large place. Would she ever return to see the finished product?

They headed outside to an area especially built for the night's production. It seemed fitting somehow that an opera about the Egyptian goddess of nature should be presented outside, under a setting sun. Antoine found their seats and, true to his word, His Majesty had arranged the seating so Louise could sit next to the Duchess.

The two women began chatting almost immediately. They found they had many of the same likes and dislikes, although it was obvious that the Duchess was by far the more outgoing.

Anne Marie leaned over to whisper. "Do not look now, but I believe someone is spouting steam from her ears."

Louise did not understand.

The Duchess opened her fan and pointed from behind it. When she closed her fan again, Louise looked in the direction indicated.

Louise had to open her own fan to cover her giggle. It might not have been nice, but it brought some satisfaction to see the King's Favorite so irritated. Having been relegated to a different area of seating, the Marquise was most certainly unhappy.

The orchestra sounded, and the opera began.

Enthralled, Louise often closed her eyes, getting lost in the music and letting it transport her to Egypt. Yet with the ballet portions, she had to sit on the edge of her seat and grip the armrests. How inventive! How wonderful! She could have joined in their dance and been carried away. As the stars came out and the light of day dimmed, Monsieur Lully arranged for lighting to be added unobtrusively. The effect was magical. Louise could not bear for it to end.

Afterward, while on the way to dinner, His Majesty motioned to her. "So, dear little cousin, what did you think?"

"The saddest part was that it must end."

"I take it the production pleased you."

"Oh oui, Your Majesty. It greatly pleased me."

"Bon. Then I will let Monsieur Lully know he may have other showings."

Louise took Antoine's arm and they began to walk away, but

she could still hear His Majesty speaking with Anne Marie. "My dear, Conté just informed me you have hired a new gardener. He is not a Huguenot, is he? That name sounds very much like one of those heathens."

The word *Huguenot* gripped her heart. Could it be someone she knew? Louise listened hard for more.

"Your Majesty, there are no Huguenots on my list of paid employees. But if there were, would that be such a tragedy?"

"My dear Duchess, to hire one of those creatures is tantamount to blasphemy. Hire an atheist if you will, but stay away from the Huguenots."

A lump settled in Louise's stomach. She should not have eavesdropped, but she had never thought to hear anything so horrid.

Looking over at Antoine, she noted a set to his jaw. Had he heard the charges? Would he be of the same opinion? Now more than ever she was grateful he had not gotten a look inside her journal.

Dinner followed, served outside on the lawn. Louise picked at her food and looked around at the festivities. She needed to forget about what she overheard and enjoy this magical night. This would be a wonderful entry in her journal. She pushed her plate away and glanced over to Antoine.

He smiled back and stood. When he offered his hand, she knew they would take another stroll around the Marble Courtyard.

Louise took his hand and they found a tranquil place next to a fountain to sit and watch the stars.

Antoine rested his arm about her shoulders. "Was it everything you hoped it would be, my love?"

Closing her eyes, she listened while the wind replayed the music just for her. She sighed. "Oh, oui. It was all I had hoped for and more."

Antoine laughed and brushed a tendril from her cheek.

"Your innocence draws me." He leaned in and stole a sweet kiss.

Louise leaned her head on his shoulder. "I think if I summed this evening into one word, it would have to be magic. My heart still pounds in my chest from the excitement."

"The excitement of this night is only the beginning. Just wait until the morrow and see what our king has planned."

An icy wind started up Louise's spine.

Antoine took no notice of her silence. "I have been told His Majesty is preparing a hunt on the morrow. We have not had one in quite a while, and it is one of his favorite pastimes. You will enjoy it, I know."

The words dropped like cold rain. On the morrow she was to go meet with Matthew. She could not go on a hunt. She also could not have Antoine go with her. Not until she spoke with Matthew first. What could she do?

"A hunt?" The words creaked out as if past an old rusty hinge.

"Oui. Have you not ever been on one?" Antoine searched her face.

Louise averted her eyes. "In fact, no. That was one thing my father never let me do. If you want to go, it is not a problem for me. I will stay here. I have much I can do."

"Nonsense. You can come. It is not difficult. You are an expert rider so if you stay by me, it will be well."

This would not do. She had to get out of going. "I am sorry, Antoine. I do not want to go on a hunt."

"Oh." The poor man. He was trying so hard. She could not explain she needed to stay at the chateau to meet with another man.

"No, it is not a problem. Please, you go and have a good time. I will be here and waiting for you on your return."

"You know that will not do. Aside from that, I would rather be with you than on a hunt."

What could she say to that? She wanted to be with him too,

but he could not go with her. No matter what she did, she would end up hurting this man she so dearly loved.

Louise took Antoine's hand. "I would rather be with you too, but there are matters demanding my care. Some feminine type matters. I need some time to myself to accomplish this. Do you understand? "

"Not really. But as you wish." He sounded gloomy, and she hated that she was the cause.

"I will come find you on the morrow in the afternoon when you return."

"But I cannot go if you are not going. His Majesty will wonder why your escort is having so much fun without you. I will be here and wait as patiently as I can."

"Very well." Though Louise agreed, she knew she would need to find a way to get to the stables for a horse without Antoine discovering her. She sent out a silent plea for help and changed the topic.

Chapter Eighteen

Claude could not believe how quickly they accomplished the trip back to Versailles. It was not even noon yet and here they were approaching the outskirts of the town. Maury began to reduce his speed, slowing to a stop.

Taking a paper from his vest, he handed it to Claude. "Do you know this area?"

The stars must have turned in his favor. Maury had put the note in his hand. Claude had never had such luck fall into his lap. He scanned the letter, committing the contents to memory. There was nothing he could use at the moment, but who knew what might come up later? Steadying his voice, he handed the paper back to Monsieur. "We are close. Follow me."

Claude led him into the woods, down a narrow riding path and through to the hidden glade at the center. "This is the spot, monsieur. So, what now?"

"I believe this is where we say goodbye. I appreciate your help, Claude." Maury took out a purse and handed Claude several coins.

Claude admired the silver pieces. He tossed one in the air and caught it before pocketing it with the lot. "It was nice doing business with you, monsieur." He tipped his hat and rode his horse in the direction of the chateau. There were more coins in the purse, but then Maury would not be going anywhere for a while. Claude knew where to find the purse and its owner later.

He rode up to the stables and left his horse. Knowing his way quite well, he headed for the nearest servant entrance.

La Petite Chateau de Versailles, though undergoing major renovation, had several extra servants in and about due to the royal visit. With so busy a group of people traversing the halls, an indigent courtier bold enough might chance a free meal by pretending to be one of the regular servants. It was this very fact that Claude counted on to get himself in to see Momo.

Once inside, he had a general idea where to search for her without causing a disturbance. It took him less than five minutes to locate the maid and pull her into a quiet corner.

"You are back." She sounded genuinely glad to see him. This day was getting better and better.

"Oui, but I was only paid in part. Come here and pay me the rest." He pulled her to him for a rough kiss.

She pushed him away. "Not here, you oaf." Tucking a curl back beneath her cap, she glared. "I am supposed to be Mimi, and she is in mourning."

He pulled her back, whispering in her ear. "Tell them you got over it and found someone better."

Momo pushed free again. "Stop. I have to tell you something." She put some distance between them and looked over her shoulder.

This was not what he had hoped for after traveling half the countryside for the wench. Yet it would do no good to fight her. He sighed. "As you wish. What is it?"

"I found another job for you."

"Another? I just got back. I want to spend some time with my girl."

"This is a big one and pays well." Her eyes gleamed.

"What do I have to do?"

"The lady who wrote that note you delivered?"

"Mademoiselle de Saix?"

Momo nodded. "She has made a dangerous enemy of someone quite powerful here at court. This someone wants you to help the mademoiselle to disappear."

"What? Ho, I've not done any killing. A bit of snatching here and there, but killing is another story."

"Well, Mademoiselle High and Mighty could have an accident. Then it would not necessarily be killing, now would it?"

"You are serious about all this?"

"Deadly." She looked him straight in the eye. "My family is in danger. If we do not help her, she will turn us in for helping Mimi. Please, I have no one else to turn to." It sounded like a purr.

He never could resist her and had known from the beginning she would have her way. She had known it too. But killing, it did not sit right with him. He would figure something out. "So be it. What is the plan?"

"There is none but for you to do it as soon as possible."

"Will this afternoon be soon enough?"

Momo's eyes widened. "Oui." Her voice whispery with excitement. Reaching out, she grabbed his face with both hands and kissed him hard on the mouth. Before he could react, she was gone.

◈

LOUISE PACED THE ROOM UNTIL SHE WAS SURE SHE HAD worn holes into the soles of her shoes. She fiddled with the ribbons on her dress, tried to write in her journal, and even snapped at Mimi. Though she had apologized, it was obvious the feelings of the young maid were hurt.

In time, the afternoon shadows began to appear. Since no specific time had been arranged, Louise packed up her journal and some supplies for something to do while she waited. She changed into her riding costume and slipped out to the stables hoping that Antoine would not see her.

Everyone appeared to be gone, presumably on the hunt. She found the stable boy cleaning out the empty stalls.

"Might I have you saddle a horse for me?"

"Oui, Mademoiselle." He leaned his pitchfork against the wall and Louise stepped back out into the yard, keeping close to the side of the entryway.

Shortly, the boy led Étoile into the yard saddled with that ridiculous red velvet contrivance.

"I do not ride with a sidesaddle. Where is the astride one I have used in the past?"

"I am sorry, Mademoiselle. That saddle belongs to La Grand Mademoiselle, and she has use of it today."

Of course, and the Duchess was at the hunt with the others. Louise bit her tongue. It would do no good to chastise the poor stable boy. He looked wretched enough as it was. With a sigh, she mounted carefully, and started off in the direction of the glade.

Louise could almost give Étoile the lead to get to the special spot without a problem. It took a mere twenty minutes to arrive at the place that belonged to her and Antoine. Antoine. Would he understand? Her conscience niggled at her. Why had she picked here of all places to meet with Matthew?

She picked this place because at the time she knew of no other.

Oh, why had she ever written to Matthew?

As she dismounted, she noticed some movement in the trees across the way. She returned her foot to the stirrup and grabbed the pommel to pull herself back up.

"Louise!"

She released her breath and the pommel. Gathering her skirts, she ran toward the blond man standing in the glade. "Matthew!"

He wrapped her in a bear hug and gave her a quick twirl.

Setting her back on her feet, he held her at arm's length. "You look very well, ma petite."

"So do you, Matthew. So do you." Breathless, she grabbed his hand and led him to an outcropping rock where she could sit and catch her breath.

❦

ANTOINE CAUGHT A GLIMPSE OUT THE WINDOW OF A HORSE being ridden out of the gate. Normally he would not have thought anything about it, but something about the posture of the distant rider looked familiar. The rider used a sidesaddle, however, and he knew Louise's opinion of sidesaddles.

His curiosity got the better of him, though, and he wandered over to the stables.

Inside, mucking a stall, the stable boy worked diligently.

"Have you by chance seen Mademoiselle de Saix this afternoon, Daniel?"

The poor lad jumped three hands high.

"Monsieur, de Crocketagné. I did not hear you. What is it you need?"

"Mademoiselle de Saix. Have you seen her?" Antoine regretted sounding so sharp. The boy had enough to do while the hunt was in progress.

"Do you mean the lady you are always out riding with, Monsieur?" Daniel leaned on his shovel.

"Oui, she is the one."

"She left just a little while ago. A bit put out she was about having to use the sidesaddle, though. I could not do anything else, since La Grand Mademoiselle used the other one for the hunt."

"Did she say where she was going?"

"No, monsieur, she did not do a lot of talking. She seemed in quite a hurry, though you might be able to catch her, if you try." He turned back to his work.

"Merci. See how fast you can get Vent saddled. There is a franc in it for you."

The boy straightened, his eyes big and round. "Merci!" Daniel dropped the shovel and ran for the horse and equipment. He had the stallion ready in record time.

Antoine flipped the coin to him and rode off.

Chapter Nineteen

Claude made himself comfortable among the brush. His horse waited, tethered close by. From his position, he could see all the comings and goings in the glade. He hoped he would be able to get this over soon and was thankful to see a young woman arrive. His question of whether she was the right one vanished as he watched Maury come out of the trees on the other side to greet her. He was sure she was the noble woman Mimi cared for—a cousin to the king or something like that.

This little intrigue had better pay very well, with all these prominent players. He watched them sit on a rock and talk, cursing himself for being too far away to hear what was said.

A beetle ran across his fingers. He swiped it away and shivered. Nasty things.

Back in the glade, Maury patted the hand of the woman a few times. They laughed over something. Though he could not hear their words, the sound of their laughter carried to his hiding place.

How long would this take? Maury had ridden for several days to reach this place just at the request of the woman. Claude settled in for a long spell.

Surprisingly, Maury stood soon after. Holding out a hand to the woman, he assisted her to her feet, and they walked to her horse. She kissed the man on both cheeks. Maury helped her up into the saddle.

Claude took that as his signal.

He waited until she was all the way up in the saddle and Maury was walking away. At least he had figured out the start of a plan. After he had her, he could determine what else to do. He might even get a bit of a ransom out of it, put the blame on Monsieur. Sure, Maury had been decent to him, but these were hard times. A man had to look out for himself.

Claude climbed into his saddle.

෴

ANTOINE HAD NO IDEA WHERE TO SEARCH FOR LOUISE, BUT instinct led him toward the glade. Why she would go there without him, he could not say. Then again, he had no clue why she had put him off about today. Or why she had decided to go for a ride.

He covered the distance quickly and only slowed when he came near the glade. Perched atop the crest, he could see down into the valley.

He found her.

A man was helping her into the sidesaddle.

They appeared friendly. She blew the man a kiss as she turned to ride in Antoine's direction.

A part of Antoine wanted to ride away, hide, do anything to keep her from seeing him.

Instead he remained rooted.

At first, the angle of the sidesaddle kept Antoine from Louise's view. But he knew the exact second she saw him.

Étoile halted. Louise's face froze in a look of panic.

Antoine stared back. His heart exploded like grape shot from a cannon.

As he picked up his reins to turn, another horse pounded out of the brush, heading toward Louise. The rider leaned as he came near her. He grabbed at her reins, pulling her along.

Louise tumbled headlong from the saddle.

Almost as if time slowed, her hands rose to catch herself. He saw her skirt catch on the edge of the saddle and rip as she plunged forward. Her hat flew off. Her hair spilled out.

He was helpless to stop her.

Louise crumpled into a heap. She lay motionless.

Antoine spurred his horse toward her.

The man from the glade ran to her on foot. "After him, man!" the stranger yelled. "I will stay with her."

Antoine obeyed without question.

The villain dropped Étoile's reins and galloped for the woods.

Antoine plunged in after him.

Daylight dimmed in the thick forest. The treacherous floor caused Antoine to reduce his speed. He found no sign of the stranger. The search continued.

Up ahead, the stranger's horse stood alone.

A twig snapped overhead.

Antoine froze in his tracks. His gaze flicked upward.

A large weight dropped on him.

Antoine and the stranger fell from the stallion. The thump to the ground knocked the breath from Antoine. His lungs screamed at him for air.

A flash of metal.

Antoine caught the glint of a blade plunging toward him. He rolled to his side.

The stranger raised his arm to strike.

Antoine lunged for the hand holding the knife. The blade sliced back at him. *My dirk, I need my dirk.*

Antoine jumped to his feet.

The stranger did likewise, lunging and slashing.

At the right moment, Antoine charged into the stranger, shoulder to the man's stomach.

The man flew over Antoine's back.

Antoine spun around.

The stranger lay still amid the fallen leaves and growth.

Keeping an eye on the prone figure, Antoine stooped and pulled his dirk from his boot. He edged closer to the fallen man. With the tip of his toe, he nudged the stranger over.

The man had landed on his knife. The hilt protruded from his chest.

Antoine gathered the horses. He tossed the dead man over the back of the villain's horse, mounted his stallion, and returned to the glade.

⚜

Louise floated on her cloud again. She could see the storm ahead and the dark clouds gathering around her. Her rider would come, though. He would be there soon. She was not surprised to hear his horse.

He called to her by name, over and over. With hand outstretched, he beckoned her.

She stretched out her hand to him.

Their fingers touched.

He grabbed her hand firmly. "Louise!"

His visor raised, and she saw his face.

⚜

Antoine led the horses back to the glade. The other man sat on the ground, Louise's head resting on his lap. He had removed his jacket, rolling it up for a pillow under her head. In doing so, he revealed a piece of jewelry pinned to his vest. It was a gold, open four-petal Lily of France with the petals in a V shape, forming something like a Maltese cross. A descending dove pendant, suspended from a golden ring, hung from the bottom petal.

Antoine had seen only one other like it. His jaw tightened. He knew the significance.

The man stroked hair from Louise's face. He spoke softly to her.

Knots tightened throughout Antoine's muscles at the thought of this traitor's hands touching Louise. Yet if he attacked the man, he might hurt her more than she was already.

"You caught him. What happened?" The stranger never looked up.

"Fell on his knife." That was more than the man needed to know. Nothing mattered until Louise was safe. "How is she?"

"I do not think she has broken any bones, but she remains dazed. She mumbles, but I cannot understand her."

"Antoine." Louise mumbled more clearly this time.

Antoine knelt next to her, taking her hand. "Louise, I am here."

"Antoine." Still her eyes remained closed.

"What is it, Louise?"

"You have come," she murmured and fell silent.

Antoine met the gaze of the other man.

"Know you of a place nearby where we can take her?"

Antoine thought quickly. The closest place he could think of would be to Mimi's family.

"Oui." He stood. "Let me secure the horses, first. She will have to be carried." Tethering all but the dead man's horse, he led the animal to the stranger and handed him the reins. "I will carry her and lead the way. You may bring him along." Antoine took Louise from the man's arms.

The bitter gall choked him. Louise—his Louise—had been with another man. She lay so helpless in his arms. Yet he burned at her touch. No matter. He would be cursed if he allowed this interloper to carry her to safety. It was his name she called so, *step aside, Monsieur.*

The stranger spoke no more, and that did not bother Antoine. There would be a lot of questions to answer later. Now, Louise needed help.

They walked through the woods to the town and up to the modest home.

Vivi played outside. When she saw them coming, she dropped her rag doll and ran inside.

By the time they arrived, Robert held the door. Annette came from the back of the house, wiping her hands on her apron.

Antoine stepped sideways to maneuver Louise through the doorway. "I am sorry to intrude, but Mademoiselle is in need of help."

"Do not worry. Bring her in here." The kind mother of seven girls added another to her brood as she guided Antoine up the stairs to a small bedroom. He placed her on the bed and stepped back.

Annette inspected the still form.

Antoine backed up further. Moving to the doorway he turned his back while Annette undressed Louise. "We could only examine her so far." Antoine's face heated even as he spoke. "You might want to make sure the boning in her corset has not caused further complications."

"Wait outside, Monsieur. I know what I am doing." Annette stood and met him at the door. Patting his arm, she steered him toward the stairs. "She will be very sore for several days, but my greatest concern is for her head. She needs to awake. Go pray. I will care for her." She shooed him out to her husband.

Antoine descended the stairs and followed Robert out the front door. He could hear the stranger trailing behind.

Robert went to the horse. Grabbing a fistful of matted hair, he raised the face of the dead man. "It is Claude Bealieu." He released the corpse, shaking his head. "I am not surprised. He is a bad man, that one. How did this happen?"

"He rode out of the woods, straight for the horse of Mademoiselle de Saix. I saw him grab her reins. She fell. I went after him while this gentleman—"

"Matthew Maury, monsieur." The stranger bowed.

Antoine's breath stopped. A slow burn began to scorch in his belly but a hand on his heart held him in check. He must learn all the facts before saying the wrong thing. Focusing on Maury's face, he continued the story. "Monsieur Maury remained with la mademoiselle. I chased the rider, Bealieu, into the woods and lost him. He jumped down on me from the trees and attacked with a knife. We fought. In the scuffle, he fell on his own knife."

"I see." Robert nodded thoughtfully. "It might have been better to leave him in the woods for the animals. Transporting him in may bring about an investigation."

Antoine ignored the implication. "Where shall we put him?"

Robert shrugged. "He has no family here. Perhaps Father Francois would know what would be best."

Antoine looked at Matthew and snorted. "Do not worry. I will handle the arrangements." He led the horse down the street to the small chapel.

What had happened to cause this nightmare? Antoine kicked a pebble out of the way. It bounced and thumped on the cobblestones. What had Louise been doing meeting with Matthew Maury? Was she a Huguenot spy after all? Could he have misjudged her so badly? His stomach tied into knots. She told him she had some secrets. He had never let himself believe they could be so devastating.

Antoine entered the vestibule. The same priest who cared for the chapel in the town also ministered at the chateau. The gentle man was lighting candles when Antoine located him.

"Father, I have a dead man outside. He fell on his knife while trying to attack me. I do not know where to take him." It was best not to mention Louise or Maury, though he owed the stranger nothing.

The priest replaced the wick and turned to Antoine. "Show me."

Antoine led the way.

"Oui, I knew the poor soul. I am not surprised. There may even be a price on his head. Bring him around to the back. You can help me to clean him. I will pray over him, and then we can bury him across the way."

Antoine nodded. He led the horse to the back.

It took both Father François and Antoine to lift Claude from his horse and carry him. The priest had cleared a table. They stretched the lifeless body across it.

Antoine then stepped back.

The priest gently washed the man and prayed for him.

"He died trying to hurt a woman." Antoine's temper simmered just below the surface. He had little patience left.

"So you say." The priest continued his duty.

"He tried to kill me." Antoine watched him rinse and wring his cleaning rag.

The basin water turned blood red.

"You told me that too."

"Then why all this kindness, the gentleness? The man does not deserve it."

The priest stopped. His blue eyes pierced Antoine to his soul. "None of us do, my son. Yet God in His mercy decided to be kind to us anyway. Can I do any less?"

Antoine hung his head. "I will be back in an hour to help you bury him." He turned on his heel, leaving through the back door.

Chapter Twenty

Louise was awake. She was not sure she wanted to be, though.

Her head hurt with any movement or sound. Each breath brought a wave of pain. Her ribs were bruised from having the wind knocked out of her in the fall.

Those seemed to be the only physical injuries.

The emotional one of seeing Antoine's face before her fall hurt more than all the rest. He looked as though he had been betrayed. How could she ever explain? Where was Matthew?

Madame Roché said that Antoine and another man brought her to their home. Could the other man have been Matthew?

"There is someone here to see you, Mademoiselle." Bibi peeked her head in the room. "Are you well enough?"

Louise pulled her covering a bit higher. "Oui."

Expecting Antoine, she was surprised to see Matthew's blond head with smiling face steal a look from around the door.

Louise tried to motion for him to come in, but everything just hurt too much. He understood, coming to her and sitting on a chair next to the bed.

"So, ma petite. You are awake at last. You gave us quite a

scare, you know." Matthew's tender words reminded her of the others involved.

"I am sorry for frightening you all. It frightened me too." She tried to smile but found that not to be a good idea either. "I worry for you, Matthew. I have kept your secret. I have not said anything to Antoine. He is a good man, but I am afraid he will feel the need to do his duty."

"Do not worry for me, small one. My Protector will care for me. I am not afraid of what mere man can do to my body."

"Have you spoken with Antoine?"

"Not really. He has been very protective of you." He stroked the back of her hand with his finger. "He also is dealing with what happened out in the woods."

"What do you mean?"

"Your Antoine chased the man who tried to grab you. They fought in the woods. I understand Claude fell on his knife in the fight. Antoine knows he was within the law, but it is hard to deal with the fact that a man died."

The burden of her whim fell heavy on her heart. "All because I wanted to see you again."

Matthew stopped his gentle touch and grabbed her hand in his own. "Do not blame yourself, Louise. Claude made his own choices, as did I. Rest, and I will come back and see you again." First giving a gentle squeeze, he released her hand and stood.

"Matthew, keep yourself safe, please. I will understand if you must leave."

"I am only going in the other room. Now rest and I will see you again soon." He bent over her, brushing hair from her forehead.

Louise nodded.

Matthew walked to the door, turned and waved, and then stepped out.

ANTOINE ENTERED THOUGH THE FRONT DOOR AS MAURY came down the stairs. The sight of the man stirred a tumult in his brain.

"I think that you have some questions for me, Monsieur de Crocketagné."

"Oui, I do. Shall we step outside?" Maury embodied all that made the world fall apart today. Wanting to lash out, it was an effort to try to remain calm until they were both outside and out of earshot at the back of the house.

Antoine knew not where to start. All he wanted to do entailed beating the man to a bloody pulp. He closed his eyes and breathed deep. Start with what you can prove. "I noticed your pin, the one on your vest."

"I thought you did."

That was it? That was all he could say? Antoine wanted this man to suffer. "I also recognized your name."

"Now that is interesting since I had never heard of you before today."

This heretic had heard of him today? Louise had spoken of him. Antoine had no idea if that boded well or not. He chose his next words carefully. "I was warned to be alert for you."

"You were? May I ask for what reason?"

"Why do you think?" Antoine exploded. He had no reserve left. "You are a Huguenot. You blaspheme against the church and teach others to betray our king."

"Is that what you think?" Matthew laughed and shook his head. "The papist propaganda has been at work."

Did this man have no understanding? His very existence lay in Antoine's hands. "You deny these charges?"

"Oui, of course, I do. I do not blaspheme against the church of my Lord Jesus Christ. I denounce the papist mutilation that so many blindly accept as the true church. As for His Majesty, he would be hard pressed to find better citizens than his so-called Huguenot subjects."

Finally, some passion from this scoundrel, le andouille.

Maury's eyes revealed a fire. "We uphold His Majesty as the true head of the government—not the Pope in Rome who has no understanding of France or her ways. We support our king with our taxes, our revenues, and our industry. *Reformees* have complained little although, year by year, our rights are being taken from us. Our fathers fought hard for the Edict of Nantes, believing we would finally have the peace to worship as God calls us. Instead, little by little, we are forced to choose between our love for our country and our God. As much as we love France and will fight and even die for her, when given that kind of choice, there is no contest." Folding his arms across his chest, Maury stared back at Antoine. "Have you more questions, Monsieur?"

Antoine did not know how to reply to Matthew's charges, but yes, he did have one more question.

"What part does Louise play in all this?"

Maury laughed. "You want to know if she is a spy or if she played you for a fool?"

Antoine did not reply but stood his ground.

The Huguenot relaxed his arms. "She is not a spy, monsieur. And the only way you could be made the fool is if you let her slip away. Will that be all?"

Maury turned to leave.

"How long have you been in love with her?"

He jolted to a stop.

Ah, Antoine hit a nerve.

Pausing, he took a breath and let it out slowly as he turned back to Antoine. "I did not think it showed. I have loved Louise for as long as I can remember."

"Yet you have not tried to convert her or marry her?"

Maury's eyes became slits as he bored holes through Antoine with his gaze. "You really do not understand, do you?" He shook his head. "Her life would be in danger should I disciple her. If we were to marry, the union would not be recognized by the State. All of our children would be considered illegitimate." His voice softened. "In truth, I have longed to tell her, but until the Lord releases me to do that, I cannot. Instead, I answer her questions when she chooses to ask, without much detail. The Holy Spirit will do with it what He wishes." He paused. "There is one other thing you should know."

Had not Antoine heard enough? "What is that?"

"She is not in love with me."

There was no way this Huguenot could know the gift he had just given. Antoine rolled his shoulders, releasing tension and antagonism toward the man. Yet it solved nothing. "What are you going to do now?"

"I thought I would retrieve the horses and then see about finding a place to stay for a few days."

"Is that safe?" Antoine spoke the thought aloud.

"I did not realize you cared. Louise asked me the same thing. I reminded her that it is not those who can kill the body that we need to fear."

The words reminded Antoine of his promise to Father François. "As you wish. You fetch the horses. I will help you find lodging when I return. For the moment, I have an appointment to keep with a dead man."

Antoine could see Matthew wanted to say something more but changed his mind. Perhaps he thought Antoine was off to turn him in. Very well, he'd let him think it awhile. He ambled back to the chapel.

☙❧

THE GUARD WALKED OFF. MATTHEW SCANNED THE STREET, getting his bearings before starting off in the direction of the glade.

The walk felt longer than it had coming from there to the town. No one had thought to see if he remembered his way, but then he was a pariah, not worthy of concern. At least not in this situation.

Shadows deepened in the woods matching his dark and weighty feelings.

He began talking aloud to himself. "I could have said 'no' to Louise instead of dropping everything and coming here. Perhaps I should have. I thought I was doing what the Lord Jesus would have done."

His conscience pricked him.

"Of course, I hoped she would see my love for her." He shook his head at his candor and realized his sin. He had not stopped to pray before he left. Rather, he let his own wants and desires guide his actions.

Now one man was dead, Louise hurt, and he faced some serious accusations from those in charge.

If he had been the only one involved, he would not have worried about it. "I do not worry so much for me. I well understand the risks." The scrutiny never stopped. If anyone believed he proselytized, he could be arrested. If anyone thought he taught or preached to those of his faith, he and they could be arrested. If he had more than thirty people in attendance for any meeting, be it at the celebration of Christ's birth or Resurrection or even a christening or funeral, all in attendance could be arrested.

Nothing was exempt.

These were the rules by which he and his neighbors lived. They understood.

The people here, and even dear Louise, did not understand.

"I do not fear what might happen if I break one of the rules, Lord. If Your Holy Spirit says to do something, that supersedes the law of man." Matthew had seen others taken away, legs tied beneath their horses' bellies or tied and dragged off behind. Men and women bullied to recant their profession of faith. He lived with the knowledge it could happen to him anytime, without warning.

"Oh, Lord, others are involved this time. These others do not understand their risk."

Matthew arrived at the glade. The horses stood where the guard had tethered them. He sat down on the rock he and Louise had employed earlier and closed his eyes.

"Lord, I have made a mess of things. I am sorry for not inquiring of You before setting out and ask for Your forgiveness. Lead and guide me where You choose. I am Yours and will go where You send me."

Quieting himself, Matthew listened with his heart. He closed his eyes and heard Paul's words from the Book of Philippians.

Let your forbearing spirit be known to all men. The Lord is near. Be anxious for nothing, but in everything by prayer and supplication with thanksgiving let your requests be made known to God. And the peace of God, which surpasses all comprehension, shall guard your hearts and minds in Christ Jesus.

A peace the world could not explain rolled over him. He drank it in until it became part of his being. Comforted, he rested in the knowledge he was supposed to be here in Versailles.

The Lord is at hand? Perhaps there is someone here who needs to hear a word of hope. Oh, the sweetness of sharing the Good News.

Matthew began praying for each person and household, with thanksgiving for the opportunity given, allowing the Holy Spirit to lead and guide him. He did not know what would happen in the future, but he did not have to. He was in God's hands.

Nothing would ever remove him.

Chapter Twenty-One

❧❧❧

Antoine returned from the chapel as Maury brought the horses to the house. He removed two packs from behind the saddle and handed one to Antoine. "Louise's."

Though light in weight, it represented a burden Antoine feared. He had not been to see Louise as of yet. What would he say when he did? Madame Annette had already informed him that Mademoiselle was now alert.

Antoine feared little. He had seen battle and known hardship. Yet the thought of facing the woman upstairs twisted his entrails into a bulge.

With a sigh of resignation, he climbed the steps to Louise's room. Even then he paused in front of the door before raising a fist to knock.

Mademoiselle Bibi answered and inquired of Louise as to whether she was prepared for a visitor. Apparently, she consented. Antoine was ushered in.

Sitting in the chair next to the bed, Antoine stared at the pack in his hands. His voice fled. He cleared his throat.

"How fare you?"

"I am very bruised." The words seemed to come with effort.

"Madame Roché believes you will be recovered with enough rest."

She reached for his hand.

It burned like an acid. He pulled from her touch. The pain of her betrayal scorched his soul. "Stop. I cannot do this." He stood to leave. As he reached for the door, he remembered her pack, still in his hands. He turned back and focused over her head, afraid to meet her pleading gaze. "Monsieur Maury brought this back for you." He set the pack by at the foot the bed, turning once again to go.

"Wait, please." With great effort, she stretched for the pack. Unable to reach it, her eyes pleaded for help.

Antoine picked it up and held it open for her.

She took out a book and held it out to him. Her journal. "Antoine, please, take this with you. You do not want to see me now. I know. I will not try to keep you, but if you will read this, then perhaps you will understand. Please." Her hand trembled. Whether from the physical strain or her emotions, he knew not.

He shook his head, not trusting his voice, and dropped the pack down where it had been.

"Please." Her gaze found his.

He closed his eyes to the sight of her misery, but it still haunted him. Grabbing the book, he strode from the room.

Out in the hall, he stood next to her door, back against the wall. He put his hands on his thighs, breathing as if he had run all the way from St. Germaine. With eyes closed, he tried to slow his racing heart.

Why was life so hard?

After a time, he made his way downstairs.

Maury sat in a chair at the table. "Did you say something about knowing of a place I could stay?"

"Oui. Follow me."

Matthew picked up his bundle and followed.

Antoine decided to see if Madame LeSuere might take lodgers. Huguenot money was as good as anyone else's. There was no telling what type of reception they might receive. He almost explained the situation to Maury but changed his mind. Madame LeSuere and Monsieur Maury could share their secrets as they wished.

He knocked at the door, but there was no answer. While he knocked again, Maury walked toward the back of the house. Antoine gave up and followed.

She knelt in her vegetable garden, picking and weeding. Glancing up long enough to see who entered her yard, she returned to the task at hand.

"What do you want?" Her tongue was as sharp as ever.

"This gentleman needs lodging. I hoped you might put him up."

She stood and wiped her hands on her apron. "What makes you think I need your help?" Her gaze hid none of her contempt. "Never mind. You will break your fast at seven. I will do no washing or ironing for you. How long do you plan to stay?"

"At least two or three days."

Antoine looked at him with surprise.

"You can pay me now--ten francs." She held out her hand.

Now Antoine looked at her with surprise.

Maury merely pulled out his purse and paid her.

She examined the money, then put it in her pocket and motioned to them. They followed her into the house, and she showed them where Maury would sleep.

Antoine then excused himself to return to the Roché home. They could make their own introductions as they wished.

Walking back to the house, Antoine debated within himself. Should he stay close by in case Louise needed something? He was still her guardian. Or should he get out of the way and return to the barracks for the night?

Vivi played a game of hoops in front of the house. She ran to him as if he were her closest friend and grabbed his hand.

"Mama has prepared your supper. It is on the table. Come. She worries for you."

Antoine found himself pulled and cajoled into the dining room and seated before a bowl of *ragout* and a chunk of bread.

"Eat, Monsieur," Madame Annette encouraged. "You have had a very bad day. You need nourishment. I will keep my girls out of your way. When you are finished, then I will make you a bed so you can be close for Mademoiselle."

Antoine opened his mouth to argue but Madame Annette waved her hand at him and *tsked* under her breath as she walked away. He conceded and picked up his spoon and bread.

He had not realized he was so hungry, wolfing down the food without tasting it. As he shoved the bowl away, he remembered Louise's journal.

Picking it up, he peered again at her precise handwriting on her title page. Was it only yesterday she had tried so hard to keep him from reading it? Now, today, she offered it to him, begging him to read the words.

He took a deep breath, steeled his heart, and turned the page.

Louise wrote how she purchased the journal in Paris, her hope being to record her thoughts and observances about this first visit to Versailles. Antoine noted she was in the habit of writing in the morn after her prayers, though she had not written every day.

Antoine had experienced much of what the journal shared along with Louise. Yet to read her private thoughts revealed much more.

She searched for something. He was not sure whether it was as distinctive as searching for God, or merely His purpose for her life. Perhaps somewhere in between.

I do not understand how one so benevolent and kind as His Majesty has been to me could turn and do such an odious act as was done to Madame LeSuere. My heart broke each time I viewed her last evening. Has His Majesty no compassion? She is his subject and has suffered so greatly. Yet I have heard from his very mouth words of wisdom as he entreats the Almighty to guide and direct. I am at a loss.

She asked many questions of herself, of God, of life. Antoine had not realized the depth of her.

How is it that I may enjoy the carefree life of nobility at Versailles when so many are in need just outside the walls? The village is home to many who struggle to find their food and keep a roof over their heads. Yet a mere stone's throw away, lavishness is tossed about with great caprice. Guilt assails me when I find joy in the frivolous. What kind of creature am I to frisk and play while others serve at my whim?

He read how she struggled with her feelings for him.

My heart has taken hold of my senses and my brain has given up control. It makes little sense for love to have blossomed in such a short interval. Yet, I cannot deny the fact Monsieur Antoine Desaure Permonette de Crocketagné has captured my heart. What will come of this, I know not. I am learning he is a good man and to be trusted. My love for him grows daily though I do not know how.

Though Antoine understood and struggled with the same thoughts, he could not believe this tender woman loved him. She loved him, and he had tossed it all away like refuse. He did not deserve her.

Father, I pray You will protect and guide my love in all he does. Do not take him from me, I beg You, Lord.

She prayed for him.

Antoine's hand began to shake as he turned to the most recent entry. *Today Antoine found my journal. My heart ceased to beat, and breath would not come. What if he should discover about Matthew? What if he learns we are to meet? I begged and entreated the man to return my property. I know he teased, but how frightened I was he would find and read my entries. Perhaps I should no longer record what is in my heart of hearts.*

Yet, I know if Matthew and Antoine were to meet, they would become fast friends. I do not know if Antoine shares His

Majesty's cruel assessment of Huguenots, but I know Antoine to be a reasonable and intelligent man. How I wish to share my life with him, yet, some secrets are not mine to share. I pray Matthew will release me from my promise, at least where it concerns Antoine. Then I might tell Antoine of the great friend I have in this older and wiser brother. I do not like keeping things from my love.

When I meet with Matthew today, I will persuade him to let me tell of our friendship to Antoine. I know he will have no need to worry. Antoine will keep him safe.

Maury was loved, but only as a dear friend, a brother.

Antoine closed the book. Every faithless thought he had harbored against Louise rushed back and poured like hail pounding against his memory. He had misjudged her. There had been no guile, no betrayal. In truth, it was Antoine who had betrayed Louise.

She was no Huguenot spy. Her only secret had been the protection of her friend.

Now it was his turn. He would protect them both, one way or another.

For Louise, he would do that.

ॐ

Mimi made her daily pilgrimage to the chapel and returned to put the chamber in order. Mademoiselle would most likely come back from her ride desiring a nap before preparing to attend *appartement* this evening.

However, after putting the room in order and looking for more to do, the time passage began to bother Mimi. She peeked out the window but noted nothing of interest. Her view into the hall yielded the same result. Mimi returned to the window.

The door flung open behind her.

Mimi jumped.

Momo let the door slam. "Is she here?"

"Of course not. You could have known that without scaring the wits out of me." Mimi's heartbeat returned to a normal pace.

Momo paced the room like a caged tiger.

"What is amiss?"

"Nothing." Momo lied.

Mimi knew she lied and that Momo knew her twin knew.

Momo stopped her walking back and forth. "Claude was due back today, and I am anxious to see him."

Mimi accepted this for the moment but only because Mademoiselle concerned her more. Perhaps she enjoyed an extended ride with Monsieur de Crocketagné or a deep discussion with her newfound cousin. The hunting party had returned some time ago.

Momo left.

Evening shadows deepened and though Mimi tried not to worry, she gave way to fear. The worst was not knowing whom to trust for help. Something must be terribly wrong. Most in authority would laugh at her fear. Who would be able to help?

Servants were to be in their quarters by eight o'clock, according to the prescribed rules set forth by the Prince de Condé. Still she would have to take a chance. Rules, there were so many empty rules—no dueling, dicing, playing cards, visiting the theatre or swearing in the servant housing. Yet they could be enforced at the whim of a noble.

Of course, there were exceptions to the rules, but that usually meant that one was on a special assignment. Mimi was on no such special assignment and, though dueling, dicing, cards, the theatre or swearing were not likely to be a part of the evening, it was after eight o'clock now.

Mimi shivered.

Throwing a dark shawl about her shoulders, she slipped out and headed for the barracks. She hid in the shadows as best she could and knocked at the door.

It was opened by Monsieur de Grillet. "Mademoiselle, what has happened?"

"Is Monsieur de Crocketagné here?" She glanced past him into the sparse hall. It was a sign of nobility to do your duty and serve your king with the least amount of luxury.

Monsieur de Grillet stepped outside with her, closing the door behind him. He guided her to the shadows. "No, he is not. Might I be of service?"

Mimi made a decision. She must trust the man. "I am concerned for Mademoiselle de Saix. She left at midday for a ride but has not yet returned. I am hoping Monsieur de Crocketagné accompanies her, but I feel something is wrong."

"Have you inquired at the stables?" Monsieur did not laugh at her fear.

"No, I thought to come here first."

"I will help you search. Come." He took her by the arm and guided to the stables. His presence bolstered her nerve.

At the stables they found Antoine's black stallion missing as well as Louise's favorite, Étoile. Monsieur called for a stable hand. A sleepy-eyed Daniel answered.

Monsieur de Grillet stood, feet apart and arms crossed at his chest. "Do you know where Monsieur de Crocketagné and Mademoiselle de Saix have gone?"

Daniel's face filled with fear, but he answered straight away. "No, monsieur. I first saddled Étoile for mademoiselle. She was not pleased to ride the sidesaddle, but today I had no other for her. After she left, monsieur asked for her. I told him the same thing, and he had me saddle Vent for him."

"They have not returned?"

Daniel shook his head. "I have not seen them since. They did leave in that direction." He pointed toward the town.

Monsieur de Grillet leaned in close, his breath tickling her ear. "Do you ride?"

Mimi shook her head.

"Do not worry." Monsieur turned to Daniel. "Saddle my horse."

Daniel did as requested and had Albert's white mount ready faster than Mimi would have imagined possible.

Albert settled into his saddle and held a hand down to Mimi.

She hesitated. The moment their fingers touched, she filled with courage. Taking his hand, she swung aboard behind him and wrapped her arms about his waist.

He spoke over his shoulder. "Hold tight."

She did.

Chapter Twenty-Two

Albert sped out the same way Daniel had indicated, galloping straight for the village. True, either Antoine or Mademoiselle might had taken any of the side roads between the chateau and the village, but he and Mademoiselle Mimi could work their search back from there.

Clopping down the cobbled streets, he scanned the roadsides, looking for any sign. He was nearly upon them when he spotted two black horses. Antoine's stallion, Vent, stood tethered with the white-faced mare. He stopped and helped Mimi down before dismounting himself. By the time his feet hit the ground, she was already flying through the front door.

A woman he recognized as Mimi's mother stood in the doorway, her arms about her daughter. "Sh-sh, all is well. Mademoiselle is upstairs."

The women moved into the house.

Albert decided to follow.

A man stopped him at the door. "Monsieur, you brought our Mimi to us?"

Albert removed his hat and bowed. "Oui. Albert de Grillet, at your service, monsieur."

"Robert Roché. Welcome to our home." The man stepped aside allowing Albert to enter.

Antoine appeared disheveled from the back of the house, his face bruised, his eyes wide. "Louise. Is there a problem? How does she fare?"

Several girls of varying ages, all looking very much like Mademoiselle Mimi, rushed into the room.

Madame Roché put her hand on Antoine's shoulder. "She is well and rests. Our Mimi arrived with your friend. We will let you talk in peace." She turned to her girls. "Come, let us go to the other room. Mimi, you may go upstairs. Mademoiselle is resting. Bibi will tell you more." The family disappeared so quickly Albert had no time to object.

Antoine motioned to the table.

Albert took a seat, put his elbow on the table and leaned his chin onto his fist.

Antoine sat opposite him. "A man attempted to take Louise today at the glade. She fell when he grabbed at her reins." Combing his fingers over his crown, Antoine paused before continuing. "I chased him into the woods, and we fought. He fell on his knife and died. This was the closest place for help." Antoine spread his hands on the table.

Albert stared at his friend. They had known each other too long not to hear the unspoken. What did Antoine not say?

"You left Mademoiselle de Saix on the ground alone, injured, while you chased the fugitive? You did not go to her first?"

Antoine did not meet his gaze.

Something was amiss. He knew the man who sat across from him—knew him better than a brother. This was not like him. "My friend, is that all of it?"

Raising his head, Antoine looked him in the eye. "It is all that I can say for now."

Albert accepted the statement. This was not the time nor place for more. "How does she fare?"

"She will be sore for a while, badly bruised. Nothing seems broken. Madame Roché believes rest is the best thing for today. On the morrow, we can help her try to move around so she will not become stiff."

"What would you have me to do?"

Antoine shook his head. "I do not know. At this moment, I do not even know what I can do."

Silence lingered. Antoine opened his mouth to speak and closed it again, lowering his head.

Albert waited. The words would have to come from Antoine. He could not supply what he did not know.

Looking back up, Antoine rubbed his chin. "Would you go back to Versailles and get word to Monsieur Colbert and to the king as well, about what happened? Tell them Louise is recovering. She cannot be moved at this time."

"That will start an investigation. You know that."

"I know. The priest identified the assailant as Claude Bealieu. He buried Bealieu in the plot of the pauper. There was a price on his head."

"That may be enough." Albert stood. "I will leave Mademoiselle Mimi here with you and take word back to the household that the royal cousin is alive and will quickly recover. Will that do?"

"Oui." Antoine looked relieved. "And, Albert? Merci."

Antoine stood and offered his forearm.

Albert grasped it. The thanks, Albert knew, was not only for what he said he would do but also for what he did not say. He clapped Antoine on the back and strode out the front door. Albert had no idea what Antoine had gotten himself into, but the man was more brother than friend. He swung aboard his horse and left to keep his word.

LOUISE WANTED TO TOSS AND TURN THROUGHOUT THE

night. She wanted to but could not. After lying still for so many hours, the parts of her body that had not been injured in the fall now screamed at her.

Though they did not scream as loudly as her conscience. Or was it her heart, broken into a million pieces. Her heart and soul bore bruises as well as her body.

Madame Roché and Mimi helped Louise eat some porridge and then washed her face and hands.

"That is all the pampering for now." Madame Roché stood and kissed the top of her head. "You will have to get up and move around or you will be too stiff to recover."

Louise did not argue. She did not like being cooped up in bed all day.

Mimi pulled the bedclothes back and her mother guided Louise to a sitting position. Louise inched her feet over the side of the bed and, with the two women each supporting an arm, she rose to stand.

It felt good.

It hurt a great deal.

Standing there in her chemise, Louise took in a breath and tried to straighten her spine a bit. That helped. She motioned for the women to step back. "I want to try on my own." Louise took one shaky step and looked up with a grin. Progress. She took one more and heard the door below slam.

Hurried feet stomped up the stairs.

Louise took her third step, her confidence growing.

The bedroom door burst open. Momo exploded into the room. She lunged for Louise, knocking her to the floor.

Louise's head banged against the floorboards.

Falling on top of her, Momo pounded with fury.

Dazed, Louise tried to put her hands over her face and ward off the attack. Then she was free. Glancing up, she saw Momo held back by her mother and twin.

"Have you lost your mind?" Madame Roché shook the girl.

"No! I have lost Claude!" Momo pointed at Louise. "He is dead, and she is to blame! She killed him!"

Louise scooted against the wall, wishing it would swallow her up.

"Momo, she did not kill him." Mimi reasoned. "He tried to kill her. He was caught and fell on his own knife."

"No, she should be the one that is dead, her and that holier-than-thou attitude. Why are you not dead?" Momo struggled toward Louise.

Louise pulled herself into a tighter ball, her heart beating a hole in her chest.

Annette ushered her distraught daughter out of the room and closed the door. Mimi remained with Louise. "Mademoiselle, let me help you to the chair."

The shaking began in earnest. Louise had never beheld such fury. "Why? Why did she do that? What did I do to her?"

Mimi sat next to her. "Nothing, Mademoiselle, you did nothing to Momo." She stroked Louise's hair. "Momo has always been envious of those with title and money. Please understand, I love my sister very much, but I am not blind to her ways. Versailles is a two-edged sword to her. She loves to be among all the opulence, but she wants to be the one being served. She finds no satisfaction in doing a job well and would prefer a shortcut to riches. I think that is why she and Claude were so attracted to each other."

Louise looked at Mimi. She shook so much she did not think she could ask but needed to know. "Who is Claude?"

"Claude Bealieu is the man who attacked you in the glade. No one had mentioned his name, and so I had no idea it was he, but I am not surprised. My family has never approved of Claude, so Momo had not told anyone but me that they were planning to be married as soon as he had enough money. Only it was never enough. He must have hoped to get a great deal of money for you so they could marry." Mimi folded her hands in her lap. "Apparently, word has gotten back to the chateau that he died trying to hurt you in some way."

The shaking subsided a little. Louise tried, but could not make sense of what Mimi explained. "Why does she hate me so?"

"Because you are doing all that she has wanted to do but cannot. It is not you, personally, although she thinks it is. That is her way of justifying her greed."

"But she blames me for . . . Claude?" Was that his name?
Mimi nodded.

"She blames me for Claude's death. It is my fault. I never should have been out there." Louise leaned her head onto her knees.

"No, you must not blame yourself. Claude was a bad one and bound to come to trouble." Mimi put a tentative arm about Louise's shoulders. "I hurt for Momo, though, because I know how it feels. Whether he was good or bad is not the point when it comes to her feelings for him. She loved him, and now he is gone."

Louise fell over onto Mimi's lap. "So, what will happen now?"

"I do not know, Mademoiselle." Mimi stroked Louise's hair. Soft, gentle soothing stokes. "Only God knows."

Louise grabbed onto the phrase and held it tight in her memory. Only God knew. It would have to be enough.

Chapter Twenty-Three

"Monsieur, I need to speak with you a moment?"

As Antoine returned from caring for the horses, Madame Roché met him at the door. Her face foretold she had something serious on her mind.

He nodded, and she led the way outside.

"I need your help, Monsieur, for my daughter."

"But of course."

She held up her hand. "This is very difficult, Monsieur, and I need to know you will do all you can to protect her."

"You have my word, Madame. I do not know what I would have done without your help yestereen. Anything I can do, I will. Tell me, what is the problem?"

"I know who was behind the attempt on Mademoiselle."

"What? Who?"

She put a hand on his arm.

With great effort he pulled his focus back to her.

"My daughter, Momo—Monique, she is Mimi's twin…"

He nodded at her questioning look.

"Momo was caught at the chateau and blackmailed into helping to protect us all. Claude was her . . . suffice it to say they were a lot closer than either Robert or I knew. Claude was a bad one, but I doubt he would have come up with something like this on his own." Madame Annette sighed. "I have learned the Marquise de Montespan hired him."

Could His Majesty sanction such a thing? No, this had to be from the Marquise without his knowledge.

"The Marquise has held a grudge against Mademoiselle for some time now. She wanted Claude to get rid of her. I am sorry to tell you this, but I thought you should know. Momo has no proof but for the money she was given. The Marquise could always say she stole the money. Can you help us?"

Antoine shook his head. He knew the Marquise did not like Louise. She was well known for her volatile temperament, but he had no idea she would take things to such extremes. He put his hand on Annette's shoulder and gave it a little squeeze. "I will do all I can. In fact, I will leave for St. Germaine to see the authorities now. Please tell Mademoiselle, that I… tell her I will be back as soon as I can."

A look of relief lit up Madame Annette's face. "I will tell her, Monsieur. God's speed." She returned to the house.

Antoine saddled his horse. Then he realized before he could carry out his plan, he must make a detour. He spurred Vent on and rode hard for Versailles.

At the barracks, he inquired for Albert and learned he was training a new recruit.

"You are back. How fares Mademoiselle?"

"She improves." Antoine stood for a moment and caught his breath, looking from Albert to the stranger being trained. "I have news. It appears a special favorite of His Majesty is behind the incident." Antoine knew to choose his words with caution and even now feared he had said too much.

"You know this how?"

"An accomplice confessed."

Albert stared back at Antoine, his cocked eyebrow saying more than words.

Antoine framed his next sentence with care. "If it becomes known about this accomplice, it could be very bad for others."

"I have already spoken with Monsieur Colbert and His Majesty. They know about the incident and want to know more."

Antoine nodded. "Perhaps I need to take this to the Office of the Marshall of France?"

"One moment." Albert motioned for another guard to come. "Take Tobin to the armory and show him the weapons." He waited until the others had gone and turned back to Antoine. "What would you say?"

"I will think of something."

Albert grinned. "This I will need to see." He followed Antoine back to the stables.

The horses were saddled in record time.

Albert mounted. "Are you ready, my friend?"

"As ready as I will ever be." Antoine pressed his heels, and Vent responded. Man and horse flew as one over the eight miles to the palace of St. Germaine.

The Marquis agreed to see the men without appointment. Antoine explained what had happened, leaving out Maury and Momo's parts, but naming the Marquise de Montespan as the one behind the attempt.

Albert summed up. "We realize this is a very delicate situation, monsieur, but we felt you should know. The abductor is dead, and Mademoiselle is recovering. She would prefer to not have to think about this business any more than necessary. As she is scheduled to go home as soon as those on the excursion to Vichy return, she respectfully asks that we not prosecute the offender."

"You have been the escort of the lady, no? Is this your understanding on the matter?" The Marquis squinted directed at Antoine, making him want the retreat. Give him an enemy with weapons and he could be fierce. But someone of power who could destroy with the scratch of his quill?

"Oui, monsieur, it is. The lady is not one to carry a grudge. She would prefer this matter to be dropped."

"Well then, if she is sure, I will take this to His Majesty and explain the situation."

"It is, monsieur. Merci, monsieur."

Antoine and Albert bowed and exited, hurrying back out to the stables on the other side of the palace.

"I do not know if that explanation will work with His Majesty." Antoine still worried.

"The Marshal of France accepts it. God willing, so will His Majesty. What will you do now?"

Antoine sighed. "I need to make peace with a certain mademoiselle. If she will see me."

"Very well."

"Merci, my friend." Antoine embraced Albert before climbing onto his horse. He needed to see Louise and could not put it off any longer.

❧

MATTHEW KNELT BESIDE THE BED HE HAD SLEPT IN AND began his morning ritual. Prayer, Scriptures, and then his journal. It was a routine that fed his spirit, nourished his soul. He put his mind on things of God and started to pray.

"It will do no good in this house."

Matthew jumped to his feet.

Madame LeSuere stood in the doorway. "God does not hear the prayers from inside these walls."

Although startled, Matthew determined not show it. "I beg to differ with you, Madame. God hears all prayers, in here and out there."

"Think what you like, but I know better. I knocked, but you did not answer. It is time to break your fast." She closed the door on her way out.

Dropping back to his knees, Matthew continued. "Lord, You

know what has caused the pain in her heart. If it is Your will, help me to show her Your love that she might know You hear all the prayers of Your children. In Jesus's Holy Name, Amen."

He stood and brushed at his knees. Later he would finish.

She placed a bowl of porridge out for him and a mug of steaming tea.

He sat. When he bowed his head, she looked away. "Merci, Madame. It smells delicious."

"It smells, but it will keep your stomach from growling." She turned away.

"Have you lived here your whole life?"

"If you are desiring my life story, you can stop. I live here alone. Versailles gobbled up my husband and son, and I am merely waiting for God to get tired of tormenting me and let me die. Enough for you?"

Matthew put his spoon down. The weight of her pain staggered him. "I am truly sorry for your loss." It was the most honest and only thing he could think of to say.

She appeared surprised he did not ask more.

He returned to his food.

After eating, he cleaned up after himself and then fetched water and firewood for Madame LeSuere.

She did not say anything.

He then went to the garden and made sure it was weed free. Bringing in fresh vegetables for her, he placed them on the table before going to visit Louise.

Matthew knocked on the door and Mademoiselle Bibi gave him entrance. "Monsieur de Crocketagné is not here. My sister, Mimi, is with Mademoiselle. Would you like to speak with the lady?"

Matthew nodded. "Oui, please."

"I will go and let her know you are here. Please wait." She hurried up the stairs.

A moment later Vivi raced through. "You wish to see Mademoiselle? She is upstairs with Mimi." Vivi grabbed his hand and began to pull him along. "Mimi is another of my sisters. She is a twin, you know. Did you meet all my sisters? Papa gave us all special names because he says we are his special girls." She continued breathlessly, pulling Matthew up the stairs as she went. "I bet Mademoiselle wants to see you too. Monsieur had to leave early this morning. Are you all friends?"

Matthew chuckled since he could not get a word in between her observations.

"It is something like that." Matthew tousled her hair. By now he stood in front of the door. "Would you ask if it is permissible for me to see Mademoiselle?"

"But of course." She knocked and opened the door at the same time.

Someone chided Vivi for not waiting for the knock to be answered. Vivi explained. There was a sudden rustle and bustle in the room and then the door was opened to him.

"Come, Monsieur. Mademoiselle will see you now." Vivi curtseyed with formality and left the room. As soon as the door closed behind her, the women burst into quiet giggles.

"She dreams of working at the chateau," Mimi explained. "We will leave you two to talk." She and her sister exited, leaving the door properly ajar.

This time Louise sat in the chair. She wore a wrapper with a lap robe placed across her legs.

"You are looking much better, ma petite. How are you feeling?"

The smile on Louise's face began to tremble. She looked at him and tears began to trickle down her cheeks. Before she could say a word, she was sobbing.

Matthew knelt before her. "What happened? Did that oaf say something? Where is he?" Matthew demanded. "Oh, dear one, do not cry. Here." He produced a clean handkerchief and shoved it into her hand.

She threw her arms around his neck and cried all the harder.

What had that dolt done now? *Un pied!* He had no words and could only kneel, stunned.

The door burst open.

Someone grasped Matthew by the shoulder and hauled him to his feet.

Turning, he saw the fist just before it smashed into his mouth.

Matthew staggered backward. Gaining his balance, he charged in return and landed a punch to de Crocketagné's eye.

Louise screamed.

He froze, fingers gripping Antoine's collar, his fist in the air.

De Crocketagné, one fist full of Matthew's shirt, the other cocked in the air, did the same.

Both men stared at Louise, who continued to scream.

People crowded into the room.

"Stop it, stop it, stop it!" She swiped her arm under her nose and pointed to Matthew. "He did not hurt me." Hiccupping, she pointed at Antoine. "And he did not make me cry."

Matthew dropped his hand. "Then what is it, ma petite? Why are you crying?"

Annette grabbed Antoine by the ear.

Matthew chuckled until she grabbed his ear as well.

She dragged them both from the room. "The two of you put together have shown about as much intelligence as a flea." Though she whispered, her words were quite clear. She released their ears and put her hands on her hips. "Do you not yet understand? That young lady is frightened. She has been through a rough morn, aside from what went on yestereen. She hurts in places she did not even know she had. And *that,* my dear friends, is why she is crying. She will probably cry again before this is all over." Her finger wagged in Matthew's face before doing the same in front of Antoine's nose. "Stop using it as an excuse to make the other look bad. You will go in and be kind and patient with her. No more fighting—not in my house. Am I understood?"

"Oui."

"Oui, Madame Roché."

She left them alone.

Matthew pressed at his lip. "You have a strong right hook."

"You have a powerful punch yourself." Antoine touched his cheekbone. "This should make the other one black as well."

Matthew sighed. "You honestly love her?"

"Oui." There was no hesitation.

"Even after knowing about me?"

"Oui."

"Then you had better tell her." It was not what he wanted to say, but what he knew he must. "I think she needs to hear it. I will be downstairs." Matthew laid a hand on Antoine's shoulder and gave him a nod towards the room.

"Perhaps you are right." Antoine opened the door.

Matthew turned and went down the stairs.

❧

"Monsieur, might I speak with you a moment?"

Antoine pulled his gaze from Louise's miserable face. He finally had words and courage all at the ready. Yet, he nodded to Mimi.

The maid motioned him over by the window and spoke softly. "I do not know if you are aware, but Mademoiselle was attacked again this morn."

The bottom dropped from Antoine's stomach. "How? Who? I believed her safe here." He did not attempt to hide the anger in his voice.

"She is. My sister rushed in. My mother and I stopped her. She has calmed, and I know my mother gave you needed information in exchange for protecting my sister."

"If I had known…" Antoine's fist clenched.

Mimi touched his arm lightly. "Monsieur, she had just heard her lover was dead. She was wrong, and she knows it. It will not happen again. However, that is why Mademoiselle is in such a state."

Antoine looked over his shoulder at Louise. She sat staring into space like a lost little girl.

"I understand. You are not to let your sister near her again. Am I understood?" If he could only hit something.

Mimi nodded and patted his arm before leaving the room. She adjusted the door, leaving it open a crack. Her footsteps echoed down the stairs.

Antoine turned and stared at Louise. She looked so frail and small. It wounded him.

Kneeling in front of her, he took her hands in his. "Louise."

Her gaze found his, revealing the fear that seemed to choke the life from her.

"Louise, my love. I am so sorry. I was wrong to think what I did."

A tear trickled down her cheek.

"Can you ever forgive me, love?"

"Do you still love me?" She spoke so low, he almost missed it.

His jaw dropped. She thought he had stopped loving her?

Antoine gathered her gently into his arms and held on. "Oh, my dearest love, I will always love you. I never stopped loving you. I never will."

She cradled into his shoulder and poured her tears over his coat. Her body heaved sobs, over and over.

His throat constricted. To think he had contributed to her pain. He had been an even greater cad than he imagined. "I am so sorry, Louise. So very sorry."

Louise raised her head in an obvious attempt to garner breath. She tried to speak, gasping for air and hiccupping all at the same time.

Antoine looked for a cloth to wipe her face. Even with her eyes so red and her nose dripping, he could not help but think she was lovely. He saw her inner beauty and it held him spellbound.

Finding a handkerchief, he blotted at her eyes and face. When he handed it to her, she blew her nose.

"Would you like a drink of water?"

She bobbed her head and he poured her a cup. Her hands shook as he put the cup into them. She drank a few sips and calmed.

"Antoine, I—" She hiccupped. "I am—" Another hiccup. "Sorry." She took a slow breath, and he waited while she gained control. "I never should have written to Matthew. He has been my friend since we were children." Another hiccup. She paused. "I do not understand what he believes, but when I have a problem, he is very good at helping me sort it out. I am not a Huguenot. The Huguenots I know are kind, but then I know people who are not Huguenots who are kind. I could not betray Matthew, and I promise I did not betray you." Her lip quivered.

"I know. I know." Antoine pulled her close again. "I read your journal. You are the better person, my love." He pulled back and tipped her chin up with his knuckle. "Do you believe me?"

She nodded. "I am just so frightened. I do not know what lies around the bend in our road. I do not know who will ride out to grab me or burst through the door and shove me to the ground."

"No one will, my love. Never again. I will keep you safe, now and always." He pulled her close. "Now and always."

Chapter Twenty-Four

I will help you. Take one step at a time."

Louise nodded and held tight to Antoine.

She had passed a better night, physically since she could move more readily and better emotionally since she trusted Antoine. Letting him take care of her problems lifted some of her fear.

Now, by this second day of recuperation, Louise was anxious to try navigating the stairs.

She was not all that steady on her feet yet but, with Antoine by her side, she ventured all the way to the table.

Vivi applauded her, and Annette brought her a plate of ragout and some brown bread.

Grateful to get out of the bedroom, every little thing seemed a thrill to Louise. Even food tasted better while seated at the table.

"Now that you are safely in your chair, I will go look after the horses. They tend to want to be fed daily." Antoine winked and kissed her cheek before leaving.

Mimi sat across from Louise.

The girl's presence brought about uneasiness. Finally, Louise had no other recourse than to just say it. "You have been so kind and patient with me. Your whole family has treated me as one of their own."

Mimi's open face registered confusion. "That is how it ought to be, Mademoiselle. I already know you would do the same for me."

"But I behaved badly the day of the accident…the day before yestereen." Was it only two days ago? Louise looked down at her food. "I owe you an apology and am very sorry for my behavior when you have only offered kindness and help."

Mimi's hand covered hers. "Consider yourself forgiven if you feel you need to be. I hold no grievance.

Louise smiled as more weight lifted from her shoulders.

"Monsieur Maury and Monsieur de Crocketagné seem to be getting along better today." Mimi pulled her hand back and leaned on her elbows, fingers weaving a rest for her chin.

"They are? Oh, I hoped Antoine and Matthew would become friends."

Mimi laughed. "I would not call them friends as such, yet, but at least they are behaving in a civilized manner toward one another. That is something."

"They probably talk about horses all the time." Louise snorted and giggled behind her hands.

Mimi's eyes twinkled, but she patted the table next to Louise's food. "You need your nourishment, mademoiselle."

Louise picked up her spoon. "It has been good here." She paused and smiled. "Most of the time." She set the spoon back down on the table. "I almost wish I did not have to get better so I could stay on. I envy you your family."

"There are days I would sell them to the first gypsy I found. Yet most of the time I am very grateful to have them." Mimi cocked her head. "You have no family?"

"Only my father. Since I started traveling, I have not seen him. I have no brothers or sisters. Tante Marie, though, is a dear." A dear who would be ready to leave for home as soon as she returned from Vichy.

"I cannot imagine having no sisters, mademoiselle." Mimi sighed.

"Mimi, please. Enough *mademoiselle.* It is stuff and nonsense. You are my friend, and I am Louise."

"I thank you, and I understand. However, if I get into the habit of calling you by your given name, I might slip and use it at the wrong time." Mimi folded her hands and pulled them below the table.

Louise shook her head. "There will be no wrong times or slips. You are my friend and I will defend the right to have my friends address me as I choose. Are we agreed?"

The question hung in the air.

Mimi paused before nodding. "I agree."

"His Majesty's entourage will move back to St. Germaine by the end of this week. Today in fact. When I can move about better, we should plan something. Perhaps a meal in the palace gardens. Antoine and you and me."

Mimi shook her head. "I would just be in the way. It would feel very awkward. I am happy to chaperone but not participate."

"What if we ask Matthew to come along?"

"What if we ask Matthew to come along to what?" Matthew inquired as he strode into the room. He kissed her on both cheeks and sat on the bench next to the wall.

"I think we should have a celebration when I can better move. I want Mimi and you to come along."

"I do not think that will work, ma petite." His smile looked sad.

"Why?" Her bottom lip protruded as if it had a mind of its own. She thought better of it, though. It was time to grow beyond being a pouting child.

"I think you know." His look was quite pointed.

Louise received the reminder.

"Aside from that," he squeezed her hand, "I need to leave for home soon. I notice you made it down the stairs. You must be feeling much better."

"I am, but that does not mean you need to leave right away." She reached for his hand.

"It is time. I will most likely depart on the morrow. That is all the time I can afford to stay."

"But Matthew…"

He stood and coming close, he drew her hand to his lips. "No 'but Matthews.' We had a nice visit, once we got through the drama. For the sake of everyone, I must return home. I know you understand."

"I do understand. I do not like it, but I understand." She held his hand against her cheek. "Merci beaucoup for all you have done. I have missed you and our talks so much. You must come and see me before you leave."

He pulled his hand back but did not meet her gaze. "I will, I promise. Now I will let you two talk while I go to find your Romeo." His chuckle did not reach his eyes.

"Oh, men." Louise smiled, though she could not help but worry about Matthew while she watched him walk away. Her silly letter had placed him in grave danger. She would not again do something so frivolous. Turning back to Mimi, she resumed their conversation. "Now what do we do for a fourth for our celebration?"

"Do not worry about me. You do not need to include me in the plans." Mimi looked uncomfortable, but that only made Louise want to convince her. She needed to do something for her in a way that proved she was a true friend.

"Oui, we must include you." Who could she invite who would convince Mimi to come not just as an attendant? "I know, that friend of Antoine. Monsieur de Grillet. He has seemed lonely as of late. He is nice. Would you be comfortable if we asked him?"

"This is your party. You may invite whomever you choose, Louise."

She could not help but grin at the sound of her name.

Mimi smiled, but looked down.

"Very well then, shall we start planning?"

JOSEPHINE HEARD THE DOOR OPEN.

"Madame LeSuere." Monsieur Maury called out. The sound of his boots scraping clean carried into the house.

"I am cooking."

Never had she met anyone quite like Monsieur Matthew Maury. No matter how cross her words, he remained gentle and non-judgmental. She even caught herself doing little things for him, like his laundry, or baking something extra.

It was not due to any physical attraction. She was old enough to be his mother. Yet there was something special about the man. He brought an ounce of joy to her house, and it gave her purpose to have someone to care for again.

"You are soon back." She came out to him, wiping her hands on her apron.

"Oui, Mademoiselle was in deep conversation with Mademoiselle Mimi, and I was in the way." He laughed.

She pleasured in the sound.

"Mademoiselle, she improves then?"

"Oui, she does, merci. In fact, I think she is doing well enough that I can plan to go home."

Had he thrown cold water in her face, it would not have startled her more. He was leaving so soon? The days passed much too quickly.

"I have enjoyed your hospitality long enough." He stared at her, concern clouding his eyes. "I would gladly stay here indefinitely if I could, but I am a businessman. I must return home."

"But of course. I understand." Though she did not understand. Not really. "When shall you leave?" She turned her back to him to conceal the tears that threatened to form. Where was her stone barrier? He had penetrated her defenses. She needed to gain control. If she began to cry, she would never be able to stop.

"On the morrow, if that is agreeable?"

So soon?

"You have done more for me than we agreed. How much more do I owe?"

Business, that is all it was.

She waved the back of her hand at him. "No, no, you are all paid up. Do not worry. I will bring your meal." She hurried to the fireplace, plating up the chicken she had prepared, especially for him. Her hands trembled.

Someone touched her shoulder.

The plate clattered to the stone hearth.

She spun around.

Monsieur Maury stood close.

Falling onto his chest, her dam burst within, and the flood threatened to drown her. She sobbed as never before.

Days, weeks, months of grief poured from her soul. For so long she had stood strong, but now there was nothing to stem the tide. All poured forth on this stranger.

When her sobs began to slow, he guided her to the table, helping her to sit on the bench. He sat at her side. "Here." Monsieur Maury offered his handkerchief.

She wiped her eyes and blew her nose. This cloth would not be enough.

"Would you like someone to listen? I am skilled at that." Monsieur winked.

She took a breath and nodded, but nothing came out.

"Let me pour you some water." He hopped up and fetched a cup.

It afforded her the moment she needed.

"I did not know how much I enjoyed your stay or how much I have missed having someone here with me." She paused, twisting the handkerchief between her fingers. "I have not always been alone. My Gaston and I lived here as man and wife for twenty-five years. Our twin sons, Alain and Adrien, did not live their first year. Zoé, my beautiful daughter died of the pox. I did not want more babies, and yet I did. Our Pierre was born a year after Zoé left. He was a beautiful child. Kind and thoughtful. My Pierre knew just what to say to get his way with me, full of charm."

She chuckled, recalling his impish grin, then sobered. "I feared every sniffle, every cough. Still he grew strong and healthy. Pierre and Gaston both were stonecutters. When His Majesty decided to build his monstrosity, they were conscripted to work on the fountains." Bile tinged her tongue. She had started, she would continue, every drop of bitterness in her soul pushing itself to the surface.

"Stonecutting, building is an untidy business. The end product is a thing of beauty, but the journey is cluttered with debris and noise. But that is not allowed at Versailles. Oh, no. Work must be done at night to hide the disorder. Sounds must be muffled. Heaven forbid His Majesty be uncomfortable with the implementation of his orders. The safety of his workers means nothing as long as he is not bothered. Gaston was crushed to death only six months past. My beautiful Pierre died last week."

Monsieur took her hand. "You are still in mourning, my dear lady. I am so sorry to have intruded."

"No. I am alone, and the mourning will go on. You brought lightness to my grief for a brief time. Do not apologize." At that moment her arms ached more than ever. A physical pain in her chest told her that her heart no longer resided there.

As she met the gaze of Monsieur, she knew he saw her wounds, saw them clearly as if he could see her naked. She pulled her hand away and wrapped her arms about her.

It was easier to stay in the house and grow cold.

"I am sorry for your loss." His compassion unnerved her, made her open her mouth and reveal her secrets.

"When alone, I ask the questions. What if I had kept Pierre

with me, and we had moved away? What if His Majesty had not been so greedy? And the unanswerable one: Why? Why my family? Why did it have to happen? Why did God allow it? Why did He not stop it?" She flailed down the hill of her thoughts, helpless to stop, picking up speed. "Why did He not He heal my son? Did He just decide we were not worth His time? Did He have something better to do? Where was He when Pierre needed Him so? Where?"

She sobbed again.

He pulled her against his side and held her head to his chest, stroking her hair. "I do not think there is any pain as great as the loss of a child. Nothing begins to compare."

She nodded into his shirt.

"I know I cannot understand your pain, so I will not pretend that I do." He lifted her face and wiped tears from her cheeks with his thumb. "Yet, you now understand something of God that I cannot."

Had he lost his mind?

"I mean, He lost His only Son to death as you have too."

"If He knew how much it hurt, why did He not protect me?" She pushed away.

"Why did He not protect Mary? We call her blessed to be the Mother of our Savior but look at what that blessing cost her. She is called favored among women and she suffered, as you have suffered. Her husband was not there to hold her or share in her grief either."

"Her Son was raised from the dead after three days."

He gently turned her to face him. "Do you think she knew that would happen ahead of time?"

"No, but it was only three days. This is forever."

"Did Pierre know the Living Savior? You know that if he did, he will rise on the last day and you will see him again. Not with a crippled hand. He will be waiting for you and will embrace you when the Lord calls you home. The question for you is, will you be ready?"

Josephine softened toward him. Her gaze searched his face for truth, for hope.

"If you ask 'why' of God, Madame Josephine, you may not be able to understand His answer. His wisdom is higher than ours. If you ask 'where,' He has already told you that He will neither leave you nor forsake you. Perhaps you might ask Him what He would have you to do until He calls you home. Listen with your whole being, and He will tell you." Monsieur wrapped his arms around her and held her.

The tears continued, but softer, more gently. The flood had washed away mounds of bitter roots. This was more like spring rains on new ground.

After a time, she pulled back and dried her face. Standing, she gave him a gentle peck on the cheek and went to get his food.

Moving away from him gave her time to better ingest what he said. She wondered again about this man.

Chapter Twenty-Five

"H o." Albert pulled the reins slowing the wagon to a stop. The matching horses shook their manes in harmony and pawed at the dirt. He took a quick peek at his cargo before jumping down. A steady thumping sounded from back behind the house, but he chose to go to the front door.

Hat in hand, Albert swiped at the dust covering his pant legs before raising a fist to the doorjamb. He lowered his hand and scuffed his feet. Puffing his cheeks out, he released the air through his teeth. A deep breath, and he raised his fist again, this time following through.

The sound echoed in his brain while he waited for an answer. Perhaps she was out back with the thumping noise. He should try once more.

Just as he raised his hand again, the door cracked open. A bloodshot eye squinted back at him.

Albert swallowed and forced a smile. "Madame LeSuere, how fare you this morn?"

"What do you want?"

Simple conversing apparently was not the order of the day. "I have brought you—"

"Away with you." The door swung wide, and Madame LeSuere charged through. "Away with you and your guilty gifts. Tell His Majesty I want naught from him. He can do with it as he pleases, but I want nothing to do with him or his offerings."

"But my dear—"

"I am not your dear anything. I am no one's dear anyone due to His Majesty's pride. Now be gone and take your refuse with you." The door slammed in his face.

Albert jumped.

She had a right to her dignity, and he could not blame her for her reaction.

Still, the gifts came not from the king.

No, and she could not know how he longed to cleanse himself of the guilt of his crime. To have whipped a woman was more cowardly than running in the face of battle. No mere penance could remove this stain.

Albert returned his hat to his head and boarded the wagon seat. A flip of the reins and the horses began their trot. His fragile honor lay smashed under the cart's wheels. Tiny shards ground into dust.

Responsibility lay heavy on his shoulder. He needed to know she was cared for. Driving on to the village chapel, he hoped the priest might help. Somehow.

❧

THE LABOR HELPED. MATTHEW BROUGHT THE AX DOWN again, slicing the wood clean in one chop. He kept at the rhythm: pick up a log, set it down, split, and repeat.

Biting jealousy longed to have its way. Every time it raised its head, he cleaved another log.

The worst part was that he liked de Crocketagné, or what he had learned of the man. If circumstances were different—no Louise, no rift of faith—they might be friends.

Lord, I need You.

Chop.

Take this jealousy and heartache. I do not want them.

Chop.

Let me see Louise and Antoine only as You see them.

Chop.

Matthew stacked the wood for Madame LeSuere. The load felt no lighter. Perhaps he did not mean what he asked? He stopped and examined his motives as closely as he knew to do.

No, he meant what he prayed.

Once back at home he could put better perspective to things. Space would make it easier to come to terms with Louise's love for Antoine. Not easy, but easier.

He wiped his forehead and brushed wood chips from his clothes. Stomping his feet before entering the back way, he called out to Madame LeSuere. "I believe you should have enough wood to last you for a while."

In the kitchen, she chopped carrots with vigor. All at once he had a view of himself chopping wood and knew this was no mere meal preparation.

"May I help with something?"

She turned on him, knife brandished. "How dare he! How dare he think he can buy my forgiveness with goods and trinkets!"

"Who? Who is trying to buy your forgiveness?"

"His Royal Highness, Louis XIV, King of France." She spat the words as if they tasted foul and turned back to her chopping.

Matthew leaned in the doorway. Shaking his head, he knew he needed more information to understand. She had begun to heal earlier, but now her anger filled the room. "I am afraid I do not understand."

"Once again, His Majesty sends a messenger with goods to soothe his conscience. As if he had one to begin with. Let him suffer, if he can. I do not want his pity or his penance. He can rot, for all I care."

Matthew winced but remained silent.

"You have nothing to say? No words about loving my enemy?"

"Is that what you want? Then love your enemy."

She spat on the floor and stared him down. "He is not even worth my spittle."

"Your anger is understandable." *Lord, I need Your wisdom now, more than ever.*

"I hate him. With everything in my being, I hate him and wish him worse than dead." As her words penetrated to her hearing, her face revealed shock. The knife dropped from her hand, clattering on the floor. "Give me your words, Monsieur. I do not know how to control this anger. Help me."

Matthew strode over and embraced her as he would his mother. "Come. Let us sit." He guided her to the bench and sat beside her, taking her hand. "You are human, Madame. Anger at what has befallen you is natural. It also is toxic. It can destroy you if you do not let it go."

"How?" One word from her lips, but her eyes spoke volumes.

"On your own, you cannot. It will eat you alive like an acid. Yet look what all the Christ has forgiven. He can do it for you, if you will let him."

She grabbed his chin and stared deep into his eyes. "You believe that?"

He nodded, and she dropped her hand.

"I do believe it though I struggle at times myself." He glanced to the floor.

"You are struggling now, Monsieur?"

"Oui, but I know His help is sure. It is only my flesh that struggles. My spirit understands."

"Do you want to tell me about it?" Her hand covered his, and he remembered his mother with deep melancholy.

Shaking his head, he tried to smile. "No, but I thank you."

Madame LeSuere stood. First removing her apron, she

brushed a hand over her skirt and tucked a curl under her cap. "I will clean this later. Now I shall go to the chapel to light a few candles. Would you care to go with me?"

He stood with her. "Merci, but I think I will stay here."

Her gaze threw questions until one became verbal. "Is there a reason you cannot go to Chapel?"

Never in his life had Matthew run from his beliefs, but he did not go out looking for trouble either. She asked and deserved his honesty. Where to begin?

"My beliefs and those of the Pope do not coincide, so I worship as the Lord Jesus has shown me."

"What does that mean?" She sat back on the bench. "I cannot believe you are a heretic. I have seen your faith at work and believe your words because of how you have carried yourself. I do not understand."

Matthew knelt in front of her. "I, and those of the same faith, believe we do not need to have a Holy Father in Rome to intercede for us. Jesus was our sacrifice and is our High Priest. We know this from the Scriptures. He promised to send His Holy Spirit, and He kept His promise on the day of Pentecost. We have direct access to the Father through the Son, Jesus Christ. These beliefs do not sit well with those in political power in the Church, so I am not welcome. We are told, though, to not neglect the coming together for worship, and so I will meet with those who believe as I do when I return home." He smiled and patted her hand. "Merci beaucoup for thinking of me, though."

He stood but she remained seated.

"When you say, 'those who believe as you do,' is there a name? What are you called?" Her eyes still questioned.

"I am a *Reformé*—you have heard us called Huguenots. I believe the teachings put forth by the Protestant Reformers, especially those of John Calvin."

"You are a Huguenot? I thought Huguenots were enemies of

the king." She caught his gaze and blushed when she realized she had spoken aloud.

"The papists have put out that propaganda, and unfortunately, His Majesty seems to believe it, more often than not. In truth, we are very loyal subjects. We pay our taxes and have served often in times of war. We support his authority to govern without Rome."

An idea dawned, and Matthew sat next to her on the bench. "Have you not seen my pin on my vest? Let me tell you about it." He removed it from beneath his coat and laid it out on the table between them. "The open four-petal lily is to remind us of our mother country—France. The petals form a cross in the center and each one stands for one of the Gospels. The eight rounded points, here at the tops of the petals, stand for the Eight Beatitudes. The four fleurs-de-lis also remind us of France and the three petals on each stand for the twelve Apostles. Can you see the little hearts that are formed where the fleurs-de-lis touch the petals? That is a symbol of loyalty and the dove that comes down is to remind us of the gift of the Holy Spirit. I wear this over my heart to always be mindful of what is precious to me."

Madame LeSuere remained quiet for a time studying the pin. Finally, she stood and put her hand on his shoulder. "You are a good man, Monsieur Maury."

"Scripture says that no one is good. All have sinned and come short of the glory of God. However, when we invite Jesus to come into our hearts and lives, He brings His goodness and mercy. I am grateful that that is what you see."

She said no more but kissed him on each cheek and left for the Chapel. He did not believe she would divulge his secret. He was more concerned with whether she had understood what he had shared. He prayed that the Holy Spirit would speak to her heart.

JOSEPHINE AMBLED TOWARD THE LITTLE CHAPEL, Monsieur Maury's words whispering secrets to her heart. Though she still did not understand faith as he explained it, she would not speak of it to the priest. There was no need to bring trouble to the man after he had been so kind.

A wagon with matching horses and without the driver stood outside the chapel. Had that guard brought the goods here?

Her ire rose. Why had he not gone back to the king?

Storming though the door, she stopped in her tracks. The priest looked up from where he stood with the man.

"Madame LeSuere, we were just speaking of you. Might I introduce you to Monsieur de Grillet?"

The guard stepped forward. "We have met." For a man of his stature his voice tremored like that of a frightened child.

"Of course, we have met. He attempted to bring that wagon load of guilty penance to my door a bit ago." Father François should have known that fact.

"Oui, that was I, but we met before that. Madame, I came on my own. This is not from His Majesty." The man stood nearly bent from some invisible weight.

"I do not recall meeting you in the past and cannot understand why you would bring me such a wagon load." Knowing His Majesty had not sent him cooled the fire in her belly, but now her curiosity roused.

"You must tell her, my son." The priest put his hand on the guard's arm and nodded.

Monsieur de Grillet raised his head. The eyes that looked on her were filled with something akin to shame.

"Tell me what?"

"I am the one who whipped you, Madame LeSuere. I was wrong to have done so and have regretted it every instant since."

For a moment, Josephine felt she might drown in the flood of emotion whirling over her. Then one buoyed her, bringing her to the surface. She found compassion for this man's suffering. It was obvious he suffered.

"I forgive you." The words cost her, but not what she feared. And with them she found the look on the man's face healing to her own soul. "Now I must go to light a candle." One to match the flame of hope rekindled in her heart.

<h1 style="text-align:center">Chapter Twenty-Six</h1>

ntoine brought Louise to the palace of *St Germain-en-Laye* the following Monday. She moved slower than normal, but at least she moved under her own power. He made the carriage as comfortable as possible, and kept the driver going at a measured pace. What should have taken forty-five minutes stretched out to over two hours.

He had been apprehensive about bringing her back to court. The Marquise was still the favorite, though Albert had delivered news that eased Antoine's mind. She had been sent on to Paris, to the Louvre Palace, to begin her confinement and would not be enjoying the fun at St Germain. Louise would be safe.

Mimi escorted Louise to her room, tucking her into bed amid much complaint, which filtered through the door. Even amidst the protests, Antoine knew Louise was grateful to have Mimi assigned to her during her stay at this palace.

When finally settled, Mimi let him in.

"I am tired of bed. Antoine, please tell her I do not need this."

"A short nap will not harm you, my love. After you rest I will take you anywhere you wish." Antoine knew as soon as he said the words, he needed to qualify them.

"Anywhere?" Her eyes danced at his expense.

"Within reason."

"Whose reason?" Louise tried to look stern, but her face broke into the smile that lit up rooms.

"My reason, and you need to rest. So, when I return, we can go where you choose, within my reason, provided you have rested. Are we agreed?"

She surrendered, lying back against her pillows. "I acquiesce only to you, my love. Do not be long."

"I shan't." He brushed a kiss across her lips, longing for more, and left her there to rest. There was something urgent he needed to gain.

The Office of the Grand Marshal most often was quite busy, but Antoine arrived during a lull. Granted an audience, he entered, hat in hand. "Monsieur, I have a need to speak with His Majesty. Might you arrange an audience?"

"Could you tell me what this is about?"

"I would prefer not to as it is personal and involves His Majesty's cousin." Antoine could feel heat rise in his cheeks while his fingers crumpled his brim.

The Marquis stared back, but soon a knowing smile spread over his face. He chuckled. "I will see if he is now available."

Antoine waited, tapping his heel, until the Marquis returned.

"You may go in." The Grand Marshal of France winked at him.

Antoine straightened his spine and approached the king with his request.

"Antoine, my friend, I understand Louise was to return to court today. Has she yet arrived?"

"Oui, Your Majesty, a few moments ago."

"You would like to confer with me regarding . . .?"

"Oui." Antoine paused, squeezed his eyes closed for a second, and plunged in. "I would like to request a small leave in order to accompany Mademoiselle de Saix to her home after the arrival of her aunt."

"For any particular reason, may I ask?" His Majesty queried, his smirk belying his intuition.

"I wish to ask her father for her hand in marriage, if that is pleasing to you, Your Majesty."

The king sat up straight, his chin slightly elevated. "And if it is not?"

Antoine's heart stopped. "I, ah, do not know." His Majesty's blessing had never been considered a problem.

"Then, perhaps you do not love her enough," he paused, "or maybe you are the loyal friend I have always thought you to be." His Majesty smiled. "Of course, it is to my liking. I am very happy for you. I grant you my blessing.

"However, I should inform you of something. I am putting together an expedition of relief to go to Crete now that the treaty with the Turks has been signed. I will handpick the group in a week and plan to include you in the group. We leave September first. You will postpone your wedding until you get back, *n'est-ce pas?*"

Breath returned, and Antoine could feel his pulse in his throat. "I have yet to ask Louise or speak to her father. There may not be a wedding to postpone. But, oui, I will let Louise know, should she agree, that we will need to wait until the spring." He bowed, though his legs shook. "Merci, Your Majesty, for your permission and most of all for your blessing."

"You are most welcome. Only remember you must be here in time to leave with the expedition. Now, do not just stand there. Go ask her so I will know. I hate the suspense." His Majesty's laughter echoed as he raced from the throne room.

⚜

RAPPING AT THE DOOR AS QUIETLY AS HE COULD, ANTOINE waited for Mimi to open. "Is she asleep?"

She put her finger to her lips and let him in.

"You do not have to whisper over there. I am awake." Louise pushed herself up higher on her pillows. Her hair splayed about her shoulders, shining soft like a halo.

"Did you rest?" He covered the distance, longing to run his hands through her tresses.

"Oui, Nurse." She tipped her chin up.

Sitting on the edge of her bed, he grabbed her chin between his knuckle and thumb, his eyebrow cocked. "Nurse, is it?"

"If you continue to treat me as an invalid, it is." She wrapped her arms about his neck. "Might we please go for a walk in the garden?"

Antoine moaned, unable to resist, but knowing he must hold her off a short while more. "How would you feel about a small party in the garden? That meal outside by the fountains you were telling me about?"

"We can do that?" Her strangle hold about his neck attempted to cut off his air.

He loosened her arms and kissed her forehead. "Oui. You dress, and I will make the arrangements."

"And Mimi is coming." Not even a question.

The maid looked about to argue but bit her lip and nodded.

"Oui, I know, I will also bring Albert." Antoine stood. Leaning over, he kissed her and left before he did something rasher than he planned to do.

⁂

"Now remember, you will need to take Mademoiselle Roché off for a walk so I might ask Louise. Or, maybe I should wait until I speak with her father. What if she is not willing, and I ask her father first?" The beat of Antoine's heart pounded so loud in his ears. He was surprised Albert could not hear it.

"Stop looking for trouble. There is enough of it in this world without you creating more from your imagination. Are you quite sure you want me to go along?"

"This is per Louise. She and Mademoiselle Roché think they have planned the outing. You are going, and you will help me. We are agreed?"

"Oui, agreed." Albert chuckled. "Better you than I."

Antoine punched him on the arm, but in spite of the teasing, he knew this was right. It was what he was meant to do. He only hoped Louise felt the same.

When Antoine knocked at the door, the two women came out, ready to go. He led the way with Louise, Albert followed behind with Mimi.

Antoine had begun preparing for this outing as soon as Louise broached the subject of a celebration. Now a table stood ready in the garden, surrounded by elegant chairs. He feared sitting on the ground might be harder on her bruised body.

Set with exquisite china and crystal, the table was topped by an enormous basket in the center.

"Oh, Antoine, you have outdone yourself." Louise squeezed his arm and planted a kiss on his cheek. He understood her message, but the gesture was highly unsatisfactory. However, in public, it would have to suffice.

The men seated the women, and Antoine played host.

"What have you provided this time, Monsieur?" Louise reached toward the basket.

Antoine smacked her hand back and wagged his finger under her nose. "Not so fast, Mademoiselle. You need to mind your manners and let me serve you."

She pouted, but only briefly. "Very well."

"First, I have some cold pheasant." He withdrew a package from the basket and passed it first to Louise, who in turn offered to Mimi. The men helped themselves after the women had their portion.

"Next, we have these delicious sauvignons which escaped the monks and their casks. The royal chef has an arrangement with a monastery near Orleans, I believe." Antoine winked while bringing forth a smaller basket brimming with delicious white grapes. He again passed it to Louise and reached back into the larger basket. "And what would this tasteful meal be without a *bondon* of Neufchatel, one per person?" He held up four small, white briquettes and handed them out with knives. A crusty brown bread followed.

"Have you nothing to drink in your magic container?" Albert held out his goblet.

"Patience, my man." Antoine scowled.

"Patience, nothing, I thirst. What have you to drink?"

Louise laughed, but Mimi still watched her fingers play with the tablecloth.

"Wait for your turn. I serve the ladies first, knave." Antoine pulled a bottle from the basket. "A lovely champagne to tickle your fancy as well as your palette."

"I believe I recall you saying something like that before." The smile on the face of his love told him she remembered it all.

"Enough talk. Just pour."

Antoine rolled his eyes. "Some people are simply born uncouth." Winking at the women, he filled their glasses before sharing with Albert and himself. He stood and raised his goblet. "A toast." While the others stood, Antoine closed his eyes and thought deep. "To kindness, to mercy, and to friends. May we always know and be known by all three."

The others touched their glasses to his in agreement and then they each took a sip.

❧

THE CONVERSATION REMAINED LIGHT AND PLAYFUL, AND in time Louise caught Mimi smiling at the banter. Her own sides hurt from laughing so much, and for the first time, she realized she would miss parts of court life. A sigh escaped her lips.

"Do not tell me you suffer from melancholia with all this gaiety, Mademoiselle." Antoine eyed her closely.

"No, Monsieur. It is not that, exactly." But then it was. "Time is drawing to a close on my visit. I freely admit I will miss all of this."

Antoine covered her hand with his own and nodded to Albert.

Albert stood. "Mademoiselle Roché, would you care to take a walk with me?" He held out his hand.

Mimi looked at her.

Louise shrugged.

A smile played at Mimi's lips. "I would be most happy to walk with you, Monsieur de Grillet." She stood to join him. He took Mimi's arm and escorted her away from the table.

Antoine leaned in close. "I saved something back for you." His whisper tickled her ear and set off familiar tingles up her spine. "Remember when I told you I had two weaknesses?"

"Oui." Louise had not been able to learn his secret, try as she might. What with the situation concerning Matthew and her accident, she had let the search for answers slip from her mind. "Though I have tried valiantly, my love, I have yet to learn your second weakness. Perhaps it is not such an Achilles' heel."

"I am not so sure. However, I have decided I will confess, as I trust you not to divulge it to anyone." He brushed a kiss against her lips. "Close your eyes and open your mouth."

Louise closed them but opened one eye for a quick peek.

"Close them or I will not share, and you will be sorry."

Sighing, Louise closed both eyes and folded her hands in her lap. Her lips parted, waiting.

Antoine touched a confection to her tongue. She bit into it and savored the sweet concoction. Part was familiar but part, the best part, was new and different and wonderful. "I can taste the strawberry, but what else is this?"

"Do you like it?"

"But of course. Tell me what it is."

"Can you not guess?"

She opened her eyes. "Oh, Antoine, do not tease me. I do not think I have ever tasted anything quite like it. I can understand why this is a weakness. Now tell me. What is it?"

Antoine held what was left of the confection in front of her. "The strawberry has been dipped into chocolate. It is a favorite of the queen, and we lower subjects have a hard time getting our hands on it. I bribed the *chef de partie* and told him it was a very important occasion. We each get two—you have had one of yours now, I am afraid."

"You had four and did not save one for Mimi or Albert?"

"Let Albert get his own." He bit into another one. "I said this was for a special occasion. I do not share my weaknesses with just anyone."

Louise giggled. She could not help it. With everything going on, her nerves had taken on a mind of their own. "What makes this such a special occasion?"

"I was wondering if you would like some company on your way home to Alsais?"

"I would love for you to come, but will you get into trouble for leaving your post?" She had caused him enough trouble to last a lifetime and still could not understand how he forgave her.

"I spoke with His Majesty after we returned this morning and explained my reasons. He has allowed me a short leave."

"What reasons did you give him?" Louise's chest grew tight.

Antoine leaned his forehead against hers and twirled one of her ringlets around his finger. "That I would like to go along so that I might speak with your father about something."

Her heart wanted to pound through her chest. "Anything that might be of interest to me?"

"Perhaps. I thought, if you do not mind, that I should ask your father—" he knelt in front of her and picked up her hand — "for your hand in marriage. You do not have an objection to that, do you?"

Louise could not breathe. She knew she was crying as she

threw her arms around his neck. "I will, I mean no, I do not have any objections and, oui, I will marry you! Oh!"

Antoine stood, drawing her to her feet. "I think I now have three weaknesses, and the newest is the greatest."

Louise melted into his embrace, burrowing her head into his chest. "What is that?"

He tucked a tendril behind her ear. "It is not a what, my love, but a who."

His knuckle rested under her chin, bringing her gaze up to meet his. She could ecstatically drown in the blue ocean of his eyes.

"My third and greatest weakness is a person. That would be you, my love," he whispered, right before he kissed her.

Chapter Twenty-Seven

The rhythmic *clumpity-clump* of the horses' hooves became a monotonous chorus in Louise's head. Day after day the carriage traveled on, closer and closer to Alsais.

Her home.

Her father.

Papa would love Antoine. He must. He would bless the match and… *What if he does not?*

The wheels took up the chant. *What if he does not? What if he does not?*

Louise put her hands to her ears.

"Are you feeling all right, Mademoiselle?" Josephine LeSuere's face mirrored concern.

Louise hoped her smile allied the woman's concern. The suggestion to employ Josephine had come from Mimi, but it was brilliant. Louise needed her, and Josephine had nothing left in Versailles. When asked, she had said, "I will bring the good memories with me, but I will leave the misery of this past year to be buried with the dead." Already Louise could tell the decision was good for both of them.

"Dear heart, does your head trouble you?" Now Tante Marie was awake.

"No, I am fit. I only rubbed at my ears." Louise glanced out the coach window. She could see Antoine, or part of him, as he rode Vent past her view. How could her father not love him? Was there ever a more wonderful man than Antoine? Well, perhaps her dear papa, but then she could not marry him. Louise smiled to herself. Oui, her father would love Antoine, the son he never had.

"Oh." The carriage jolted over bumps in the road. Louise bounced against the other two women. "Is anyone hurt?" She pushed back up into the seat.

"I am unharmed, dear heart. And you, Madame LeSuere?" Tante Marie reseated herself and brushed off her skirts.

Josephine nodded, though her eyes darted to the window.

"How fare you, ladies?" Antoine rode close to the window. "That hole did not appear to be as deep as it turned out to be. Anyone lose their teeth?"

Though she could not see his face, Louise could hear his smile. "I believe we all survived. Will we be stopping soon?"

"I will ask the driver." Antoine rode forward but returned in the space of a minute. "He tells me Auxerre is only about a mile up the road. We can stay the night there."

Louise patted Josephine's hand. "Auxerre is the halfway point." Though she had not complained, Josephine appeared ill, and her hand felt warm to the touch. "Are you quite sure you are feeling well?"

"Do not worry about me, Mademoiselle." In spite of her smile, Josephine did not convince Louise.

Leaning her head back against the seat, Louise closed her eyes, enough to make it look like they were closed but open enough to observe the older woman. Josephine's arm crept up to rest next to her stomach, making small circles against her abdomen.

Something was amiss. Soon they would be at Auxerre, and

she could ferret out the source of the problem. Louise sighed, closing her eyes completely.

Thud.

Josephine landed on top of her.

"*Aie!*" Tante Marie scrambled to get Josephine moved.

"Something is wrong. She does not wake."

Tante Marie and Louise shoved and lifted Josephine back into the seat across from them, helping her recline across the cushions. Louise waved a handkerchief out the window then returned her attention to Josephine whose eyelids fluttered.

"She is waking." Tante Marie brushed hair from Josephine's forehead.

"Sh-sh, do not move, Josephine. Please rest." Louise knelt in the crowded coach and chaffed at the woman's wrists, sharing a glance with her aunt.

Tante shrugged and shook her head.

The carriage stopped, and Antoine opened the door. "What is the problem?"

"Madame LeSuere swooned." Tante Marie sat back in her seat, allowing Antoine a better view of the situation.

"Should we call for a physician or hurry to the inn?" Louise searched Antoine's face.

"No." Though weak in voice, Josephine proved emphatic in spirit.

"Madame LeSuere, we need to see to your health."

Josephine brushed Louise's hands from her and pushed herself to a sitting position.

Louise could see that was not the best idea but did not force the issue.

"Continue the journey. I will not be a bother."

"You are not a bother, Josephine LeSuere. I know you would insist on caring for me if the situation were reversed."

"It is not, and I am paid to care for you, Mademoiselle, not the other way around. Please continue, Monsieur. Arriving in

Auxerre very soon is the best medicine for me." Josephine straightened her clothes.

Reaching out, Louise grasped the woman's hand aunt squeezed gently.

Josephine's demeanor mellowed the tiniest bit. "Please, Mademoiselle. I am well. Do not worry."

There was nothing to do but accept the woman's word. Louise nodded, and Antoine closed the carriage. Once again, they were on their way.

"What do you think happened?"

Josephine shook her head.

"I really want to know."

Tante Marie gave her a look that told her to let the subject go, but Louise could not.

With her gaze focused on the floorboards, Josephine's whisper was difficult to hear.

"My stomach has not appreciated the travel, as I am not accustomed to this type of life. I did not want to bother you, so I asked at the inn this morn for something that might soothe. The hostess offered some herbs, but they have not set well either."

"Oh, Josephine, why did you not let me help you? I am so sorry you have been ill. And you have been caring for me all this time? You must let me care for you in Auxerre."

The woman did not respond. However, her face took on a greenish hue, and her eyes grew wide.

"The door!" Tante Marie grabbed the handle and flung it open.

Josephine pulled herself to the doorway and Louise grabbed her hips, holding her secure. The morning's meal and more exploded over the road.

"Hold on to her." Tante Marie kept the door from banging back onto Josephine with her arm wrapped through the window.

"I am holding on. Help me pull her back in."

Josephine felt like leaded weight as Louise and her aunt

pulled her back to the seat. Though not completely dazed, she was very weak.

Louise returned her to a prone position across the seat and wound her shawl as a pillow. "This time we brook no argument. I will care for you, are we agreed?"

Josephine gave a slight nod before closing her eyes.

Louise looked back at aunt, who sighed.

Removing her shawl, Tante Marie handed it over, and Louise draped it across Josephine.

For the rest of the way, the coach remained quiet. Tante Marie kept a lace hanky near her nose. Granted, the odor was not pleasant, but it could not be helped.

Antoine opened the carriage door for them upon arrival. "What has happened?"

"Madame LeSuere no longer needed the contents of her stomach."

Louise grimaced at her aunt's attitude. "Josephine became ill and vomited. She is resting but needs to be inside as soon as we can help her there."

"I rode ahead to let the inn know we had an ill woman with us. They are prepared, but I am sorry I was not here to assist." Antoine helped Tante Marie and Louise from the carriage. Leaning inside, he spoke quietly before entering the coach. Soon he emerged, Josephine in his arms.

Her face now appeared as white as the unused pages in Louise's journal.

"Coachman, make preparations to have this vehicle cleaned and aired. I do not want to travel with this stench a moment longer." Tante Marie kept her nose buried in her handkerchief until well away from the carriage.

The man continued unloading the baggage. "Oui, Madame du Sine."

Louise's ears warmed, but she clamped her lips shut. Though it would only be fair to show her aunt a bit of her own medicine, the woman would not understand and would only think Louise ungrateful and rude.

Antoine led the way into the inn where a maid bade them follow up the stairs to their rooms. The women were quartered together, across the hall from Antoine, in a space housing one armoire, a vanity, and only two beds.

"Lay her on the bed by the wall, please." Louise pulled back the bedclothes.

Antoine laid Josephine on the bed, and she fell into an instant sleep.

"Where will you sleep?" Tante Marie stared, her hands on her hips.

Louise turned to the maid. "Would it be possible to find another bed?"

The servant shook her head. "No, Mademoiselle. There are no more beds. I could bring up a pallet for you, if you wish."

"I understand. A pallet will do."

"No. It will not do." Tante Marie glared.

Antoine crossed his arms. "You cannot sleep on a pallet, Louise."

"If that is all there is, I will sleep on a pallet. It bothers me not."

"It bothers me, my love." He turned to Tante Marie. "Perhaps, Madame de Sine, you will take my room. Louise can have the other bed in here, and I will take my rest downstairs."

Louise could see the wheels turning in her aunt's mind.

"Very well." She turned to the door. "See that my things are brought to my new room. Are you coming?"

The maid bobbed a curtsey and hurried out to lead the way.

Josephine moaned in her sleep.

Grabbing the chamber pot, Louise rushed to Josephine's side. "Bring me water and some cloths, please." She heard Antoine's boots on the stairs and turned her attention to Josephine. Helping the woman roll to her side, she held

Josephine's hair out of the way and rubbed her back. Was there anything else to be done?

Antoine returned with a pitcher and cloths.

Louise dampened one and began washing Josephine's face. "I do not know what else to do, Antoine. She is so sick. I have never seen someone so ill."

He stood behind her, his hands resting on her shoulders. "Do what you know to do and leave the rest to Providence."

"Will that be enough?"

Antoine kissed the top of her head. "It will have to be."

Chapter Twenty-Eight

Antoine rolled over. His cot at the barracks was more comfortable than this pallet on the floor in the servants' quarters.

Madame Josephine would need to rest at least another day, thus putting off his quest. His mission.

His nerves were already getting the best of him, and now he felt Louise's anxiety too. She said it was Madame du Sine's attitude that embarrassed her, but he had noticed it long before Madame Josephine became ill. Was she that concerned for her father's answer? Would Monsieur de Saix be likely to refuse his offer?

Antoine punched his pillow. More thoughts like these and he would drive himself mad.

So, they would remain for at least one more day, perhaps two. As long as Madame Josephine improved. If she did not… He had best come up with a plan for that, just in case.

Rolling to his back, Antoine could see a faint lightness in the surrounding dark. Dawn would be here soon. He might as well get up. There would be no more sleep this night.

He pulled on his boots and went out the back way to the stable. The soft nicker of his horse called to him.

"So, Vent, how fare you this early morn? Have you been well treated?" He scratched between the stallion's ears. Vent's nose nuzzled against Antoine's side. "Perhaps I should ask you. What would you advise concerning Madame Josephine?"

The stallion's lips grimaced, and he snorted.

"Just as I thought. You have no answers either." Antoine grabbed a brush and ran it through Vent's mane. "In that case, I will have a plan or a well-groomed horse or both before I return."

❧

LOUISE WATCHED JOSEPHINE SLEEP FROM THE COMFORT OF her own bed, moonlight spilling in just enough glow. Supposed comfort would be a better description for the mattress. However, it had to be better than the pallet provided for Antoine.

Antoine. How dear and kind he had been with Josephine, treating her with respect and compassion.

Unlike Tante Marie. What was the problem? Or had her aunt always been like that and she had never noticed?

Josephine rolled to her side, mumbling.

Louise lay still.

"No, do not leave me. Gaston." Josephine gasped. She sat up, her eyes opening wide.

"Josephine? You were dreaming."

"I saw them. My son and husband." Josephine closed her eyes, but the tears glistened with moon glow. "I wanted to remain with them, but they said no and left me. Once again."

"Oh, Josephine, I am so sorry." Louise knelt next to her bed, wiping away tears and stroking her hair. Josephine's skin felt cooler to the touch. Perhaps her fever had broken.

"Again, they left me."

Louise wrapped her arms about Josephine who did not pull away. Instead she allowed herself to held and repeated, "They left me, they left me."

"I do not want you to go, Josephine. I still need you." Louise rocked side to side. "I was afraid you would leave me, and I need you to help me with all that is ahead."

Josephine sniffed. "You are not alone. You have your aunt."

Louise shook her head. "Tante Marie is sweet, most of the time. She has never set up a household or started a family though. I have no mother to guide me. Josephine, I am afraid you have your work cut out for you."

The older woman pulled back and glanced up before patting Louise's cheek. "Then God help us both."

A giggle escaped Louise.

Josephine softly chuckled.

⁂

LOUISE HAD JUST FINISHED BRUSHING HER HAIR AND TYING it back when the knock sounded.

Peering over first to make sure Josephine still slept, Louise opened the door, a finger to her lips.

"How fares Madame Josephine this morn?" Antoine held a tray of teacups and a pot. Leaning over, he kissed her.

"She is still sleeping. You think of everything. Please, set it over there. Merci, my love."

When his hands were free again, he wrapped her into a hug. "Is she improved? Do you think she will be up to traveling on the morrow?"

"If you will continue to hold me, I think we could stay indefinitely."

Antoine rested his chin on top of her head. "If I continue to hold you, you will need to call for a priest *trés rapidement* in order for me to marry you here and now."

The heat rising in her cheeks was not from embarrassment. Louise buried her face into his shirt, hoping he could not feel the warmth radiating from her core.

A gentle tug at her chin brought her eyes to meet his gaze. "I will wait, my sweet Louise. Just know it will not be without want of you." He released her arms from about his waist and stepped back. "I will be downstairs should you need me. Enjoy your tea."

By the time her breath had returned, Antoine was down the stairs.

❧

TWO DAYS LATER, MADAME JOSEPHINE APPEARED STRONG enough to travel. Antoine knew she had gained strength when her chaperoning skills improved. As long as he kept his distance from Louise, Madame Josephine treated him like a long-lost son. The second his gaze meandered in Louise's direction, though, he became the wolf at the door.

Of course, gazing at Louise did bring out the wolfish side of him. A smirk escaped as Louise chose that moment to exit the inn. Madame Josephine followed, catching his gaze. He could tell she had read his mind and did not like the tale.

"Good morrow, ladies." He offered his assistance into the carriage.

"Good morrow, Monsieur." Louise's small hand sent waves of electricity throughout his body.

"Good morrow, Monsieur." Madame Josephine's work worn hand did not.

"Run along, now, Monsieur de Crocketagné and find your horse. Louise, get settled in here. It is time we were away." Louise's aunt, ever the taskmaster.

"As you wish, Madame du Sine." Antoine bowed and left to do as he was instructed. Soon. They would arrive at Alsais soon where he might ask for Louise's hand. Soon. Always soon and never now.

For this man of action, soon was becoming hard to stomach.

Chapter Twenty-Nine

Alsais

Papa!"

As soon as Antoine handed her out, Louise gathered her skirts and ran from the carriage to the arms of an older man. For a moment, Antoine had a picture in his mind of a young girl running toward him, arms outstretched. Someday he would like to be a father and have a daughter run with abandon to his embrace.

However, a part of him was not too keen on the idea of sharing Louise with this other man. With little imagination, he could well speculate the feeling was mutual.

"Papa, wait here. There is someone I want you to meet." Louise rushed back to his side and pulled him to her father. "Papa, might I present Monsieur Antoine Desaure Permonette de Crocketagné, second in command of the palace guards. He has been stationed at Versailles and is a favorite of His Majesty."

Antoine made a sweeping bow.

"Monsieur, I introduce my father, Monsieur Philippe Guillaume Henri de Saix."

Monsieur de Saix nodded, staring at Antoine as if he had just stolen his most prized possession.

"My pleasure, monsieur. You have a lovely home."

"Oui, that I do. And I have—what are you doing, Marie?"

"Bring the trunks this way." Louise's aunt pointed at a side entrance. "Someone has to make sure things are put in their proper place. It is good to see you, too, Philippe." With a laugh she embraced the man and returned to directing the scene.

"Since it seems Tante Marie has our arrival well in hand, we shall go inside." Louise linked arms with her father, dragging him to the door.

Antoine caught the wink she threw him over her shoulder. So, she planned to smooth the way, did she? Though he winked back, Antoine could not decide if that was good news or ill.

❧

LOUISE GARNERED STRENGTH FROM HER FAMILIAR surroundings. Recognizable smiles, eyes with more wrinkles, but the same twinkle, people dear to her reached across time and enveloped her into the daily routine that had been her life.

Before Tante Marie.

Before Versailles.

Before her heart found a new home with Antoine.

She tied on her apron and slipped down to the kitchen.

"What is planned for supper, Adélaïde?" Louise brushed a kiss on the housekeeper's soft cheek.

"Welcome home, *ma petite chou.*" Adélaïde drew Louise into an embrace. "What a beautiful lady you have grown into. I was afraid you would no longer visit my kitchen."

"Adélaïde, where else would I come to see you?"

The old woman's pinch on Louise's cheek only reassured her she was home at last. "I had planned a simple dinner of chicken and vegetables, but we must celebrate now that you are here."

"Simple is better. I am tired of fancy. Give me your chicken and vegetables any day. If His Majesty ever finds out what he is missing by not eating from your kitchen, he will conscript you in an instant."

"Bah." Adélaïde tossed a bunch of carrots onto the table. "You may chop these if you will take care of your fingers."

Louise chose a sharp knife and a carrot. "So, what have I missed? Papa looks tired. Is he still traveling as much as he did?"

"Hrmph. I am not your father's keeper. If he chooses to traipse all over the countryside when he has a perfectly grand home here, it is none of my concern."

"He is often gone, then?"

"Too often if you ask me, and you did. Otherwise I would keep my own counsel."

Two more carrots became multiple bits while Louise mulled over this news. She had hoped her father would now stay closer to home. What pulled him away?

She shook her head at the sudden thought. No, not her Papa.

Other men had done so. Men of the same age and social position as her father.

"Do you think he is seeing a woman?"

"Who knows? Surely not I."

Who knows indeed? Someone knew. And soon Louise would, if she had anything to say about it.

⚜

"Monsieur de Crocketagné, would you follow me to my study?"

Antoine stood. "Oui, Monsieur. Mademoiselle, a superb meal. Merci. Now, dear ladies, if you will excuse me?"

Louise nodded. Monsieur de Saix kissed her cheek on passing. Madame du Sine covered Louise's hand with her own.

The study proved small and tight with a low ceiling and bookcases lining the walls from bottom to top. Monsieur de Saix indicated a chair stacked with papers. "You may set the correspondence on the floor. I will get to it someday."

Antoine did as he was told.

"I do not let Adélaïde clean in here, much to her disappointment. This is my sanctuary, and I will have none in without invitation first."

"Then I am honored, Monsieur."

"Pour a cognac for me and one for yourself. Let us get on to the business at hand."

"Pardon?" Antoine nearly dropped the flagon.

"I know why you are here. You know why you are here. Shall we not get to the point, son?"

"As you wish." Antoine handed the man a snifter and took one for himself. Returning to his seat, he watched the liquid swirl round the glass as he pulled his words together. "Monsieur, I have had the pleasure of escorting your daughter about Versailles. In that time, I have come to be quite fond of her. She is, without a doubt, the most enchanting woman I have had the privilege to meet. I request permission to marry your daughter." Now that the words were out, only half the battle was over.

"I see." Monsieur de Saix took a sip and slowly swallowed. "Why?"

"Why?"

"Why do you ask my permission? Why do you want to marry her? Did something happen at Versailles?"

Well Antoine could believe this man enjoyed his games. Though being toyed with, he knew to keep his temper in check.

"Nothing that might diminish the sterling reputation of Mademoiselle Louise. I ask because I want to marry your daughter. I love her."

"What if I were to tell you Louise has no dowry? Would you still want to marry her?"

No dowry. What game did this man play? "But of course. I do not understand, though. You have this home and appear to do well."

"*Fauché comme les blés.* I am reaped like wheat."

"You are insolvent? You have no money?" The letter at the top of the stack he had placed on the floor looked to be from a creditor. Perhaps this was no joke.

"Do you still want to marry my daughter?"

Antoine set the drink aside. "Monsieur de Saix, I love your daughter. I have enough money to last me and have no need of more. Oui, I want to marry your daughter. I love her, Monsieur."

The gentleman stood, looking older than when he had first sat. "Then you shall have my blessing and the hand of my daughter." He held out his arm. "And you shall have her dowry."

Grasping the man's forearm, Antoine tried to sort out what has just been said. "You are not insolvent?"

"No more than I was yesterday." Monsieur de Saix poured another drink and downed it. "We love the same person, you and me. Only I love the girl. You love the woman. I ask you to take care of my little girl as you care for your woman."

"Oui, Monsieur, I will. Merci."

Monsieur de Saix turned and waved Antoine away.

He had been granted what he wished. So why did it feel as if something were very wrong?

❧

THE MORNING RAIN LEFT DROPLETS ON THE PANES TO RIVAL the tears dripping down Louise's face. Though she pleaded, Antoine knew he must leave if he were to return in time to ride with His Majesty.

"Do you understand?"

"Of course, I do. I just do not like it. That is all. Do not ask me to like being away from you, Antoine. I cannot do that." Louise sniffed.

Antoine handed her his handkerchief. "I will never ask you to like it. I do not like it. I want to be here together as much as you do." He grinned. "Think of all you can get accomplished with me out of the way."

A faint smile teased at the corners of her mouth. "You would not want to go for the fittings or go shopping or help sew."

He shook his head. "Probably not. However, with you there, I might be able to persevere through such unmanly tasks."

"I will not require that of you. Perhaps you should go, though, before I change my mind."

Antoine glanced about the room. Though they stood alone, the door was left open a bit. *Let them look if they want.* He pulled her close and wiped a tear from her cheek with his thumb before lowering his mouth to hers. Time vanished. In its place only the two of them existed. He drew her as close as he dared, deepening the kiss, knowing if he did not stop, he would not be able to pull away, to leave her.

Only it was Louise who pulled away. She who brought reality back to his conscience.

"Go now, my love, before I cannot let you go."

He grappled with breath and committed to memory her cheeks tinged with pink, her lashes damp with tears, every inch of her face, every feel of her touch. Running a finger along her jaw, he steeled his nerve. "I will come back for you. I promise."

"I know. I will wait. Now go."

He did.

Chapter Thirty

"Are you sure this is the color?"

"Oh, oui, mademoiselle, oui. This color is what all the most elegant and refined brides will be wearing this year." Monsieur Frederick draped the material over Louise's shoulder.

Louise let the fabric flow through her fingers. A deep rose, perhaps, or a dark blue. However, this sage green was not what she had expected. She twisted her wrist, letting the sunlight shine on the threads. "What do you think, Tante? Will Antoine like it?"

"With your orange blossoms, it will look wonderful on you, bringing out the green in your eyes. He will love it."

A glance at Josephine found her nodding in agreement.

"Very well, Monsieur Frederick, you have convinced me. When shall we schedule the fittings?"

"Let me check my calendar. We can begin Tuesday next if that is pleasing to you, Mademoiselle de Saix." He began to fold the fabric.

"That is acceptable. We will expect you at ten o'clock. If you would be so kind, please put this on the account of my father."

A strange look crossed the man's face. "I apologize for any

inconvenience Mademoiselle, but if you might pay me now, I…"

"To whom do you think you are speaking? How dare you even presume to ask such a thing?" Tante Marie spoke with her tiger voice.

Louise put a restraining hand on her aunt's arm. "No, that is no bother. I have the money for you here." She dug into her reticule and pulled out some bank notes. "Will this cover today?"

"Oui, Mademoiselle, oui. Today and Tuesday next, as well. Merci, Mademoiselle." He stashed the notes in his pocket, scooped up his things, and exited as if his coattails were on fire.

"Of all the… *C'est un débile, ce type.* How dare he insinuate your father will not pay him."

"I know, Tante Marie. I do not understand either. After supper I will tell Papa about it."

"If there were others in the area as skilled, we might go to them."

"No, Monsieur Frederick will make my gown and my bundle, but I will know why he refused to honor Papa's account."

❧

LOUISE'S STOMACH FLIP-FLOPPED ALL THROUGH THE evening meal. Somehow, she needed to ask the question. Now that supper was over, she sighed and knocked at the open door. "Papa, might I speak with you a moment?"

"Come in, come in daughter." Her father stood to greet her. "What is it, ma petite?"

Louise found a seat and clasped her hands tight in her lap. "Monsieur Frederick was here today. He brought fabric and took measurements for my gown."

"I see. You do not look happy about it."

Clearing her throat, she pressed on. "When I asked him to place it on your account, he said he could not do that."

"What?" It was the roar of a lion, a tired old lion, but one still with some strength.

Louise rushed to him. "It is no problem. Papa. I paid him from my own allowance."

"You should not have had to do that, *ma petite poupée*. I will make it right with Monsieur Frederick."

"So, there are no monetary difficulties?" Louise watched his eyes.

"Nothing that I cannot handle." He kissed her forehead and she knew no more information would be forth coming. "Do not worry your pretty head about such things. Plan your wedding the way you want and leave the finances to me. It will all be as you wish."

She wrapped her arms about his neck and kissed his cheek. "Oui, Papa. I will leave it in your hands."

When she turned to leave, Louise glanced over her shoulder. The view of her big strong Papa had changed. He had shrunk in stature and vitality. The fact stared at her and ripped away a piece of her heart.

Her papa had grown old.

⚜

"THESE WERE JUST DELIVERED BY ROYAL PAGE." JOSEPHINE carried a silver tray bearing two letters addressed to Mademoiselle de Saix.

"Oh, one is from Antoine. Who has sent the other, I wonder?" Louise weighed the two envelopes and knew she had to read Antoine's first. Breaking the wax seal, she slid out the page.

My dearest Louise,

*I miss you more with each passing day and cannot wait to
be back with you. This trip has been fruitful, and I am glad
I have been a part. His Majesty has revealed his wedding
gift to us.*

*We will soon be known as the Marquis and Marquise de
Tarn-Et-Garrone, so polish up your silver and ready your
china. We are to be counted among the nobility, but do not
let that title change any part of you. I love you just as you
are, with or without a title, ma petite. I am counting the
days, as I know you are.*

Soon my dearest. We will be together very soon.

*Until then, I remain ever yours,
Antoine*

Louise held the note to breast, her excitement making her
bounce on the balls of her feet.

"What does the gentleman have to say, dear? No, do not tell
me. I should not have asked. I beg your pardon, Mademoiselle
Louise."

"Josephine, wait. It is perfectly fine for me to tell you what
he said. He will be returning soon, and His Majesty has chosen
his wedding gift to us. We are to be titled. Marquis and
Marquise."

Nodding, tight-lipped, Josephine pointed to the other letter.

"I am sorry. His Majesty is not your favorite person,
is he?"

"Never mind that. Who else writes to you?"

"Oh, let me see." She turned the envelope over in her hand.
"I do not recognize the hand or the seal." She slid her finger
under the flap, releasing the wax, and pulled out the note. "It is
from Monsieur Charles LeBrun. Oh, my. He says he has been
commissioned to paint my portrait in my wedding dress and will

be here in a fortnight to begin. The dress will be ready, will it not?"

"You have only two more fittings to finish the gown. It should be completed by the end of the week."

Something seared into her brain. "I am about to become the Marquise de Tarn-Et-Garrone and Monsieur Charles LeBrun is to paint my portrait. Pinch me Josephine, for I am afraid I am asleep and will find this is all a dream."

"I do not need to pinch you, ma petite chou. I cannot think of anyone more deserving than you."

"Then you do not know me well, dear Josephine. I try, I try very hard, but I fall so short. I just know as soon as I start to trust in this, something bad will happen. So, perhaps you should not pinch me. I think I prefer to remain in this dream for as long as I can." Though she laughed, the familiar tentacles of fear gripped her heart. How would this dream come crashing down?

⁂

Antoine rode to the stable and dismounted. Leading Vent to the stable boy, he handed him the reins and a franc. "Is Mademoiselle Louise in the house?"

The boy, eyes as big as saucers, nodded, his mouth hanging ajar.

Taking his hat from his head, he slapped it against his thigh a few times. The dust poofed about him making the effort useless. He ran his hand over his hair and down his clothes, cleared his throat and slipped inside the back way.

Familiar voices rang from the kitchen. Antoine put his finger to his lips as Josephine's face came into view.

She started to break into a smile but worked her face into what she must have believed to be a natural visage.

He motioned with his hands, asking for Louise's location.

Josephine nodded toward the parlor with her head.

He blew her a kiss and tiptoed down the hall.

"Josephine, do you think—" Louise stepped from the room and into Antoine.

"Does she think what, my love?"

A scream, a bounce, and suddenly Antoine's air supply ceased. However, he did not need that much breath to kiss the woman he loved.

"When did you arrive? Have you been here long? Why did you not tell me you were coming?" Louise struck him on the chest before kissing him fervently.

"I did not want to waste time when I could get here as fast as any letter." How good she felt in his arms. Worth every rugged mile just to be with her.

"Come, we must let Papa know you have arrived. Now we can set a date. Oh, Antoine, welcome home."

Antoine allowed himself to be dragged along. Just before they came to the study door, he pulled Louise to him. "My darling, Louise. I need one more moment with you. I have missed you more than I can say, and the sooner we are wed, the better. I love you." He lowered his lips to hers and let her once more steal his breath.

Chapter Thirty-One

The morning dawned bright leaving only one cloud in the sky, one small worry to keep at bay. The excitement stirring in her belly kept Louise from breaking her fast. It would only help her dress to fit better. Josephine braided and pinned and made magic with Louise's hair, working her mother's pearls in just as Mimi had done back at Versailles. Back where Antoine first saw her. Back where life changed forever.

Soon she met her father downstairs. The look in his eyes reminded her of the old days when she would call out "Papa" and he would open his arms to her and spin her around. Only she was too big for that now. This was her wedding day. She was no longer his little girl.

Together, with Josephine and Tante Marie, they took the carriage to the chapel. Louise sat between the women who each held one of her hands, sending reassurances through touch. Papa rode with the driver where she couldn't see his eyes or what they might be doing.

At ten o'clock the carriage arrived at the chapel. Louise searched until she found the lone figure standing next to the chapel door. It took everything in her power not to climb over

Tante Marie and run for Antoine. She also knew the instant he saw her. His face beamed. His eyes welcomed, drawing her heart to his. Still, she waited for her papa to help her from the carriage and to walk her to the door.

Together, she and Antoine knocked. The priest opened to them, and the service began.

"Who gives this woman?"

Papa cleared his throat. "I do."

"And the dowry?"

Papa set a money bag into the priest's hand, who prayed over it and handed it to Antoine.

"Do you have the ring?"

"Oui." Antoine pulled out a simple gold band. Placing it on her thumb he began the words. "In the name of the Father." He moved it to her index finger, "the Son," and then her middle finger, "and the Holy Spirit." Finally, he moved it to her wedding ring finger. "I marry you, Wife. My Louise. My love."

At that point, the priest, who had baptized Louise, who had confirmed her in the faith, and who had given her mother Last Rites led them inside to the high altar.

She and Antoine knelt together while the priest blessed them.

"May God bless thee and keep thee. May His face shine upon thee and be gracious unto thee. May He lift His countenance upon thee and grant thee peace."

Antoine drew her into his arms and kissed the tiny cloud of worry to the back of her mind.

❧

"Hurry back to me." Antoine's whisper titillated and thrilled Louise with anticipation.

"I will, my husband, I will." Just saying the word felt odd, exciting.

She had a husband.

Quickly climbing the stairs to her room, albeit ladylike for the sake of decorum, Louise met Josephine at the door. "Oh, Josephine, I am married. I am really and truly married to the most wonderful man in the world."

Josephine opened the door and Louise twirled inside the room, heedless of anyone.

"Was it not the most beautiful of ceremonies? Did not my sweet Papa outdo himself with this splendid fête?"

"Oui, ma petite, it was a lovely wedding, and well you deserve it."

Louise stopped.

Deserve it? No, she did not.

At once, as though someone had poured cold water on her, she sobered. She did not deserve such happiness. That could only mean one thing.

Something bad lay around the bend.

"Are you well, ma petite chou?" Josephine's hand on her shoulder brought her back to the present.

Louise forced a smile to her lips and the dark thoughts from this day of all days. "Oui, I am well and blessed." She changed into the soft-pink traveling gown while Josephine inspected Louise's hair for misbehaving tendrils.

When all was in place, Louise kissed the dear woman's cheek and scurried out. The back stairs would take her out to her husband quicker and perhaps give her a moment to hug her father in private. She had not seen him at the party during the last hour and suspected he had barricaded himself in his office.

Stifling a giggle, she raised a fist to knock at the study door.

An angry voice from inside froze her hand in mid-air.

"Philippe, I do not know how you can ask. Where is your self-control? Remember who you are."

"I do not need a lecture, Marie. Will you help?"

Louise bit her knuckle and leaned in closer.

"Oui, I will help you out of the mess, this time. For the sake of the daughter of my late sister. But do not ask again, Philippe. Do not give me cause to tell you no."

"Very well. I will have the papers drawn up."

Fear of being discovered made Louise hurry back up the stairs. What had she heard? How bad was the trouble her papa had gotten into?

Chewing on her bottom lip, Louise came back down, this time by way of the front staircase. Friends and family stopped her every time she made another step toward her beloved husband. Yet with each step, worry settled deeper in her soul. Something was terribly wrong with her father. Was it right to leave him now? Who would take care of him?

Antoine glanced her way, drawing her to his side with his smile.

At that precise moment, her papa entered the room, his eyes, sad and old, tugged at her heart.

There they stood, the two greatest loves of her young life. She must go with her husband, leaving her father to fend for himself.

Her husband. Her father.

She had made her choice.

What had she done?

❧

ANTOINE HEARD THE SNIFFS. HERE IT WAS ONLY THEIR second night together and his bride tried to hide her crying. He had been as gentle as he knew how, and she had responded with an amazing passion. So why the tears? *Ask her, you fool.*

He stoked her hair from her cheek. "*Ma amie*, what is it?"

Louise turned to him, her face glittering wet in the sparse moonlight. Clambering to him she soaked his chest with her sobs, her fists clenching his shirt.

He enveloped her while her body heaved with misery. Moving his fingertips in gentle circles over her spine, he waited.

And waited. At last she seemed to melt into him and only the random shudder and sniff remained of her tearful episode. Antoine softly kissed her temple. "What causes such sadness, dearest? Can you not tell me?"

She shook her head, soft tendrils floating under his nose. He wiped them down and asked again. "Louise, what is it?"

"I am afraid." She hiccupped. "I cannot explain it. I am sure you think me touched, but that is why I cried." Another hiccup.

"You are safe, my love. I will not let anything happen to you. I promise." Antoine tipped her chin up and focused on the dim outline of her face. "You believe me, oui?"

She hesitated the briefest of moments before nodding, punctuating her answer with a sniff. "I believe you, my husband."

Antoine pulled her secure, tucking her head beneath his chin and stroking her hair. With his eyes closed, he breathed in her scent, holding it in his lungs until he thought it might burst forth like truth. Then he released the air slowly, letting his breath ruffle her hair. Truth. It nagged at him, circling like a dog to settle at the back of his mind. Still it sent its message up to his last wakeful thought. Did she lie to him or to herself?

Chapter Thirty-Two

Wheels crunched on the oyster-shell covered drive as the carriage turned toward the house. Though the imposing structure breathed a persona of wealth, Antoine knew looks could be deceiving. The family who resided within those walls needed his assistance from time to time. But that was no hardship as far as Antoine was concerned. This was the home of his sister.

Louise clutched his hand as children ran from the house, waving their greetings. Antoine mentally checked off each child as he came into view. Four boys ranging in ages from fifteen to three. He squinted and gave his wife's hand a little squeeze. *Where. . .?* A girl, about twelve years of age, ran from behind the house and into view. Antoine smiled, relaxing into the seat. All there.

The carriage jostled to a stop. Antoine opened the door, stepped out and held up a hand for Louise.

"*Oncle* Antoine!"

He barely had Louise on terra firma when he was grappled about the legs.

The girl ran back to the house. "*Maman*, he is arrived! Oncle Antoine, he is here! *Vite!*"

Antoine was seized and clamored over and climbed, nearly tripping over his own feet. He let go of Louise's hand just in time to keep her from losing her balance. Still his nephews embraced him from head to toe.

"Ho! Allow me breath." Antoine shook his head and stared at the gangly lad before him. "You, you cannot be Alexandre! You were just a boy when last I saw you and now you are nearly as tall as I."

"But it is I, Oncle. See what happens when you are gone so long?" If possible, the boy had added another inch to his height.

The shortest one of the lot tugged at the leg of Antoine's trousers. "And I am Sébastien. Do you remember me?"

Scooping up the raven-haired child with the piercing blue eyes and serious countenance, Antoine looked the boy over—in the lad's ears, behind his neck, and under his arm—then solemnly nodded. "I believe you must be Sébastien, but I do not know how this is so. You are the same size and weight as Richard." He set the excited boy down. "Richard, Richard—are you here?" Antoine searched and searched over the head of the child jumping up and down, waving his hand in front of Antoine's nose. "Oh my, Richard, is that you? I cannot believe it. How has this happened? And where then is Jeannot? I suppose you will next tell me he is that one who looks like Alexandre used to look."

The child referred to, with the same shining black hair of his siblings, swung his arms about Antoine's waist. "Oui! I am Jeannot. And you know that very well." He tipped his chin up to stare at his uncle. "Have we grown that very much, Oncle?"

"Oui, *mes petits hommes,* oui. You are becoming big, strong men. But please do not do it so quickly. It makes me feel old." Antoine ruffled the hair of little Sébastien who had been but a baby the last time he'd visited.

"Ah, but you are old, Oncle." Jeannot giggled and dodged the swat aimed at him. He fell on the ground in a fit of laughter, his younger brothers following suit.

"Antoine! At last!" And there she was, his sister, Aimée, who had been the only mother he remembered. He imagined the mother they shared had looked very much the way Aimée looked now—her blue eyes shining warmth with little crinkles about the edges. Antoine preferred to think the lines were there due to all the laughter that bubbled so free from his sister, but after losing her husband, he knew there were other causes.

"Aimée!" He swept her up in his arms and whirled her around, her feet flying out behind, before planting a kiss at her temple. New silver threads intermingled among the black of her hair. Antoine bit his lip.

"And you must be my new sister, Louise. I am so glad this brother of mine succumbed to my pleas and brought you. *Bienvenue*. Welcome to our home." Aimée pulled Louise into an embrace.

"I was about to introduce you to my wife. If you would only be patient one moment."

"I think the moment has passed us by, little brother. Do you not agree, Louise?" She winked, and Antoine's bride tipped her head and smiled in return.

"You might introduce me, Oncle Antoine." The girl standing next to her mother, simply a younger version of Aimée, held her hands behind her back and bounced on her toes.

Antoine's heart flipped in his chest. Surely this was not his niece but some neighbor girl who teetered on the verge of womanhood. Yet she had Aimée written all over her in coloring and voice and mannerism. "Ma petite, how you have grown!" He turned to Louise. "My lovely wife, may I present my *nièce*, Élise. Élise, this is your new tante, the Marquise de Tarn-Et-Garon, Louise de Crocketagné."

"*Enchanteé.*" As his niece curtsied, Antoine caught the glance Louise sent in his direction. Even her eyes smiled at her new name. Bon. He needed to see her smile as much as she needed to feel it.

Louise took Élise's hand, pulling the child to her and kissing both cheeks.

Élise suddenly stepped behind her mother, her face tinged a soft pink, but her eyes glittered.

Aimée laughed and looped her arm with her daughter's. "Come in," she called over her shoulder. "We do not need to stand here on the lawn all day. Come meet the baby, Joan." She led the way to the house.

Antoine offered his arm to Louise, and together they followed Aimée and Élise inside. Louise would love his sister and family and they will all love Louise. This would help. He knew it.

⚜

"Shall we?" Louise didn't know whether she asked Josephine or herself. The proper thing to do would be to offer to help with dinner. Though Louise may be a guest, Aimée was now family. Would she expect help?

Josephine nodded and opened the door for Louise, closing it after and following Louise down the stairs.

The kitchen was a bustle of activity. Aimée chopped celery, Élise plucked pinfeathers from a chicken, and a woman Louise had yet to meet kneaded bread. None looked up as Louise and Josephine stepped down into the kitchen. "Might we be of some service?"

Aimée looked up with a start then smiled. "Oh, my, no Louise! You should make yourself at home in the parlor. You are a guest."

"But we are now family. Will you not let Josephine and me help, *s'il vous plaît?*"

The pause lengthened, but Aimée's smile never faltered. "What if—." she inclined her head toward Josephine.

"Madam LeSeure."

"Oui, Madam LeSeure, merci, what if Madam LeSeure takes

over my celery and I show you around my home?" Already Aimée was wiping her hands and removing her apron.

Louise and Josephine exchanged glances. The older woman's brief nod was enough. "That would be lovely. Merci." After waiting until Josephine had donned the apron and knife, Louise followed her hostess—her sister-in-law—back up the stairs to the nursery where baby Joan still slept, and then down again through the front way.

Once in the parlor, they stopped before a window. Laughter filtered into the house from somewhere on the lawn, and Louise peeked past the drapes to see if she could locate the source.

Aimée's hand squeezed Louise's shoulder. "The boys have missed their father greatly. It is good that Antoine is here to give them that type of fun."

When Louise glanced back, Aimée's eyes were rimmed with moisture. Instinctively Louise covered the gentle hand still on her shoulder and squeezed back. Only married a little more than a week, and already the thought of being without Antoine made her heart freeze. She could not imagine what her sister-in-law must feel. Then a new thought rose up from her very soul. "I hope I may give him sons one day."

Aimée's arm wrapped around Louise's shoulder and a fierce love for the man outside bonded them. Louise tipped her head over against Aimée. She may not yet know her new sister well, but she already loved her.

❧

"Gentlemen, have you your weapons?" Antoine's sternest look descended on each nephew.

"Oui!' "I do!" Oui, Oncle!" Each boy nodded his head and stood at attention, brandishing his miniature tree branch.

"Very well, we shall begin. Remember, without the basics the warrior is not fit for battle. One must be able to perform the basics of swordplay in one's sleep. Feet apart?" He surveyed with a critical eye. "Bon, bon. And now, en garde!"

The boys rushed at him swinging at his stick. Encircling him, they giggled with delight as he danced in their middle, clashing sticks, swatting thighs, and making them run about.

"Ho! Where are my trusty companions in this exercise?" Antoine swirled around as each boy hid behind a tree or bush. "There, I have discovered one of you!" and he ran to scoop up Sébastien and hold him high overhead. The boy screamed with delight and took off running the second his feet touched the ground.

"And where are the rest?" He caught Richard and Jeannot at the same time, pulling both into a rugged embrace and swinging them around. They both dropped into heaps of giggles on the lawn.

"Who is left for me to capture? Shall I search for you Alexandre or will you come face me as a man?"

A stick tapped Antoine's left shoulder. He grabbed it and swung its wielder around to the front. "Aha! There you are."

Alexandre dropped the stick. No laughter danced in his eyes. Instead an earnestness shone that struck Antoine like a revelation. "Oncle, no more games. I am nearly a man. Can you not teach me how to fight like a man?"

"Oui, you are nearly a man and growing closer to that each day. Bon, I will show you a few steps to start, but you must practice. And remember this is for self defense and the defense of your family. This is not to pick fights with your schoolmates." Antoine stepped closer.

Solemn eyes, steady and blue, gazed up at him, only the chin did not tip up much. Within a few short years, Antoine realized, this stance might be reversed. "I understand, Oncle. I am now the man of the house. I must know these things. Shall I get Papa's sword?"

"Not yet. We can begin with these weapons." He pointed his

stick at the other boys. "You men, take a rest while I work with this recruit."

The younger ones scampered to a safer place with a good view, eyes wide with excitement.

"First you need to remember it is not all about the rapier. You must make your off hand do its part as well. Your buckler will be more effective against other cutting instruments, but your dagger can give you added help against thrusting instruments. The buckler will help you with defense but the *main-gauche* is helpful for offensive strikes. For now, we will stay with the buckler and leave the left-handed dagger for another lesson." Antoine scanned the lawn for something to use as the small shield and noticed his hat, tossed aside when he came out to play. "Here, you shall use this." He picked it up and brought it to Alexandre. "Grip it thus." Antoine modeled holding it so the crown faced away from the body. "There are several ways to employ it but for now, just use as a shield to your chest."

Alexandre took the hat and held it as shown.

Antoine nodded and stepped back to face the boy. "Next, you must remember, the edge is for cutting but the tip is for . . . the thrust." He was not ready to talk of killing to this boy, not yet. "Are you now ready?"

"Oui, Oncle!" The boy's eyes gleamed. Had he been that eager at the same age? Alexandre would not be so excited if he had seen the aftermath of such fighting. Perhaps he should not be encouraging his nephew with this lesson. "Oncle Antoine?"

"Very well, stand thus and face me."

Horses' hooves clattered up the laneway. "Oncle Dominique!" The three younger boys jumped up and ran to greet the horseman.

"Oncle Dominique?" Who was this other uncle? Neither their father nor Antoine had any brothers. He turned to Alexandre.

The icy stare and set mouth told Antoine there was more to this than a visit from a family friend.

"Halloo!" The rider jumped down from his horse and tousled the hair on Jeannot's head before tickling Richard and Sébastien under their respective chins.

Antoine strode over, hand extended. "Bienvenue. May I assist you with something?" The stranger quietly eyed Antoine. "I am the Marquis de Tarn-Et-Garonne, Antoine de Crocke-tagné, brother to Madam de Lefèbvre. Might I be of service?"

The stranger smiled but did not completely lose the wariness in his eyes. He took Antoine's hand. "And I am Dominique Denis Bertrand, a neighbor and friend to Madam de Lefebvre. I am pleased to make your acquaintance."

"Was my sister expecting you?"

Jeannot tugged at Antoine's arm so he leaned towards the boy. "Maman invited Oncle Dominique to supper. He often eats with us."

"I beg your pardon, Monsieur. I am rather protective of my sister, but do not mean to offend an invited guest. Shall we go in and announce your arrival?"

The three younger boys ran ahead, calling as they went.

"I do not think we will need to announce my arrival. By the time we enter the house, the whole of France will be aware." Bertrand chuckled and walked to the door as though it was a familiar habit.

Antoine stopped to look for Alexandre. The boy stood stock still, but his emotions ran free about him.

Oui, there was definitely more to this story and he would have to uncover it.

❦

"Boys, you will wash quickly. *Vite, vite!*" The sound of his sister saying such things took Antoine back to simpler times. He resisted the impulse of wrapping her in his arms.

"Oh, and you are not excused from that command, little brother. Go with the children and wash. I know you."

Antoine grimaced. He could have done without the scolding in front of his wife and this stranger. But this was Aimée, his beloved sister. She always could get him to do what she wanted. That would never change.

Louise came to kiss his cheek. "Did you have fun?" Her eyes twinkled.

"But of course. Did you?" He claimed her chin and stole a real kiss.

"I think I love your sister. She loves you so much, how could I not?"

The most wonderful women in his life liked each other. But then, he knew they would.

Louise glanced over his shoulder. "Is there a problem with Alexandre?"

"I do not know. I will speak with him, do not worry." He stole another kiss.

"Antoine!" His sister gave the look she always did when he wasn't moving fast enough to suit her.

"I am going, I am going. You are most fortunate that I allow you to boss me." He turned to Louise and winked. "Do not get any ideas," he said before following the boys upstairs.

After a quick dash into the room he and Louise would share, he deftly washed his hands and face and combed his hair. Presentable again, he raced back down to his ladies. "I suppose you will want to inspect my hands." He held them out to Aimée.

"Why would I need to do that? You are old enough to be married; you are old enough to tell if your hands are clean. And for your information, you will always be my little brother." Aimée sighed. "I am sorry. The need to care for you is a dragon that awakes from slumber when you appear. I cannot help it." She shrugged.

Antoine kissed her cheek. "You may care for me anytime. That right you have earned, though I think Louise will do a good job keeping me in line, so you do not need to worry."

Aimée and Élise chuckled, and Louise's cheeks pinked to that lovely shade he adored.

"Oh, and you have already met my friend and guest, Monsieur Dominique Bertrand."

Antoine nodded in the man's direction and smiled. "We introduced ourselves."

"Bon." Aimée looked about the room. "Since we are all here now, let us go to the table. Supper is served."

Antoine took Louise's hand and noticed Bertrand took his sister's arm as they walked to the dining room. When Antoine held the chair for Louise, Bertrand did so for Aimée, and Alexandre followed suit for Élise. The tension in the air was as thick as cannon smoke, but the women did not seem to notice. The men, however, did. Though he could not taste a thing or even remember what had been placed in front of him, Antoine made the obligatory remarks to compliment the chef. Someone took his plate and cutlery.

Aimée cleared her throat. "I wanted to wait until we were all together to make our—mine and Dominique's announcement." All faces turned to her. Bertrand sat at her left and covered her hand with his. "You know it has been hard since Martín passed away. It has been the love of my family and the company of this kind man that has saved me. We have decided to marry—"

Alexandre pushed himself to his feet, his chair crashed behind him. He slapped his palms to the table. "Never!" Kicking his chair out of the way, he ran for the stairs.

Antoine stood, too, but not as quickly as Aimée. She raced to the bottom of the steps. "Alexandre, come this instant. I will not have you behaving so rudely to our guests. Alexandre, do you hear me? Alex—"She spun around at Antoine's touch.

"Allow me to speak with him."

"What is the matter with him, Antoine? I do not under-stand?" A tear squeezed itself from her eye to outline her nose and the corner of her mouth.

"Oh, my sister." Antoine pulled her close. "You of all people should know. You, who were my mother when I had none. Do you not understand? You have removed Alexandre from his position as man of the house."

Aimée pulled back, her eyes round pools. "I never thought— Oh, no. Antoine, he must know I love him. Why can he not accept I have found love again, a love he cannot give?"

"Would you have accepted another woman as my mother after you had been caring for me? How would you have felt if Father had remarried?"

"What must I do?" Her voice was a mere whisper and another tear streaked her cheek.

"First, allow me to speak with Alexandre. Second, I must—"

A clanging sound followed by rapid feet on the stairs. Antoine and Aimée looked up to see Alexandre armed with his father's rapier and buckler.

"No, Alexandre, you must not!" Aimée reached for him, but he pulled away.

Antoine grabbed the boy by the arms. "Stop, you must stop this right now."

Alexandre fought and pulled. "Who will stand for my father then? Who?" He stared into Antoine's eyes. "Do you agree with them? Does this seem like what my father would have wanted? This man has no business putting his hands on the wife of my father!" A quick twist and he was free from Antoine's grasp, rushing into the dining room. "You, you will pay. I challenge you on the field of honor." He struggled to pull the rapier from its scabbard.

Antoine grabbed his elbow. "Alexandre, do not be foolish. You have had but a small part of one lesson. You would kill yourself!"

"Better to die than see this man usurp my father's place."

Bertrand stood before the boy. "I will not fight you. Not today, not ever. I will leave now, but Alexandre, know this. I love your mother. I have not done anything unseemly. I cannot take the place of your father. But I can be a good husband to her and perhaps a friend to you as well. I will let you think on it." He lightly touched Aimée's fingers before walking out the door.

Alexandre sank to his knees. Antoine caught him and nodded to Louise and the other children, hoping she understood to keep them in the dining room. Then he helped his nephew though the doorway and back to the bottom step, sitting next to him.

Aimée sat on Alexandre's other side and attempted to brush the hair from his eyes. He slapped at her hand. "Still you treat me as a child! Why? Why could you not have come to me and discussed this? I am the man of the house. It is my job to care for you and my brothers and sister. Not the job of some stranger!" He dragged his sleeve under his nose. "How could you do this to us? To me?"

"I am sorry, my son. You are right that I should have come to you and asked your opinion. Do you know what you would have said if I had done so?"

Alexandre's eyes turned to slits. "I would have said 'no!'"

Antoine turned the boy to him. "Why, Alexandre? What have you against this man?"

"Would you allow your sister to marry a Huguenot?"

Chapter Thirty-Three

Somehow the breath in Antoine's chest became thick, and the beats of his heart slowed to deliberate blows in his pulse. He attempted to turn to face his sister, but it was as if he sat underwater, and he fought to move his head even that slight distance. When his eyes met Aimée's, he knew the boy spoke the truth. He opened his mouth, but the words were not his. "Alexandre, being a Huguenot does not mean a person is evil or dangerous. Many good men have served at His Majesty's command and have been of the Huguenot faith."

The look of gratitude in Aimée's eyes overcame the shock of what he had spoken. He had no idea where the words had come from, but his sister apparently needed to hear him say them. "Allow me to speak with your mother, and then we will both come speak with you. Please wait in your room." Alexandre stood. "And leave your father's sword and buckler with me for the moment."

The boy laid the weapons down and dragged his feet up the stairs.

Aimée scooted next to Antoine, and he wrapped his arm about her shoulders. "Do you love Bertrand?"

"Oui, very much." She leaned her head on him.

"And he will love the children?" Even as he said it, Antoine remembered how the younger boys all ran to Bertrand and he seemed to enjoy them.

"He loves them as his own. Dominique's wife died soon after they married. They had no children. Though those of his faith encouraged him to remarry quickly, he could not. Martín and Dominique were neighborly, not that Martín was home enough to make friends outside of the army."

Antoine nodded, his cheek rubbing against the top of her head.

"As soon as Dominique heard about Martín he came to help. Neither of us thought of again marrying, but as time passed, we became friends and then fell in love." She lifted her head and looked Antoine in the eye. "He is a good man. A decent man."

"He is a Huguenot." His words held no condemnation, only facts.

"I know. He did not ask me to convert, but we could not be married in the church. Therefore, I asked more about his faith. I find nothing to which I disagree, therefore, I will become a Reformeé when we marry."

Antoine's throat constricted. "What of the children?"

"It will be their decision, but I hope they will see the truth in Dominique's goodness and kindness toward us all."

"You are sure this is what you want?"

"I was. Now I do not know what to do with Alexandre." Her eyes filled with tears.

He stood and held out his hand. "Then let us go speak with him and see what can be done."

Aimée took his hand and they went up the stairs to Alexandre's room.

LATER THAT NIGHT WITH LOUISE IN HIS ARMS, ANTOINE

recounted all that had been said. "No boy wants to think of his maman as having those kinds of needs or desires. I have a hard time thinking of my sister. . ." He shook his head.

"Men." Louise sighed and snuggled closer. "And so, what will happen now?"

"Alexandre and I will call on Monsieur Bertrand and question him. If he answers to our satisfaction, Alexandre will give his consent. And Alexandre knows he must be reasonable and give the man a fair chance."

Louise leaned up on her elbow to look him in the eye. "But if Monsieur is Huguenot, what will happen to your sister and her children?"

"I do not know. Before I met your Monsieur Maury, I would not have accepted it. Now I am willing to at least give the man an opportunity to share his mind."

Louise grew quiet, and at first Antoine thought she had drifted off to sleep. Then she ran a finger down his cheek. "I watched you play with the boys this afternoon."

"You did?"

"Oui, I did. I think you will make a wonderful father."

He hugged her close. "You will make the most beautiful mother in the world." It was strange how he could feel her blush in the dark.

"I do not know about that, however, I enjoyed watching Aimée when she was with her children. She loves them dearly, and they are such good children. While you spoke with Alexandre, little Sébastien curled up on my lap and Jeannot must know every story ever written. And Richard, sweet, quiet Richard. Oh, I helped Élise with her hair when she readied for bed. I want sons and daughters, Antoine, many sons and daughters. A house full of children to laugh with and cry with. I do not like that I had no brothers or sisters."

"There were days I would have sold you a sister." Antoine laughed.

Louise punched his chest. "Oh, you!"

He took her hand, opened it and brought it to his lips. "My love, we can have as many babies as you want to have. Whatever will make you happy." *Whatever, my love.*

⁂

ANTOINE HELPED ALEXANDRE UP BEHIND HIM ON VENT, and the two of them rode for Monsieur Bertrand's home. Alexandre had promised to be reasonable and to listen. There wasn't much else Antoine could ask of the boy. He had a few questions himself, but those would be better to ask man to man.

The Bertrand home was closer than Antoine had imagined. They could have walked if he'd realized. A lovely country home, he could picture his sister and her children living here. No, he must not get ahead of himself.

He and his nephew dismounted before he tied Vent to the rail.

Apparently, Monsieur Bertrand saw them approach as he greeted them at the door before they had mounted the steps. "Welcome! Come in." Though he smiled, Antoine noticed a nervous look in the man's eyes. Did he have something to hide? Or was this meeting with Alexandre that important to him?

Monsieur Bertrand led them to the parlor. "Please sit. I'll send for some tea."

"None for me." Alexandre was a bit quick on his reply.

Antoine gave him a look that he hoped reminded the boy of his promise.

He got the point. "No, thank you, sir."

"I will take some, thank you." Antoine almost felt sorry for the man. Accepting a cup of tea wouldn't hurt and might ease the tension.

Their host stepped from the room. It would have been the perfect time to verbally remind Alexandre, but at this point the boy knew. Anything more would just push him into a corner. Antoine glanced about. "It's a nice room."

Alexandre nodded.

"The house looks quite large. I imagine Monsieur Bertrand does well."

"Oui." His nephew squirmed in his chair. "But there is more to this than a nice big house."

"You are right, Alexandre. On that we are agreed." Monsieur Bertrand entered the room in time to see the boy's face turn to crimson. "I apologize. I should have made more noise coming in. I wasn't trying to sneak up on you."

Antoine liked him for that. He was honest and aware of the gravity. This was good.

Taking a seat, their host smacked his hands to his thighs. "Shall we get started? I know my housekeeper will be in in a moment with the tea, but I feel like we all want to get this into the open."

"I agree, sir. Alexandre, do you want to start?"

The boy pulled out a folded piece of foolscap, opening it slowly. Was he rethinking this? Alexandre cleared his throat. "Why do you want to marry my mother?"

Bertrand smiled. "That question is easy. I love her very much. I would like to make a home with her and your family. I know that it is not enough to love only your mother. I also know I am not a replacement for your father. But I can offer my home, my care, and a relationship that would be unique to us."

"What can you do for my mother and brothers and sister that I cannot do?"

The housekeeper brought in the tea at that moment. The room became silent until she left, closing the door behind her.

"Alexandre, the love between a man and a woman is not the same as the love between a young man and his mother. For one, she will always see you as her son no matter how old you are. It is the way of the world. Also, there will come a day when you will want to have a family of your own. You will have less problems with that if you do not feel you must put your mother's needs above your own. That is something I can do—put her needs, and those of her children, above my own. God willing, on the day when the last of your siblings have married and started a family, I will still be with your mother. We will have each other to love and care for. Does that make sense?"

Antoine knew the man had been thinking this through. His answers showed he'd worked to form his emotions into thoughts he could convey. He'd also referred to Alexandre as a young man, respectful yet accurate. Antoine glanced at his nephew.

"Oui, it makes sense." Alexandre slowly folded his paper and put it away. "You have not treated me as a child today. Thank you for that. What would I call you?"

"Well, you would not have to call me *papa*. For now, we could stick with Oncle Dominque, or perhaps another name will seem fitting that we can decide on together."

There was a lengthy pause where it felt like the room was losing air. "I have one last question. Must I become a Huguenot?"

Antoine had wondered if that would be asked. Better coming from Alexandre than him though.

"That is something you will have to decide, Alexandre. I am not making it a requirement. My faith is mine. I am happy to share it, but I will not force it on you. When forced it is not faith."

Antoine was proud of his nephew. He'd asked good questions. Even more, he opened the door for Monsieur Bertrand to elaborate enough to satisfy his own questions. The only thing left was to learn if the answers satisfied Alexandre.

The boy took a breath, clearly mulling things over in his mind. Standing, he walked to Monsieur Bertrand and held out his hand. "I give you permission to marry my mother."

Bertrand pulled Alexandre into a hug and kissed him on both cheeks. "Merci. Thank you, Alexandre. You do not know how much this means to me."

Antoine had the feeling, however, that one day the boy just might.

"PLEASE COME AGAIN! I WILL MISS YOU SO MUCH!"

Antoine laughed as Aimée, baby Joan on her hip, pulled Louise and then him to her.

"You must write to us and let us know how things fare with you and I will write to you, as well."

Louise's head bobbed up and down. "Oh, oui! We must write. I am so glad Antoine brought me here. Thank you for your hospitality."

Antoine began to maneuver Louise toward the carriage.

"It was my pleasure! I would have been crushed if he had taken you all the way to Tarn-Et-Garrone without stopping here first."

"You know I would not have done that. I fear your wrath much too much." He tweaked Aimée's chin.

"Do not think you are too old for me to make you behave." She grabbed him by the chin before kissing him soundly.

Once she released him, Antoine turned to his niece Élise and tugged on her braid. "You will be good and help care for your maman?"

"But of course, Oncle Antoine."

"And you will stop growing so lovely." He winked.

"That is out of my control, Oncle." She laughed, and he pulled her into an embrace.

After clearing his throat, Antoine called his nephews over and hugged each one. When he arrived at Alexandre, he leaned to his ear. "You still must behave as a man. Keep a close eye on your brothers and sisters. This is a very big job. Think of Monsieur Bertrand as help. We know he is a good man, no?"

"Oui, Oncle, he is a good man, and I will try to do as you ask."

Antoine raised an eyebrow.

"Very well, I *will* do as you ask."

Pulling him into an embrace, Antoine held him a moment.

"That is the young man I have grown to love as my own." He kissed him on both cheeks and followed Louise into the carriage.

The visit had been far too short.

Chapter Thirty-Four

Tarn-Et-Garrone, 1670

When the knock at the door sounded, Antoine looked up in time to see Josephine go to answer it. Her excited voice could be heard in the parlor.

"Monsieur Maury. It has been a long time. How good it is to see you."

Antoine hurried out to welcome the man.

"It is good to see you, too, Madame LeSuere." Matthew greeted Josephine with a kiss on both cheeks. "Where is everyone?"

"If you are referring to the Marquise, I expect her to come running about… now." Antoine laughed as his wife rounded the corner.

"Matthew! Oh, it is you. Come in, come in." Louise hugged Matthew and accepted his kiss before dragging him into the parlor.

It had been some time since Matthew had visited. He had traveled to Tarn-Et-Garrone soon after they had returned from their wedding trip.

Antoine had an inkling this would not be the same happy occasion. The eyes of the man gave him away.

Matthew looked around the room. "You are doing quite well, I see."

"My inheritance from my father has kept us from being paupers." Funny, before that might have needled Antoine, but now he accepted Matthew and read no more into the statement.

"The portrait of Louise is now hung." Matthew walked over to the mantel for a closer look. "Monsieur LeBrun outdid himself." Louise, in her sage-green bridal gown and her mother's pearls with her serene smile and orange-blossom bouquet. "Of course, he had wonderful inspiration."

"I agree."

"Oh, you two." Louise swatted at them and Antoine drew her close. "Have you eaten, Matthew? I can have something readied." Louise did not wait for a reply. Instead she squirmed from Antoine's side and raced from the room. Antoine suspected she would have her kitchen staff work on a meal for Matthew vite, in spite of the protests.

"To what do we owe this unexpected pleasure?" Antoine waited until Louise left the room. "You have a serious look about you, friend. There is a problem."

"Oui, but I should wait until Louise is here. It concerns her, but you are right. I have news."

Louise breezed in and sat in the chair nearest their guest.

"My dear, Matthew has brought us news. We were waiting for you so he could share it."

"I am here, and you have my full attention. What is your news, Matthew?" Her face lit up.

Matthew stared at his shoes.

The news must be worse than Antoine thought.

When the man looked up again, Antoine moved closer to Louise and put a hand on her shoulder.

Matthew cleared his throat. "Small one, this has to be the hardest message I have ever had to deliver. It is your father."

Louise opened her mouth then clamped it shut, her eyes focused on her old friend.

"He passed away the Monday before last while in his sleep. Adélaïde found him on the morn. I came as soon as I knew the facts. I am sorry, ma petite."

Her face began to crumble, but she caught herself and took a breath. A lone tear trickled down her cheek.

"Louise, my love, I am so sorry." Antoine drew her closer. "We had no clue. Had he been ill?"

"Not that anyone knew. He would never say he felt unwell." Matthew stared back at his shoes, again.

"There is something more, is there not, Matthew?" Louise laid a gentle hand on Matthew's arm.

"I had thought to discuss this with just Antoine, but you should hear, as well." He shifted from one foot to another. "Oui, there is more, much more, and I am so sorry to be the bearer of such ill tidings. You know how much your father loved the card tables."

Louise mutely nodded.

"He had incurred some very significant debts and had already borrowed against the house and his holdings, leaving nothing to use to pay off the debts. I believe he had already given you many of your mother's things, Louise, but anything he did not put into your hands is now gone. I am sorry."

The room grew very quiet. Antoine could feel the rigidity in Louise's body. "How large of a debt exists?"

Matthew named the figure.

Louise gasped.

Antoine stood and paced. The figure was quite large indeed. Though many of the nobility ran up debts and lived off their titles, he could never do that. He would not do that. It was wrong.

Yet to leave the debt of his father-in-law unanswered would be just as wrong. The man had shown him the greatest kindness in the world by allowing him to marry his daughter. For that, he would be indebted to Monsieur de Saix forever.

"I will pay it."

"Antoine." Louise's eyes glowed wide.

"I will draw out the money and send it back with you. Will you make sure it goes to the right people?"

Matthew nodded. "Oui, but what will you live on?"

"I do not have it all figured out, but I know I have enough to pay off his debts. We will not have a lot left, but I cannot let the debt remain. He was my father-in-law. He gave me the gift of my wife. I will do this for him and her."

"Merci, my husband." Louise took Antoine's hand.

"The gesture is quite honorable, Antoine. I am concerned, though, about how you will live if you have no resources left to you." Matthew paused before he continued. "I have an idea, though, if you would be interested."

"I am willing to listen."

"I own a rather lucrative salt and wine export business—in truth, I am one of three owners. The brothers Fontaine and I share equally. I am in need of an agent who would be willing to travel two or three times a year. It would not be often, but the trips would be extended for a month or two. The business is quite profitable, and you would be able to live in comfort. There would need to be a few big changes, though."

"Such as?" Fear tinged Louise's voice.

"First, you would need to move to Bordeaux."

"We would have to leave Tarn-Et-Garrone?" She looked to Matthew, who nodded and then to Antoine.

He clasped her hand. "We would have to give up our titles, since nobles are not permitted to be merchants. But then I lived quite satisfactorily without a title for many years."

"Is that all?"

Antoine shook his head. "There would be no more *de Crocketagné*. We would be plain Monsieur and Madame Crocketagné." He took her face in his hands. "What say you, my sweet wife? Shall we leave this fine home and all its trappings to live as merchants?"

Louise squeezed her eyes closed. When she opened them again, she met his gaze squarely. "Whither thou goest, my beloved husband, whither thou goest."

Antoine did not care that Matthew would see. He encircled Louise in his arms and covered her sweet lips with his.

A moment later Louise drew back and placed her hands on either side of the face of her husband. "My home is with you, Antoine, and as long as I am with you, I will be content." She turned to her old friend. "Merci, Matthew. Now I will let you two talk and go speak with Josephine. I am confident about what she will say, but I prefer to ask rather than assume."

Antoine knew she would weep with Josephine for her father but did not correct her. He worried for her. But this was not the time. After their guest was in bed, he would hold her and do his best to make things right.

He turned to Matthew. "And so, my friend, what must I do first?"

Chapter Thirty-Five

Louise should not have become comfortable. No, she had become too happy and settled in her life. That was never a good thing. Now look at what had happened. Her father gone, his reputation destroyed, and the sacrifices Antoine made out of his love for her.

True, she still had Antoine, but for how long?

And a family. She longed to have children, babies to care for and love. Even that was denied her. Had she done something terrible? Perhaps as a child? Were her sins not forgiven? Would she be forced to pay penance every day of her life?

Too many questions and not enough answers.

She wrapped one more dinner plate of her mother's china in a rag and placed it in the box. None of the pieces had broken in transport from Alsais—a truly amazing feat. The trip from Tarn-Et-Garrone to Bordeaux would be just as long. Did she tempt fate again?

If it were not for Antoine and Josephine, she could not have born it. Even with them, she might go mad waiting for the next punishment from God.

Josephine brought more rags. "Madame Louise? Why do

you not go rest? I will wrap these as if they were my own. You go on."

Louise nodded and handed the plate she had started to Josephine. Her grief drained her. Just when she thought she had no more tears left, a new collection appeared.

As she climbed the stairs, her hand lingered over the balustrade. This was a lovely home, her first home with Antoine, the home where he was born and raised. She would have enjoyed growing old with him here. Still no home would be sufficient without him. Any home would bring contentment in his arms.

Stretching out on her bed, Louise closed her eyes. As the warmth of the day lulled her, she determined to look forward to being with Antoine, no matter where that may be.

❧

"LOUISE, LOUISE!" ANTOINE took the steps two at a time and burst through the door to their room. "We have heard from Matthew. He sends his regards and says he has found a house for us. We should have all of our affairs in order within another week, and we will be off to Bordeaux."

Louise appeared sleepy. She rubbed her eyes and stretched before sitting up on their bed.

"Were you napping? I did not think and have woken you."

"No, no. There is too much to be done. I only laid down for a moment." Standing, she straightened her dress and checked her hair in the mirror. "Tell me what else Matthew writes."

"He says he has found a satisfactory house with large grounds just outside the city. There are stables and plenty of room for Vent and Étoile."

"Have I ever properly thanked you for purchasing Étoile for me?"

"I am sure you have, but let us pretend you have not. How will you ever thank me?" He grabbed her wrist and spun her to him.

"You are quite sure of yourself, Monsieur."

"That I am. I hold the fairest woman in all the land in my arms. She is mine. Have you any reason to doubt my word?"

She leaned her head against his shoulder, her breath warm on his neck. "None whatsoever, Monsieur."

"Bon. Then you need to get back to work." He swatted her backside.

"*Ouille!* Just see if you deserve a kiss for that." She pulled free.

Antoine slammed the door as she raced for it.

She turned and climbed across the bed.

Taking advantage of how her skirts slowed her movement, he trapped her on the bed and tumbled on top of her.

"What was that you said about a kiss?"

"None. I said you would get none." She started to giggle.

"None, is it? Then perhaps I shall keep you pinned until Josephine has all our worldly possessions packed."

"You would not."

Antoine waggled his eyebrows at her.

"Oh, you would."

"You could just kiss me, but I have to confess, I am very comfortable. Shall I become more comfortable?"

She grew very still before wrapping her arms about his neck. Pulling his head to her, she kissed him with a passion that heated his soul. "Oui, Antoine. I want a baby. Make love to me now."

Her plea was the only encouragement he needed.

❧

ONE MONTH AND NOTHING. ONE WEEK OF GETTING READY, two weeks of travel, and one more of trying to set up housekeeping. The first visitor was her monthly friend, on time as always. Louise had cried when she awoke with cramps, not because they hurt that much but because of what they meant. No baby.

The activity of setting up their home while Antoine was away learning the business made the days fly.

However, the nights were long and lonely.

Then the days and nights became months. And then a year.

Louise had been sure she would have been with child by this time. It was not from a lack of effort. However, the more time that passed, the more she began to fret.

There was no one to talk with about it. Though Josephine had confided in her, she was not ready to share this deep disappointment. It was too private. What if she had done something so wrong, so bad, that God would not allow her to become *gravid*? Not having her own baby to hold in her arms seemed like a punishment too large to bear.

Instead, she cradled guilt.

Every time Antoine looked at her, she knew she was not the woman he deserved. If she could not bear him children, would he then leave? He already spent so much time away with his new work, to think of him gone forever left her crazed.

❧

"I THINK THAT IS ALL WE CAN DO FOR TONIGHT." ANTOINE yawned and stretched in the chair before leaning his head on his arms, crossed on the desktop.

"You are doing well, Antoine. Almost as if you were born for it. Business has increased in this last year, and it is due to your hard work." Matthew leaned back in his chair. "I can see you are tired. I should send you home to Louise."

"Have you seen her lately?"

"No, I have been moving my holdings to Bordeaux. The more this region develops with the wine trade, the more important it is to have holdings here. Why do you ask?"

Antoine ran his fingers through his hair and sighed. "She is changing, Matthew. I do not know what the problem is, but I think it has to do with the fact we as yet have no children."

Matthew did not reply.

However, since the gate had unlatched, Antoine let charge out all the worries that had claimed him. "When I arrive home, I will be able to tell she has not slept for days. The dark rings under her eyes give her away. She has lost weight, and her emotions range from one extreme to the other. This might sound strange, but I believe she worries I will leave her if she cannot have a child."

"Would you leave her?"

"No! Never would I leave her, Matthew. I love her more today than I did on the day we wed. I could never leave her."

"Have you told her so?"

"I tell her I love her. I show her I love her. I do not know what else to do." Antoine rested his head back on his arms.

"Have you taken this to God?"

The rueful laugh escaped before Antoine thought better of it. "No. Honestly, I did not even think to." He raised his head to search Matthew's face. "Yet that was your first thought, was it not?"

"Oui. It seems only natural to share my concerns with the One Who has the answers."

"How can you be so sure? What if it is something scientific? Perhaps the fact that Louise has always preferred to ride astride has something to do with it."

"Antoine, what if it does?" Matthew leaned forward in his chair. "Do you really think that could keep God from giving you two your own child if He so chooses? Do not tell me the 'God is punishing you for something' theory. You are among the most honest and honorable people I have ever met. I have seen many people with very little honor or honesty that have a large brood. So, although I may not know the reason, I know Who can take care of any problem that comes. In His time and in His way. Knowing that, I just trust that this is all a part of His plan. My job is not to give my plan to Him, but to search for Him and His kingdom in the place He has led me. Does that make sense?"

"More than you know." Now that He had brought up the subject, Antoine could not let the moment go. "Matthew, I have to confess something. I see you and know that God is real to you, not just something or someone you talk about because it is the pious thing to say. It is not just what you say, but what you do and how you live. I am envious."

"Why? Do you not know you are seeing Christ in me? He will come to you and make His home in Your heart just as well as mine. I do not have exclusive rights." Matthew's stare probed deep into Antoine's soul. "Do you want to know the risen Son of God as your personal Savior and Lord?"

"Oui!" The exclamation came from his heart before Antoine had time to think.

Matthew knelt and motioned for Antoine to do the same.

Antoine joined his friend.

"I will pray, Antoine, and you pray the same."

Antoine nodded.

"Our Father in heaven, one of your children calls out to You. He knows he needs Your forgiveness and direction. He has carried this load as long as he can and now lays it at the foot of the cross. Jesus, let him feel the refreshing cleansing of your blood. Release him from anxiety and grant him Your peace. Lead and guide him for Your Name's sake. Claim him as Your own in this world and the next and welcome him into Your fold, Great Shepherd. In Jesus's holy name we pray. Amen and amen."

"Father, I ask of You all that Matthew has spoken and one more thing. Please help Louise. Amen."

Matthew clapped him on the back.

Just as Antoine looked up, a cloud finished passing in front of the sun and the rays of light illumined the room with a new brilliance. Joy and lightness filled him. His grateful heart overflowed.

When they were seated back in their chairs, Matthew undid

the small Huguenot cross he always wore and laid it on the table between them.

"Antoine, you must know, must understand what you have done. By inviting our Lord into your heart, you will be required, undoubtedly soon, to make a verbal confession of faith. This is not because of something I say you will have to do, but because God will allow you to be put into the position of having to declare your faith or recant. I will pray for you and will be there for you if I can, but this will be your moment of truth. Will you deny your Lord or serve Him no matter the cost?"

Antoine searched within himself. Is this what Aimée had to ask of herself? At what cost could he remain true?

Matthew leaned in. "The cost will be quite steep before very long. Already I know of men and women dragged from their homes, their children left to starve while their parents await sentencing and sometimes death. You can ask any of the Fontaines about their family's story—the murder and treachery they have all lived through due to their faith. It is growing very bad again. I believe it will quite soon come to the point where we of the Protestant faith will have to recant, escape, or die for what we hold dear as our forefathers did."

Could Antoine do that? Could he die for his faith? What of Louise? Could he remain true if it cost him her life?

"I do not tell you this to frighten you, but so you will know the gravity of your decision. Should you choose to hold true, this is for you." Matthew slid the pin in front of Antoine.

The questions were hard. There was no way to lie to God or himself. "Pray with me for strength."

Matthew nodded and prayed for the both of them.

When the prayer finished, Antoine soberly picked up the pin and attached it to his vest, over his heart. "Merci, my friend."

Chapter Thirty-Six

When Antoine arrived, Louise raced to the door. He had guessed correctly. Deep purple shadows circled beneath her eyes. When had she last slept?

"You are home. I missed you so, Antoine." She threw her arms about his neck.

Embracing her he could feel the looseness in her gown. More weight lost. He buried his face in her hair. "And I you, my love. I am home for now."

"Bon, then come into the parlor and tell me of your adventures." She led him into the room and pushed him into a chair before climbing onto his lap.

Antoine laughed. "You do not believe me? I will not run away, I promise."

"I believe you. However, I feel better making your escape more difficult." She leaned her head against his shoulder while he wrapped his arm about her waist. Her hand roamed up his chest and paused. "What is this?" She pulled his jacket back, revealing the Huguenot cross pin.

For the first time, Antoine worried about what Louise would say.

"This looks like Matthew's pin."

"It is."

She sat up and stared at him. "Why would you…" The light of understanding grew in her eyes. "No, no." She shook her head and jumped off his lap.

"What is the matter, ma petite?"

"You are a Huguenot? When? Why?"

"Matthew and I have talked. This afternoon I knew I wanted the peace, the understanding he has. We prayed together. Louise, it was as if I was suddenly stones lighter. Breath even came easier."

"Are you mad? You cannot be a Huguenot."

Antoine stood and reached for her.

She pulled away.

"I do not understand, my love. You have no problem with Matthew, and he is a Huguenot. You said nothing when Aimée married Dominique. Why do you have a problem with me?"

"Matthew is not my husband."

"No, I am. And I want to understand."

"Will you recant?"

"Louise! Of course not. What is the problem?"

"Have we not made God angry enough? You must become an obstinate? A protestant?"

"Made God angry?" Antoine shook his head. "I feel closer to Him than I ever have. Louise, do you not want to know this peace?"

Tears coursed down her cheeks. "Peace? There is no such thing. There is only the calm before the storm. I cannot, nay, I will not do this just because you did. Oh, Antoine, how could you?" She turned, running out of the room and up the steps.

Antoine could hear the slam of the door all the way in the parlor.

"WHY, WHY DO YOU TORMENT ME LIKE THIS?" LOUISE clapped a hand over her mouth. Only this very morn she had recited her prayers once again on her knees beside their bed, and now this evening she shouted at God as if He would not strike her dead for such blasphemy. "You are a wicked, wicked woman, Louise Crocketagné."

"Nay, you are not."

Louise spun around to see Josephine in the doorway. She opened her mouth to yell, but her voice refused her. At this moment she needed her mother, and Josephine was as close to a mother as she had. "Oh, Josephine, why did he do it?"

Josephine walked to the bed and patted it. "Come, sit here awhile."

Louise obeyed and waited.

"The bigger question is why are you so upset?"

Louise shrugged. "I am not sure. Am I losing my husband?"

"No, ma petite chou, you are not losing him." Josephine took her hand. "Did you notice his face when he came in?"

Louise nodded. She had seen a difference, a quiet, visible assurance in his eyes. "He puts himself in danger."

"He stands for what he believes."

"You side with him?" Louise pulled her hand away.

"I side with what is right. Why are you so against this?"

Louise shook her head. Even if she could form the words, did she dare speak them?

"Are you frightened?"

"Oui." Louise hung her head, shamed to admit this weakness.

"Ma petite, go and hear the heart of your husband. Listen with your own. Even if you do not join him in faith, you can trust his heart." Josephine slipped out.

The room waited for Louise's decision.

❧

"Tell me."

Antoine looked up. Louise stood in the parlor doorway. He had not heard her come in. "Tell you what, my love?"

"Tell me why."

Worry knocked at his heart, but he could not turn back. Whispers of encouragement crept into his head. *You have shared your heart with her. Now share Who is in your heart.*

Peace grew. Drawing his beloved wife onto his lap, he began to tell her what Matthew had said.

"His Majesty has nothing to do with Huguenots. I am his cousin. He would make me choose." Louise stared at her hands.

"You must do what you must do."

"Do you think I could choose against you?"

"I did not think you would, but I will not force you into anything you cannot believe. Ma petite, hear me. I have not stopped loving you. I will never stop loving you. And I will protect you however I need to. I am but a man, though. He is God and much better at protecting His children. I am just learning this, but I have seen His hand at work in Matthew's life. So have you. And in Aimée's life and Dominique's. I have chosen to trust His hand."

Louise sat in silence. When Antoine had finished, she folded her hands in her lap, her eyes still glued on them. "This is the peace I see in you, is it not?"

Antoine nodded.

"I have seen it in Matthew for years." She sighed. "You know I love you. I will follow you anywhere, my husband. But I cannot do this because you have."

Antoine's heart sank.

She raised her head. "But I will think on it."

Leaning back in the chair, he stroked her hair and breathed again. For now, he would settle for that. For now.

Chapter Thirty-Seven

April 1672

Louise tucked the final Venetian lace napkin under the gleaming silver set. It had been her mother's—the silver, the hand-painted china, and the crystal goblets. She ran a finger around the lip of her glass. The crystal sang.

"What think you, Josephine? It must be perfect."

Josephine smiled. "It is, child. Your table looks beautiful."

"What of supper?"

"The duck is roasting as we speak. Everything will be ready for Monsieur, ma petite chou. Let us go ready yourself, and then you can wait in the parlor. I will come back and finish with the food. After three months, it will be good to see Monsieur home again."

Louise leaned over and kissed Josephine's cheek. "Oui, his letter promised he would be here by supper."

Wandering across the hall to the stairs, Louise wondered how she had survived with Antoine gone. She raced upstairs, Josephine trailing behind. Three years as of today she had been married to the most wonderful man in the world.

Upon opening her bedroom door, she found a basket of rose

petals waiting on the bed. "Oh, Josephine, merci!" Louise kissed the cheek of the older woman who blushed and waved her away.

A new gown lay ready on the bed. As she shimmied into it, the tightness where the boning rose higher in the bodice only made her smile. Josephine helped secure the dress before slipping out to the kitchen. Louise sprinkled the bed with the petals letting them trickle down onto the floor and down the steps while moving back downstairs to wait.

The other servants had been given the evening for themselves. Only Josephine remained to offer discrete assistance.

With everything at the ready, all she had left to do was pace and check the window every three or four minutes. Feeling foolish, she sat and shuffled through some papers lying on the table. Nothing of interest there.

Her Bible, a gift from Matthew, lay on the table mocking her fears. Louise closed her eyes. *C'est bien.* "Where shall I read?"

Open the book.

The Bible fell open to the Gospel of Matthew.

For this reason I say to you do not be anxious for your life, as to what you shall eat, or what you shall drink; nor for your body, as to what you shall put on. Is not life more than food, and the body than clothing?

Look at the birds of the air, that they do not sow, neither do they reap, nor gather into barns, and yet your heavenly Father feeds them. Are you not worth much more than they? And which of you by being anxious can add a single cubit to his life's span?

And why are you anxious about clothing? Observe how the lilies of the field grow; they do not toil nor do they spin, yet I say to you that even Solomon in all his glory did not clothe himself like one of these.

*But if God so arrays the grass of the field, which is alive
today and tomorrow is thrown into the furnace, will He not
much more do so for you, O men of little faith?*

*Do not be anxious then, saying, "What shall we eat?" or
"What shall we drink?" or "With what shall we clothe
ourselves?"*

*For all these things the Gentiles eagerly seek; for your heav-
enly Father knows that you need all these things. But seek
first His kingdom and His righteousness; and all these things
shall be added to you.*

*Therefore do not be anxious for tomorrow; for tomorrow
will care for itself. Each day has enough trouble of its own.*

She blinked. Of course, she felt anxious, but not for clothing
or food. Her anxiety was for the arrival of her husband. She
thought not about the morrow. She only wished for Antoine to
be here with her tonight.

Louise closed her eyes, pondering the words. The room
faded away.

A gentle hand caressed her face. Her favorite voice whispered
her name. Louise's heavy lids rose. A blurry Antoine knelt
before her.

Antoine!

Bursting from her chair, she threw her arms about his neck,
tackling him onto the floor. Oh, to touch him again.

He pulled her close, kissing her.

She kissed back with everything she had saved for the last
three months.

He stole her breath away.

Louise rested her head on his chest, taking in his scent of
outdoors and sweat. He must have worked hard to arrive here in

time. Her eyes flew open. "Oh, supper!" She jumped up, nearly tripping on her skirt.

"Supper can wait. Come here." He pulled at her hand.

She stooped down and kissed him again. "I have planned a very special evening for you, and you will appreciate it—or else." She attempted to waggle her eyebrows as he did.

Antoine laughed. "Can I not appreciate it from down here?" He scanned the room. "No one seems to be around."

"Josephine is, and she worked hard to help me make things as perfect as possible. I promise you will like it." She held out a hand to help him up. "Trust me."

One eye closed as he stared up at her. He could have pulled her back to the floor—she knew that, and part of her wished he would. Instead, he nodded, took her hand, and escorted her to the dining room.

Candlelight glistened off her mother's crystal, sending prismed rainbows about the room. Josephine stood ready to serve. Anticipation tickled beneath Louise's ribs, and she chewed the inside of her cheek

Antoine held her chair before taking his own. For one brief instant, she could have sworn they were back at Versailles.

Often through the meal, Louise stopped, fork to her lips, just to drink in the sight of her husband. He stifled a yawn, and she shoved her chair back. "The food and wine, it makes you want to sleep, no?"

Antoine covered her hand. "I am not that tired, my love.

Louise stood and whispered in his ear. "Oui, you are but no matter. Count to one hundred and then come up the stairs."

"Ninety-seven, ninety-eight."

She kissed him. "One, two, three…

He nodded and continued, "Four, five, six…"

She flew up the stairs. Once in their bedroom, she found her new lavender negligee laid out. Once again Josephine had thought ahead.

Louise wiggled and squirmed her way out of her dress,

muttering curses against the fasteners she could barely reach. Dropping it onto the floor, she kicked it under the bed.

"Ninety, ninety-one, ninety-two…"

Already he was at the stairs.

Gathering the negligee, she slipped it over her head and poked her arms through the holes. Could he not give a lady an opportunity? Her hands slid down the silky fabric, smoothing it in place.

"One hundred." The door opened, and the most wonderful man in the world stood in the doorway.

Antoine came to her, their passion ignited. Scooping her up in his arms, he carried her to their bed. It had been far too long. She melted at his touch, his kiss. A sigh escaped her lips before hungrily finding his again.

His hands began to explore up her thigh, caress under her gown.

Excitement coursed through her. As he came to her abdomen, she could feel his hesitation. Louise held her breath. She had not been sure before he left, and her dresses did not yet reveal her secret. Could he feel the change in her body?

At once he was on his knees, on the bed beside her. He stared at her belly. In the moonlight she saw his eyes glow big, asking the question.

Louise grinned and nodded. Finally.

Antoine let out a yelp of joy, his hands in the air.

Giggles bubbled up from her toes.

All at once he leaned over and kissed her belly.

Louise laughed out loud.

Falling back against the pillows, Antoine pulled her into an embrace and made love to her as if it were the first time.

Louise floated again. She had not dreamed this way since her visit to Versailles. The cloud was peaceful, and looking over the

side, she again saw all the wonders she had before. She rolled to her back, enjoying once again the dance of the constellations. Music of the heavens sang her a lullaby. Her soul smiled.

Rolling to her stomach, she looked back down at the green treetop islands and the glimmering mirror of the lake below. Familiar and sweet, it was like visiting an old friend. Her Antoine would soon arrive. She began to look for him.

The bright mountain of light appeared up ahead. She had forgotten about that, and the familiar feeling of danger returned. So did the Scriptures from earlier in the evening. Do not be anxious.

Why should she be anxious? Her Antoine would be there soon. He would take her to safety.

She heard the whinny. The flying horse of Antoine headed her way. He flew closer, his visor up revealing his handsome face.

He reached for her.

She stretched out her hand. An eternity seemed to elapse until she could feel the touch of his fingers. She grabbed hold.

Instead of his pulling her to him, he landed and stepped down from the horse letting it fly away. They stood together, alone on the cloud.

Anxiety rose again. Holding on to Antoine, she began to tremble. Then, from somewhere inside her, the voice spoke again. Do not be anxious.

At once, Louise felt herself rising above her cloud. As she looked down, she could see that it had a definite shape, like that of a hand, large and protective. Slowly, gently she was lowered back onto the cloud. Peace flowed throughout her very being.

Louise relaxed and rolled into Antoine's arms, opening her eyes.

The room was dark. Antoine's left arm held her close, his right hand was entwined with her left.

Peace remained in her spirit. She did not know what the dream meant, but for this moment, the future did not frighten her. Tomorrow the fears may return, but for now, Antoine was here.

Chapter Thirty-Eight

Knock.

J osephine, someone is at the door." Louise listened for footsteps. "Josephine?"

Whether the heat was due to an unusually warm summer or the fact she was beginning her eighth month, Louise did not know. All she knew was that it was hot.

Knock.

Tossing her fan aside, she pushed herself from the chair and waddled to the door.

"May I help you?"

"Oui, Madame, might I speak with the man of the house?" The gentleman noticed her swollen belly about that time, his cheeks glowing pink. He swiped his hat from his head and kneaded it in his hands.

"He is not in at the moment. Might I give him a message? I am his wife."

"Madame Crocketagné?"

"Oui."

The man seemed to relax. "So glad to meet you. I am the Reverend Jacques Fontaine."

"Fontaine? Are you kin to—?"

"Oui, the brothers are my cousins. I had hoped to meet with your husband."

"Come in, Monsieur, come in. Antoine will be home any minute. He is not traveling at this time." Louise held open the door.

"Well, ah, if you are quite sure. Is anyone else here?" He remained outside.

"Oui, Monsieur. Madame LeSuere is here. We are not alone."

"Very well. He wiped his feet and stepped into the house.

"Make yourself comfortable Reverend Fontaine, and I will have Josephine start us a pot of tea."

"Merci."

Louise excused herself and went in search of Josephine, finding her coming in from the back. "We have company."

"Oh, my, I did not hear the door. Shall I prepare tea?" She dropped an armload of vegetables on the table.

"Oui, and until Antoine is home, you need to make your presence known."

Josephine nodded and grabbed the teapot.

Louise returned to her guest, finding him standing at the window where she had left him. "Please be seated, Monsieur." She lowered herself into the chair and picked up her fan.

Reverend Fontaine sat once she was down. His long fingers steepled under his chin.

"So, Monsieur, what brings you to Bordeaux?"

"I am visiting families in the area, looking to see how you fare, and what needs if any I may find."

"You are only visiting then."

The Reverend nodded.

What else could she say? Conversation with a married woman did not seem to be his forte. "With whom are you staying while here?"

He scuffed a foot on the carpet. "I have not found lodging

yet. In truth I have not looked for a place as I thought to meet the families first."

Josephine entered at that moment carrying a tray. "Madame Louise, Monsieur Antoine just rode into the stable." She set the tray on the table by Louise's elbow.

"Merci, Josephine." Louise poured fresh milk in the cups before filling one with tea for her guest. "Here you are, Monsieur. My husband should be here momentarily."

After preparing a cup for Antoine, she fixed a cup of tea for herself and leaned back. How nice it would be if only the hot tea would warm her inside enough to feel cooler on the outside.

"There you are, ma petite." Antoine entered and leaned in to kiss her cheek. "I understand we have company."

The Reverend stood, hand outstretched.

"Monsieur, may I present my husband, Antoine Crocketagné. My husband, our guest is the Reverend Jacques Fontaine. He is visiting families in the area." Louise remained in her seat and hoped her guest would forgive her. This baby had better come soon, or it would be bigger than she.

Antoine shook hands with the man. "Fontaine?"

"Oui, the brothers who employ you share a great grandfather with me."

Antoine sat and motioned for the Reverend to do the same. "What families do you plan to visit in the area, Monsieur?"

"Réformees families, Monsieur Crocketagné. I have studied the doctrine for the ministry and am working at increasing communication between Réformé communities."

Antoine leaned forward. "Where all have you been?"

"I spent a little more than a week in Nîmes and several days in Orange before working my way west. It is much worse there. Though our brothers have remained strong, the persecution has increased."

Louise set her cup on the table. "Monsieur, we have heard rumors of atrocities. I cannot believe all that I hear."

"Ma petite, perhaps you would excuse us men to speak?"

"I should know what is happening, Antoine, or I will become frightened of what I imagine. This is an area where I do not want to be surprised." Would Antoine insist she leave the room? She preferred to stay and hear to having to stand and waddle out.

"Very well. Reverend Fontaine, please spare my wife the details, but I would like to hear what you have learned."

Unfolding himself from the chair, the young man clasped his hands behind his back and began to pace. "I have seen the atrocities with my own eyes, held the broken bodies while they breathed their last. The dragoons have no fear, nor heart. I do not need to describe the carnage, since if you can imagine it, it has happened, only worse than you can imagine. Thousands of our countrymen are tortured, killed, or sold as galley slaves."

"Then the rumors of women forced to watch their babes starve, children left homeless, or forced into convents and monasteries to learn their catechisms, these tales are true?" Louise felt the old familiar clench to her heart. "I am cousin to His Majesty. Surely he does not condone such action."

"I am sorry, Madame, but I am afraid the rumors are true. Your relationship with our king may afford you some protection. However, I come not to bring fear. I ask for the Body of Christ to pray fervently for each other. I hope by keeping you informed, you will be able to draw strength from our Father and understanding of what He would have you to do."

Antoine stood. "Merci, Reverend Fontaine. We will talk again, but for now I think, for the sake of my wife, we should table the discussion until another time."

"Perhaps you are right. I need to see others in the area as well."

Louise scooted to the edge of her seat. "Antoine, the Reverend mentioned he needs a place to stay. We have room."

"Of course. You will honor us with your presence, Reverend?"

"Oui, for one night only, I would be delighted. Merci."

Antoine led the way and the Reverend followed, leaving Louise alone with her thoughts.

❧

"I HEARD THE MARTEIHLE FAMILY HAS LOST THEIR HOME IN Bergerac." Antoine picked up his goblet and drank.

Josephine took Louise's plate. "What happened, Antoine? Where will they go?" He must have gleaned this from the Reverend before he left.

Antoine slid a hand over hers. "Ma petite, the family runs out of money paying off trumped up fines and exorbitant taxes. Once they have nothing left, the state and church can fight over the land while the family is displaced. This is why Dominique and Aimée sold everything and left before it became too late. Do not fear for Jean Marteihle, though. He prepared for this day."

"We did not plan well, though did we, love?" She looked down and rubbed her growing belly. "It is not the best time to bring a new life into this world."

"Man may plan, but the plan of God is what will be, ma petite. We will protect our child. Matthew and I are working on an idea."

Louise closed her eyes, trying to recapture the vision of the hand and find calm.

❧

EARLY ONE MID-SEPTEMBER MORNING, A COMMOTION outside the house woke Antoine from a sound sleep. He could hear Josephine shouting that Monsieur Crocketagné was not at home.

He hopped up, running to the bedroom window. "Never mind, Josephine. Oui, I am here. I will come down to you," he called.

Louise sat up.

"No, you stay here, ma petite. I am ready. We knew this might happen, but I had hoped for more time." He drew her close, kissing her forehead. "I am not afraid, but I hate to leave you now. Pray I will be released before the baby comes."

She looked up at him, and a knot clenched in his gut. Could she turn to prayer?

Antoine ran his finger across her cheek to catch a tear. He reached for his clothes and hurried out with a small bundle.

❦

LOUISE WATCHED FROM THE WINDOW. A GUARD OPENED Antoine's pack. Only an extra set of clothes and his Bible were revealed.

Another guard had him mount up on one of their horses. The one in charge said something to Antoine, but Louise could not make it out. *Please do not let them tie his feet beneath the horse.* She waited, holding her breath. A guard carrying rope moved toward Antoine, but the commander motioned the man back to his own horse. Louise let out the breath she had held. The archers mounted their horses, and they all left together.

"Josephine, vite, find Jean-Paul, and bring him here quickly." If the stable boy could follow, she would be able to know what became of her dear husband.

Louise could not explain her lack of panic. Yes, she was anxious, but when she'd thought of this day she was sure she would become hysterical. But now that the day was here, there was no panic. Mystified, she wiped her cheeks and drew away from the window. Her time of confinement was well underway, so visiting the prison was out of the question. Confinement or no, she still needed answers.

Jean-Paul did not return that day or the next. Louise hoped he was just being careful. No neighbor came by the house to see to her situation. However, that was not unusual. To be seen at the house might put a person under suspicion. Even a few of their servants had taken for the woods out of fear.

Josephine, however, never left Louise's side.

⊗

"THERE WILL BE NO TALKING WITH THE OTHER PRISONERS. You will keep to yourself and do as you are told. If you follow these directives, you will find your stay with us more pleasant."

Antoine bit his tongue to keep the taunting quip at bay. The last thing he needed was to call attention to himself with mocking comments. Standing in the back of the crowd, he surveyed the other prisoners, some of whom had been incarcerated for a while. Others, like himself, were new to the prison. He found Matthew near the other end of the group. This was not good, though it did not surprise him. He had hoped Matthew would take care of Louise while he was away. Obviously, that was not to be.

The guard finished his speech, and the prisoners began to spread out.

"Our Father, who art in heaven—" Antoine recognized Matthew's voice as it carried over the courtyard.

"What do you think you are doing?"

"I am praying, Monsieur. I pray to our Heavenly Father at this time every morning. You would have me not talk to God?"

Even from his position, Antoine could see the guard did not know what to say. "Very well, pray then, but do not disturb the rest."

"If I disturb someone, perhaps it is because his heart is not right with God? Where was I? Hallowed be Thy name. Thy Kingdom come, Thy will be done…"

Other prisoners took notice. The quieter they got, the louder Matthew sounded.

Well, Antoine may not be able to talk with his friend, but he could pray with him. "On earth as it is in heaven."

Matthew looked up.

Antoine caught his gaze and smiled.

They continued in unison. "Give us this day our daily bread. And forgive us our debts, as we also have forgiven our debtors."

More voices joined in.

"Do not lead us into temptation but deliver us from evil. For Thine is the kingdom, and the power, and the glory, forever."

The *amen* echoed throughout the courtyard as each man said it one at a time.

Matthew was going to make it hard for Antoine to stay unnoticed.

Chapter Thirty-Nine

Y ou, get up."

Antoine's eyes flew open, but he saw no one. He got up and peeked. Guards had come for Yves, a young man new to the faith. Faced with recanting or torture, what would he choose?

Matthew had noticed as well. He began praying using Scripture. "Father, I pray that You would keep me strong in the Lord and in the strength of Your might. I put on the full armor of God that I may be able to stand firm against the schemes of the devil with Your help, Lord. For we know our struggle is not against flesh and blood, but against the ruler, against the powers, against the world forces of this darkness, against the spiritual forces of wickedness in the heavenly places. Help me to remember this and forgive those who hold me captive."

Antoine listened and prayed in silent agreement.

"Lord, I take up the full armor of God, that I may be able to resist in the evil day, and having done everything, I stand firm, having girded my loins with truth, and having put on the breastplate of righteousness, and having shod my feet with the preparation of the gospel of peace. I take up your shield of faith with which I will be able to extinguish all the flaming missiles of the evil one. Lord, place your helmet of salvation on my head and wield your sword of the Spirit, which is the Word of God. I am Your ambassador in chains, O Lord. May I speak boldly as I ought to speak."

The guard banged the hilt of his sword against Matthew's bars. "You are speaking too boldly, Maury. It would do you good to pray silently."

Matthew's answer carried clearly. "Forgive him, Lord. He does not know what he does."

"Silence yourself, or I will show you what I know to do."

The words of his friend's prayer called to Antoine. *May I speak boldly as I ought to speak.* Before he could think, the words bubbled up from inside him. "Forgive him, Lord."

Then from another cell, "Forgive him, Lord."

Soon prisoner after prisoner called out asking forgiveness for the guard.

Antoine looked over at Yves.

The young man stood taller, his eye clearer, his face resolute.

Kneeling in his cell, Antoine prayed for Yves's family.

◈

DAYS PASSED INTO A WEEK, AND ONE WEEK BECAME TWO. Antoine began to doubt he would see his child come into the world. He even doubted if he would see Louise again in this life. No one had called him for questioning, and though he thought that strange, he also thanked God each evening for a day without physical torment.

"Get up, Crocketagné. Get your things."

He had known the day would come. Now that it was here, he prayed for strength and resolve.

"This way."

Following the guard, they stopped by Matthew's cell. He was told the same thing and made to come along. They continued until at the office of the treasurer.

"Messieurs Maury and Crocketagné, you have enjoyed our facilities for too long. If you will kindly pay for your upkeep, you may be released."

Antoine imagined his countenance mirrored the incredulous look on the face of his friend. For Louise's sake, he bit his tongue. "How much to we owe for your services, Monsieur?"

"Let me see, mmmmm." He ran his finger down a column of figures. "It appears two hundred francs apiece will suffice."

"Two hundred francs?" Matthew sputtered and spat.

Antoine placed a hand on his arm and caught his gaze before addressing the Treasurer. "Done. I do not have the cash on me at this moment. Might I sign a voucher? Will that be acceptable?"

The official nodded and placed a quill and ink bottle before him.

Antoine dipped the nib and signed his name. "I will send someone with the cash as soon as I arrive home. Is that satisfactory?"

"Quite. And you Monsieur Maury?"

Matthew acquiesced and soon they were out of the prison, free to return to their homes.

Antoine took a deep breath of fresh air and turned to Matthew. "Take care, my friend, on your journey home."

"And you, Antoine. This is only the beginning. There will be more ludicrous fines. You know that."

Antoine nodded.

"At least you should be home in plenty of time, long before your child arrives."

"Not if I do not start walking. We will speak later."

Antoine embraced Matthew before heading for home.

"Madame! Madame! Monsieur is coming. He is coming home." Jean-Paul called from the foot of the stairs.

Louise waddled from her room as fast as her legs could carry her bulk. "Have you seen him?"

"Oui, Madame. He is on the road outside."

She hurried down the steps as rapidly as she dared and grabbed the boy. "You have seen him? With your own eyes?"

"Oui, Madame. He is coming home."

Pushing past Jean-Paul, she rushed to the front door, yanking it open.

Antoine stood in front, staring up at the windows.

"Antoine!"

He ran to her before she could waddle to him.

She wrapped her arms securely about his neck, and every lonely moment she had endured dripped from her eyes and down his back. "Oh, my love, you are home. You are finally home."

Antoine scooped her into his arms and carried her into the parlor.

So wonderful, leaning her head against his shoulder. He let her feet drop to the floor, and she stood with her face buried in his shirt.

"I need a bath."

Louise giggled. "Oui, you do. You have been gone so long, though, I can stand it for a few moments."

He ran his fingers through her hair, pulling out the ribbon that held it back.

"Very well, I will have Josephine pour you a bath, and I promise to scrub your back."

His breath tickled her ear. "See that you do."

What was he about? She was in no condition to meet his passions. Louise pushed away. "I will tell Josephine."

He grabbed her hand, weaving his fingers with hers as she turned. "Louise, my love, I will not start something we cannot finish. Just know, I have missed you more than I can say." Drawing her hand to his lips, he kissed it.

"As I you, my love. Let us get the stench of prison off you."

He nodded and released her.

⚜

AN HOUR LATER, HE WAS STRETCHED OUT ON THE PETITE coucher in their room with his head on what was left of Louise's lap. She ran her finger across new worry lines etching the forehead of her husband. His time in the jail had aged him. Gray hairs at his right temple, new since his time away, boldly sprouted, though he had yet to see his thirtieth birthday.

Antoine stirred, and she stroked his head again. Worry, more than the prison experience, had worn on him. If only she could take it all away for him.

He opened his eyes and stared at the ceiling.

"I believe I have an idea. Matthew is at the home of his brother-in-law. I will go there for a few minutes and see what he thinks." Antoine stood and stretched.

"But I just now have you home. Must you go?"

"Oh, my sweet wife. Yes, I must." He leaned over, caressing her chin. "But then, you already know that." He kissed her and left the room.

She did, but it didn't make it any easier.

⚜

RIDING VENT, IT TOOK ANTOINE ONLY ABOUT TEN MINUTES to reach the house. A modest cottage in Bordeaux, it sat along a busy thoroughfare. Matthew himself answered the knock.

"Is there a place we could talk?" Antoine asked.

"Certainly. Come in. Follow me."

Matthew led the way upstairs to the room where he stayed.

"How fares Louise?"

"She is well enough, though I still worry." Antoine sat in the chair Matthew indicated. "That is what I want to discuss with you. Would you believe I dreamed an idea?"

Matthew chuckled. "I can well believe it. Tell me your idea."

"I do not want to wait until we are out of money and there is no choice about where to go. Though I have led Louise to believe I have plan, the truth is until this evening, I had nothing. I have been afraid to upset her more, especially after I received news that my sister and family have gone into hiding. But while I dreamed of my last trip for the company, I recalled a conversation I had with Sir Edward Spencer. Do you remember him?"

"Oui, he lives in England, in Bath, does he not?"

"He is the one. When I was last there, he said something. I put little stock in it at the time, but his words returned in my dream. Something about it not being the first time the Church of England had opened her doors to the persecuted. I had never thought of the Church of England doing anything like that, so I dismissed it. Then I relived the conversation in my dream." Antoine leaned forward. "I believe we are to go to England." He paused, watching Matthew's face.

Matthew tugged on his lower lip and sighed. "I understand. It is not as if you are a man alone. You have Louise and the baby to consider."

"I keep thinking that if the stories are true, about what the dragoons have been doing, how long before they are brazen enough to come to the major cities? I served His Majesty faithfully. I would rather leave than take up arms against him."

"I understand. So, when? How?"

"We need to hold on until the baby arrives. Louise should not have to think of traveling when she is in confinement." Antoine stood and began to pace. "I will have to convert what I can to cash, preferably *pistoles*. One of those gold coins can buy a great amount. But I'm afraid Louise will need to leave behind many things, so that it will not appear that we are leaving for good until we are safely gone. What do you think?"

"I think you have been thinking on this. It would be less conspicuous for someone you can trust, who is not of our faith, to convert the money for you."

"I believe I know the man. I cannot guarantee he will help, though I know I can trust him."

"Then all that is left to do is pray. If this is how the Lord is leading you, may He open wide all doors. We will also pray that if His plans are different, He will put that on your heart and turn you back to His path. We will lift your friend, that the Lord will prepare his heart for you. I will be praying for traveling mercies for a safe trip and that you will arrive back in time for the arrival of your son."

"I am not brave enough to claim this baby is a boy." Antoine grinned. "I do thank you for your prayers, though."

Kneeling beside Matthew, they prayed for each other. A shock crashed through Antoine as his friend's words poured over him. This might be the last time they would see one another in this life. He had not realized how strong the bond of friendship between them had grown.

When the prayer was complete, Antoine embraced Matthew before slipping out for home and Louise.

Chapter Forty

Louise helped him pack up the portmanteau.

Antoine watched her efficient movements, still not sure this was the right thing to do.

She pressed something onto his palm. "Take this. It will bring a good price."

Antoine held open his hand to find a white velvet bag. Her mother's pearls and the aquamarine set lay nestled inside.

"Are you sure?" A lump swelled in his throat.

"Oui, before I change my mind." She brushed a kiss across his cheek before searching for more for him to take. She had locked her fear away from him and at times seemed like a prisoner having come to terms with her sentence.

Once the packing was complete, they fell into bed. He wanted to leave at first light.

Louise curled up next to him, as close as her bulging belly would allow.

He put his hand on her abdomen, feeling for a kick. "I hate to leave you now."

"I know." Her fingers stroked his jaw.

"What if I do not come back in time? What if no one believes I am traveling on business?"

"Rest, my love. There is no other choice." Her whispers puffed soft against his cheek until she drifted off to sleep.

Concerns he had tried to shove to the back of his mind wandered into his sleep causing him to wake with a start. *What if I am wrong? What if I am rushing the strategy God has designed or, worse yet, dragging innocent people into a dangerous plan?*

Antoine rubbed his hand over his eyes and got up, tiptoeing down to the parlor.

His Bible lay on the table by his chair. Opening it, he turned to the book of Proverbs. The wisdom of the ages called from each page. Wisdom. How he yearned for that.

He turned another page. All at once a part of the text seemed to have a light shining, causing the words to glow and rise off the page.

Startled, Antoine snapped the book closed.

He shook his head. Perhaps he dreamed it.

He opened it again.

The portion still glowed.

He slammed the book closed again, his heart racing.

Taking a deep breath, a third time he slowly opened to the Proverb.

The glow remained.

Drawn, he could not resist. Antoine read the text.

But as for the upright, he makes his way sure.

There is no wisdom and no understanding and no counsel against the Lord.

The horse is prepared for the day of battle, but the victory belongs to the Lord.

Antoine read the Scripture over and over. *He makes his way sure. The victory belongs to the Lord.* Peace blanketed him.

Kneeling, he thanked the Lord for His mercy and guidance, and gently closed his Bible, trailing fingers over the supple leather cover.

He had to know. Once more he opened to the Proverb.

There was no difference in the appearance between the verses he had just read and the rest of the Scriptures.

He set the book aside. Perhaps he had dreamed it.

His heart knew better.

Returning to their bedroom, he gathered his things. Faint light outlined where Louise lay sleeping. His heart hurt. Leaving her was the hardest part. Yet he knew he must, for her sake and that of their child. He bent to kiss his sleeping wife.

Louise put her arms around him, holding him.

When he pulled back, he realized she had been awake all along. With one more look at her beautiful face, he left.

✦

IT HAD BEEN SOME TIME SINCE THE TWO FRIENDS HAD SEEN one another. France was a big place. One could not easily get together with friends when three hundred miles lay between them. Though Antoine had made it a point to stop by whenever he was on his annual trip, Louise had not seen their friends since the day they left Versailles.

After nearly a week of hard travel, by boat and over land. Antoine was ready to collapse. Now that he was close to his destination, he needed to determine whether to go on to the home at night or wait until morning.

He was so tired, but time was too short. Spurring his horse on, he arrived soon after sunset and rapped at the door.

Mimi answered and, with a cry of joy, pulled him into the home. "Antoine is here!"

Albert reached him before Antoine could set down his bag. Handing their squirming toddler to Mimi, Albert enveloped Antoine in a bear hug and then kissed him on each cheek.

"What are you doing here, my friend? We did not expect you until next spring."

"Be prepared to tell me all about what is going on with Louise. I will be back as soon as I have this one prepared for bed." Mimi held the child out toward Albert. "Say good night to your papa and give him a kiss."

"Pa pa pa pa." The little one squished his father's cheeks between baby hands and planted a slobbery kiss.

An intense longing wrapped about Antoine's heart. He must complete this mission and return to his family.

Mimi took the baby upstairs while Albert led the way to the parlor. "Let me take your hat and cloak. Then you can tell me what is wrong."

"What do you mean?"

"Something is not right. I can see it in your eyes. Is it Louise? The baby? Tell me what I can do."

Antoine sat, running his fingers through his hair. "I hesitate to bring you into this, but I know of nowhere else to go." He sighed. "No, that is not true. I prayed about this, and the Lord put you on my heart. Therefore, I am here. However, I will understand if you cannot help."

"Do not be foolish. Tell me what it is I can do, and consider it done."

"I need to convert some things to ready cash, preferably *pistoles*. The arrests have started in Bordeaux, and that can only mean one thing. It is the beginning of the end. I do not know for sure that the dragoon squads do what they are rumored to do, but I cannot put Louise and the baby at risk."

"Has the baby arrived? We have been waiting to hear."

"No, and he could come at any time."

Albert chuckled. "You know, God sends little girls too."

"So I have been told. But, no, he or she is not here, and Louise is waiting, so I must hurry. I had to be careful what I took from the house. We want to leave enough there so that it appears we are returning."

"Show me what you have."

Antoine pulled opened the case, laying out item after item. Albert helped him sort according to what would be easiest to sell and what would bring the most cash.

"I remember those pearls." Mimi had slipped in unnoticed.

Another knock sounded at the door.

Antoine's heart jumped.

Mimi stepped out, closing the parlor door behind her. "Good evening, Father." Her voice clearly carried.

Antoine mouthed, "Robert?"

Albert shook his head and motioned to his collar.

The priest?

"What brings you out tonight, Father?"

"Might I come in, Madame de Grillet? I need to speak with your husband."

Albert jumped up, motioning for Antoine to put away his things. He slipped out, drawing the door closed behind him. "Good evening, Father François. What can we do for you?"

Antoine listened, stuffing all the items back into his bag.

"It is not what you can do for me, but what I can do for you."

"What do you mean, Father?"

"May I come in and sit? This will take some explaining."

Albert cracked open the door and peeked inside.

Antoine nodded.

"Oui, but of course." Albert opened the door, revealing Antoine seated in one of the chairs.

"Monsieur Crocketagné, it has been a long time." Father François extended his hand. "I am glad you are here. Now it makes much more sense."

"What does, Father?" Mimi asked.

"I am here to help you."

Antoine stared at the priest, then at Albert, and then back at Father François. Had he heard correctly?

As if in answer to his unspoken question, the priest replied, "Oui, my son, you correctly heard me. I am here to help you." Father François sat across from Antoine. "I know, Monsieur, you most likely consider me as one of the enemy because of my faith. I must reassure you, that is not true. I do not agree with the politics of what is happening in Rome, but I believe the Church of our Holy Savior is Catholic in the truest sense of the word. It is universal. The Church encompasses all those who have received the gift of salvation from our Lord. If you can agree with me that Jesus Christ is the only begotten Son of God, the Savior of the world, and that no man comes unto the Father except through the Son, and, if you have received the precious gift of our Lord, then we are brothers in Christ, no matter the title. Are we agreed?"

"Oui, on this we are agreed."

"Then let me say, I believe the persecution of the Huguenots is immoral. It is not of God. Those who continue in this way will be responsible for the downfall of France and may lose their souls in the process." He leaned in. "Now I will tell you something. I am not sure you will believe me, but I will swear to my dying day that it is true.

The glowing words of Scripture flashed through Antoine's mind. He knew what he was about to hear was true. Antoine drew closer to Father François. Albert and Mimi did the same.

"I had finished saying Mass and had gone to my cell. A visitor waited in the room for me. I do not know where he came from, nor how he got in, but he was there. He told me I would find a man in need at this home, and that I was to help in any way that I could. As a sign, I am to tell you that you have a pair of aquamarine combs in your pack. Do you have such items?"

Antoine's heart stopped. He could only stare at Albert.

"Louise wore a set of combs like that when she was here," Mimi whispered.

"I brought them at her insistence." Antoine had not realized he spoke aloud until he heard his own voice.

"Then I believe the only question left to you, Monsieur, is do you trust me?"

Antoine could hear the Scripture in his mind. *There is no wisdom and no understanding and no counsel against the Lord.* This he did not understand. *But the victory belongs to the Lord.*

That was a surety. *But for the upright, he makes his way sure.* Antoine closed his eyes and silently prayed.

Not even the sound of breathing could be heard.

The heart in his chest began to beat again. "I believe you."

A collective release of breath caused Antoine to laugh.

Father François joined him, followed by Albert and Mimi.

"I will make some tea while you men get to work." Mimi slipped out.

"Here is what is needed." Antoine explained his plan to the priest and opened the bag.

When he took out the aquamarine combs and placed them in the father's hand, the priest began to tremble. "I have trusted in You, O Lord, and You have not failed."

The words seared into Antoine's soul.

An hour later, Father François left with the promise to return the next evening.

Chapter Forty-One

Are you quite sure, my love?" Albert whispered into Mimi's ear as they lay in bed. The house lay silent while they held each other close. He could feel her nod against his shoulder.

"I always thought Momo went to England. It would give us an opportunity to find her."

"True. You must remember, though, it would not be like here. We would be the ones treated as heretics due to our faith."

"I know," Mimi mumbled into his chest.

"I cannot stay where my best friend is considered a criminal because of how he chooses to worship God. I am afraid a time will come where I would have to take up arms against those like him. I cannot do that."

"I know."

"You are very wise." He burrowed his fingers in her silky hair. "Do you also know I love you very much?"

"I know." She tipped her head back, her eyes danced. "Every so often, though, I like to be convinced."

"Then I will have to convince you again." He kissed her, enjoying a chance to put her doubts to rest.

TRUE TO HIS WORD, FATHER FRANÇOIS RETURNED THE next evening.

The weight of the purse shocked Antoine. "I could not have hoped to have made so much money." He opened it to see more gold coins than he had ever seen in one place.

Albert nodded to the purse. "You will be quite vulnerable to attack, traveling with all that gold."

"God has supplied thus far. I will trust Him to see me home."

"I cannot deny what I have seen and heard here. I believe I have an idea that could be part of the plan of God."

Antoine eyed his friend. "Tell me."

"I will ride back with you and help you bring Louise here. Then together our families will leave for England."

Antoine's legs failed him. He sat.

"Do you know what you are saying? You are not under persecution here, but you would be there. This is where you are safe."

"This is where I may be forced to take up arms against those whose only crime is worshipping God. I cannot do that, nor can I raise my son in such a place."

"What of Mimi? What does she think of this plan?"

Albert smiled, but it was a sad smile. "She thinks she might find her sister in England."

Antoine thought he had put aside his feelings against Momo. Perhaps he would need to deal with them again. "When did you decide this?"

"We talked it over last night. You will not change my mind. I am ready to ride with you at first light."

Trying to talk past the lump in his airway, Antoine cleared his throat and blinked. "Make sure you are right, then go ahead."

"So, what is the plan?"

"I had not thought in detail beyond coming here."

"Would anyone like to hear what we think?" All eyes turned to Mimi, who stood with Father François. "We have an idea, if you are interested."

"Then tell us, Mimi, Father. What is your plan?"

Mimi linked her arm though the arm of the priest. "First, Antoine, you must go back with Albert. Once the baby comes, you can purchase tickets to sail for Nantes and come up the river to Blois. From there you can take a coach to here where Louise and the baby can have time to recover before we leave for Normandy and England."

Father François nodded. "And since you will be returning here, you do not have to take all the gold with you. Madame de Grillet can keep it safe. If anyone should ask, you can say you are taking the newborn to see his royal cousin. No one would dare to stop you."

"And with you two strong men to protect them, Louise and the baby will make it without a problem. She might even get to bring along a few extra things that way."

Antoine laughed. "If only you two could be put in charge of your own regime. I think that is a fine plan. As we leave at first light, I must make my goodbyes and go to bed." He held out a hand to the priest. "Father François, I cannot thank you enough."

The priest pushed aside Antoine's hand and wrapped him in an embrace. "May Almighty God bless and keep you in His care, my son."

"And you, Father. And you."

❧❦❧

ALTHOUGH THE WEATHER HAD COOLED SOMEWHAT, LOUISE could feel the sweat on her forehead. Something was different.

Antoine could return at any time, but that was not what was strange.

A low backache seemed to come and go. Walking in her garden helped a little. She lugged an old basket to hold pears from her trees. As long as she kept walking, the pressure eased. She would miss her garden and the orchard. Why did she have to leave? Why must there be such cruelty against the Réformés? *And those who love them.*

Yet the change in Antoine this past year, his depth of faith, and his ability to release everything to remain true to his faith, only increased her respect of him.

It also frightened her.

And irritated her at times.

Like now.

This was her garden, her orchard. When she and Antoine leave, who knows what will happen. And what of Étoile? True she had not been able to ride for some time, but her horse still knew her and waited each morning for her carrot. It was impossible to search for a good home for the horse for fear someone might prematurely learn of their departure. Her mother's china and crystal—much of her jewelry—all needed to be left as though the Crocketagné family planned to return.

"Why? Father, I have tried hard to be good—a good wife and hostess. I do not understand why all this is being taken away?"

Will you let me walk beside you in place of these things?

Things. Beloved things, but nonetheless things.

Will you let me care for you?

"Lord, I know You can. I'm just not sure that You will."

I will, if you will let me. You are in the palm of my hand.

A plump pear dangled just within reach. She stretched up to pluck it when a new sensation grasped her.

"*Aie!*" Louise dropped her basket and grabbed for the tree trunk.

A belt wrapped around her middle, back to front—a belt that was being cinched too tight.

Just as she thought the tightness would not stop, it began to ease the way it had come.

She felt for the closest bench. She needed to catch her breath so she could return to the house. "Oui, Lord, I will let You. Please, help me to the house."

"Madame Louise, let me help you." Josephine rushed to her. "I saw from the window, you need help. Let me take you into the house."

The tightness fled as quickly as it came. Louise looked up at the cloudless sky and breathed deep. "I am well. I do not know what happened, but I am fine."

Josephine sat next to Louise. "Oui, you are well. However, your baby is telling you something."

Louise glanced into Josephine eyes as understanding dawned. "Now? My baby is coming now? Antoine is not back. It is not time."

"Babies come when they are ready, dear one. Shall I help you into the house?"

Louise nodded.

They walked together up the steps, and Josephine guided her to a chair in the parlor.

"Sit here while I bring you some pillows."

Though Josephine tried to help, there was no becoming comfortable. Louise squirmed and adjusted cushions. Just as she found a good position, the belt started to tighten again.

The truth was plain. Her baby would be born this day. She had promised to let God take care of her, and now this. Couldn't He have started with something smaller, easier? Her hands grew clammy and her knees shook. No longer must she only dream of becoming a mother. Her dream was about to come true.

Would her baby be well? Would she be a good mother? Would Antoine return to them?

Josephine helped her up the stairs.

Louise undressed to her chemise, and Josephine helped her into the bed, covered with clean sheets.

"Antoine has not returned. He needs to be here when the baby arrives."

"God willing, he will be." Josephine pulled a sheet up over her.

"How long do you think this will take?"

"Too long and not long enough."

"What does that mean? Oh." Another pain began.

"You will soon understand, ma petite chou. Soon."

Five hours later, Louise understood. Her pains were coming at about three minutes apart. Just as she would get as comfortable as possible, the next would be upon her.

She'd stopped asking where Antoine was and put her faith in knowing God would get him there somehow. Another pain shot around her belly, and this time it began to push downward. She felt a pop before the bed under her legs grew moist.

"Your waters have broken, ma petite. Now the pains will increase. Tell yourself it means your baby is almost in your arms."

The next pain did not even wait a full minute before starting. Louise tried to keep from crying out, but so great was the intensity, the sound escaped her lips.

❧

A SCREAM.

"That was Louise!" Antoine jumped from his horse, tossing his reins to Albert before flying up the steps to the house. He took the stairs two at a time and burst through the bedroom door.

"Antoine!" Louise reached for him. "Oh. Another comes." She tipped her chin to her chest, straining.

"Push, dear one, push." Josephine stood at the foot of the bed. "Keep pushing, ma petite chou. Your baby wants to be out and with his mother."

Louise took hold of Antoine's hand. Her grip nearly broke his fingers before it relaxed.

"Antoine, I must tell you something."

"It is of no concern now, my love. I am here, and you can tell me after our baby is here." He stroked the damp tendrils from her face.

"No, I must tell you now. I told God I would let Him care for me, that I would trust Him, and then the baby started to come."

Josephine patted Louise's shin. "Now wait, let me adjust. Bon, that is good. We will wait for the next pain and push again."

Antoine kissed her forehead. "Then He will take good care of you."

His hand became caught in the vise of her grip. "Oh—Antoine!"

"Oui, I am here, Louise. *Aie!*" Louise's grip on his fingers tightened while she strained, her back arching from the pillows.

All at once she fell back with a sigh.

A wail pierced the moment.

"He is arrived." Josephine held up the newest member of the Crocketagné family.

Antoine's focus glued itself to the baby while Josephine deftly wiped him clean and wrapped him in a soft blanket.

"Here, Papa. Here is your son." She placed the bundle in his arms.

Son. He had a son. With trembling hands, Antoine brought his child to his lips, kissing the scrunched forehead. He then held the baby for Louise to see. "Son, this is your mother. She has worked very hard to bring you into this world. Be kind to her." With the greatest of care, he tucked the baby into the crook of Louise's arm and kissed the top of her head. Watching them, the flood of emotion nearly knocked him to his knees.

Louise stared at the little face, her fingers caressing the flawless cheek. "Antoine, he is so perfect." When she turned her face to him, tears dripped.

Antoine grasped her hand and leaned over to watch his son. His son. The most beautiful words in the world.

Something wet plopped onto the sheet. Antoine wiped his hand over his face and found tears of his own.

His son chose that moment to announce his displeasure.

"Save your strength, my boy. Your adventure is only just beginning." At that moment, Antoine understood. He, too, stood on the brink of adventure. A new life for all of them. He was a blessed man.

Antoine gently kissed his two favorite blessings.

Epilogue

Louise closed her eyes, letting the wind blow against her face. It let her relive the sensation of floating, like in her dream. With a smile of realization, she opened her eyes and looked up at the landscape as their ship drew closer to the English shore.

The white cliffs of Dover loomed large ahead, and at once Louise was reminded of that part of her dream. The bright, large object she had seen from the cloud looked very much like the cliffs ahead. Only now, fear no longer had a place. She knew her family was in the loving hands of Almighty God, her heart thrilled at the mercy He had shown.

So much had been left behind, but then it was only items. The best of God's gifts were always with them. It had been hard to leave Étoile and her mother's china and crystal, but God promised to provide for their needs. In reality, china and crystal and even her beloved Étoile were not needed.

Louise gazed at her small family. Whatever the future held, God would see them through.

Her wonderful Antoine stood by the railing holding their most perfect son, Gabriel Gustave Crockett, a tiny duplicate of his father.

Although they named the baby after his paternal grandfather, they would now be in a new country. Antoine decided they should all begin with a new name—Crockett. A name with enough of the French influence to help them remember their heritage, but different enough to help them let go of the past and embrace the leading of their Heavenly Father.

Antoine handed the little one to Josephine. She stood back and crooned to the infant.

God had indeed blessed them with this sweet-natured baby. He would carry on the new name.

Louise snuggled up to her husband. Their future stood wide. Louise Crockett had no clue where God would lead. He had led them to this point, though, and would be there the rest of the journey.

Antoine drew her hand to his lips. "We must remember to teach little Gabriel Gustave what the Lord shared in the Scriptures. We must teach all our children. *Make sure you are right, then go ahead.* Perhaps they will someday pass it on to their children.

"Do you believe we will have more babies?"

Antoine looked her in the eye. "I have no doubt, ma petite. You were born to be a mother."

Somewhere deep inside, she believed him.

It was then the rays of the sun glinted off the cliffs. The brilliance nearly blinded. Louise remembered once more that she did not have to see the future. It was enough to trust the One who did. With a heart overflowing with gratitude, she squeezed Antoine's hand.

Cast of Characters

Bold denotes a mentioned historical figure. Italics denotes fictional characters.

- **1. Antione Desaure Permonette de Crocketagné (Crockett)**
- **2. Albert de Grillet**
- **3. King Louis XIV of France**
- **4. Louise de Saix**
- **5. Jean Baptist Colbert**
- **6. Moière (Jean Baptiste Poquelin)**
- **7. Antoine Coysevox**
- **8. Niccoló Machiavelli**
- **9. Cardinal Jules Mazerin**
- **10. The Marquis d'Heudecourt**
- **11. Prince de Condé**
- **12. Matthew Maury**
- **13. La Grande Mademoiselle Anne Marie Louise d'Orleans**
- **14. Queen Marie Therese**
- **15. The Duchess Louise-Françoise la Valliere**
- **16. The Marquise de Montespan**

- **17. Jean Bapiste Lully**
- **18. Philippe Quinault**
- **19. Philippe Guillaume Henri de Saix**
- **20. Monsieur Charles LeBrun**
- **21. the Reverend Jacques Fontaine**
- **22. Sir Edward Spencer**
- **23. Jean Marteihle family**
- *24. Michele (Mimi) Roché*
- *25. (Tante) Marie du Sine*
- *26. Danielle (Didi) Roché*
- *27. Monique (Momo) Roché*
- *28. Josephine LeSuere*
- *29. Jean-Luc de Turenne*
- *30. Pierre LeSuere*
- *31. Simone*
- *32. Robert Roché*
- *33. Annentte Roché*
- *34. Beatrix (Bibi) Roché*
- *35. Cecile (Cici) Roché*
- *36. Genevieve (Gigi) Roché*
- *37. Violette (Vivi) Roché*
- *38. Father François*
- *39. Claude Balieu*
- *40. Gisele*
- *41. Adélaïde*
- *42. Monsieur Frederick*
- *43. Madam Aimee de Lefebvre*
- *44. Alexandre de Lefebvre*
- *45. Sébastien de Lefebvre*
- *46. Richard de Lefebvre*
- *47. Jeannot de Lefebvre*
- *48. Élise de Lefebvre*
- *49. Dominique Denis' Bertrand*
- *50. Jean-Paul*
- *51. Yves*

Afterword

Do you enjoy reading about this period of history? Would you like to know more about King Louis XIV, the Sun King? I have a short story (it developed from cut scenes from *Patriarch*). Go here (https://dl.bookfunnel.com/g3akoy67f3) to download it now.

Then come back for a sneak peek of *The Sojourners: The Crockett Chronicles: book 2.*

If you enjoyed this book, please leave a review. Reviews can be as simple as "I couldn't put it down. I can't wait for the next one" and help raise the author's visibility and lets other readers find her.

Acknowledgments

First, thank You, Lord, for the inspiration, the words, the desire as well as the genetic material. Without You there wouldn't have been a story—You are faithful to a thousand generations.

Though *The Patriarch* is not the exact same book as *The Huguenot*, you would not have the former without the latter. So, my thanks goes to everyone who helped from the inception:

To my friend and mentor, Esther Bailey—thank you for believing in me, encouraging me and editing me. You are the true meaning of a Godsend.

To Terri Barraco—thanks for your encouragement!

To Debbie Atkinson, Wanda Chiles, and Lois Rogers Lamb who edited the original story—thank you!

To Beth Bowen—I can't imagine what I would have done without your careful help of my Google Translate French. Thank you!

To Diana Brandmeyer—thank you for your friendship and wonderful editing of this new and improved story. Sure wish you lived closer!

To "my friend Jen," Jennifer Crosswhite—your talents amaze me. Your know-how blows me away. Thank you for your generosity, guidance, and help.

To Jacques de Fountaine—your memoirs are not only fascinating, they answered my questions and help me to understand. So good, in fact, they helped with two stories! Thank you for your forethought, and for passing the torch.

To my family, that has grown quite a bit since I first tried my hand at this writing thing, thank you for your love, encouragement and patience. I love each one of you!

To my sweet husband who believed in me when I stopped believing in myself. You are the best, a true gift from God. I love you.

And to my EB—I still miss you.

Reader's Guide

1. Davy Crockett is a familiar figure, especially due to over 150 years of media press. Knowing now about his ancestry, did that change how you view him? What surprised you?
2. What previous knowledge do you have about the Protestant Reformation, John Calvin, or the Huguenot movement? Has this had an effect on the story as you read? How? In what way?
3. What previous knowledge do you have of seventeenth century France under King Louis XIV and Versailles? How has this effected the story for you as you read?
4. Antoine seemed to change his mind about his assignment quickly after meeting Louise. Does this speak to a flaw in his character? Would you call him brash? Or flexible? Or typically male?
5. Louise is characterized by the king and others as "pious." Have you known someone who seemed to do all the right things and looked "pious" or "religious" but didn't have a relationship with Jesus?

What was the one thing that you noticed about them that stood out to you?

6. Much has been written about King Louis XIV, the most popular and longest reigning king of France. The direct quotes from his memoirs used in the book show him to be a man with knowledge of God as his source of knowledge and power. Yet he openly kept mistresses and sire illegitimate children. What does this say about his character? How might this have had a direct bearing on present day France?

7. The Catholic Church was going though some major turmoil during the era of the Great Protestant Reformation. How believable is it to you to read of a priest who could reach across the denominational lines of that time?

8. The persecutions of the Huguenots drove off most of the merchant and artisan class in France and sent them to other countries. What might have been the shape of world powers today if France had chosen to embrace the movement rather than wipe it out? What effect might it have had on the history of the United States?

9. What is the one thing you hope to find out about in the coming sequels to *The Patriarch*?

10. What part of the story would you have changed? What was your favorite part?

Author's Note

Dear Reader,

Thank you for taking this journey with me. This is a story that has been on my heart for decades. It took me at least one just to get in onto paper. Then I produced it as *The Huguenot*. That was a learning experience. I didn't know more than I realized I didn't know.

Now, another ten plus years later, I did my best to honor these people whose DNA I share. I've learned a lot since that first version. Think of this as the six million dollar man/book; it is bigger, bolder, better. At least, I think so. Hope you agree.

Most of the characters in this book really lived and are set in the correct time and place. The rest is my imagination run amuck. I gave them memories and passions, thoughts and words. When possible, I culled from their own quotes.

Josephine LeSuere was elaborated from an incident mentioned where Louis XIV had a woman beaten—a onetime occurrence and a bit of a political nightmare for him. And, though I put the words in her mouth, the Sun King did outlive his son and grandson. He was succeeded by his great-grandson.

The Marquise de Montespan never got her wish. She was ousted by her children's nanny who, after the queen died, became the king's morgan wife—wife without title.

The telling of the Huguenots is as accurate I as I could make it. It was difficult finding data. Too much has been lost. Many of the wars and the bloodshed has been forgotten rather than taught. Sadly the difference this group of believers made to France and the void that was left when they were driven away is buried deep or destroyed. France never recovered. However, during World War II, Huguenot families who had settled hundreds of years before in the remote regions of the French Alps were instrumental in protecting many Jewish children from their Nazi predators.

If you would like to know more about Huguenot life in the seventeenth and eighteenth centuries, I suggest *The Memoirs of a Huguenot Family*

(https://en.wikisource.org/wiki/

Memoirs_of_a_Huguenot_Family).

Jacques de Fontaine, the real one, wrote about his experiences. I included his firsthand observations also in the second book of this series, *The Sojourners*. He gave me wonderful information, and I owe him. Making him a character is my way of saying thank you.

For more information on life at Versailles, I suggest the nonfiction book, *Daily Life at Versailles* by Jaques Levron. It is filled with letters, journal entries, and all sorts of other anecdotal records. It is an enjoyable read.

Also, I'd be remiss if I did not tell you that the seed of the idea for this book came from a collection that is now out of print but housed at the library adjacent to the Alamo. Volume six of *Notable Southern Families* contains two paragraphs that first sparked my imagination about my great-great-great-grandfather's great-great-great-grandparents, Antoine and Louise. The first Crocketts.

And so, thank you again for reading *The Patriarch*. Until we get to meet again on the pages of *The Sojourners*…

Abundant blessings,

Jenny

About the Author

Jennifer Lynn Cary is a direct descendent of Davy Crockett making Antoine and Louise her ancestors as well. A retired elementary teacher, she resides in Arizona with her husband where they enjoy family time with two more generations in the Crockett linage.

You can find her at www.jenniferlynncary.com

facebook.com/authorjenniferlynncary

Sneak Peak of The Sojourners: The
Crockett Chronicles book 2

County Donegal, Ireland 1698

She was gone.

Joseph teetered on the brink of insanity. Could someone feel numbness and anguish at the same time? He didn't trust his mind.

Joseph could feel Father's arms. Mama softly cried. Others, heard above the rush of the wind, sniffed in dignified grief. Then everyone grew quiet. The Reverend Fontaine spoke.

He was trapped in the now, filled with all its agony, as they laid his wife to rest.

Kathleen.

Mama wept.

The wind, as it cried through the trees was the answering call to the empty wails of his heart.

"It is time, son." Father's hand rested on Joseph's back. The coffin bearing his life rested at the bottom of the grave. Yet, for him, there was no rest.

He picked up a handful of dirt. Panic inched its way to his soul. Kathleen loved being with people. Now she lay alone.

The reverend's words filtered through. Kathleen was not in

the grave. She lived with her Savior. What they buried today was an empty shell left behind by her faithful spirit.

Deep inside Joseph, the words rang true. Kathleen, free of earthly cares and woes, no longer knew pain. Rather it was his own soul sliding off faith's edge.

He unclenched his fist, letting the dirt slip through trembling fingers onto the coffin. A simple task, yet it rent Kathleen from his grasp.

He could not let her go.

Too late, he grabbed at the dirt. His hand, like his heart, remained empty. He watched the lightest of the particles drift from his fingertips to the pine box below.

Release her. Cling to Me. The voice cajoled, invoking the image of a heavenly hand reaching down to him.

The same hand that snatched Kathleen away.

"No."

He fled the cemetery.

❧

"I ache for him, Antoine." A salty tear pooled at the corner of Louise's lips. "I understand he is a grown man, but he is still my son. My child. I want to take away his pain." She dabbed at her eyes.

"*Je sais, ma petite,* I know." Her husband drew her close. "He will need time."

Louise walked with the love of her life to their home. Others followed.

Antoine glanced over his shoulder at the entourage following them back to Edenmore, their estate. "We will have much company today." Family and friends, both young and old, gathered to pay their respects.

The manor came into view. Louise sighed. They had landed on English shores with only what they could carry. So much had happened over the past quarter century.

Antoine guided her through the door of their home—the home where her children had been raised.

"Josephine, we are arrived." Louise removed her cloak, tying on her apron before slipping upstairs to the nursery.

Josephine LeSeure, more family than servant, had remained behind this day to care for Louise's new grandson. Wee Joseph slumbered in Josephine's arms, unaware that his mother also now rested.

Louise stroked her grandson's feathery hair. He favored Joseph at that age. "How I would love to coddle you, ma petite, but I have work to do."

Leaving the babe to Josephine's care, Louise returned downstairs to examine the sideboard. *Oui*, there were enough savory oatcakes and black tea for those wanting refreshment before leaving.

By sunset, most of the callers were gone. That is, except for Sarah Stewart. As far as Louise was concerned, she might as well be one of her brood. As Louise watched the girl help her daughters put the house to rights, she was struck by how the freckle-faced tomboy who could outrun the boys bloomed into a willowy and spirited young woman.

While the guests departed, Louise noted the lass slipped upstairs, presumably to check on Wee Joseph. Now that all the visitors were gone, Sarah sat in the nursery rocking the baby, cooing in his ear.

"*Merci*, Sarah. I thank you for all your help today." Louise leaned over the young woman's shoulder, looking on her grandson again for the hundredth time.

"I'm glad to help. He's so…small." Sarah turned a misty glance at Louise, and then back to Wee Joseph. "I need to be telling ye something."

Louise waited. Sarah's profile showed her fine bone structure and classic features. All were enhanced by delicate freckles and rogue tendrils of russet-tinged hair. Oui, she had grown into a beauty.

Sarah continued to focus on the baby. "Kathleen and me, we had a talk about a week ago. Back then I told her it was stuff and nonsense, but now I'm thinking she might have known something like this could be." She rocked slower as she spoke.

"About what did you speak, dear heart?"

"We'd been going through all the wee things she made, and our talk turned to whether the babe was to be a boy or girl. She turned to me and she says, 'Oh, I know tis a boy.' 'Oh, ye do,' says I, and she says, 'Aye, he'll be a fine, strapping boy and we'll name him after his father.'"

Sarah's voice grew taut. "Then she says to me, 'Sarah, if something should go wrong…' I stopped her and said nothing would go wrong, but she held up a hand. 'If something goes wrong, please tell me you will care for me men. Both of them. Promise me. Joseph won't be knowing what to do, and this babe will be needing ye.' 'You're talking foolishness,' says I, but she says, 'Promise me, and I'll be talking no more foolishness.'" Sarah's voice softened to barely a whisper. "I told her 'Aye, I promise,' and we spoke of it no more."

Continuing to rock, she took a slow breath before turning to meet Louise's gaze. "Now I have a promise to keep." Tears ran down her cheeks, glistening in the firelight.

A glimmer of hope flickered in the darkness of Louise's grief. Perhaps in the flurry of Sarah's words was the answer to her prayers for Joseph.

Bending, she kissed the top of Sarah's head. "Never in all my days have I known a more loving person than you, Sarah Stewart."

⁂

The wind pushed Robert Crockett along, hurrying him like some dilly-dallying child. In many ways, Robert saw himself that way and didn't like it. Here he was, at twenty years of age, still running errands for his mother.

Of course, he would have done it without her asking, if only he'd thought of it first.

Lights peeked through the cracks of the Stray Dog, gleaming slashes against the dark. A *shebeen*, though barely a pub and little more than a stall, it had hosted many a celebration. The Stray Dog was a handy place for the men of the area to share their news, give advice, and drown their sorrows. The host, a discreet little man with a pleasant grin and a mildly shady repute, went by the name of Cullen O'Keefe. With a heart as big as his girth, he served Catholics and Protestants alike. Most turned a deaf ear to the rumors concerning Cullen's past and considered the Stray Dog an oasis of truce.

Another time, Robert would have heard Cullen call out a hearty greeting and ask, "What'll it be, lad?"

Tonight, though, he just gave Robert the briefest of nods and motioned with a quick shake of his balding head to a back table.

Robert followed the direction, finding what he'd expected. Ignoring the chatter and the sour smell, he made his way through the less than half-filled room to his brother.

Joseph's hands were buried under his dark mane. The golden bottle of whiskey at his elbow emptied. His brother made little sounds, more like a child's cry than drunken snoring.

Robert pulled up a crate and sat, wondering if he should wake him or let Joseph sleep it off. Apparently, the liquor had failed to alleviate his suffering. Even in his stupor, Joseph reeked of devastation.

A noisy entrance across the room drew Robert's attention. A swirl of auburn hair stormed in. "What in the world is Sarah doing here?"

Most of the regular patrons held their tongues in respect for the lass, but one drunken lout pushed up from his bench by the hearth and staggered toward her.

"Aye, an' looky what the wind's blown in, laddies. Come on o'er here an' give us a kiss, lass."

"Twill be the back of my fist you'll be kissing, Christopher Dougherty, or maybe ye should be thinking more about the hands ye should be kissing if your sainted wife finds out how yer talking to me."

Sarah's retort only added fuel to Christopher's fire, but all he could do was stutter and sputter.

Robert sprang to Sarah's side, beating some of his neighbors to her defense. He overheard Christopher muttering something about a tran targer as Robert steered Sarah toward Joseph's table. There were many things he could think of to call Sarah at this moment, but that wasn't one of them.

"What are ye doing here?" He grabbed her elbow and whispered in her ear. "This here's no place for the likes of you."

"I can handle meself, Robert Crockett." Sarah hissed back. "I've come to find Joseph and take him home."

"Then we're of the same mind." He led her to the table Joseph held down with his head.

"Well, what are ye waiting for? Ye take one side. I'll take the other, and we'll *oxtercog* him out of here."

Robert sighed, and with Sarah's help, struggled to haul Joseph to his feet.

Sarah gritted her teeth and glanced at Robert. "Maybe tis a blessing we both came looking."

Robert merely grunted.

Out cold, Joseph gave no resistance or help at all. His arms slid to his sides as gravity pulled his body toward the floor.

Finally, with Cullen's assistance, Robert flung one of Joseph's arms around his neck and Sarah did the same.

Joseph's head lolled from side to side as they maneuvered three abreast around tables and benches.

Cullen held open the door. The wind threatened to tear the plank off its hinges.

Robert stumbled out with his load into the nearly starless night, dragging Sarah along on Joseph's other side. The door shut tight behind them, and at once the world became black.

Howling winds made it too difficult to talk. That didn't stop Robert from berating himself with every step for not thinking to bring a wagon. Drunk like this, Joseph was as heavy as an ox. He surely must be a strain on Sarah, although she never complained. Perhaps the wind kept her complaints at bay.

What was she doing here in the first place?

Robert knew why he was here. He was the dutiful son, responsible now that Gabriel studied in Glasgow and Joseph no longer resided at home. That left James and as the only other brother at home, yet he wasn't there either. How did that big brother get elected the family messenger? One by one, Robert's brothers, all grown men, made their way into the world and left him behind. He could feel the familiar resentment begin to rise.

But he had no time to dwell on it. The faint outline of the two-room stone cottage Joseph built for his bride came into view. Robert needed to get the three of them inside.

After he fumbled with the door until the latch gave, he shoved it open with his shoulder. They stumbled in, struggling to get Joseph the last few yards to the bedroom. Despite Robert's best efforts to be gentle, Joseph dropped with a thud on the bed.

Sarah turned her back and lit a lamp while Robert undressed his brother.

He drew a handmade quilt over Joseph's intoxicated form. "I'll fetch something to get this fire started. You'll stay with him?" Robert knew the answer even as he spoke.

"Aye, I'll be keeping watch." Sarah brought the lamp closer to the bedside.

He paused at the door, observing as she pulled a three-legged stool next to Joseph. With a shake of his head, he left.

❧

Silence filled the room. Sarah, fists opening and closing at her side, viewed the sleeping figure of her childhood friend. Joseph had always been her favorite of the Crockett brothers. "Aye, and ye still are, Joseph." He didn't stir, so she braved more whispers. "I always could tell ye my secrets. And since ye are asleep, I'll tell ye one more." Her gaze traveled to the doorway and back. "I've kept every letter ye sent me while ye were away to school."

She had memorized each one from reading them a thousand times over.

"Oh, Joseph, why my cousin? Why Kathleen? I loved her like a sister. Never will ye know how ye killed me inside."

Sarah had silently watched while Joseph and Kathleen married and began a family, dying a thousand deaths it seemed. And now? Now she had this promise to keep.

This would be so much harder than she thought.

She squeezed her eyes shut, took a deep breath, and slowly counted to ten. It was an old trick she used to handle her temper, one she should have remembered back at the Stray Dog. Only this time, it wasn't her temper that was out of control.

Slowly she let out her breath and glanced about the room. Spotting a bucket, she set it on the floor beside the bed.

Just in case.

And because sitting still only made things worse.

Lamplight carved shadows over Joseph's face, making him look older that his twenty-two years. His beard showed coarse on his hollowed cheeks. A sable-colored forelock tumbled across his brow. The sight tore at her heart.

He stirred and mumbled.

She leaned forward and brushed damp curls from his face.

Raising his arms, he pulled her to him, his azure eyes glassy. "Kathleen."

Her soul ached at his touch.

"I'm not Kathleen, Joseph."

Instantly his eyes focused, his face flushed. As if she had burned him, he jerked his hands from her. "Oh, God." A sob choked his voice, followed by the heartbreak of another. And another.

Unsure of what to do, she moved to the edge of the bed and held Kathleen's husband.

She was still consoling him when Robert brought in the peat.

After giving her a sympathetic nod, the younger brother went to the hearth. Moments later, the earthy smoke of the fire seeped into the room. She could hear him brush his hands over his breeches before taking a seat in the front room.

When at last Joseph's grief had spent itself, she eased him back to the pillows. Restless sleep claimed him.

She wiped his face once more and drew the coverlet over him. She moved into the front room with Robert and eased herself into the rocking chair Joseph had made for Kathleen.

"What happened?" Robert leaned back with his eyes closed. "I thought he was out for the night."

"Nothing. He just thought me Kathleen 'til he saw the truth of it." And it broke his poor heart. "He's out for the night now, I'm thinking."

"Aye." Robert sighed. "Still, twill be a long night."

She nodded, sure his prophetic words were understated.

"So why were you at the Stray Dog?" He almost sounded uninterested, but not quite.

Sarah had asked herself that question more than once. "I'd overheard Ann Wallace carrying on about how Joseph had run off. I didn't want yer mother to worry."

In truth, Sarah hadn't wanted to worry.

"She wasn't worried. She sent me." Now a touch of irritation crept into his voice.

"Oh." Well, she wasn't about to explain about the promise she'd made to Kathleen. Robert would never *ken*.

And he might tell Joseph.

She leaned back in the rocker and closed her eyes.

"Twill be a long night."

The peachy-pink fingers of dawn pulled the sun up over the eastern horizon as Sarah cracked opened her eyes. She rubbed her sore neck and gazed about the room.

Robert still slept in his chair, looking remarkably like his brother, only without the etched pain.

She noticed his blanket before realizing that she too was covered. He must have put a quilt over her and taken one for himself while she dozed.

She stretched and stood. Wrapping the coverlet about her, Sarah walked over to stir the fire and start the water for tea. That done, she tiptoed outside, breathing in the crisp morning air.

This was her favorite time of day. Most days she reveled in the newness. Today her heart was sore.

Robert came out and joined her.

She suddenly wished she'd taken time to rebraid her hair. Loose as it was, it must be as wild as a lion's mane. "What say we let him get all the sleep he can? I'll fix us something to eat." She needed to do something, anything.

"Aye." He stared at the horizon.

She went back inside, poured them each a cup of tea, bringing his to him. "The *brochan* will be ready in two shakes of a lamb's tail." She retraced her steps.

After making her hair more presentable, she prepared the porridge. She folded the borrowed blankets and put them away while it cooked.

Kathleen always kept a tidy home.

When the porridge was ready, she called to Robert but received no answer. The only sign he had been there was the empty cup resting on the sill.

"Now how am I to keep a watch on Joseph here and still go to take care of Wee Joseph?" She brought in the cup.

Her hope that Robert would stay with his brother while she went for the baby was postponed for the time being. She wasn't too concerned, though. What with his grandmother and Josephine, not to mention his three new aunts—Lucy, Mary

Frances, and Sarah Beth—that little one would receive a lot of attention.

The sound of blankets being thrashed brought her to see to her ward. Joseph sat on the edge of the bed, elbows posted on knees, his hands clutching his head.

She averted her eyes from those long legs.

"Morning, Joseph." That was too happy. *Don't sound so happy.*

He minutely turned his head to the side, peering at her from the corner of his eye. "What are you doing here?"

She winced. "I'm here to help."

"Not s'loud, woman. Where're my pants?" He waved off her explanation. "Just point."

Obediently, she indicated where Robert had tossed them, then left the room.

A minute later Joseph stood in the doorway, needing the support of the doorpost.

"Sit and I'll dip ye up some brochan." She held up a ladleful.

One look, however, and he retreated to the bedroom.

She could hear the bucket being used. Perhaps porridge hadn't been the best idea.

Soon he staggered back, this time making it as far as the front door. He stood on the threshold, leaning against the post.

She brought him a cuppa.

He took the tea, tried a sip or two. "Thanks."

She waved her hand. "'Tis nothing." The awkward silence became unbearable as she rocked back and forth onto her toes. "I'll be in the kitchen." So it was a cowardly retreat. After last night, what might he be thinking?

The porridge pot bubbled, so she stirred and moved it away from the flame before gathering up the things to be washed. All the while she kept an ear out for Joseph.

However, after an extended quiet, she peered around the door.

She was now alone at the cottage. Oh, that man. Sarah

plopped in the rocker. Just like his brother. There one minute and gone the next. Not even a thank you for sleeping in a chair all night or keeping watch. Nothing. Why did those Crockett men have to always be going somewhere?

She rocked harder. She should have just let the ungrateful oaf suffer. Except, God help her, it hurt to see someone suffer. Especially when she cared for that someone very much.

A tear dripped off the end of her nose as she pulled the rocker to a halt. She swiped it away. She would not cry. It had been foolish to think she might ease the man's pain.

However, there was Wee Joseph to think about. No matter what, she wouldn't—couldn't—go back on her promise to his mother.

God, what should I do?

Sarah listened but heard no answer. Pulling her shattered pride and feelings together, she rose. Who knew better how to handle Joseph than his mother? She would speak to Mistress Crockett.

For Wee Joseph's sake.

To pre-order The Soujourners, go to https://amzn.to/2mp3JMu.

www.ingramcontent.com/pod-product-compliance
Lightning Source LLC
Chambersburg PA
CBHW032144050726

47591CB00001B/73